THE
SIGHTSEERS

–

THE SIGHTSEERS

ROBERT WESTFIELD

Storied City

NEW YORK

STORIED CITY

First edition May 2021

ISBN: 978-1-7354821-0-1 (paperback)
ISBN: 978-1-7354821-3-2 (ebook)
Library of Congress Control Number: 2020919297

Westfield, Robert.
The Sightseers : a novel / Robert Westfield.

Subjects: BISAC: FICTION/GENERAL. FICTION/LITERARY.

New York photography by Colin Winterbottom
Cover design by Alexander Von Ness
Cover illustration by Mia Heller

Storied City
630 Fort Washington Ave
New York, NY 10040
www.StoriedCity.co

For my mother

THE
SIGHTSEERS

THEY COME AT YOU at five hundred miles per hour. That's how it starts; it's that kind of job. They speed toward you at five hundred miles per hour, break through the clouds, and drop out of the sky. You're soon surrounded and asked, sometimes ordered, to show them everything. *Everything* keeps you busy. A few days later, they lift off from the ground and disappear over the horizon. Then another jet soars into view, and another invasion force swarms into baggage claim in search of you. They don't care how tired you are. They have spent a lot of money, waited almost a year, and traveled half a day to get here, so they expect you to put on a smile and show everyone a good time.

Sometimes these planes, with passengers whose paperwork has your name printed all over it, pass each other in the sky. These are *doubles*, one flies out as one flies in, and doubles are disorienting. The people, with whom you just spent three or four or even five days, hug you, tip you, thank you and cheer for you, take their final pictures with you, and by the time they're boarding their flight for home, their trip winding down, you're starting all over again, introducing yourself, and trying to remember the names attached to a fresh batch of faces.

If the groups happen to cross in the same terminal, you almost question your sanity. You watch your departing group wearily walk through security and around the corner just before your next group (which looks exactly like the first group) bounces back out. Through what kind of Dr. Seussian machine slide these star-bellied sightseers?

What kind of injection are they given to replenish their energy? All season long, from March through June, students, teachers, and parents travel here from across the country. You wear them out, send them on their way, and then meet more of the same. But they keep coming, these worthy adversaries, they keep coming from California and Idaho, Mississippi and Texas, with the identical buzz of excitement, while your own resources are depleted, as your heels begin to throb, as your eyelids droop and smile fades.

They tend to blend into one large group, but they are not all alike. They only seem that way when you're tired or not paying attention. They only seem interchangeable when you first meet them or when, looking back at the end of a long season, your brain cuts together a montage so that all you can see over your shoulder are vaguely featured people with hair or hats, trudging behind you and taking pictures of whatever it is you're pointing toward.

But every group is comprised of individuals, I have to remind myself, each face desperate to break free from the mob that swarms around it. In the card they sign for you at the end of the trip, more than half will feel the need to add, beneath their names, a reminder: "the one who drank Dr. Pepper"; "future Fox News anchor"; "the dancer with the dimple"; "Red Sox #1." Some will keep in touch with you after the tour. Some you barely recall will reconnect with you online or through the post office. They will send you emails or ship you a care package from home. You will marvel at the variety of packaged nuts the regions of this country have to offer, and the t-shirts you wear at the gym will be adorned with mascots from schools you never attended.

The trips you remember are the ones with an element of the unusual. You won't remember all the groups that took the ferry to the Statue of Liberty, because almost all of them do, but you will remember the group who went out on a morning so frigid that dozens of people were literally crying on the dock. Likewise, you won't remember every ride to the top of the Empire State Building, but you will remember the evening when a thick expanse of clouds floated at the eightieth floor as far as the eye could see, so that you and your sight-seers were alone in the dark blue sky with the tops of the Twin Towers poking through in the distance, the rest of the city completely covered, while the lights of the buildings *almost* tall enough colored portions of the fluffy floor purple, green, and gold. You will remember the time you had to rush forty-one Californians to JFK by subway after their bus broke down at the hotel on a rainy Friday afternoon, the collapsed sidewalk grate that almost killed a grandmother from Michigan, the car speeding from a jewelry heist that rear-ended your bus of Hawaiians, the blizzard that kept forty Nevadans on the East Coast for an additional three days before they at last escaped by taking Amtrak and flying out of Baltimore, as well as the euphoric Texans photographed by a hundred paparazzi as they rode the Central Park Carousel with Angelina Jolie.

And you will remember very well the group for whom everything fell apart, the tour in June of 2008 that lost a student and was abandoned by a chaperone, that had a suitcase stolen and was haunted by a ghost. You will remember almost everything about that tour, because at one point you cursed at an eighth-grade girl and at another point you found yourself in your living room wearing only a towel with two of the adults who should have been at the theater. You won't be able to forget a tour like that, because those are the ones that are followed up with letters and emails from *numerous* participants, people who want to relive the trip, explain their behavior, and apologize or thank you.

One will send you photographs shot on the tour, and even though the objects in those pictures have already appeared on a million post-cards, these will be close-ups from angles you have never seen and will change how you think about those parts of the city, those tiles, light bulbs, and handrails. You'll blow up some of those photos to hang in your apartment and then think of that trip each and every time you ponder the wall.

One letter in particular will arrive that will make you rethink and reevaluate the tour from start to finish.

Most groups come and go too fast for you to really process who they are, but others linger, they leave fragments behind so that afterward, long afterward, you're able to piece most of their trip together and understand that the reason they came to blows at Ground Zero was complicated but had something to do with the Civil War, a sexual assault on the subway, a black dress, a memory of prom, a poll taken on evolution at Planet Hollywood, and, of course, tardiness. Always tardiness. You'll think back, dissect the itinerary, identify the eight or nine who determined the tour for everyone else, and you will replay their stories in your mind, remembering what you saw, filling in what you didn't, beginning with their arrival, with the two teachers, who bravely, though unwittingly, led their groups into battle.

So, a couple years ago…

Or eighty-two groups ago…

Or three thousand four hundred twenty-three people ago…

DAY ONE

Thomas Ledcke High School
Arrive LaGuardia Airport 4:02 p.m.
United Flight 396 from Seattle via Chicago

K.C. Crown Middle School
Arrive LaGuardia Airport 4:15 p.m.
Delta Flight 234 from Savannah

4:30   Meet Guide and Tour Bus at LaGuardia Airport

4:45   Bus Tour into Manhattan

6:00   Chinatown

7:15   Dinner in Little Italy

8:15   Bus to Empire State Building

8:30   Empire State Building

10:00   Grand Central Terminal (Time Permitting)

10:45   Check-in at Hotel

Thomas Ledcke High School
(Seattle, Washington)
2 chaperones, 2 adults, 15 students

CHAPERONES:
 Pete Troiano (LEAD)
 Lu Takahashi

ADULTS:
 Barbara Swope
 Dennis Brewer

STUDENTS:
 Ryan Mendive
 Cody Swope
 Laurie Albright
 Jenny Zhang
 Brittany Brewer
 Dana Spencer
 Jacob Heller
 Sun Tzu
 Tracy Powell
 Melanie Sadler
 Michele Baroody
 James Chappelear
 Bobby Fields
 Jennifer Ferrell
 Tommy Newman

K.C. Crown Middle School
(Sherrodsville, Georgia)
4 chaperones, 3 adults, 10 students

CHAPERONES:
 Kelly Mitchell (LEAD)
 Ramona Harrison
 Nancy Davis
 Wally Williams

ADULTS:
 Penny Tucker
 Travis Tucker
 Dina Burns

STUDENTS:
 Clint Williams
 Faith Hutsell
 Alice Tucker
 Pamela Burns
 Brandon Burns
 Brandon Nervik
 Brandon Ellerbe
 Lash Dautenhahn
 Ashley Schmidt
 Zach Kurlansky

Thomas Ledcke High School
Arrive LaGuardia Airport 4:02 p.m.
United Flight 396 from Seattle via Chicago

AS PETE TROIANO would describe it to me over dinner that night, paintings on loan from the Metropolitan Museum of Art were lining the runways at LaGuardia when they landed. Van Gogh, Rembrandt, Mondrian, and O'Keefe were all represented beneath protective glass, atop easels made of polished marble. Even better, opera singers, from the other Met, were now directing the planes as they taxied. Dozens of brawny baritones and even brawnier mezzo sopranos were striding along the tarmac, spears aloft, pointing pilots to appropriate ports. Year in and year out, he was convinced, the city of New York reinvented itself as the cultural capital of the universe. What other city employed its opera singers as parking attendants? In the distance, a luggage truck bearing a corps de ballet stopped alongside a 737, and the dancers, in tights and tutus but wearing thick canvas gloves, began leaping to the ground to await the cargo. Their backs, their knees! They might never dance again. Impossible! This was impossible.

Pete snapped his eyes open. His right hand instinctively flew to his mouth to wipe drool out of his beard. The plane was pulling to its gate. He had slept all the way from Seattle to Chicago and most of the way to New York. He felt like a drowsy grandpa, but to be fair: he had needed to meet his group at Sea-Tac almost nine hours earlier, four thirty in the morning Pacific Time, which meant he had had to leave his house at three forty-five to be on the safe side. This required him to be in the shower at two forty-five, and though he tried to go to bed at ten, he couldn't fall asleep until twelve, so he was working on fewer than three hours of sleep when they boarded the first aircraft, and despite the nine hours already together and the ten months planning the itinerary with his account manager—recruiting interested students, passing out forms, collecting deposits, helping with fundraising,

arguing with the tour company about its sneaky little insurance sur-
charge, conducting meetings with the kids and their parents, and re-
turning countless phone calls—this, right now, was the moment the
trip really began.

The extinguishing of the seatbelt light and the accompanying bell
worked on Pete like a starting pistol. His was the first belt unbuckled,
and in four deft moves he was standing in the aisle, his overstuffed
backpack swinging from his shoulder. He preferred to be among the
first off the plane and liked to sit as close to the front as possible,
which meant, since he was a public school teacher, behind business
class. When the door was popped open, Pete followed the seven men
and women who would spend the rest of their week raising interest
rates or "going to contract" or bundling mortgage-backed securities
or performing credit default swaps. As soon as he stepped off the jet,
however, he leaned slightly forward and overtook each and every one,
swerving and dodging, squeezing between the walls of the carpeted
tunnel and the purposeful strides of the suits, to enter the terminal
in first place. Then, after all that, he stepped to the side and turned to
wait for his students. He ignored the glances of the business class who,
no doubt, wondered why in the world someone would rush by them,
with the speed and urgency of an ER nurse, only to stop and stand at
the gate. This man, they thought, must be unstable. Pete would not
disagree: he taught in the American public school system, and nothing
was crazier than that.

This is what the energy of New York always did to him. It first
happened when he came with his parents to visit colleges in the North-
east. (He had Columbia chosen before he even saw the campus, much
to the dismay and horror of his parents, who failed to see the allure of
New York in 1977.) It happened whenever he returned to the city at
the start of each semester, and it had happened every spring since June
of 1990 when he began bringing high school students from Seattle for
four days in the Big Apple. 1990? 1977? He scratched his beard and
set down his heavy backpack between his feet. It was mind-boggling

how these dates which he remembered with such clarity had receded so quickly into the past. How could so many years have crammed themselves between 2008 and 1977? Pete was as old as Lincoln Center and, like Lincoln Center, the wear and tear was showing.

The first of his group to emerge was Tracy Powell, the only sophomore on the trip. Since Pete taught upperclassmen, he didn't know her very well, but she seemed a sweet-natured girl—chubby, curly-headed, and freckled—who took a quick picture of the unimpressive terminal before joining him.

"I'm in New York City," she said with astonishment and then, as a bold affirmation: "I'm in New! York! City!"

Next came Pete's fellow chaperone, Lu Takahashi, the new drama teacher. Twenty-four years old. To Pete, that seemed as impossible as opera singers on the tarmac. Closer in age to the students than to many of her colleagues, Lu bonded effortlessly with the kids. In her first year, besides directing the school plays, she volunteered to sponsor the Class of 2011 and assist with student government. She arrived in the terminal encircled by four of her student council officers, class of '08, recently graduated.

The former president proclaimed, "Mr. T! We need a Starbucks immediately."

The treasurer seconded, "James owes us all mochas."

"He was the *Celebrity* loser," Lu said, as if that made any sense.

Pete answered, "Let's hold on. We didn't fly twenty-four hundred miles from Seattle for a Starbucks."

"Do they have a Tully's?" the secretary asked.

"I'm glad you got my point."

The flock Pete was going to lead to baggage claim was spilling out of the tunnel. Two of the girls ran past, shouting about the restroom, which somehow gave license to others to follow or buy a snack. When Pete announced that they would meet outside of the bathrooms in five minutes, they all dispersed. His flock had become a pack of feral cats. He waited for the other two adults in the group. Parents had the potential to undermine a teacher's authority, and Pete had long ago learned to carefully interview each parent who voiced interest in joining the trip to New York. Barbara, the stepmother of the school's star quarterback, and Dennis, the recently divorced dad of one of the younger girls, had both been Pete-tested, Pete-approved. He waved and smiled when he saw them. He repeated the instructions and pointed to their meeting spot.

Just before he turned away, he saw one more recent graduate emerge. Her name was Melanie, and her hair was blue. Pete, who taught Latin and Honors English, had never had her in any of his classes, knew little about her except what everyone else saw: her fingernails were painted black to match her clothing; her ears were each pierced six times; her lip just once. She was courteous and always the first to turn in her forms and payments. That surprised Pete, but he reminded himself that just because a student was pierced didn't mean she couldn't be punctual.

He informed her, "We're all using the restrooms."

Melanie pulled her thumbs from underneath the straps of her backpack and held them up in front of her face as if to say either *Got it!* or *Look what happened to my thumbs.* They walked side by side. She hadn't proven herself a talker at any of the meetings, so after asking her a couple of questions about her day so far, questions answered in nods, Pete concentrated on tracking down his cats who were scattered up and down the corridor.

"Can I get you a latte, Mr. T?" Lu called from an espresso line off to the left.

"No, thank you," he answered. It was the principle of the thing. The clock was ticking.

There were three girls inside a store on the right already shopping for souvenirs from a city they hadn't yet experienced. He didn't bother to remind them that there would be cheaper places, because they weren't children and they were not broke. At least four in the group came from Microsoft money. The trip itself cost over two thousand dollars, and only three of the students participated in any fundraising. The others just asked mom and dad who paid the full price. Most of these kids had hundreds of dollars for their four days in the city, and a few had credit cards. But this trip, as Pete repeated several times at each of their meetings, was *not* a shopping spree.

—Yes, there will be opportunities to shop, but we are going to New York to explore a cultural capital, to attend theater, visit museums, and broaden our horizons. We're not spending two thousand dollars for four days to shop at the Gap.

—Oh, Mr. T! We don't shop at the *Gap*.

—I'm glad you got my point.

Five minutes became ten and were now approaching fifteen. The coffee people were now in the bathroom and the bathroom people were in line for coffee. Their carry-on luggage appeared strategically placed across the carpet as a barrier against anyone trying to pass. Pete was relieved that his fellow chaperone began to take the initiative. Lu urged the group to move to one side, pointing out the obstruction. One of the students asked, "What obstruction?" and then did a pratfall over an abandoned backpack.

When the student council vice president was back on his feet, Pete did a count. He was here, Lu was here, the two parents were here, he saw their two children, Pierced Lip was listening to her iPod, there were the computer boys, the shoppers were back, I-am-in-New-York-City was coming out of the bathroom, the student council made four…seventeen, eighteen.

"Who's missing?" Heads swiveled, and shoulders shrugged. He counted again. There were only eighteen people. Someone was still in the bathroom, and he decided that this was the perfect time to give yet another reminder: "Guys, we have to shape up. This has taken fifteen minutes. We only have four days for our entire trip. We want to see as much as we can. Am I right? We've talked about this. We're on a tight schedule and, if we're not careful, we can miss appointments, we can miss meals, we can be late to the theater." Silence. "We can miss valuable shopping time." Anguished groans. "And remember: we're sharing this trip with another group. We're not the only ones. This group is going to be too large to wait on one person again and again."

"Oh my God, Mr. T.," said one of the shoppers, "you're so East Coast all of a sudden."

"Well, when in Rome…"

"But we're kickin' it. We're good."

"We're not kicking anything," Pete argued. "We're still not here."

Lu, his fellow chaperone, said, "I think we are."

"We're missing one."

"I count eighteen."

"We're *nineteen*."

"You're counting Tommy." That is exactly what Pete was doing. There followed a moment of silence when each person withdrew, and the group that had just been blocking the entire corridor now almost disappeared into the wall. Since Christmas, nineteen had been their count. Throughout the winter, nineteen was their count, and into the spring, four adults and fifteen students (nineteen) remained their count. Until the Monday after prom. The empty seat on the flights here belonged to Tommy, the extra tickets and meal allotments in Pete's heavy backpack belonged to Tommy.

Thinking an apology would only make it worse, Pete said enthusiastically, "Well, then we're all here! Great! Onward!" He began to lead the way, repeating to himself "eighteen, eighteen, eighteen" while two of the kids, in their own attempt to lighten the mood, speedwalked past them all, pumping their arms and saying, "We're East Coast, we're East Coast."

K.C. CROWN MIDDLE SCHOOL
ARRIVE LAGUARDIA AIRPORT 4:15 p.m.
DELTA FLIGHT 234 FROM SAVANNAH

AT THE OTHER END of the aiport, in Terminal D, Kelly Mitchell had her sixteen lined up right behind her like ducks: ten eighth-graders-going-into-ninth; a dad; a mom; a grandma; her vice principal; as well as her fellow teachers, Ramona and, bringing up the rear, towering over them all, Wally, whose ten-year-old son was the group's youngest member.

Kelly was walking faster than usual to keep a few paces between herself and the trip's mother, who had just made her seventh complaint since the morning: "Isn't somebody from the tour company supposed to be here?"

When Kelly answered that they would connect at baggage claim, because greeters weren't allowed to come to the gate anymore, Dina Burns, world traveler that she was, snorted, "Since when?" as if the tour company had pulled another fast one, taking advantage of poor Kelly, inexperienced goober that she was.

"Since September 2001." Kelly felt a twinge of satisfaction at how fast that shut her up, and that was when she made a break for it. Just get to baggage claim, she told herself, keep Dina distracted. If you stand still, she'll find something to gripe about. Kelly regretted letting her sign up, but Dina wouldn't let her two children travel without her, and Kelly needed the numbers to defray the cost for everyone else.

This was Kelly's second time as leader, and she felt so much more relaxed. Having done it once, she knew she could do it again. She also had capable chaperones—Ramona and Wally, as well as Nancy, their vice principal, who would drive Ramona insane, but whose mere presence would keep the kids in check—so, with the exception of Dina Burns on her tail, Kelly was able to relish the carefree walk through Terminal D.

"LaGuardia is a magical place," Kelly would tell me two days later over the potent, off-duty, alcoholic drinks that followed our group's meltdown at Ground Zero.

I would agree: "Hours can disappear while you're waiting on your flight."

But Kelly was referring to Heidi Hubbard, the teacher who preceded her at the school. On the fourth day of *her* final trip as leader, as her group walked into the diner for breakfast, she spotted her boyfriend in a booth with a long-stemmed rose on the table. Their guide and another teacher knew about the surprise and sat everyone else while Heidi tentatively approached her boyfriend, who was supposed to be hundreds of miles away. As they hugged, Heidi noticed his brother and her own sister standing in the back of the diner recording their embrace with a video camera. The three of them had driven all the way to New York to sweep her off her feet and to document that sweeping. Heidi was not going home on the airplane that day with the rest of her group; she was going to spend an extended vacation with him and then take a road trip back home. Her eyes were glassy throughout breakfast, as they whispered about the different things he had planned, and she waved goodbye to her students. By the time the group arrived at the airport—this was legendary now—the tour guide had received the phone call to let everyone know that the young man in the diner had taken Heidi to Central Park, rented a boat, and proposed on the Lake. "And Miss Hubbard just said yes." The women and girls screamed so loudly and at such a high frequency that air traffic control over LaGuardia was disrupted for the next twenty minutes. Kelly was not on that trip, she only knew Heidi through photographs, but she had heard the story so often that she started telling it to friends. It was her favorite proposal story, and she related it as if she had been there, one of the women screaming on the departures curb at the airport.

"But why is *LaGuardia* magical?" I would ask since the proposal took place in Central Park, which was a far more romantic locale than Terminal D out in Flushing.

"Because Heidi flew *into* LaGuardia expecting to fly *out* of LaGuardia, and her entire life changed before she ever made it back."

"Right, but it changed in *Central Park*. Or at the diner that morning."

"Oh, Jack!" Kelly could never convince me that there was magic or romance at LaGuardia, but for her that airport vibrated with the possibility for change and love. She claimed she didn't have these same associations the year before when she brought her group through Newark, but here at Terminal D, with her sixteen behind her, she focused her eyes on a door at the end of the corridor, the door leading to baggage claim, the same door that Heidi Hubbard passed through, blissfully unaware that she would not see that door or that corridor again. Kelly slowed down and then stopped at the door, expecting it to open automatically. Magically.

"Ya gotta push it, Miss Kelly," she heard one of her students say. Kelly did. It opened.

—Aw, crap. Our leader can't even open up a door.

—Well, she's not used to the big city and all their fancy contraptions.

Kelly ignored the jokes and led her giggling gaggle down a short escalator. Among a throng of drivers holding signs, Kelly saw a family of three women with two small children. Tied to the strollers were four Mylar balloons. "Welcome Home!" The women and children were dressed up, and Kelly could almost smell their perfume and minty breath. She led her group into the fenced-in area off to the left, found their flight number on a display board, and directed them all to the carousel. After they passed her by, she stood to the side and watched the family. The girl, who looked four years old, was wearing a yellow sundress, and the boy, a two-year-old, wore dark blue jeans and a small white polo shirt. He pulled at the strings of the balloons and let go. He gave a dance as he watched the silver bob above him. The wife was the first to break off from the family. She ran forward. The object of their affection had arrived. On the breast pocket of his tan fatigues was his name: RUIZ. Ruiz dropped his duffel bag, grabbed her around the rib cage, and pulled her to him. They kissed before they said a word. The others stayed back and quietly watched, especially the boy who stood in his tiny Timberlands taking in this man who was eating his mama's face. They kissed and hugged as more people came off the escalator searching for their names scrawled on rectangles of folded paper.

"I don't see anyone from the tour company." This from Dina, the miserable mom.

"I'm sure they'll be here soon. Do you have your bag?"

"None of them are out yet." Dina let loose a groan over the ineptitude of the airline. "I'm goin' out for a smoke while we're *waiting*. Brandon's gettin' my suitcase. Don't leave without me."

"We won't," Kelly said with four spoons of sugar.

Ruiz and his wife were still hugging. Kelly pulled her cell phone out of her purse. The couple was whispering now. The wife reached behind her back and took one of his hands before turning. They both looked at the boy, standing his ground, playing with his fingers. Had they not met? Had Ruiz been away that long? They were two yards apart, the father and son. Ruiz leaned forward. He didn't scare the boy with an outstretched arm but instead put his free hand on his own knee. He said something Kelly couldn't hear. Still, the boy felt the need to retreat. He moved behind the legs of his grandmother. The father didn't push it. He was a smart one, that Ruiz. He focused his attention on the others, giving his son his space. It was going to take a little while for the boy to get used to the man in such big boots.

"God, I love LaGuardia," Kelly whispered through tears. Her boyfriend was going to surprise her. She was convinced. She felt it likely he was somewhere nearby, so she called their home number, expecting it to ring into voicemail, confirming her suspicions. She looked toward the escalator where Hunter might appear any second.

Hunter answered the phone and said, "Hey, baby."

Startled that he picked up, she said, "Oh, hey. We made it."

"I figured. I have the news on and didn't hear about a plane blowin' up." So he wasn't in hot pursuit.

"Do you miss me?" she asked.

"Sure do. You bought your dress yet?"

"Hunt, I'm in baggage claim. Tomorrow is our shopping day."

"I thought they did everything fast up there in New York City. Like it's already Friday or something." Kelly smiled. "You let me know when you get that dress. Send me a picture to my phone. We need to look smokin' hot. Red carpet hot."

"We will," she laughed. Across the way, she could see Wally chasing some of the boys off the conveyer belt. The three Brandons. Inseparable since kindergarten, the three amigos, the three musketeers. A big bear, Wally affectionately swiped his oversized paw against the head of one of them. The three then surrounded him. Sparring commenced.

"What are you doing?" Kelly asked. Her new scenario involved his packing his suitcase for a road trip up north like the one Heidi Hubbard's husband took. "Catching up on your sleep?"

He pretended to be insulted: "I know you did not just say that. I woke up early to drive you over sixty miles to the airport and then turn around and come back to start working on the yard. I'm about to mow the lawn…"

"Oops, Hunter, I have another call. I think it's the tour company."

"Have fun."

"I love you so much."

"Um, love *you*, baby," Hunter said less earnestly, removed as he was from the romance and magic of LaGuardia.

Kelly pressed the talk button and said hello.

"Oh! OH! Kelly Mitchell? It's Elaine Caine, listen, I've been trying to reach you. Oh! Oh! Did you get any of my messages? I'm with the Seattle group, that's who I was supposed to meet, and Jack, that's your tour guide, was supposed to meet your flight, but he's departing a group he just finished with at US Air which is in another part of the airport and WE'RE IN ANOTHER PART OF THE AIRPORT and so are you all right? No problems? Listen, Jack is on the way to you and since the bus wasn't in the area when I called just a few minutes ago, I decided to bring the Seattle group to you. You'll love them, they're so sweet, I just didn't want us to wait around at United twiddling our thumbs, so I made the executive decision, and we all got on one of the shuttle buses, which was a LITTLE PROBLEMATIC, but this gentleman right here driving us is an angel. You're an angel, sweetheart, what's your name? Reggie? Great, Reggie, YOU'RE GREAT, you're an angel, so, Kelly Mitchell, we are on the way to you, DON'T PANIC, we're almost there, I can see your terminal up ahead, and then we'll call the bus and all of you will roll into town. Do you have all your bags? Is Jack there yet?"

"Not yet."

"Okay, he will be, DON'T PANIC, and we'll be there in a second, A MINUTE, we'll be there in a minute. Step on it, Reggie, you're an angel, you're a sweetheart…" The phone call ended. Kelly was relieved Elaine Caine was not their tour guide.

"Got your bag, Miss Kelly," said a voice behind her. It was Lash Dautenhahn, the quietest, shyest, most polite boy on the trip. Also the most country. His family sharecropped. Many of their kids lived or worked on farms, but Lash worked the hardest, sometimes arriving at school smelling of fertilizer, and while all of the kids needed to do some fundraising in order to help their parents pay for this trip, he had to raise every last penny. What Lash didn't know was that he was just over two hundred dollars short and Kelly, whose trip as the leader was free, made up the difference out of her own pocket.

"Thank you, sir. Always the gentleman."

"Yes, ma'am," he replied with a nod, eyes down, embarrassed by praise.

Kelly saw Dina coming back from her smoke, and before she could open her mouth, Kelly said, "They're bringing the Seattle group to us as we speak, Mrs. Burns. Life is good."

4:30   Meet Guide and Tour Bus at LaGuardia Airport

THE SEATTLE GROUP was packed aboard a terminal-to-terminal shuttle where one of the larger suitcases protruded from an upper shelf, pressing against the side of Barbara Swope's head and forcing Barbara, the stepmother of the school's star quarterback, to stare at the woman who spoke without stopping for air: "We're almost there, Reggie, then you're done with us, we'll be on our way and you'll forget all about us by US Air, you're an angel, Reggie, YOU'RE AN ANGEL, don't hate us, you hated us a little when we got on, I could tell, but you're saving the day, Reggie, YOU'RE SAVING THE DAY…"

Tonight, Barbara thought, one of Reggie's kids would be spanked without knowing why.

Barbara had been the first to speak up in baggage claim after Elaine Caine barreled her way through the crowd of recent arrivals, shouting, "Seattle? Seattle?" Barbara already had her suitcase and was waiting to the side as the rest looked for their luggage. Many in the crowd were from Seattle, so twenty different people nodded to Elaine Caine, which compelled her to consult a sheet of paper in her hand. Barbara didn't think this woman was there to meet a high school group, because if she were, wouldn't she have simply walked up to the only pocket of high school students in sight?

When the strange woman began calling out the name of their school, Barbara raised her hand and the woman grabbed it. "Oh! OH! You're here, I ran straight over from Continental as soon as I got that group off, you wouldn't BELIEVE how many groups are coming in today, your tour guide is departing a group at US Air, and so I'm picking you up and don't even know if Jack will get to the other group in time, Jack's his name by the way, did you just get here? I hope you just got here, are you ready to go? I'll try to call the bus, I'm Elaine Caine, by the way, and that's a beautiful outfit you're wearing, VERY CHIC. Nowadays most people on planes look like they're taking the

Greyhound, makes you wonder what the people on Greyhound are wearing. Are you the teacher? No? He's right where? I'll go introduce myself, thanks so much, you're an angel, you're a SWEETHEART, maybe I should call the bus first…"

She pulled her phone from an oversized bag. Her thumb then flicked it open too quickly. The phone went flying, hitting the floor and skidding between the legs of a man holding his laptop in one hand and typing with the other. Elaine bent over and reached between the man's legs. When he looked down at her, she looked up and said, "Funny we always meet like this, I'm joking, sorry, sorry, my phone, you're an angel…" When the group was gathered, she told them that their bus wasn't at the airport yet, but that they couldn't just stand around—if they waited for the bus to pick them up and then had to drive over to pick up the Georgia group, they would be losing valuable sightseeing time.

One of the shoppers cried, "We can't lose ANY time in Chinatown."

"Then it would make more sense to hop a shuttle and meet the other group at D."

Barbara, considering all the luggage, thought this was a deranged idea, but Pete, their fearless leader, seemed to wilt in Elaine's presence—when on the East Coast, do what the East Coasters do—because before Barbara knew it, they were all hurrying through the automatic doors into the warm, fume-filled air and clambering aboard a small bus with a driver, who looked at Elaine like the crazy woman she was.

This was a far cry from the other time Barbara had come to New York. Seven years earlier, Christopher (the fiancé who did not become her husband) brought Barbara with him on a sales awards trip. They flew business class, direct, non-stop, from San Francisco into JFK, where they were met by a tall young man in a black suit with green tie, holding a laminated sign with both Christopher's name and the Lexus logo. He shook their hands, welcomed them to New York, asked how their flight had been, and listened to the answer as if they were the only couple to have flown on an airplane in the last thirty years. Then he held his arm out toward the appropriate carousel. Their bags were the first to come into view, and the young man briefly disappeared and returned with a wheeled cart, transferred their bags himself from the belt, made a phone call, and led them to the proper door where, as if on cue, a limousine pulled up to the curb. The trunk popped open. The driver, an African American gentleman in livery (*Simon*, she still remembered) came around the car for their bags. The young man in the suit opened a rear door, informing them that Lexus had provided chilled champagne and sparkling water for their ride into the city and that he hoped they would have a wonderful stay in the Big Apple. And they had. That Friday through Monday, no one, anywhere in the world, had a more perfect weekend.

That glamorous vacation was why she told Michael (the fiancé who *did* become her husband) that she was interested in joining her stepson on his trip to New York. So far, the glamor was elusive.

Their group stumbled off the shuttle. The doors shut behind them, and the bus screeched away as if Reggie were deliberately trying to pepper Elaine Caine with gravel.

Tracy, the chubby girl next to Barbara, said earnestly, "We get to see another terminal at LaGuardia!" Barbara wasn't very impressed with the first one but smiled at the nerd.

Elaine Caine was already across the street and moving into the building. Pete was right behind her, and the rest of the group was following, chatting, laughing, enjoying anything thrown their way. Barbara wished she could feel like they did, but how could she, with memories of her previous trip outshining the present, eclipsing the image of the yellow cab speeding toward them from the right? The taxi stopped; the driver pressed into his horn. Barbara didn't make eye contact. She concentrated on pulling her suitcase with carry-on strapped to it and keeping her purse on her shoulder. It would have been nice had her stepson offered to help with a bag. Where was that man with the green tie? Where was Simon?

And now, she realized as she reached the curb, they were about to merge with the other school: the Georgians. She chanted, "Please be Atlanta, please be Atlanta."

This terminal was dingier than the first one. This was not the New York City she remembered—a city of high ceilings, walls of marble, great expanses of glass, giant arrangements of flowers placed beneath elaborate chandeliers. This was a low-ceilinged room with ugly brown tiles that were smeared monthly with a dirty mop after the toilets overflowed.

Barbara looked up from the floor to see the Georgians. City dwellers they were not. There was also something wrong with their students. The kids appeared smaller than theirs. Either the students were severely malnourished, or this was a middle school. There was one boy who looked even younger. He couldn't have been more than ten, standing next to a giant of a man whose name Barbara would wager was Bubba or Jimmy Joe. A couple of the adults, grown women, were wearing t-shirts and denim shorts. One of the boys was wearing a t-shirt with the Confederate flag on it. Many from Seattle would joke about the wording of the apparel later. On the front, the shirt read: "Have I offended you?" On the back: "Good, you've made my day." Barbara was appalled. There was an African American boy standing right next to the boy wearing that shirt, but she decided that he couldn't have been too traumatized: he seemed to be a friend of the young rebel soldier.

The two groups were facing each other now. Elaine Caine introduced them. Their leaders shook hands, like team captains before a championship match. Barbara thought the Georgian leader was a beautiful young woman, wearing ironed Capri pants and a fitted blouse. Size 4, Barbara would guess, which would make her one of the few southerners not waging a battle with diabetes.

The giant shouted out, "HOWDY, Y'ALL! YOU READY TO WHOOP IT UP?" His group laughed heartily. He was obviously the clown. Barbara's group laughed nervously.

"There he is, everyone," Elaine Caine continued, *continued* because she had never really stopped talking. "That's your guide! Theeeeere's Jack!"

And this is where I came in.

Elaine's announcement called for a theatrical curtain lift, an orchestral flourish, some kind of tumbling routine with sparklers. But I was just a guy walking past a newsstand that sold Doritos and candy. The crowd turned to look at me. All those eyes. All those eyes homing in. One hundred eyes had just left me at Terminal C. The eyes that had been looking to me for three days to tell them what was what, what to do, where to go, and when to be back, were now scanning their boarding passes for their departure gate. Outside, on my walk from US Air to Delta, I had been anonymous. No one looked at me. I didn't have to perform for anyone. But now, here were more eyes, dozens and dozens of eyes, all aimed at me.

I was on the seventeenth day of a twenty-day stretch and had this one four-day tour remaining before a two-day break. If only I had known. If only I had been fresh. Alert. Awake. But I was burned out, numb, and desensitized. I was like a screener for the TSA who, in the morning, vigilantly stops and inspects a plastic bag of candy canes but, by the afternoon, yawningly overlooks a suitcase packed with hunting knives and handguns. If only this had been *my* Day One. I would have been better prepared for what was coming. Or would it have mattered? Looking back now—as I reread their emails and letters; as I try to recall everything they told me over meals, on subway rides, while waiting in lines, during walks to and from the hotel; as I try to remember what I myself directly observed on sidewalks, in lobbies, on buses and boats; and as I try to imagine what they didn't tell me, fill in what I didn't observe—I realize that this tour was doomed from the start.

Besides feeling groggy, I was also now completely bewildered. Why was Elaine Caine at Delta and why was my half of the group so large? Or was this her half? Had I misread the itinerary? Was I supposed to be at United, meeting the people from Washington? A beautiful woman with long dark hair stepped out of the crowd, her face glowing, and threw her arms around my neck. Did I know her? I returned the hug with her level of enthusiasm. Clearly, I was supposed to recognize her.

I greeted her cautiously, "Hey, *you*!"

"I'm so glad we got you again," Kelly said. Smiling, I stepped back. I needed the space to jog the memory. "I requested you way back in September." After I had a couple of seconds, she did look fuzzily familiar. I told her I was thrilled to see her again and then turned to face the rest.

"Hey, everyone! Welcome to New York City!"

What followed were the usual *WOOOOOOOOOs*.

I asked, "Now is this just the Georgia group?" Barbara Swope, standing in the back of the Seattle group, looked as if I'd just slapped her in the face.

Elaine Caine explained what she had done. I asked her how, did not bother with why. She started one of her rambling monologues about how it wasn't so difficult and that the driver of the shuttle was an angel and it was easy, easy, easy. I had a hard time believing that and was annoyed, because, not only had she dug a hole for me by alienating the Seattle group at the outset of their trip, she had stolen my buffer time: when our bus arrived, instead of chatting casually with the Georgians on our way to the main terminal, I would have to begin giving a tour to everyone in the next ten minutes.

"Great!" I lied.

"I'll call the bus!" Elaine flicked her thumb, caught her phone before it was airborne, and made the call. "John, John, John, it's Elaine Caine, I'm glad you're there, you're an angel…" She walked away until she was out of earshot, though, in some sense, her voice was never out of earshot. It tended to rattle around in your skull for a few days.

The woman I would come to know as Dina, or the Miserable Mother, approached and told me, flat out, how nice it was that I showed up. She said it, as southern ladies often do, with a smile, as if merely teasing. I refused to answer her directly and looked to those around her. I apologized for being three minutes late.

"I just finished with another group literally five minutes ago. Usually, I have more time between groups, but it's peak season right now. I'm *so* sorry you had to wait *so* long."

Kelly said, "We haven't been waiting at all. We just got our bags."

I looked back at the Monstrous Mother with three facial expressions that read, in sequence: "How interesting…I am now utterly baffled by your performance…I'm memorizing your face and will not forget this or you."

When I first started guiding, I would zero in on the people not enjoying themselves and start catering to them, but experience taught me that those people *never* enjoy themselves, that they prefer instead to suck the life out of anyone who looks them in the eye. Since that epiphany, I stopped trying to warm up people who wanted to be cold. Let them shiver in their shadows.

"HE'S ALREADY IN THE AIRPORT!" Elaine was back and shouting. "HE'S PULLING UP TO THE CURB! HE'S PULLING UP TO THE CURB!" She was wildly waving at us. I calmly joined her, whispering for her to relax. Thirty-five people followed us. Barbara from Seattle felt that they were now part of a mob whose pell-mell movement made the shuttle experience seem choreographed. There was bustling and fumbling, wheels rolled over toes, satchels swung into hips, people bumped along, modifying their pace, adapting, adjusting, some breaking out in front, those in the back having to stop now and then, all trying to find their natural rhythm within the mindless mass. The vehicle awaiting was a large white coach bus. It was clean, brand new, but sadly for Barbara, the driver was not Simon in his livery but a Korean man wearing black slacks and a white shirt. He was opening the luggage bays at the bottom of the bus. As the crowd pressed toward him, Barbara stepped to the side and escaped the melee.

Eventually, her stepson, Cody, their school's star quarterback, stepped up to her, reached out his hand and spoke quietly with an exaggerated drawl, more Texan than Georgian, "Lemme take that thar suitcase from ya, little lady." She suppressed a smile, squeezed his shoulder and quickly extracted herself from the hurly-burly to board the bus.

The kids in front of her oohed and aahed when they climbed up the curving staircase, and she admitted it was a luxurious bus—with brightly patterned seats, clean windows, the new car smell—but it was still a bus with gaping luggage bays, not a limo with a trunk popping open. She saw Dennis, the other Seattle parent, sitting at a window, and she took the seat next to him.

Dennis said, "There she goes." Barbara leaned over and looked past him to see Elaine Caine waving her arm at the bus windows. She was rushing off, Barbara assumed, to terrify another incoming flight. The tour company hired this maniac to greet groups. Maybe it was strategic. If you could get through her, you would enjoy New York so much more.

Barbara leaned back into her seat just as one of the girls from Georgia yelled: "LOOK! They got a BATHROOM on this thing!!"

4:45 BUS TOUR INTO MANHATTAN

TRACY, THE SOPHOMORE from Seattle, was so excited she was pressing her lips between her teeth to stifle the squeals, so every minute or two a high-pitched sound squeaked through her nostrils. Whenever that happened, and I looked her way, she pretended that she was trying to get her ears to pop. She was in New York City! Tracy Powell was in New York City! She was sitting in a seat right up front, in the row directly behind the one I claimed for myself above the driver. The two lead teachers took the first two rows on the other side.

I was standing in the aisle and fiddling with the microphone, "Hello, testing, hello." Shouts of hellos filled the bus. "And welcome again to New York City!" Cheers and hoots replaced the hellos. "First off, who's been to New York before?" Eight or ten hands were volunteered. "Okay, so how many—raise your hands high and proud—have *never* been here before?" Arms were raised throughout the coach, a garden of five-fingered sprouts. "Good, good. Lots of first-timers. Very exciting." I was not at all excited, but I forced myself to keep that smile big and bright. While we waited for the driver, I jumped right in. "You're now in the largest city in the United States. Does anyone know how many people live in the five boroughs that make up the city of New York?"

—A MILLION!

—A BILLION!

—LOTS!

—WHAT'S A BOROUGH?

—EIGHT MILLION!

"That's it!" For middle school groups, I always come armed with a bag of Starburst candies, sweet bribes for their attention, and I flung a red one toward a kid five rows back.

"There are over eight million people who live here," I tell all my groups, so my mouth was on autopilot. "If New York were a state, it would be the twelfth largest in the country. It's about the same population as Virginia! It's almost as populous as the next three American cities—L.A., Chicago, and Houston—combined. One out of every thirty-seven Americans is a New Yorker. Seattle, by the way, is a little over six hundred thousand. Atlanta? Fewer than that. Manhattan alone has a larger population than both those cities. There are 1.6 million residents on a skinny island that's only about 13.4 miles long. Just under twenty-three square miles. That's it. But twice as many people as Alaska. About seventy thousand people per square mile. So you have hereby relinquished all claims to personal space. We are going to be sharing sidewalks with thousands, so we'll have to talk about how to navigate without getting…"

Kelly from Georgia said, "I thought Atlanta was in the millions?"

With that, I pivoted back to numbers: "Only if you count the suburbs, the sprawl around a city center, the *urban agglomeration*, but if you want to talk urban agglomeration, then New York has a population of about twenty million, the third largest in the world." I held up another Starburst. "Can anyone name a city with more people?"

Kelly shouted, "URBAN AGGLOMERATIONS *ONLY*, PEO-PLE!" I was remembering her now. I liked her; she'd be fun.

Tracy, the nose squealer, stammered, "LON-LON-LONDON!"

"Nope." Others tried.

—CHINA!

"That's a country."

—INDIA!

"Same problem."

—TOKYO!

"There you go, largest in the world," I tossed a Starburst through the air and wondered where the hell the driver was. We should have been moving by now. "With around thirty-five million, Tokyo is the biggest urban agglomeration."

—THEY'RE SMALLER PEOPLE SO THEY DON'T TAKE UP AS MUCH ROOM!

—URBAN WHATSAHOOZ?

Through the window, I saw the driver finishing a cigarette. Bastard!

"Now the other city is south."

—MIAMI!

"Southern *hemisphere* and, remember, it can't be in the U.S. because New York…"

Tracy wouldn't give up, "BUENOS AIRES, SYDNEY, BANG-KOK, SOMETHING IN AFRICA! SOMETHING IN AFRICA!"

"JAKARTA, INDONESIA!" shouted one of the kids from Georgia and claimed the Starburst with Tracy's name on it. I could have just tossed Tracy one for the effort, but for some reason (i.e., power trip), I was very strict with the candy. Our driver joined us at last; I told him we were ready to go. The coach eased out to the left and accelerated past another bus, a few cars, and a lonely prayer rug.

At LaGuardia's Terminal D, underneath the exit ramp from the Departures curb, in the patch of dirt and wedge of air just before the concrete returns to earth, is a prayer rug for any taxi driver wishing to face Mecca before his next fare. Sometimes, in its place, is a piece of cardboard, but usually there's an actual rug. It's the kind of thing I would love to point out on my tours, but to do this the group has to take Delta and fly into LaGuardia. And I'm reluctant even if they do. If you introduce yourself and immediately point to an Islamic prayer rug, the worst groups, committed to keeping their boundaries clearly marked, will start spitting venom about Muslims, and even the best groups will grow concerned that they're embarking on a four-day tour of 9/11. From Terminal D, it's safer to direct their attention to Flushing Meadows where they can see the stadium where the Mets lose (for the baseball fans), the U.S. Open complex (for the tennis aficionados), the remnants of the 1964 World's Fair (for the history buffs) that look like flying saucers that were used in *Men in Black* (for the cinephiles) and were designed by Phillip Johnson for the New York State Pavilion (architecture) and are right beside the ice skating rink that housed the temporary headquarters of the United Nations (political science), all of which are on land that was once a giant ash heap that figures prominently in *The Great Gatsby* (literature).

The tour into the city was my chance to figure out who these people were. I plied them with information, numbers and stats, trivia and stories, to hear their responses, to see what they deemed interesting, and to gauge how familiar they were with a variety of references. Since their itinerary restricted them, as usual, as always, to Manhattan, I took five minutes to tell them about the two hundred eighty-two square miles that constitute the other four boroughs. I asked a question, tossed a Starburst, expanded on the answer. In this way, we covered the Yankees, hip hop, the whale of Long Island, Xerox machines, advertising, supermarkets, Louis Armstrong, Coney Island, hot dog carts, chewing gum, and the neglected or forgotten borough, the one that threatened to secede in 1993…

—STATEN ISLAND!

I threw a Starburst to the father from Seattle. Eyebrows were raised. Adults were eligible for Starbursts? This made the game harder. With everyone on the bus in full participation, we moved into the numbers and discussed the subway, yellow taxis, and the millions of dollars a day New York paid to get rid of its trash, at which point, post-garbage, I decided to take a break and confer with the two teachers about their itinerary. This permitted the group to chatter about what they saw through the windows—small houses connected with tiny front lawns and miniature driveways, gas prices posted at the stations, stores they recognized, or didn't, from home.

—These people don't got no yards.

—They don't got *any* yards.

—Where are all the trucks, the pickups?

—I hear they don't got Walmart up here.

—This part reminds me of Tacoma.

—I think my uncle used to live in Queens. But maybe New Jersey.

—Where's Delaware?

Tracy Powell from Seattle had no one to talk to, but she didn't mind. She was taken by the view, rendered speechless, squealing through her nostrils, and absorbing all the trivia rattled off about the boroughs. She was the youngest person in her group, the only one from her class. She would be a junior this fall. She hoped to make some friends on this trip, seniors-to-be to whom she could wave in the hallways next school year. She took from her backpack a list she had drafted at home.

TO DO IN NEW YORK CITY!!!!!

Take pictures of everything.
See TWO Broadway shows.
Ride in a taxi cab. (Hail one too.) (I hope it's the Cash Cab.)
Ride in a horse carriage.

Ride on the subway.

Eat a New York City hot dog from a cart in a park.

Eat a New York City hot dog from a sidewalk cart on a sidewalk. (And compare.)

Eat a New York City pretzel.

Eat a New York City bagel. (With a shmeer???)

Eat a New York City pizza.

Eat a New York City cheesecake.

Eat a New York City cannoli.

Eat a New York City pickle.

Eat a New York City beeawlee.

Visit an Irish pub. (If they let me.) (Just to see one.) (There are Irish pubs in Seattle.) (Have I been?)

Mail a postcard from New York.

Buy an I ♥ NY t-shirt.

Pet a police horse.

Shop at Tiffany's. (Something cheap, just for the bag.)

Sit on a bench in Central Park.

Row a boat in Central Park.

See the statues of Balto, the bull, and the Flying Gold Man.

Buy a shawl.

Sit on a staircase and people watch. (Try for a STOOP.)

SEE A CELEBRITY! GET MY PICTURE TAKEN WITH HIM/HER! (Hopefully THEM.)

Stand outside the Today show with a sign.

Take a picture with the lions at Library. (Or is it City Hall?)

Visit as many sites as possible from The Great Gatsby, Sex and the City, Gossip Girl, Friends, and Seinfeld.

Have a coffee at Central Perk.

There was nothing to cross off yet. Her greatest fear, and the reason she made sure to show me her list early the next morning, was leaving a location only to find out that *that* had been the neighborhood where the Naked Cowboy sang or where they sold the best pickles. She would have to keep her eyes wide open.

At the group's first full view of the Manhattan skyline, I got back on the mic to point out individual buildings and to make sure they saw that there were two distinct outcroppings of skyscrapers: downtown where the World Trade Center had been and midtown where the Empire and Chrysler Buildings stood. As my mouth rambled, my brain was assessing the traffic—we'd be through the tunnel ahead of schedule—when our driver dipped down an exit ramp and took a right for the bridge. Had I not asked him to take the tunnel? I couldn't recall. But this route, a more scenic tour, would add another thirty minutes to my already taxed voice.

"So we're going to take the bridge!" I announced, as if that had been the plan. The traffic down on these streets was scarce, which is maybe why our driver went rogue, and we were soon making a turn and beginning to climb the cantilevered structure that would take us from Queens to Manhattan. I mentioned the television programs and movies that used the bridge and asked if anyone knew the name of it.

"Hint: it's a Simon and Garfunkel song." For the adults.

—BRIDGE OVER TROUBLED WATER!

—THE FIFTY-NINTH STREET BRIDGE!

"Right. Also known as the Queensboro."

"From *The Great Gatsby*!" Tracy exclaimed.

"Yes!" I was impressed and handed her a Starburst from my bag. Yellow. The one flavor she didn't like, she told me later. She thought it tasted like wood polish, Lemon Pledge, but she ate it anyway. It was a prize, her reward. Tracy thought she heard someone mimicking her, "From *The Great Gatsby*." A few people laughed. From her school. This was why she had been pressing her lips between her teeth. She decided to stay quiet for the rest of this bus trip. She didn't want people to turn against her. Maybe they would forget what she said, since there was so much to look at. I elaborated, "There's a memorable scene in *The Great Gatsby* when Gatsby and Nick are driving into Manhattan, and Nick thinks, and I'm paraphrasing here, that the city seen from this bridge is the city seen for the first time, every time, in its wild promise of all the mystery and beauty in the world. Anything can happen once we slide over this bridge."

Tracy chewed on her first Starburst and smiled.

Anything can happen once we slide over this bridge.

"Oh, I hope so," Tracy whispered.

IN THE BACK of the bus, ten-year-old Clint asked his dad, "You get one of them questions right, will you give me the candy?"

Wally, the giant chaperone from Georgia, whose bulk could easily be seen from the front of the bus, wasn't sure he would get any of the questions right, and the pressure that his son expected him to wasn't going to help things. He wanted more questions about the Yankees or the Mets, the Giants or the Jets. Wally was a gym teacher. He also taught math. What about a word problem? The bus leaves LaGuardia traveling at forty-five miles per hour...

"Will you, Dad?"

"Son, you don't need any more candy. You went through that whole bag of Skittles."

"Naw, I shared that," Clint defended himself. "You know what else we need?"

"What?"

"More cameras."

"How many you use?"

"Two."

"You took two rolls at the airport?"

"*Two* airports! And the plane! I took a whole mess of pictures on the plane." Clint was Wally's youngest child, and Wally knew he would be buying more cameras. "Look out for that tram he said was from *Spiderman*. I'll look out this side, you look out the other."

Wally looked to his left across the aisle where the blue-haired girl from Seattle was sitting low, her knees up on the seat in front of her, iPod wires in her metal-studded ears. Two of her classmates were behind her—nice future computer programmers who were making up for her lack of attention. In the row in front of Wally were the three Brandons taking a break from their fart jokes to listen to the tour.

Wally looked back down to his right at an island with tall apartment buildings stretched below the bridge in the middle of the river. He wondered if that was Long Island but then remembered the bus was leaving Long Island because Queens was part of Long Island. He knew home and the surrounding counties like the back of his hand, and he was rarely anyplace where he needed a map, but here he didn't know what direction he was facing, what was behind him, where the sun was. He knew as much as his ten-year-old did, and that was a peculiar feeling.

"Now over there to your left, that part of New York is not part of New York or even part of the United States…"

What the heck? Where? What? What?!

"It's international soil. That complex is the United Nations. Radical architecture at the time. The tall building with the green glass is where the administrative offices are. It's called the Secretariat…"

Like the thoroughbred, Wally thought. Ask a question about the Triple Crown…

"…short building with the dome is where the General Assembly and the Security Council meet. And that giant black building there is currently the tallest apartment building in the city."

—I BET THAT'S AT LEAST A HUNDRED A MONTH!

"You bet right," I said.

—DO I GET A STARBURST?

"I didn't even ask a question. Also, I should say not every question will be a Starburst question." I wondered how many more bags of Starburst I would have to buy before the season wrapped up. "And now, as we finish sliding over this bridge, welcome to Manhattan!" Cheers. "There's the tram in its port. Notice the grid, the straight avenues and streets. Avenues run north-south, streets run east-west…" And then

I was off, talking about the grid and blasting rock and leveling hills and draining swamps to create what was, up to that point, the largest artificial landscaping in the history of the planet. As I tried to provide a sense of orientation, describing downtown, midtown, uptown, and the respective neighborhoods they might know, Wally still felt out of his element, though he did recognize some familiar names. He needed to get himself a map pronto.

The bus passed Serendipity, Dylan's Candy Shop, and Bloomingdale's. There were squeals at each of the spots.

"You can drop us off right here," said one of the women up front.

"Are we going to be in this area?" one of the Seattle girls asked.

"We'll be on Fifth," I told her. "You can walk over. Up to your teacher."

"Let's talk about shopping when we're shopping," Pete said.

Back to the tour. Wally wondered how much of it he would remember. He wondered how much the kids were going to keep in their heads. Clint was looking out the window taking it all in, loving it. His vice principal had asked if Clint weren't too young for a trip to New York. "Will he be able to appreciate it?" Wally told her that Clint, at ten, was still a sponge. His brain wasn't poisoned by hormones yet: "He'll recollect more than most of the eighth graders." And probably more than me.

"We're about to cross Park Avenue. When we get the green light. This is one of the city's widest avenues and every day, underneath Park Avenue, about six hundred sixty commuter trains run in and out of Grand Central. You'll see a median strip planted with flowers and…"

Clint asked, "How'd they get all those trains under us?"

"I'll tell ya later," Wally answered. "It's tricky."

Cameras were raised—there were quick glimpses of flowers and small trees in between scores of yellow cabs—and the bus shot through the intersection.

"Okay, next up is Madison Avenue."

Well, that was fast, Wally thought.

Madison Avenue, a street of shops and boutiques, came up next, but the bus was past that even faster.

A Brandon shouted, "WHERE ARE ALL THE HOBOS?"

"Hobos?" I repeated. "They're back in the 1930s, riding boxcars and cooking beans by the side of the tracks."

"WHAT?"

"I'm joking with you. On your right is the Metropolitan Club…"

Wally took a deep breath. He was going to have to start writing this stuff down. He didn't have to remember everything, but he thought it would be nice to step off the bus with a little of what was said still in his mind. He ran through what he had learned so far. There are eight million people in New York, it would be the twelfth biggest state, *Spiderman* was on the Fifty-ninth Street Bridge, and so was some book about a magician. The U.N. is not part of the U.S., but I could have told you that. The grid, Park Avenue, shops on Madison…

"…Fifth Avenue, and Central Park starts right here." The bus turned left, and there was a surprising amount of green on the right. "I hesitate to tell the Georgians here, but do you see that gilt statue there with the angel?"

You couldn't miss it, Wally thought. There was a golden man, a soldier with a sword, sitting atop a mighty horse with a winged woman walking alongside.

"That's General Sherman on his March to the Sea." There were boos from the Georgians—nothing bloodthirsty about it, not viperish hissing, it's just what you did whenever Sherman's name was mentioned. I thought I'd have fun: "Notice the general there is sitting back in his saddle. He doesn't want to go. He doesn't want to take his place in history, he doesn't want to partake in this total warfare, but the angel will not let him refuse. She pulls him forward, leading him on a mission ordained in heaven." I was laying it on thick. "In her right hand, she holds the reins of the horse that is trampling the Georgia pine, and with her left, she herself crushes the palm frond representing the South."

Wally smiled, told Clint I was just "cuttin' up," and that it was time to play the "good ol' boy."

"THAT AIN'T NO ANGEL THEN!" Wally shouted. Several laughed, so he rattled off another. "I LIKE HOW YOU CALLED IT A GILT STATUE CUZ IT HAS GUILT WRITTEN ALL OVER IT!" And one more for good measure: "AND NOTE HOW THE YANKEE'S MAKIN' THE LADY WALK!"

Wally couldn't tell if the Seattle group appreciated his jokes. Most of them were near the front. He looked around his section of the bus to see how his comedy had gone over. The blue-haired girl was still listening to her iPod, but the computer boys across the aisle were smiling. Almost immediately, though, they turned their attention to a glass cube on the plaza through the window on the left.

"…on this next corner is where they lived…"

Who lived? Wally was still thinking about his jokes.

"…and it's supposedly where we got the phrase, 'Keeping up with the Joneses.' The wealthy were following the Joneses uptown, up Fifth Avenue. Now I'm going to point out the stores which you can visit tomorrow. I'm going to talk fast, here goes…"

You've been talkin' slow? Wally marveled, but he did notice the pace picked up: F.A.O. Schwartz, Bergdorf Goodman, Louis Vuitton, Niketown, Tiffany's, Trump Tower, Harry Winston…and his ten-year-old was taking pictures of them all.

"Clint, stop taking pictures out the window. There's too much reflection."

"Dad, we're in trouble," Clint said, solemnly looking up at his father. "We should've brung a whole bag of cameras."

IN THE MIDDLE of the bus, Lash Dautenhahn, the most country of them all, the one whose trip was secretly subsidized by his teacher, a boy with even fewer cameras than Wally and Clint, was sitting next to a girl he believed was the world's most beautiful high school student. He didn't know how he ended up among the Seattle group. When he took his seat, he was sitting in front of the Brandons who were his best friends on the trip. He would have sat in their row, but he wanted a window, and then they must have hopped back a row when he wasn't looking. All Lash knew was that he was surrounded by high schoolers and the one that looked most like a model lifted right out of a fashion magazine was sitting down next to him.

Miss Teen Seattle. She was very nice about taking the seat. She just smiled and said, "Is this free?" Lash didn't say anything back. He couldn't. He just cleared the seat for her by picking up his carry-on, which was just a plain backpack, nothing fancy, and placing it on his lap.

"...known as the Diamond District. Ninety percent of all the diamonds that come into the United States—that's nine-zero—go through this one block in Midtown Manhattan. Over two thousand companies operate on this one 750-foot-long block."

Lash found himself suddenly relieved that he had his carry-on in his lap. Then again, if Miss Teen Seattle wasn't sitting next to him, he probably wouldn't need a carry-on in his lap. This was one of his vocabulary words from last month: a *conundrum*.

"...an architectural joke...who would rob a bank if they could be seen doing it from the street?...built a glass bank with the vault on the sidewalk right through the window."

A vault right on the sidewalk?! Now this was something Lash had to see. There was a glass building off up to the right with silver trim. All the lights were on inside, but he didn't see a vault. People in the front of the bus were oohing, but he still didn't see it...now he did. Yep, right there, next to the sidewalk was a giant steel round door with the kind of handle you see on a submarine. That was a pretty amazing thing and maybe worth a picture. Lash only had two disposable cameras that had to stretch over four days. His mom bought three at Walmart, but she took one for a get-together, so he had to be careful not to waste any pictures. Too late: the bus was already past the bank and moving through a busy intersection. People were just running, Lash observed, like crazy folk. Where were they off to? Lash understood running that fast if you were running *from* something, but running *to*? No sense.

"The largest research library in the U.S. after the Library of Congress. The lions out front were nicknamed *Patience* and *Fortitude*, the two qualities Mayor LaGuardia said you needed to have to be a New Yorker."

—WHAT'S FORTITUDE?"

"Strength of mind to face adversity with courage."

—WHAT'S ADVERSITY?

Kelly called back, "BRANDON NERVIK, YOU'RE EMBARRASSING US!"

That library was worth a picture, Lash decided. The bus was stopped at a red light right between the lions. He aimed his camera at the building, but it wouldn't fit in the frame. There was nothing he could do about it. He clicked the button and sat back, hoping it took. Miss Teen Seattle leaned in and took a picture with her own camera. Digital. Lash could smell her hair. Very different. Very nice. Coconut? That jojoba thing from the commercials?

"I'm sorry," she said, leaning back.

"That's all right," he replied and then added, "*I'm* sorry."

"For what?" she smiled.

Lash had no answer and looked out the window. Her hand patted his arm as though she understood her own powers.

The bus was moving again. I was now probably talking about Ray Hood, the architect who designed New York's first modern skyscraper, the American Radiator Building, which stands behind the library on Fortieth, but Lash wasn't paying attention to the story. He was more obsessed with the words themselves. On our way to breakfast on Day Three, Lash would tell me that no one in his house talked as much as I did. Sometimes, maybe his mom, on a special occasion, if she had "some of her peach alcohol." He would ask how long it took me to get used to being in front of people. He couldn't picture anyone in his family ever talking on a microphone, anyone in his family ever raising their voice. Lash couldn't imagine how he would even muster the courage to call out an answer for one of those Starbursts. He couldn't speak in front of all these people.

The Seattle kids surrounding him looked rich, and they had been pointing out stores the whole way since the bridge. Compared to him, though, everyone on this bus was rich. Lash didn't get an allowance. Once, he asked his dad for an allowance, and his dad had a good laugh. Not mean or spiteful. The question just cheered him up somehow. His parents were happy for him when he came home and said he had raised enough money to go on the trip, and his brother said he would do his chores while he was away as long as Lash brought him back something from New York. His mom bought him the two cameras, and in the school parking lot, where the bus picked them up to take them to the airport, his dad gave him forty dollars of spending money. The two twenty-dollar bills were still in his wallet, unbroken and un-touched. From the stories Lash heard, Chinatown was the place for him. He could buy all sorts of things for forty dollars, but he didn't want to be out of money by the first night. He had written down some numbers on the airplane—how much to spend on his brother's present and the presents for his mom, dad, and baby sister. He still wasn't sure if he could buy anything for his grandparents, who always sent him a postcard whenever they went down to Tampa. Maybe he could just do that for them. How much would he have left over for himself?

As Lash worked out his finances, I introduced the Empire State Building. "We'll be back here after dinner, but you'll get a great view of it from the right side of the bus."

A voice of pure exasperation cried out from the fourth row: "Dang it!" It was the grandmother on the trip. Her name was Penny Tucker, and people called her either Grandma Penny or Mother Tucker. This was one of her Mother Tucker moments. "Everything's on the right side of the bus. The Rockefeller Center, the Diamond Street, the glass bank, the library…"

I reminded her, "St. Patrick's was on your side."

"We're not Catholic," she pouted.

"Trump Tower?"

"I can't stand that man's hair or his ego."

I smiled in response. What did she want me to do? Turn the bus around and drive in reverse? Strap her to the roof for a better view? Then she would complain about having to dodge the traffic lights.

RAMONA HARRISON, WHO was sitting next to Kelly in the second row, across the aisle from Tracy, might have taken me up on my offer for a rooftop seat. She wanted off the bus. First of all, she couldn't stand me, because I was rambling on about how great this was and how great that was and this was the tallest and this was the first and this was the largest and this was the last and this was the priciest. At least I was animated, she conceded to Kelly in their hotel room that night. I wasn't a "droner." I didn't overuse the words "like" or "actually." It was the content that troubled her. I had brushed off the question about homelessness with "semantic nonsense," and I hadn't said word one about how difficult it was for a single mother to raise a family on wages that would be laughed at by some of the teenagers on that bus.

For my part, I was well aware of Ramona, mainly because she was one of only two black people on the trip (the other being one of the three Brandons), so I would spend the next couple of days making sure that I wasn't looking directly at her when I discussed Harlem or the African Burial Ground. At Ellis Island, after describing the miserable conditions in steerage on the ships that carried the immigrants, I would remind everyone that, when it came to trans-Atlantic crossings, the Africans had it much worse.

Ramona was also a history teacher and not the dates-and-battles kind of history teacher, but the social-cultural, primary-source-document, what-were-the-little-people-doing kind of history teacher, and so when Madison Square appeared off to the left of the bus—trees and greenery filling three blocks—and I spoke of the Flatiron Building, the Met Life Tower, and how the park had been home to the hand and torch of the Statue of Liberty when funds were being raised to build her pedestal, Ramona wanted to add that this was also a park where people made out and drank too much and got arrested and proposed marriage and broke up and met with friends and debated politics and gossiped and lived life. For Ramona, New York was not an assortment of landmarks; New York was a place of people. (Way too many people, pushing up against each other, crowding each other, sucking each other's air.)

I would later learn that Ramona grew up near D.C., though every summer, from ages ten to sixteen, her parents sent her to stay for a month with an aunt in Brooklyn. She would arrive just in time for her to witness many of the neighborhood kids leaving for camps upstate as part of the Fresh Air Fund. Watching the kids, playmates for about a week, evacuate the city for healthier climes bothered Ramona. Why was she being exposed to the summer pollution that all the other children were fleeing? Her aunt was fun, however, as were two of her three boyfriends. She was kept entertained. She fondly remembered a roller rink and wheeling around on the smoothest wooden floors to the sounds of Donna Summers and Kool and the Gang. There were good times, but why couldn't she go to the camps in the mountains with her new acquaintances? Or, better yet, why couldn't she stay in Maryland with her year-round friends?

—Because your aunt wants time with you.

—Why the whole stupid month?

—Because it's her only time to see you. She saves up her sick days and vacation time.

—Well, why do I need to lose my vacation time?

—Don't talk back. It's complicated.

"It *was* complicated," Kelly later told me. "Turns out, Ramona's aunt was her mother."

As Ramona herself explained weeks later in an email, New York was full of these kinds of surprises, these secrets and lies. There were multitudes hidden from the naked eye. Ramona was not a fan of

America's largest city. She would much rather be at home with her family and her dog in the middle of the woods enjoying her summer break and not prolonging her school year by chaperoning students on a glorified field trip, but Kelly, her favorite co-educator, had begged her to come along, and Ramona promised she would. A trick of the mind: what had seemed a tolerable four days when she agreed to the trip last fall now felt like an unbearable ninety-two hours.

Part of what made it so impossible was the person on the bus who aggravated Ramona even more than I did: Nancy, their vice principal, sitting directly behind her and sharing pearls of wisdom collected on her one two-day trip to New York more than fourteen years ago. Three times now, Nancy had pointed out something and been corrected, which was two times more than most people needed to keep their mouths shut.

When the bus reached Union Square, Ramona had to listen as Nancy told Zach, their school prodigy, that after September eleventh the park was full of flowers and candles because the police were not allowing people south of the park. She knew this from TV, but she made it sound like she'd been there. Six days a week, Ramona had to put up with this woman—five days at school as well as on Sunday, when they always seemed to end up at the same restaurant after church and Ramona had to watch Nancy feign to be the most pious, good-hearted Christian with whom the good Lord ever graced the state of Georgia. All of this had grown more difficult since that day in April when Nancy had informally called Ramona into her office at school and gently suggested a different way for her to teach.

"Now we're crossing Houston Street, which means we're south of Houston, which means we're in…? Starburst question!"

—SOHO!!

A cherry-flavored Starburst soared to the back of the bus, and Ramona thought, *When one of those scratches a cornea, how much do you think your tour company will pay toward medical bills? That's a Starburst question for you.*

Having only read that Starburst question in her facial expression, I did not answer it. I talked instead of cast-iron architecture and the invention of the elevator, without which there would be no skyscraper, no urban density. The elevator was what gave the city, in Ramona's words, way too many people, pushing up against each other, crowding each other, sucking each other's air.

"The first building to have a safety passenger elevator is coming up on your left..."

I pointed out to Mother Tucker that the building was on her side of the bus, but Mother Tucker was asleep. Her head was back, her mouth wide open, as if waiting for a dentist.

"Okay, everyone, we're almost in Chinatown."

There were cheers from numerous seats. We had made good time, so the group had an hour before meeting back to walk to dinner. After conferring with the teachers, I gave the instructions: the high school students from Seattle had to be with at least one other person; the middle schoolers from Georgia had to stay with an adult. I gave a quick tutorial on haggling and told them they weren't allowed to buy the baby turtles or laser pointers.

—WE WANT PURSES!

"And here's the deal with those. *Nothing* is real here. Please don't come back to us having spent all of your money on what they've told you is a real Gucci, a genuine Prada, an authentic Coach. All of those are counterfeit," I stressed, and then my autopilot mouth added, "and it's a multi-billion dollar industry that's taking a major cut out of the U.S. economy."

—WHERE DO WE FIND THESE PURSES?

"Well, the bags displayed openly are perfectly legal..."

One of the girls was saying, "The good stuff's in the back of the stores! They have these tiny rooms with hidden doors."

"Those still exist, but because of all the raids, they've had to get more clever."

Ramona spoke up, "Tell them who's raiding the stores."

"The police." Ramona wanted me to elaborate. "This is illegal." She egged me on. Ramona wanted me to 'tell it like it is,' a mantra of hers. "As soon as you step off the bus, people will approach you with pictures of handbags, and they'll want to take you several blocks away into the basements of old buildings where they're now storing their merchandise. Obviously, since you don't know the city, it's not the wisest thing to do—to follow strangers several blocks down winding streets into the basements of old buildings."

Pete, the Seattle teacher, borrowed the microphone to say, "No one in my group is to leave the designated area." Kelly took the microphone next and repeated word for word.

"WHAT'S THE DESIGNATED AREA?" one of the Seattle girls asked.

"You'll be on Canal Street between Mott and Broadway. We're turning off of Broadway now. So from this corner here until the street where we're going to get off the bus. You can also walk up and down Mott which has many stores and which is the original Chinatown. Let me give you a quick history of the neighborhood, because it's pretty fascinating. This is the oldest ethnic neighborhood in New York…"

The same shopper asked, "CAN YOU SHOW US WHERE THE STORES ARE THAT HAVE THE ROOMS IN THE BACK?"

"I don't know," I lied. "They change all the time."

—HEY, THAT MCDONALD'S HAS CHINESE PICTURES ON THE SIGN!

—LOOK AT HOW MANY BAGS THAT WOMAN HAS!

—EVERYONE I KNOW WHO'S BEEN TO NEW YORK COMES DOWN HERE FOR BAGS, WHETHER THEY'RE COUNTERFEIT OR NOT.

"Yeah, that's true. And it's irritating that people come all the way to New York to buy fake handbags." Ramona was looking at me, nodding, encouraging. "You know, one of the greatest ironies in New York is that so many of its tourists who vote against immigration and send their sons off to 'fight terrorism,' are the same people who will come here and buy dozens of purses, in effect, funding both illegal immigration and terrorism." I almost stopped myself there—why was I still talking about this? I think I'd just read an article about the snakeheads in *The New Yorker*—but I felt the words gushing out of my chest. "The 1993 World Trade Center bombing was funded almost entirely by the sale of counterfeit Hard Rock NY t-shirts. The Madrid train bombing four years ago? It was funded in part by the sale of pirated music CDs here in the United States. Terrorists are moving into counterfeiting, because for every one arrested, only a handful are prosecuted, so the sale of bootleg DVDs is much safer and has a higher profit margin than the sale of heroin or cocaine. And the impoverished Chinese, smuggled in by the snakeheads who are funded by the sale of this counterfeited junk, are the ones sitting in puddles of urine in tunnels below Canal Street sewing onto purses labels that say Kate Spade, Marc Jacobs, and Louis Vuitton. So anyway, I don't want to tell you how to spend your money, but if you buy those purses, you're supporting terrorism and illegal immigration."

—AWW, WHY'D YOU HAVE TO TELL US THAT?

—THEY CAN'T ALL BE TERRORISTS!

The vice principal from Georgia said, "I'm not sure we should stop here from the sound of things."

Oops. I had gone way too far. I needed this free time to treat myself to a foot and back massage on Grand Street.

"No, no, no, there are plenty of legitimate souvenirs. And this is a great neighborhood just to walk around. Expose yourself to other cultures. If you walk up Mott instead of down Mott, you'll see the open air markets with live fish and eels, live frogs in buckets…"

—EW! WHO EATS FROGS?

—I DO. I ATE FROG LEGS BEFORE.

—THAT'S DIFFERENT.

—FROG LEGS COME FROM FROGS!

"Walk into the grocery stores and see what they're selling. Buy a dumpling, try a bubble tea with tapioca balls…"

"I'm getting purses," one of the Seattle girls bitched, "I don't care what he says."

—CAN YOU BUY FIREWORKS?

Kelly shouted, "NO, YOU CANNOT BUY FIREWORKS!"

—NOT EVEN THEM SNAPPING THINGS?

"NO, NOT EVEN *THOSE* SNAPPING THINGS."

The bus pulled over to the curb.

"Okay, you can leave your bags on the bus. Bring what you need for shopping and dinner. We'll get back on the bus after dinner to go to the Empire State Building."

—CAN WE LEAVE OUR BAGS ON THE BUS?

—YES, DUMMY! HE JUST GOT DONE SAYIN' THAT!

"Remember: we're meeting back on this corner. Seven o'clock, seven o'clock, seven o'clock. Check in with your chaperones, so they know who you're with."

People began standing up. Finally. Ramona relished the opportunity to stretch her legs and walk a while after a long day on a bus, an airplane, and another bus. She followed Kelly out of their row and thanked me for the commentary, particularly for the hard facts about Chinatown. That's what she wanted these kids to learn about—the oozing pus, the nefarious machinations underneath all the glossy postcard propaganda of the Big Apple, and she stepped off the coach into the stale, acrid air that let her know for certain that she was back in New York, New York.

6:00 CHINATOWN

AS THE GROUP DISEMBARKED, I leaned over from my row above the driver to tell him that we would meet him at Grand and Centre.

"Grand Central, okay," he said.

"No, not Grand Central! Why would I want you to meet us at Grand Central?"

"Right here."

"No. Not right here. Grand Street. And Centre Street." I pointed northwest. This was a standard pickup spot: drop in Chinatown; pick up in Little Italy. I felt like I had done this three hundred times in the last four months.

"What time?"

"Around eight, but I'll call you." I didn't trust this driver at all. Grand Central! I programmed his number into my cell phone, unsurprised to see this as the fourth "Driver John." All of the drivers for this bus company were Korean or Chinese, and most had taken "J" names—four Johns, three Joes, and a couple Jims. My favorite driver was James for a couple of years until he picked up my group one day, complained about all the "J" names at the garage, and told me his name was now Duncan.

I hopped off the bus to see my group filling up the entire sidewalk, already infiltrated by women with pictures of purses, belts, and watches. "You're blocking the sidewalk!" I called to my group. "Start walking, start walking!" Standing with their shopping buddies, the kids and chaperones immediately broke off, two by four by three by two, and floated down the streets, absorbed into the shops along Canal and Mott.

The father from Seattle was left standing beside me, "Not even a 'Bye, Dad.'"

"People go crazy here," I said warily, afraid this man expected to walk around with me. I was only five minutes away from a massage, from fingertips and knuckles pushing into the pressure points in my neck, on my feet, between my shoulder blades.

"The kids have money in their pockets now, but just wait: by the last day, they'll be holding our hands."

"So true, so true," I said, inching away. I felt slightly guilty, though that was quickly assuaged when I reminded myself that I had just taken them on a much longer tour than planned. I hurried into the crowd crossing Canal Street, because the longer I waited, the less time I'd have to nap on the massage table. I made an extravagant show of glancing at my watch, telegraphing my need to be somewhere very important. As far as he knew, I was confirming the reservation at the restaurant, I was going to the bank, picking up crucial paperwork, anything. I walked up Mott, thinking to myself that what I really needed by the end of a tour season was not a massage, but a good old-fashioned opium den. Yes, if I had been giving tours of Chinatown a hundred-odd years ago, I would most certainly have had my favorite opium den on speed dial.

BRANDON 1: Look at that barrel thing on that roof. That's in *Grand Theft Auto*.

BRANDON 2: I watch a whole mess of movies, but I don't take stock in where they are. All cities look the same.

BRANDON 3: That's not a movie. That's a video game.

BRANDON 1: That you played, dummy.

BRANDON 3: That we ALL played.

BRANDON 2: Oh, yeah. I don't remember that barrel thing.

BRANDON 3: Hey, what the heck's a kneeling bus?

BRANDON 1: LOOK OUT!

BRANDON 2: RUN!

BRANDON 3: Man, these people don't care.

BRANDON 2: That Chinese lady almost got it.

BRANDON 3: I'm not goin' anywhere near a taxi. They don't know how to drive.

BRANDON 1: Yeah, they do. They could do NASCAR.

BRANDON 2: They'd win.

BRANDON 3: That Chinese lady didn't even think of hurryin'. Cars comin' at her, and she just moseys along…

BRANDON 1: How much you pay for that cologne?

BRANDON 2: Fifteen dollah, fifteen dollah!

BRANDON 1: You coulda got it for ten dollah, ten dollah.

BRANDON 2: It started at twenny dollah, twenny dollah.

BRANDON 1: Did you hear Faith back at the place on the corner?

BRANDON 3: Yeah, that was funny.

BRANDON 2: What? I didn't.

BRANDON 3: The Chinese man told her the hat was twenny dollah, and Faith got all serious and said, "I'll give you nineteen."

BRANDON 2: That's a hard bargain right there.

BRANDON 1: The Chinese man said, "You very stupid girl."

BRANDON 2: No way!

BRANDON 3: Man, you believe everything everyone says.

BRANDON 2: Do not.

BRANDON 3: I want one of them big old samurai swords.

BRANDON 1: They're not gonna sell that to you.

BRANDON 3: Why not?

BRANDON 1: You're a kid.

BRANDON 3: So?

BRANDON 1: And the teachers won't let you. They said no on laser pointers and firecrackers, you think they're gonna let you buy a samurai sword?

BRANDON 3: It's different, it's like art.

BRANDON 2: And they wouldn't let you bring it on the plane.

BRANDON 3: I could pack it in my checked luggage.

BRANDON 2: It just couldn't be a really, really long sword.

BRANDON 1: All right, let's see.

BRANDON 3: Mr. Wally! When we're done here, can we find one of them stores that sells samurai swords?

WALLY: Not a chance, Knucklehead.

DENNIS, THE DAD from Seattle, was still on the corner of Mott
and Canal, in the exact same spot, when I returned from my day's
shortest, stingiest hour, but I was in a post-massage haze, iced coffee
in hand, ready to take on the rest of the tour and evening.

"The sidewalks are sticky down here," I told him. "If you don't
move around, you might not be able to leave."

"I haven't been here the whole time. I walked up to the open air
market for a bit. I thought of popping into one or two of the neighborhood stores to see what was being sold, but in the end I didn't
bother. It's not as if there aren't Asians in Seattle." There were three in
his group—the drama teacher was a Takahashi, one of the computer
boys was a Tsu, and one of the shoppers a Zhang. "I came back early,
because I got anxious that Brittany was getting her face slashed in one
of those old building basements."

I struggled to swallow the iced coffee I'd just sipped. "I'm-I'm sure
she's fine."

"Or fondled by one of the boys she's running with. Do you ever
notice how much teenagers hug each other?"

I took another sip and was relieved to see Wally and the boys
crossing the street to us. As soon as they reached me, they started
pulling souvenirs out of their orange plastic bags and telling me about
the unprecedented deals they'd struck. Others emerged from the shops
and crossed the street and eagerly compared purchases, holding up
shirts, rubbing the fabric, trying on the hats, posing with the sunglasses. Dennis was still looking for his daughter. Her posse—two boys
and four girls—came running up Canal with two minutes to spare.

—That was SO fun.

—Our Chinatown isn't like this one at all.

—We bought so many bags.

—But we didn't go into any basement.

—This lady on Canal...

—Where we were *allowed* to be.

—…down near McDonald's because Laurie had to go to the bathroom.

—He doesn't need to know that.

—Well, we're waiting for Laurie in a store, and this lady pushed us into the back and opened this tiny door that was all camouflaged…

—You wouldn't have seen it if you didn't know.

—…and she opened the door and we went in, like six of us, and it was so cramped, but it was FULL of bags.

—And we knew they were fake and all, but they're very good, and I don't think any of the people were terrorists.

"That's good," I said.

One of the girls, who had four purses, three pairs of sunglasses, and a roll of t-shirts, asked, "Is the bus picking us up here?"

"No, we won't see the bus until after dinner."

She chewed the side of her mouth, and I learned this one was Brittany, the daughter of Dennis, because he quickly answered her unasked question: "I'll carry your bags, sweetheart."

"Thank you, Dad!" She kissed his cheek and relieved herself of her cargo. "One of the shirts is for you."

"Which one?" he asked, but Brittany was already back among her friends.

Kelly told me that her group was present and accounted for. She turned and thanked them for being on time. On the Seattle side, the drama teacher told Pete they were missing one.

"Who's not here?" he asked. "We can't just be missing one. Everyone was supposed to be with a buddy." I wasn't worried. First of all, thanks to the massage, life was copacetic; second, I had padded the time, unsure of the reliability of my new friends. I didn't think I knew the group well enough to identify which of the eighteen was missing, but I looked around anyway and quickly noticed the absence of a particular shade of blue.

"The girl with the blue hair," I said quietly to Pete who was pushing his way into the middle of the pack for a better view of his charges.

"Melanie? Who was with Melanie?" There was no response. "Did anyone see her?" Pete pulled from his back pocket a card printed with the cell phone numbers of everyone in his group. He dialed her number.

As we waited, I reminisced with those around me about the old days. "When I first started tour guiding, there were no cell numbers. Lost kids had to find a pay phone and call the 1-800 number for the main office. Someone in the office would then page me, and I would seek out a pay phone. Then we would all have to walk three miles up-hill in the snow without shoes."

Melanie turned the corner. She had no shopping bags. Pete stepped up to her, said something, and shook his head. After she apologized, once to Pete, once to anyone who could make out her voice, Pete gestured to me. I looked across Canal Street at the pedestrian signal and waved to the front of the group. Our blob morphed into a triple-file line that turned two-by-two by the time we reached the other side of the street. I looked to the far back. Wally, the giant from Georgia, was bringing up the rear, and I noticed that Brittany was walking with her friends, five or six rows in front of her dad, who was alone, and carrying all of her shopping, looking miserable.

AS DENNIS BREWER, the last of the eight main players, would later explain to me at an Ethiopian restaurant on Forty-seventh Street, in order to join his daughter on her trip to the East Coast, he had to promise Brittany that he would not, at any time during the four days and three nights, embarrass her in front of her classmates or teachers. When his ex-wife dropped Brittany at the airport, he did not shower his daughter with kisses. Instead, he held open his arms and allowed her to determine the length and intensity of the embrace. Then he kept his distance and read his book, knowing she was excited to be traveling with her friends. In return, he received several smiles throughout the day, and it wasn't until baggage claim that he saw his daughter's eyes open far beyond their irises, a sign he had committed an egregious affront to her social standing.

Dennis had arrived first at the airport and checked his suitcase, completely unaware that all of their luggage was to be tagged with uniform yellow cards sent by the tour company. His was not. Who cared? They were claiming their own bags at LaGuardia; the luggage wasn't being transferred to a cruise ship. He had his own means of identification, and that was what disturbed Brittany when she saw the familiar suitcase slide through the rubber flaps with a bright, oversized Star Wars luggage tag featuring Yoda, Jedi Master. The quick turn of her head; the astonished gaze; the incriminating glare; the speed with which she squeezed past the seven or eight fellow passengers: all these meant his sixteen-year-old was upset.

"Is that your bag?"

"Yes."

"With the Star Wars thing?"

"Yoda?"

"Why? Why?"

"So I could pick it out at the airport."

"You promised me."

He couldn't see her dilemma. He knew Star Wars was just as popular with her generation. He knew the boys in her school would appreciate a Jedi bag tag. Dennis was bending down to reach for the suitcase when Brittany grabbed his arm.

"Please don't, please."

"What?"

"Leave it."

"Leave it?" The suitcase crept slowly past. "I need my luggage."

"You promised me!"

"Brittany, we can't just leave my bag at the airport. All my clothes…"

"We have to think," she whispered. "We have to *think*!"

After three seconds, she was off, maneuvering through the crowd and rounding the turn, appearing in the smaller crowd on the opposite side, her eyes on Yoda as he inched toward her, breaking the stare only once to remind her father of her displeasure. Quickly, she pulled his suitcase off the belt, tipped it on its side. While pretending to look for distinguishing marks, she used her right hand to rip the luggage tag cleanly from the handle.

"This one isn't yours!" she shouted. She returned the tagless bag to the belt and let it disappear through the rubber flaps. He understood that on the second go-round he would be able to claim it. He also understood that he was going to be punished for his crime. His sentence? To wander Chinatown, without companion, *in solitary*, for a term of sixty minutes. His only reason to come on this trip was to spend time with his daughter. During the bartering of custody, no discussion ever took into account the third parent in the room—high school. Her life away from home took more and more of her time and turned his meager two days of the week into really just one, if he were lucky. A sleepover. A brunch. A movie. A dinner. *A* as in one, as in single.

Dennis was one of the last to enter the restaurant, and he was surprised that by the time he walked to the back of the large room, the six tables were mostly filled. Like a game of musical chairs, people had pounced into their various arrangements. "Someone should have been in charge of seating in Little Italy," Dennis would later say to me with a slightly accusatory tone. As if I had known who made compatible seatmates. I did notice that Dennis was the odd man out, the only one standing. I saw the final place setting before he did and pointed Dennis toward the only empty seat at a four-top with three Georgians.

Two evenings later, I would tell him, "If I'd known you then and how that dinner was going to go, I'd have asked the owner to seat you somewhere in the kitchen."

7:15 DINNER IN LITTLE ITALY

THE SALADS WERE SET on the table; forks were already at work. Dennis stowed his daughter's bags underneath his chair before he sat.

One of the women, Dina, the Miserable Mother, said, "Looks like you bought a lot."

"These belong to my daughter. I'm just her Sherpa."

"You're her what?"

"Sherpa," Nancy, the vice principal, repeated and explained. "It means slave in Tibet."

Dennis was on the brink of correcting her when the man at the table lifted a bag from the floor and said, "I'm my daughter's slave too. I'm Travis." The men shook hands. Dina and Nancy introduced themselves.

"Did you have fun in Chinatown?" Dina asked. Dennis lied with a nod. "Me too. I bought four of them purses and jewed 'em down to thirty bucks each."

Dennis stared at her. Had he heard her correctly? Did she really say "jewed 'em down" or did she say "chewed 'em down" as if the buyer's task were to nibble at the sales price?

Nancy told Dennis, "It's an expression. A little outdated."

Dina said, "Outdated? I mean, you know, bargain, talk 'em down. Outdated?"

Dennis also wanted to challenge Nancy's word choice. For a second time.

"I guess it is outdated," Dina said. "You used to never see a poor Jew, but now, Zach's family, for example, they ain't rich."

Nancy expanded, "Zach is sitting over there. He's our prodigy."

"Now that there's not outdated," Dina said. "Jews are very smart."

Nancy considered this and made another small amendment. "They might not be smarter, but they put more effort into their academic pursuits."

"When did you have to get up?" Travis asked, changing the subject to Dennis's relief.

"We had to be at the airport at four thirty."

Dina bellowed, "WAY too early! That's very bad planning. It turns everyone into a zombie, and it's very difficult to enjoy the trip. You can't sleep the night before a trip anyway."

"Because you're so excited," Travis said.

"Because you're nervous, you're going to sleep through your alarm clock and miss your damn flight. Then as soon as you land, Mr. Encyclopedia starts giving you all these figures and facts, and it's hard to remember any of those things."

Travis disagreed, "I thought that was interesting. I coulda been on that bus another hour. I liked Chinatown, but I liked hearin' about all the places more."

"How far is your drive to Atlanta?" Dennis asked.

Nancy said, "We flew out of Savannah. We're about an hour from Savannah and four hours from Atlanta."

Travis said, "We live way in the country."

"Where exactly?" Dennis asked. "I've been to the South a few times."

"You know where East Bumfuck is?" Travis grinned. "We're 'bout ten miles down the road."

Nancy disapproved. "We live near a college. Zach's parents teach there. There are many cultural events. They bring in speakers from all over…"

"Aw, no, we're country. A lot of our kids are from farm families. I bet none of your kids are farmers."

"No, I don't think they are."

Nancy asked Dennis, "What do *you* do?"

"Software development."

"Computers?" Travis asked. "You ever meet Bill Gates?"

"I haven't."

Nancy said, "I was surprised that the tour guide let all your kids just wander around Chinatown on their own."

"That was up to Pete."

"They just landed in New York, and now at the first stop they're alone in the middle of illegal aliens and terrorists."

"They're high school. And they all spend time downtown."

Dina interrupted, "But Seattle is like only six hundred thousand people…Hey! I remembered something from that tour."

"Seattle's still a major city."

"Why're y'all comin' way across the country for another city? If I lived in a city, I'd take my vacations at the beach."

Dennis took a bite of bitter lettuce dripping with an extremely tangy dressing. As empty as he felt wandering Chinatown, like one of those fish on Mott flopping and flapping in an open box, he would have felt even more pointless at a beach. What kind of vacations did he like? Maybe camping. There was a purpose in the setting up and the dismantling of the site. In the mealtimes. There were tasks, assignments. Things to do.

The waiter, an older man with sunken cheeks, wearing black pants, a white shirt, and bow tie, appeared above them, listing the choices of entrée. Everyone at the table had difficulty making out exactly what he was offering. Dina stood up with a cigarette in one fist and a lighter in the other, which she placed on the waiter's arm.

"Honey, what are you tryin' to say?"

"...pezhana...balls...eeseravee...sanya..."

"You bring me what you like best," Dina patted his arm and jammed the cigarette between her lips. She looked at the table, raised her eyebrows—*Can you believe this?*—and headed outside for a smoke. The rest guessed at their orders.

"Are you a farmer?" Dennis asked Travis.

"No. My people were, but I'm a welder."

Nancy added, "He travels all over the country welding for different companies."

"Mainly through the South."

"What do you weld?"

Travis looked confused. "I'm an ironworker. All sorts of things."

"I know someone who welds. He makes abstract sculptures. Not that abstract actually. He takes automobile hoods and makes art out of them. Maps sometimes, faces, different things."

"No kidding?" Travis said. "Naw, I'm just a plain welder."

Nancy asked Dennis, "And what does your wife do?"

"She's an optometrist." Dennis didn't mention the divorce. There was something in the way Nancy asked her question that seemed nosy. She reminded him of a woman in his office who had taught him never to divulge any more information than was absolutely necessary. Whenever he did, he ended up on her blog.

"Where's your wife now? She couldn't come on the trip?"

"She had to work," he said and turned the tables, "What about your husband?"

"Oh, well, this isn't exactly a vacation for me. I'm the vice principal of the school, so I'm here in an official capacity."

Dennis surprised himself by asking her what her husband did for a living. He was working to keep on the offensive.

"He works at International Paper in Savannah. He's also a deacon at our church."

"What's a deacon?" Dennis asked. "Is that like a janitor?"

Nancy bristled at this, but Dennis didn't mean anything by it. A deacon sounded like a kind of custodian. While Dennis was often castigated for saying something inappropriate—his ex-wife's favorite term of affection for him was *social moron*—he was frankly amazed that he had been able to offend someone at a table whose recent conversation had centered on the "outdated qualities of the Jews."

"He's an officer of our church. He helps counsel members and their families." The slightest pause and then, "Do you not go to church?"

Dennis answered with a short laugh as though she had asked if he treated fevers with leeches.

Dina returned to the table; she was still harboring her frustration with the indecipherable waiter. "Well, I don't know about you, but I hope I don't get served cow brains or something like that. I don't even know how many languages I heard today, and they say it's supposed to be a wonderful thing to have this many languages. What did he say about that Queens? So many languages. But how can you be an American without English? How can you do a job without speaking like everyone else? And I'm not bein' a racist. Do you know why? If you think about it? Why it's important to have the same language? Jury duty. There was a Mexican woman in my jury selection room, and she kept getting dismissed because she didn't speak English. I thought, 'Señora, you are not a citizen of these United States. You are not one of my peers.' If you can't sit on a jury, then you're not an American. Are we going to have different courtrooms? Different schools? I thought we were supposed to be against segregation? Isn't that interesting? The people who are so against segregation are the same people who want to keep separate languages. You ever notice that? I just thought about that now."

Dina held her eyebrows impossibly close to her hairline.

"Do you know what I was also thinkin' about out there? How much this trip is. How much do you figure they mark this up? I paid eighteen hundred dollars for this trip for myself and for my two kids. Each! How much of that is air fare, how much of it is hotel? We're sharin' the rooms, so that has to bring down the price. I was lookin' at the menu outside, tryin' to figure out what that waiter was sayin', and I got to perusin' the prices. This place isn't very expensive, and you know there's got to be a group rate because they bring so many people here. Then you have the tour guide to pay, but we all share *him*, so that's nothin'. And the bus, there's that, but most of the time we're gonna be walkin'. How much you think they take?"

Southerners do like to talk, Dennis noted, but he enjoyed this topic, which was numerical, and he could lose himself in the figures. The entrees were delivered, and Dennis mentally drifted away from the table. He broke down the price (the Seattle trip cost twenty-one hundred each) by hypothesizing a few potential markup amounts, subtracting them from the total, and listing what he would assume each facet of the trip would cost a tour company. They were halfway through the meal when he announced his results, guessing a twenty percent markup or four hundred dollars made on each individual customer.

Travis asked, "Been doing that in your head all along? You're like a computer yourself."

Dina was less passionate about the answer. It was the question, he assumed, that got her riled. Now she seemed to be worked up about the shooting on an American campus that was the lead story on the televisions in that day's airports. Dennis followed the news when they were waiting at their gate in Chicago, watching the SWAT teams scurry across a quad and into a building where the shooter had, of course, shot himself. Is footage of breaking news transmitted from helicopters ever good?

"Mm-mm." Nancy swallowed a piece of meatball and commented on how sad it was that someone had become so angry with the world that he would take his rage out on others. If only someone had been able to get to him beforehand. "But they keep the church out of so many universities." It was Dennis' turn to bristle. It couldn't be more obvious that Nancy was drawing him out, but this was a topic that infuriated him, and she was a vice principal of what he took for granted was a public school.

"If only the killer had God?" Dennis asked. "There are probably several things that the shooter didn't have that could have prevented the carnage—a better GPA, a girlfriend, loving parents, I don't know, but what's more important, I think, is not what he didn't have but what he did have. In his hands. Which he aimed at several of his fellow students and teachers." The three at the table sat up tall and stiff as if Dennis all on his own, right then and there, were about to repeal the Second Amendment.

"This has nothin' to do with guns," Travis said, amiably enough. "Guns don't kill people…"

Dennis interrupted, "The God delusion does."

Silence fell upon the table. This was exactly the kind of thing Dennis did that drove his wife from so many dinner tables and eventually out of their marriage. He knew better than to keep on talking, which he desperately wanted to do, to build his argument, but he learned a long time ago that people weren't interested in the reasoning behind the arguments. His wife had repeatedly instructed him that as soon as one of his SMBs (*Social Moron Bombs)* detonated, he needed to close his mouth and let others clean up the debris. People shut down when confronted, she explained, or they retaliated with their own explosive weaponry.

Travis said, "Where we're from, guns are a way of life."

"There are plenty of guns in the Northwest."

"And they're not just to hunt. They're to defend. They're to protect my family from little assholes like that kid today. Someone like that comes onto my property, and he's gonna go off my property with a lot more holes in him than he came in with. I got an arsenal in my house. If you want to mess with me, you'll have to go through a lot of hardware."

"I won't mess with you," Dennis pledged. "I'm software only."

Travis took a second and then said, "That's right, that's right. You're software."

The men smiled. The women finished their main course. Dennis was pleased with himself. No scene. It could have been much worse, he thought, not realizing that, like a soldier or militant, he had just dug a hole with a trowel, gingerly fitted it with an explosive device, and carefully concealed it beneath a few layers of dirt. It did not go off that night, but our group would be covering a lot of ground over the next few days—lots of traipsing around, lots of careless feet.

PETE, THE LEADER from Seattle who dreamt of paintings and ballet dancers handling luggage on the tarmac at LaGuardia, was the only one at my table when the two of us noticed a few of the eighth-grade boys nearby spooning tomato sauce into a glass of Coke. They followed it up with pepper, salt, and a glob of melted mozzarella. Then they stirred. One of the boys, a Brandon naturally, picked up the glass.

"Did you ever teach middle school?" I asked Pete.

He shook his head and said, "Middle schoolers are like patients in an asylum, removed from the general population for three years before being reintroduced into society."

We continued watching. The Brandon was not sipping. He placed his glass back on the table before adding a shiny linguini noodle. Pete told me he was grateful that his high school students were beyond the stage of blending Italian food and soda, but he was also aware a probable reason was because they had dealers and other people responsible for manufacturing their highs, that they were well into experimentation with hard-core drugs, and might, in fact, even have shampoo bottles filled with vodka in their luggage for later on tonight. At this moment, though, they were sipping coffee, as teens from the Northwest were wont to do.

Then there it was again. The restaurant played its music on a loop, and it was time yet again for the opening chords of the most famous Mafia anthem, the theme to *The Godfather*. This was their background music? On each reprise, Little Italy felt less and less authentic to Pete. The neighborhood seemed more genuine when he ate here as an undergraduate, less than a decade after Joe Gallo was shot to death down the block in Umberto's Clam House.

As the waiters cleared the tables, our companions returned from the bathroom.

Grandma Penny said, "I cannot wait to see Broadway. I was thinking of getting myself and my granddaughter extra tickets for a matinee. Maybe *The Sound of Music* or *My Fair Lady*."

"They're not on Broadway," I told her.

"What? They're two of the biggest shows ever. Broadway should have them playing every night. What about *Cats*?"

"Coughed up its last furball eight years ago."

"Well, what the heck is playing? *Hello, Dolly*? No? Is *Phantom of the Opera* on?"

"Yes, we have tickets to that one," said Kelly, Pete's counterpart, the leader from Georgia who, like Pete, saw magical things happening at LaGuardia.

"I do like the opera," Penny said. "I went to Atlanta every year when the Metropolitan used to tour. The last time I went, they did

Carmen. I love that music." She lowered her voice. "But they had a *black* woman playing Carmen." I told her that wasn't unusual, and she went on to say, "She had a pretty voice, but it was very distracting. Now, listen up, I don't mind that opera singer havin' a job, but she should be playing a more suitable part. It gets confusing."

Kelly smiled and threw her arm around the old woman's shoulders, "That's why we love Penny. She just says whatever comes to mind."

"What? What'd I say?"

Screams of disgust and triumph filled the restaurant. The Brandon had taken a gulp of his Coke and Cheese. The restaurant's other diners, who didn't hail from Seattle or Georgia, glared at us all.

"Wally steps away for one minute…" Kelly left the table for a chat with the Brandons.

Dessert, a chocolate mousse cake, soon came out of the kitchen carried by a line of waiters. The manager led the line, carrying a piece of paper, the payment voucher for me to sign. I added up the number of dinners and turned to Pete for confirmation.

"So you said on the bus that you were down to eighteen?" I asked.

"Yes. Four adults and fourteen students."

"Did someone have to cancel?"

"We had to cancel for him."

"Bad grades?"

Pete didn't reply. His mouth was full of cake. I waited, but he took a long time chewing. A long time chewing mousse.

I wouldn't know much about the missing student until after the trip when Pete would send me a lengthy email of thanks, explanation, and photographs of the city in close-up.

The cake was not enough for Pete. They'd travelled thousands of miles. He wanted something more authentic. He asked me if Ferrara's were still open or if it had been firebombed by Starbucks. Did he have time to run over there and buy a box of cannoli? It would be better than the entire group stopping there, so I made sure he knew where it was and how to find the bus in case we left before he got back. He did; he knew his way around.

Pete told the drama teacher, laughing with her student council, that he was going to buy some treats and would meet them at the bus. Pete wondered how she could still be laughing after sharing jokes and playing games with them for well over twelve hours. He escaped the restaurant before *The Godfather* theme could play again.

Out on Mulberry, the sidewalks were crowded. A street of restaurants, lined with chairs and tables. He recalled his college days and all the young women from Barnard he had taken here on dates. Was Little Italy more authentic then? Everything was more authentic in the late Seventies. They would have pasta and wine, discuss and debate Dante and Boccaccio, share stories and gelato, and then return to campus. It was less safe, that was for sure, but he was young, so that didn't matter. At Grand Street, he looked up and saw the familiar sign, vertical and neon with blue and green: *Ferrara. Since 1892.* He opened the glass door and looked down the length of the display case stocked with cream pastries, cookies, cakes, and, finally, with cannoli. *Cannolo,* singular; *connoli,* plural. He could taste the sweet ricotta and the flaky crust.

"Yes, what you need?"

Pete smiled and said, "*Vorrei venti cannoli, per favore.*" And then, in English, because the woman at the counter was Chinese.

8:15 BUS TO EMPIRE STATE BUILDING

AS WE LED the group two-by-two-by-three up Mulberry, onto Grand, and over to Centre, Kelly quoted her favorite Grandma Penny gem, a critique of the Golden Gate Bridge: "That bridge ain't even *gold*. Do you know that? It's *red*!" Grandma Penny cracked Kelly up at home, but what was extra funny was watching the reaction in the faces of people who weren't from Down South.

I repeated my favorite quote: "'I don't mind that opera singer havin' a job.'"

"Hey, she blows my mind too." Kelly knew how many different kinds of people lived in her state, but she also knew that the people from Washington were going to go back home quoting Penny and Travis and perpetuating the myth that the entire Southeast was comprised of rednecks and hillbillies.

I told her that back in March, a grown woman from California asked a man from South Carolina if it were true that southerners ate "frozen mayonnaise" for dessert. "Like popsicles."

Kelly burst out laughing, and I said, "She wasn't joking! Someone had told her that."

Wally's ten-year-old appeared between us, "What's so funny?"

"Nothing," Kelly put her arm around his shoulders, "What'd you eat for dinner, Clint?"

"Cheese ravioli."

"And you liked it?"

"I thought it was good. I was scared of foreign food goin' in there."

"Italian's foreign to you? Don't you eat spaghetti and pizza?"

"Sure I do, but my *mom* makes it," he said. "You know what? I thought Little Italy was goin' to have all them boats."

"What boats?"

"You know, with a guy rowin' and singin' songs."

"That's real Italy. And just in Venice."

"They got 'em in Disney." Clint looked behind him as we reached the bus and declared, "Disney Italy is better than New York Italy."

"Italy Italy is the best," I said and held up my hand. He jumped, slapped my palm, and scampered onto the bus. I followed him on board, grateful to see that Pete was there, his Ferrara's box tied with string in his lap. The bus repopulated with rejuvenated sightseers ready for their next stop. "Empire State Building, please," I said to the driver, and the bus pulled away from the curb. The lights inside the bus snapped off, and many of the kids made *oooooo* noises as if they could now do whatever they wanted because no one could see them in the dark. "Quick, on your right, this is one of my favorite buildings. It's the old Police Headquarters, which was why that gun shop back on Grand claims to be the oldest gun store in America. They opened in 1911 when the police worked here."

"I saw that store," said Travis, the ironworker who had his own arsenal.

Kelly's phone vibrated; she had a text.

Got that dress yet? Hunter.

Her fingers typed, *No fool. Tomorrow!!*

"This is the Puck Building, which was a publishing enterprise. You'll see Puck cartoons at Ellis Island. The funniest thing about the Puck Building..."

will it b pink w bow?

Bridesmaids r wearing pink so no.

"The Cooper Union was the first building in the world with an elevator shaft. Not an elevator, mind you, just the shaft. They knew elevators..."

o

what r u up 2?

"So a man comes to speak in the hall at the Cooper Union. People laugh as he walks to the stage. He's tall and gangly..."

missing u

—ABRAHAM LINCOLN!

I tossed a Starburst to the seat behind Kelly, to Zach, their school's prodigy. Because he was usually so quiet, Kelly later predicted, the Seattle group was unlikely to remember him when they told their redneck stories, though he would probably score higher on tests than any student on the bus. He had already earned more Starbursts.

i'm nekkid. just sox.

behaving urself?

missing u

"The only president born in New York City? Anyone?"

—LINCOLN!

—JEFFERSON!

—EISENHOWER!

—ROOSEVELT!

"Which one?"

—THE ONE BORN IN NEW YORK!

"Very funny."

—FRANKLIN!

—THEODORE!

"Teddy it is. Within five years, he goes from police commissioner to Rough Rider to governor to vice president to president."

call me tonite & well fonesex it up

rooming w/ramona so no we wont

"The Empire State Building is once again, since 9/11, the tallest building in New York. The most amazing thing about this skyscraper is, are you ready for this?…"

awwwwwwww. off 2 sniff ur pillow. Imagining Hunter sprawled out on their bed, wearing only socks and hugging her pillow was both funny and arousing. It gave her a sensation not wholly appropriate for a chaperone on a bus with her students.

She slid down into her seat and tried to pay attention to the instructions I was giving: "the first elevator will take you to the eightieth floor—at a speed of twelve hundred feet per minute—and the second will take you to eighty-six. When you get to the top, look at your watch, give yourselves twenty minutes, and then start heading down. You don't need to be down in twenty minutes, but you need…"

Kelly's phone vibrated. She read the text: *All done.* She didn't reply to her man of the insatiable desires. She had to exit the bus and help pass out tickets.

8:30 EMPIRE STATE BUILDING

BRANDON 1: Are we takin' escalators all the way to the top of this thing?

BRANDON 2: That's gonna take forever.

BRANDON 3: Naw, dummies, we're only goin' to the second floor on this.

BRANDON 1: I thought he said these went at twelve hundred feet per minute?

BRANDON 3: The *elevators*! Not the escalators!

BRANDON 2: If the escalators went that quick, do you have any idea how fast you'd have to jump off when you got to the top?

BRANDON 1: Most people wouldn't make it.

BRANDON 3: That's why they don't do it.

    PAUSE.

BRANDON 2: You'd have to have some kind of net to catch everybody.

PEOPLE FROM ALL OVER the world were here, in this large, dimly lit room, to be pulled to the top of the Empire State Building, and tonight Tracy Powell was one of them. She looked at the line wrapping back and forth to see if anyone famous were standing there. It didn't look like it. She figured if someone famous visited, they wouldn't have to wait in line anyway. They would take a private elevator to the top, so she planned to keep her eyes open once she got up there. A uniformed man directing people from the escalators into the metal corral spoke with a real, bona fide New York City accent, and when Tracy passed him, she applauded.

Entering the corral, she soon saw that she was completely surrounded by Georgians, but she didn't feel the need to wait for her school. Back in Chinatown, she had had a difficult time joining a group. She walked from stall to stall with different packs, but no one knew she was "with" them. She just tagged along, thinking someone was bound to realize she was hoping to share haggling techniques or laugh with them at the jokes on the t-shirts. It was the same at dinner. No one actively excluded her. They were just unaware, and she couldn't take it personally. It wasn't as if she didn't have friends, she wanted to tell the Georgians for some reason. She had friends from her class and friends she worked with at McDonald's. Her friends were planning on taking the trip in two years, but she couldn't wait until then. She had to see New York now. Do not put off till tomorrow what you can do today. Her uncle, for example, was supposed to go to New Orleans for the Fourth of July in 2005, but he had to postpone and now everything down there was "post-Katrina." Tracy herself never got to see the World Trade Center in person. Who knew what New York would lose next?

She looked at a few of the girls from Georgia who were behind her in line. They seemed young, which was probably how the upperclassmen saw her. Tracy was stuck at the wrong age. It didn't matter. She told herself: Look busy, take pictures, pretend you don't care, smile, be nice to people. Be nice to people, and they'll be nice to you.

As the line shuffled forward, she pulled her to-do list from her new Louis Vuitton look-alike and then dug for her pen, a bulky ballpoint that illuminated at every other click. The room was dark enough to justify the light, but unfortunately the glow failed to spark a conversation. No one had noticed. Tracy's eyes scanned her list and, rather than checking anything off, she added: "Call Grandma from top of Empire State." Two weeks earlier, the two of them had spent a rainy afternoon on the sofa watching *Sleepless in Seattle* and had a long discussion about the Empire State Building and *An Affair to Remember*, which she intended to watch *after* her trip. Tracy loved watching movies set in New York and thinking, "I hope I'll get to see that," but she also looked forward to watching movies and thinking, "I was standing right there!"

Off to the side, she heard another New York accent telling everyone that they better buy tickets for the New York Skyride, some kind of 3-D movie that made the whole experience worth it. Apparently, if you just went to the top, it wasn't so impressive. She wondered if they were going to do this Skyride. Her ticket didn't mention anything about a movie. It occurred to her that she could use this to strike up a conversation.

She said to one of the girls, "Do you know if we're going to see that Skyride?"

"I hope not. I throw up on those things." The girl went on to tell a story about a county fair and how she rode all the rides, but all the rides were spinny rides, so by the time she stumbled off the tenth one, she felt queasy and had to search for a garbage can, and she puked up cotton candy and hot dogs right underneath where everyone was sitting for the horse show.

This wasn't really a conversation, Tracy thought. It was a speech, and it was delivered mainly to her friends. Again, Tracy wasn't being excluded, she was free to listen in, but the girl never looked at her after those first two sentences. When the boys in front of her moved up, Tracy reluctantly followed, leaving a gap behind her. In the three seconds it took the girls to join her, they had already somehow separated. Tracy tried to remember if she had any vomiting story worth telling. Or county fair anecdote. Or "spinny ride" tale. The girls were soon talking of something else. Tracy faced the front of the line. They were almost at security anyway.

She bided her time by watching the different people pack the gray plastic cartons on the conveyer belt and stand at attention before walking stiffly through the metal detector. She had never noticed before, but people seemed to stand up taller and straighter before passing through, as if the machine were screening for scoliosis instead of weapons. This was an observation she could share with the Seattle Urban League when she lectured them about New York. That was the stipulation agreed upon when she approached them to help fund her trip east.

Tracy was not from a wealthy family, like several in her group, and she was surprised at how little her McDonald's money added up. When their teacher distributed the handout on fundraising, most of the students threw it away, but she scanned the paper methodically, knowing full well that her grandparents were raising her and her sister on a fixed income that did not allow for extravagant four-day vacations which cost more than two thousand dollars. She sold candy, and she spent two Saturdays washing cars—three of her friends helped with this, but, as a result, she only made a quarter of the profits, and then she had to work her shift at Mickey D's smelling of sponges, car soap, and wet rubber. So then she took the advice of the handout and approached a few local charities and community boards, which offered scholarships. By the time Tracy was done fundraising, she was shocked to learn that not only had she paid for the entire trip but she had more than five hundred dollars to spend on it.

She realized she could chat with these Georgia girls about fundraising, but it was her turn now to empty her pockets and stand at attention. She secretly hoped the machine would beep, so she could have a chat with the security guard. But it didn't. She collected her belongings and followed people down a much brighter corridor. They filed through a glass-enclosed bridge that overlooked a first-floor hallway.

Tracy saw me down below listening to a couple acquaintances, women who were holding red umbrellas, fellow guides who had ambushed me as I headed for a place to sit down. That spring, one of the companies for which several of us worked was trying to compel us to sign non-compete agreements, daring to treat us like employees instead of the contracted, freelance labor we were. A revolution was in the works: a sternly-worded letter would be mailed. Tracy waved to me, and I waved back, happy to see that a part of my group had reached the elevators. I had at least twenty to thirty minutes to grab a drink and read a chapter of the novel I had been carrying all day if only I could find a means of escape.

I was always relieved that giving tours kept me out of the inane fray of office politics, but now and then I would find myself on a boat, in a hotel lobby, or in a skyscraper corridor with two or more guides who would, right before my very eyes, put together a water cooler and begin to whisper. There was the usual gossip and shop talk, as well as insecure questions about why one of them hadn't been called for a certain lucrative gig that everyone else seemed to be working. There were recriminations targeted at someone's failure to share his or her part of the work on a recent program, and there were complaints about back injuries sustained from lifting luggage or sciatica from standing on a curb holding a sign for six hours. There was occasional value in the talks—you picked up jobs, warnings about upcoming street closures, and recommendations for shows and exhibitions—but too frequently I stood around comparing myself to the socially dysfunctional people who tended to work as tour guides.

Was I one of them? People told me I wasn't. My groups told me that I was different. Not as quirky. I was drawn to the job because I loved the city, because I loved to explore, discover, and then share what I had found; but as time passed, the early research became more specific, obscure, as I grew obsessed with learning as much as I could. I had a bookcase and part of a storage locker exclusively reserved for books about New York. I collected antiquated guide books which I read from cover to cover, the only way I felt I could truly experience the 1939 World's Fair or what it was like to run with a fire company in 1845. On days off, I visited Governor's Island or Jones Beach, not to sunbathe or swim but to take notes and pictures that I would xerox and share with future tour groups. But even tour groups were not as interested in the minutiae as I was. Sometimes, I had to admit, the only people intrigued by my esoterica were other tour guides. Like it or not, I was a member of that quirky fraternity.

"You should be on the committee," one of the women broke me out of my stupor.

"Definitely," the other said, "because then we'd get Phil and Jimmy to sign."

I said, "I can't commit to being on any committee right now."

"Are you doing a show this summer? Where are you going?"

"No, nowhere, I'm kind of taking…a break from that." It was scary hearing myself admit it, but I was in the midst of giving up the theater, singing and acting, because I was tired of all the running around for the pathetic career I was failing to carve out. The last two roles I landed had been Nazi guards—and not the Nazi guards with songs, but the Nazi guards who escorted the leads on and off the stage. I was a tour guide. Who was I kidding? Most, if not all, of my income came from out-of-towners. I was no longer an actor who gave tours or a singer who gave tours; I was a tour guide who gave tours.

Somewhere, I had made a massively wrong decision. My older brother was a successful lawyer in Chicago, and my younger brother back home in Ohio had just had twins. They both had families, real careers. And what was I doing? Bicycling around Manhattan comparing all the buildings designed by Gordon Bunshaft. What kind of life is that?!

The women were now repeating themselves, a hazard from working with eighth graders. They were saying the exact same things, filing their grievances without even bothering to rephrase their earlier gripes, and I was growing more desperate for a drink. Or at least a chair. With the amount of time we spent on our feet, why were the three of us not sitting down?

Eventually, one of their phones rang.

"You're already on the bus?! How'd you get past us?" (Easy. We weren't standing near the exit.)

"We'll be there in two minutes." She turned to her partner. "They're already on the bus!"

"Let's go!"

"Jack, we'll talk."

"That's what we do best!" I called after them.

I could have followed them out and made a quick stop at the pub, but by then I knew it was too late. My people, now hundreds of feet above my head, would soon be dropping down around me like paratroopers. I had to station myself in the lobby to meet them.

The first to arrive would be Lash Dautenhahn, the most country of them all, the one with forty dollars and a pair of disposable cameras. He was astounded by the crowds. How could you live in a place like this without bumping into people every three seconds? He tried his best to curve and contort his torso to keep from making contact, but there was still jostling, apologies to be made. He had been with Wally and Clint but lost them on the eightieth floor. He tried to step out of the way to wait for them, but the crowd pushed him around the corner where he found himself in line alone for the next elevator with complete strangers who were talking English with an accent from some other country. They were teasing each other and saying *fecking* a lot, which Lash guessed was "like the cuss word but not as bad." Lash was supposed to be with a chaperone, but a guard was ordering him to go into an open elevator so he obeyed. The *fecking* people walked inside with him. It was just Lash with a whole mess of *fecking* people. They all knew each other, and they were making fun of one in particular.

"...fecking maid about something something." Lash couldn't really follow what they were saying. As the elevator dropped, his ears filled up like they did on the plane, and though the people were shouting and laughing, they sounded quieter than they did at the top. He swallowed, his ears popped, and it was "fecking stoolid drap me." Or something.

In the lobby, at the bottom of the escalator, I was talking on my phone with Carol, the operations manager of the tour company, who had called me to see how everything was going. "Whatcha doin'?" I complained that she had given me another mismatched combo group—a middle school and a high school, country mice and city mice, red state and blue state. She didn't listen, because she was really calling to ask if I could work longer the next evening. "Just get them to dinner and the theater." I told her that, after today's double, I would need the next evening off. I had to sleep. She tried to bribe me with an extra ticket to *Phantom of the Opera*.

"Are you kidding me?" I told her. "I saw that show eighteen years ago and still can't get the songs out of my head."

Lash saw me before I saw him. He stepped off the escalator and up to me, awaiting instructions.

"Hey! You're the first. We'll start gathering over against that wall."

Lash obeyed and walked to the wall, gathering with himself. Making sure he was out of the way, he slid down the wall to sit on the floor, to give his feet a rest, but as soon as his butt hit the marble, another guard cried out from the door, "Up, up, up!" Lash hurried to his feet, his apology stuck in a constricted throat. I gave him a small smile, so he wouldn't feel bad and told Carol I had to go.

I looked at my watch—how many times a day did I check my wrist?—and asked Lash if the others were behind him. He didn't answer. He seemed surprised to be alone with the tour guide for some reason. I had been addressing the whole group since the airport and now, here I was, talking only to him. I could tell that Lash thought it weird.

"Did you see anyone else in line with you?"

"Yes, sir."

"Great. Was it a nice view tonight?

"Yes, sir."

"Did you have a chance to walk around all four sides?"

"Yes, sir."

"You don't have to call me *sir*," I told him. "So you're in Ms. Mitchell's class?"

"Yes, sir."

"I bet she's a wonderful teacher."

"Yes, sir."

Lash was uncomfortable talking to adults unless there was some kind of structure to the relationship. Some hierarchy. Student-teacher.

Son-parent. Nephew-uncle. He figured he was a tourist, I was a guide, so he decided to ask me a tourist-guide question.

"Do you know where I could get another of these?" He held up a brochure for the Empire State Building that was creased in the middle. "I wanna get one that looks new."

I pointed to the information table just a few yards away and watched as Lash eagerly stepped up to it as if it were an ice cream counter. He came back with a brand new brochure.

"Mine got wrinkled," Lash explained. A silence followed, and then he added, "I couldn't afford the stuff up there. That must be where the rich people go."

I smiled, "Yep, Bergdorf Goodman, Prada, and the top of the Empire State Building. Best shopping in the city."

"I guess so," said Lash, taking me at my word. "I saw a snow globe up there that was thirty dollars. That's almost all my money." Lash didn't buy much in Chinatown, because he wanted to save his forty dollars, but he was now thinking that might have been a mistake. That might have been the only place in New York he could afford if he wanted to bring back presents for his family. "I was lookin' at a model of the Empire State Building when a foreign lady grabbed it out of my hand. She went and bought it. Maybe she knew I couldn't afford it." He showed me his brochure. "But this is good. It has pictures of the Empire State Building at day and at night and has numbers about how high it is and everything. So."

"And it's free," I said. "You can't beat that."

"No, sir."

Wally and his son came down the escalator.

"There you are," Wally said to Lash.

"I told you he was down here," said Clint.

"We were lookin' for you. You gotta stay with the adults, son."

Lash explained, "The man told me to get in the elevator."

I recognized several more familiar faces from Georgia and Washington. The guard that yelled at Lash yelled at more of the kids as soon as they dropped to the floor. "UP, UP, UP!" They complied before the *Up, up, up!* finished echoing.

—Why can't you sit on the floor?

I told them, "Because it's dangerous. People could trip over you."

—Not if I have my legs in.

—It's retarded you can't sit on the floor.

I said, "I'm sure you can't sit on the floor of a public building in Seattle."

—I bet you can.

—Well, in Seattle we have chairs. People can actually sit down in seats.

The guard told them, "A woman who worked here fell right over kids like you and broke her elbow. Do you know how much she sued for?" No one did. "Ten million dollars."

—Ten million dollars?

—What does she do with that elbow?

—How come her elbow is worth that much?

"Beats me," the guard said. "But she sued."

"This is New York," I said. "It's crowded. Elbows are the most important part of the body. You try getting through Times Square without using your elbows. As a licensed guide, my elbows are insured for five million each."

—WHAT?!?!

—ARE YOU KIDDING ME?

I laughed, checked my watch again, and called the driver for our pickup.

—Anybody know why the lights up top were yellow?

—Aren't they always?

—No, remember Jack said it's different every night.

—Like red, white, and blue on the Fourth of July.

—Oh, that would have been pretty.

—You mean the lights in the gift shop?

—No. On the very top. Outside.

—Above where we were. They change them.

—Someone told me it was for Colorectal Awareness Night.

—Eww! Gross!

—Colorectal *Cancer* Awareness.

—We came to the Empire State Building on Rectal Awareness Night.

—*Colo*rectal.

—It should be brown then.

—Brandon!

Kelly came off the escalator with Grandma Penny and gave me a thumbs-up, but Seattle was still waiting on people. Two of them broke away and sat down on the floor. "UP! UP! UP!" Pete arrived, at last, with the girl with the blue hair. We headed out.

Clint asked me, "We're goin' to the hotel now?"

"Grand Central, then the hotel."

"Does the hotel have a pool?"

"No."

"Man, I brought my swimsuit all the way up here for nothin'."

"It has a bathtub. You can fill your bathtub and go swimming."

"How big are y'all's bathtubs?"

We hit the revolving doors, which both Georgia and Washington were guilty of stuffing, and so the guards yelled, "ONE AT A TIME!" Outside, we declined the invitations of the limo drivers and walked a block south where our bus was waiting with open door.

In the horde pushing on, Lash noticed Miss Teen Seattle standing next to him, and as they neared the door, he got up the courage to say, "You wanna see out the window?"

"I can see where I am," she smiled. "You keep the window." She turned to her friends and then back to him. "Thanks for asking though."

And she squeezed his elbow.

Which felt like ten million dollars.

10:00 GRAND CENTRAL TERMINAL
(Time Permitting)

GRAND CENTRAL TERMINAL was listed on the itinerary with an escape clause ("Time Permitting"), but because the group was already down from the Empire observatory and we had the bus until eleven, time permitted. I had been hoping we would head straight to the hotel for an "early" check-in, but, at dinner, both group leaders told me that Grand Central was a must-see, and knowing it would be easier to check it off tonight than to try squeezing it into our schedule on another day, I asked the driver to take Madison to Forty-second.

Grand Central also makes for a more beautiful and stress-free stop at night, when the commuters are at home in Westchester or Connecticut, eating ice cream and watching *Law and Order*, when the space is less congested and harried, and when you can see the floor and marvel at the architecture. I unwrapped a throat lozenge and popped it in my mouth, committing myself to one last performance for the day. There is so much to show at Grand Central, and I can rarely bring myself to omit anything, so, if time or fatigue are issues, I just speed up my spiel.

We would do Grand Central, but we would do it quickly. Here we go: Off the bus at Forty-second, Beaux-Arts façade, Starburst for the Roman gods, love for the clock, see the eagle?, now look at the Chrysler, ooh-aah, picture-picture-picture; moving on, cross the street, through the door, Jackie O Starburst, Roman ramps, like the Colosseum; into the waiting room, knock on the wall, hollow, only a decade, look up, chandeliers, exposed light bulbs, think of Times Square, world-changing!; down the next ramp, heads tilt back, eyes up, the 9/11 flag, cerulean ceiling, ooh-aah, picture-picture-picture; regroup and pick up the pace, here we go, clock, famous icon, ten or twenty million, opal on all four sides; to the ceiling, big mistake, everything backwards, no one cares, tiny hole to fit the rocket, northwest corner, see the black square?, used to be the whole ceiling, mostly nicotine, Cancer the Crab joke, don't smoke!, movies, television, flash mobs and viral videos, secret about the departure board, secret about the room downstairs, Hitler sent spies!, with sand!, eastern staircase, slaughterhouses but now the U.N., hundred-dollar question, no one ever knows, share the answer, people don't believe, number of platforms, two levels, all underground, air rights!, FDR, polio, abandoned train car, "but during the morning rush a full train passes it by and arrives here every fifty-eight seconds."

I felt lightheaded, having forgotten to breathe since we regrouped, so I stopped for a few breaths. Picture, picture, picture. And then I led them all downstairs for our final stop of the night, a choice that turned out to have repercussions.

THEY COME AT YOU at five hundred miles per hour.

And sometimes you wind up giving them a tour at almost the same speed.

But there are dangers when you're moving too quickly. Especially when you lack vital information. You know nothing about them. What they've packed. What they've brought from home. What they're carrying with them.

For example, there's no way of knowing that, back in April, Nancy, the white vice principal from Georgia, had asked Ramona, the black history teacher, to come to her office during her planning period. This information is in none of your paperwork. Ramona was irritated and assumed that whatever needed to be said could have been said in the hallway in the time it took Nancy to make the invite. Nancy didn't have that many friends and used her job to force interaction with people who wouldn't otherwise give her the time. Ramona resented losing her planning period and was further aggravated by being kept outside the office while Nancy finished a phone call, which was not nearly as important as Nancy pretended it was. Nancy finally waved Ramona inside and closed the door.

Nancy was *concerned*, a favorite word of hers, about some rumblings she had been hearing. Rumblings, unlikely. One student or one parent probably. That's all it took to radically alter the teaching curriculum these days. And Nancy had called Ramona into her office to make sure they saw eye-to-eye, to make sure they were on the same page. The page where Nancy wished they were, Ramona was soon to realize, was the page *after* the slavery unit. They only had one year to get through "so many centuries of American history" (*Only about four*, Ramona almost interrupted), and word had gotten back to Nancy that one teacher was spending a good deal of the year, longer than most, teaching about the ills of slavery and even referring to those ills after the chapter where slavery had been abolished. This teacher had brought in artifacts from the slave days—a whip, shackles, and a branding iron. She had shown an edited version of *Roots* for two entire days in the classroom.

"It's best not to dwell on any one unit," Nancy said.

Ramona was a teacher who wanted to wake her students up, to make history real, connect the past to the present. She wanted to show how decisions made centuries ago still played out in her students' daily lives, that a chain of cause and effect went back long, long before something as brief as a presidential administration, or even a generation. You turned a page and retained the contents; you didn't turn the page and say, "That's over." Chapter Three informs Chapter Four which makes sense of Chapter Five and even Chapter Eight.

She saw herself, and all history teachers, as champions of the unseen, the ignored and forgotten. She wanted to make the past vivid to keep it from being dismissed. Her mission: to tell it like it was.

Nancy said, "Yes, slavery, in many circumstances, was horrible…"

"In *many* circumstances?" Ramona asked.

"Oh," Nancy stumbled but recovered. "I see where you're coming from, but what I mean is that there were many stories about slaves having close relationships with the owners…"

"Stories."

"Primary source documents."

"And who was usually the primary source?"

"We're getting off the path. I'm against slavery, of course. Obviously, I'm against slavery. What I'm saying is that it's not as much a part of Georgian history as one might think."

"For almost half of Georgia's existence, slavery was an institution."

"But which half are you teaching now? It's springtime. I think it's the constant referencing that's the problem…"

"There are only two states in this country that have more black residents, so it's very much a part of our history and the social fabric of our state…"

"But…"

"You don't think the Civil War is still playing out in our politics? When we still have debates about the Confederate flag?" For Ramona, the electorate was simple in the South: During Reconstruction, the white southerners voted for the Democrat, because the Republicans represented the anti-slavery North, Lincoln and Grant, but by the time Civil Rights rolled around one hundred years later, with Democrats sponsoring these bills, the white southerners swung to the Republican side.

Somewhere around this point of the conversation, came the line that shook Ramona to the core, that she had never heard growing up in Maryland but had heard several times since moving farther south: "*The Civil War didn't have as much to do with slavery as people think it did.*"

"What?" Ramona said. No one had previously said this to her face.

"There were several other…it's a grade school narrative to make it all about slavery. This was about the encroachment of the North, of northerners trying to impose their political preferences on another part of the country."

Ramona looked at her desk, to see if Nancy were reading from index cards, and then she shot back, "If that was what really made the South so angry, I wonder why so many southerners are happy about invading Iraq and imposing our political preferences on another part of the *world.*"

"Now let's not go globetrotting," Nancy replied. "And I wouldn't say that's what we're doing. We're fighting terrorists over there, so we don't…Anyway! The Civil War was about northern industrialists imposing a ridiculous tariff on the South, about states' rights."

"States' rights, sure, but the prerogative of the states to operate with the institution of slavery. In the articles of secession for every Confederate state, slavery is spelled out as a chief reason…" Ramona stopped arguing—pointless to argue with this blinking fish—and instead simply stared at Nancy, stared at her in her own special way. Nancy began to melt.

"Listen, we all have our own interests and obsessions, but we need to be *aware*."

Ramona stared.

"It's good sometimes for our own obsessions to be brought to our attention."

Ramona was still staring.

"If you were teaching home economics, cooking, let's say, and you loved cupcakes and you kept bringing in recipes for chocolate cupcakes…"

Still staring.

"I didn't mean that in any racial way. I mean the flavor, you know, chocolate cupcakes, vanilla cupcakes, yellow cupcakes, all the colors, I mean cupcakes, and the only thing, or one of the only things the students were learning, was how to make a cupcake, I'd have to call you in and let you know that there were other foods to teach."

Still staring.

"You know. Other things to bake and cook. You know, otherwise, you graduate a class of pastry chefs. Pastry chefs who only know how to make cupcakes." Nancy laughed.

Ramona turned up the stare by lowering her eyelids one centimeter.

Nancy said, "Though right now, a cupcake sounds scrumptious, doesn't it?"

And this went on and on.

At last, Ramona stood and promised her vice principal, "You have my word: I will not bring a single cupcake recipe into my classroom." She exited, leaving Nancy unsure as to whether they had reached an agreement. But this tête-à-tête had not been forgotten, and, along with their cameras, shoes, and outfits for the theater, Nancy and Ramona had both packed the memory of their debate and brought it with them to New York.

So now. The incident.

We were all standing downstairs, just above the dining concourse, up the ramp, in front of the Oyster Bar, underneath the domed ceiling made of smooth tiled bricks, a Guastavino ceiling better known as the Whispering Gallery, and I was telling this group, as I tell all my groups, about ancient acoustics, that in the outdoor theater of Epidaurus in Greece, if someone stands on a disk in the middle of the stage and snaps his fingers, all fifteen thousand spectators will hear it as if the fingers were being snapped at the openings of their ear canals. Simple geometry and physics: sound carries from one end of a curved surface to another as long as the surface is made of a solid material like stone. I told them all to break up into four groups, to turn their backs on each other, to face the corners, and to talk at a normal volume.

"The sound will carry from one corner to the opposite corner, from one mouth right into the ears of the other person. As if you're wearing an invisible headset. Now don't stand there and wait to hear something, someone has to talk. When you get to your corner, start talking."

I gave myself a Starburst; I only had twenty minutes, thirty tops, before I dropped them at the hotel and headed for home. There was laughter by those who heard the effect, others cast dubious glances at each other and me. I pointed into the corners, told them they had to be farther inside, and reminded them not to whisper. Those who heard it refused to relinquish their places, coming up with funny things to send into the ears of their friends.

What Kelly and I were later able to piece together was that, as most of the group moved back toward me, the last remaining whisperers moved into the corners. Ramona glanced over and saw Kelly standing in a corner to her left. She noticed Nancy standing near me, safely out of earshot, and so Ramona leaned in and shared with Kelly their inside joke, Nancy's own quote: "The Civil War didn't have as much to do with slavery as people think it did."

Ramona saw Kelly laugh, but Kelly was laughing with whoever was opposite her, because Kelly knew, since she had been listening to the tour, that the sound carried between *opposite* corners.

The sound did not carry up to the dome before making a sharp right.

This meant that Ramona's inside joke traveled across the ceiling from her southeast corner and ended up in the ears of the father from Seattle who was standing in the northwest.

"THE CIVIL WAR didn't have as much to do with slavery as people think it did."

What the hell did that mean? Dennis stared into the marble corner and tried to puzzle it out. Who said that? He looked over his shoulder. Through the crowd gathering beneath the dome, he could make out the African American teacher stepping away from the opposite corner. An African American teacher from Georgia who, out of all the sentences in the world to speak into the corner (*Can you hear me? Is anyone there? Testing, testing. Greetings. Live from New York!*) chose to assert that the Civil War did not have as much to do with slavery as people think it did! Maybe she was referring to another civil war, one more timely, and one that would justify her bringing it up at the Whispering Gallery. Darfur? Zimbabwe? Then Dennis remembered the earlier outcry when the bus had passed the statue of Sherman on Fifth Avenue, the resentment still felt a century and a half after the fact. Dennis also remembered that one of their kids was wearing a Dixie flag shirt. No, the U.S. Civil War was still on their minds. They probably all spent their Saturdays taking part in Civil War reenactments.

Well, this was another good reason to live in the Pacific Northwest: a complete dearth of Civil War reenactments. Dennis wondered what the reenactments looked like in Georgia since there weren't that many real battles—just Sherman and his army marching their way to the sea. Did they build fires and roast Sherman in effigy? All off the point, he thought as he stepped toward the center. The more important question was why this African American woman from Georgia said what she did and why she chose to say it to him? He watched her, studied her. He hoped to make eye contact and raise a brow, but she didn't glance his way.

Dennis could not figure it out. There had to be a reason that she wanted to make her outrageous slavery claim to him. Maybe something he said at dinner had gotten back to her. Maybe those three hillbillies took offense at a meaningless phrase and talked about it at the Empire State Building, inflating its significance and transforming him into the kind of Yankee they reviled. But were Seattleites Yankees? Washington wasn't involved in the Civil War, wasn't even a state until 1889. Maybe anyone who didn't speak with a stupid accent was considered a Yankee.

He wanted to tap her shoulder and just ask her why she felt inclined to debate the Civil War with him, but he knew that would lead to a scene. He would let his temper get the best of him, would not be able to keep his argument muted, would drop one of his SMBs, would say something so terrible that both schools would halt their chatter and stare at him. Brittany would be mortified. She would cry and remind him that he had sworn not to embarrass her. The legitimacy of the Civil War would mean nothing at all to his daughter.

The Oyster Bar. Dennis looked at the entrance to the restaurant a few yards away, and he thought of Brittany's mother. It was the Oyster Bar that would stifle his urge to confront Ramona for almost twenty-four hours.

Again, they come at you at five hundred miles per hour, and unless someone fills you in, how are you expected to make the connection between oysters and self-restraint?

What needs to be known about Dennis and his ex-wife was that, for years, friends of theirs in Wallingford would invite them and five other couples to an Aphrodisiac Party at their home. These parties did not morph into sweaty swinging or wife swapping. They were innocent dinner parties with foods associated with love—oysters, truffles, strawberries, and chocolate fondue. Just as one family in a neighborhood might claim the Fourth of July cookout and another might spend their energy and money on making their house the destination for all trick-or-treaters, this couple put in its bid for Valentine's Day, and over the years the couples invited stopped seeing the holiday as a downtown dinner-for-two and looked forward to a festive night of socializing. Dennis never saw the guests on any other day of the year and didn't care since he never bonded with them anyway. He usually said something to elicit a signal from his wife to stop talking.

The February before last, at their final party together, he had been under strict instructions not to say anything embarrassing or controversial. "Just listen, Dennis. For once in your life, just listen and smile. No argument needs winning, not a single one."

He didn't find that too difficult during the preliminary appetizers and soup courses. This was because one of the women, Carrie, a transplant from Encinitas, California, was dominating the discussion. She had recently miscarried. After sixteen weeks of pregnancy. Traumatized beyond words. She and her husband, who was noticeably absent, had been trying to get pregnant for three years. Afterward, grief-stricken, Carrie buried her baby in the backyard. Dennis wanted to ask how this topic could be considered an aphrodisiac. She went on to say, at great length, that she visited the gravesite in her backyard three times a day for usually an hour at a time. She had been in mourning for six months. She brought gifts to the grave that would foster good energy for her baby's spirit. Rose quartz was the most powerful stone in matters of the heart. It helped to heal and maintain balance. She told them all about where she purchased the quartz, sometimes online, but there was a store in Bellingham that sold it, and because the sun can fade the pink, the winters in the Northwest were great because the rosy hue retained its power. Her baby loved the gifts, wanted more and more rose quartz, and she kept him fully stocked, the grave a garden shrine.

Molly, the host's sister-in-law, was the one who finally spoke up, "Oh, STOP it!"

Dennis gasped with relief. Fresh air filled his lungs. Someone else was going to tell her to shut up. Someone else was going to tell her that her fetus was not a junkie with a rose quartz fix, that she was out of her mind and needed serious psychiatric help. Someone else was going to do this, and his wife would be so proud that Dennis had listened and smiled sympathetically throughout. Molly was a Washingtonian, old stock, down near Olympia. She wasn't going to put up with this California horseshit.

"You're being ridiculous!" Molly told Carrie, but then asked, "Don't you think Jesus provides all the rose quartz your baby needs up in heaven?"

Dennis groaned. This had gotten worse, and he knew from the incremental rise of his wife's shoulders that he was about to say something, and it would shut this party down as soon as he did.

Now, on this trip, one year and four months after those cursed aphrodisiacs were digested and voided, he no longer had his wife's shoulders to warn him of danger, only his daughter's eyes which widened whenever he came perilously close to mortifying her. The problem with those rising shoulders and widening eyes, though, was that by the time the bodies made the adjustment, it was already too late. But Dennis remembered that the last time he ate oysters, he had dropped an SMB, and so he kept his opinions about the Civil War to himself.

And maybe I inadvertently helped by keeping everyone moving: "OKAY! HERE WE GO! FOLLOW ME!" My day was almost over. All I had to do was get them to the hotel and turn them over to the coordinator who would check them in as I hopped on the subway for home and sleep. Dennis and Ramona's war would have to be waged another day.

10:45 CHECK-IN AT HOTEL

BARBARA, THE STEPMOM from Seattle, whose last visit to New York featured limo drivers in livery and a suite at the Waldorf Astoria, the transient domicile for presidents and foreign leaders, looked warily at this hotel which appeared barely suitable for members of a town council. From the online reviews, there were bedbugs and scabies awaiting her, prostitutes working out of rooms on every floor, and an understaffed maintenance crew at work around the clock to repair the air conditioners.

The head of a clown in a fright wig rose from the stairwell at the front of the bus, and Barbara almost screamed. It was Elaine Caine, the woman from the airport who was not just their greeter in baggage claim, but their hotel representative as well. Elaine, ever flustered, couldn't figure out how to power on the microphone so she began shrieking her welcome and moved right into hotel policies. She let them know that the room doors slammed shut if they weren't careful and asked them all to keep their volume down, especially at night. Wouldn't want to disturb the prostitutes, Barbara thought. The driver was down below pulling the suitcases out of the bus, and Elaine told them that bellmen could bring their luggage to their rooms, but that it would be faster if they all took care of it themselves. Barbara looked wistfully at the sidewalk, remembering with longing that on their arrival at the Waldorf, they were escorted directly into the hotel toward a hospitality desk and that when they stepped into their rooms, high above Park Avenue, their suitcases were already waiting for them at the foot of their bed.

This evening, as she looked through the window of the bus, she saw a skinny man in jeans and a black t-shirt walk in front of the chatting bellmen, lean over behind the driver, lift one of the suitcases by the handle, and roll it away.

When Barbara's voice finally came to her throat, she cried out that someone had just stolen a bag, and everyone on the bus jumped toward the curbside windows. Elaine stepped down the stairs and reappeared on the curb, locating Barbara's face in the window and then pointing to one of the suitcases as if she were asking, *Is this the bag that was stolen?* Infuriating! Idiot! Barbara pointed in the direction the thief had gone, and Elaine held a hurried conference with the bellmen, one of whom strolled off in tepid pursuit. Barbara was the only one confident that her bag was not the one stolen three seconds after hitting the sidewalk of Eighth Avenue. Others scanned nervously and shouted with relief whenever they spotted theirs. The two lead teachers appeared on the sidewalk to talk with Elaine and to guard the rest of the luggage. Soon the leaders were waving their respective groups to disembark, and Wally, the giant from Georgia, reminded everyone to take all their belongings from around their seats, but his choice of words ("Take everything off! Take everything off!") made the teenagers laugh.

The bus hemorrhaged its tourists. They spilled all over the sidewalk. They clumsily groped for their suitcases and then rolled or lugged them toward the front door. Barbara could see her bag deep inside the luggage bay where the driver was working in a squat. She spotted one suitcase that had to be thirty years old, with a handle and no wheels, the kind you would see onstage in a high school theater production, a suitcase donated to the props department years ago and recycled in every musical since. It had been patched up in places with silver tape. It belonged to one of the skinny eighth-grade boys from Georgia, Lash, the boy with two cameras and a ten-million-dollar elbow, who seemed happy that it had not been stolen, though Barbara doubted anyone would have risked criminal charges for the contents of that particular suitcase. That was the safest bag of the bunch. It was the chubby girl from their school—the one with the to-do list, the one who had been thrilled to see two terminals at LaGuardia—who was left standing with Barbara when Barbara's bag, the last one, was pulled off by the driver.

"You don't see yours?" Barbara asked, unzipping part of her suitcase and pulling out the handle that snapped into place. Tracy shook her head as she peered into the empty compartments beneath the bus. Barbara asked, "Was yours…blue?"

"Yes," Tracy said. She wisely inferred, "And if I'm the only one without a suitcase…"

Barbara bit a side of her lower lip and patted the girl's shoulder, guiding her toward the front doors, "Well, let's tell your teacher…" Barbara blamed Elaine Caine, the incompetent twat, and the indifferent driver who was already pulling out into the busy eleven o'clock traffic.

Just as Barbara had expected, the lobby bore only the slightest resemblance to the photographs on the hotel's website, and all thirty-some of her fellow travelers were pressed shoulder to shoulder on one side, just below the corner where the miracle-working photographer must have squeezed himself before screwing the deceiving lens onto his camera. There appeared to be confusion over the room assignments—one room had boys and girls, another room of students was on a different floor completely removed from everyone else.

"Now where's Tommy Newman?" Elaine asked. Barbara grimaced along with the rest of the Seattle group. Tommy was going to keep coming up, no matter how much they tried to enjoy their vacation. Pete explained that he was no longer with the group. "Oh, that's great! That means we can shuffle everyone around more easily." She hurried off to the front desk.

Lu Takahashi, the drama teacher, standing next to Pete, saw the empty-handed Tracy. She walked over and placed her hands on the girl's shoulders, asked her how she was.

"I spent two hours packing that bag. Now someone else has it."

"He has a nicely packed suitcase. It was very thoughtful of you."

Tracy smiled, "I should have put a bow on it."

The four student council graduates, having discovered their favorite teacher a full eight feet away from them, reattached themselves to her hip and asked Tracy what she lost, telling her she could borrow anything she needed. The Georgia group began passing out key envelopes and squeezing by for the elevators. A few of the women asked Tracy if they could help. Tracy seemed to savor the attention.

Pete announced to the group that the room situation was almost straightened out and all the students needed to be in those rooms by eleven thirty, lights out by twelve. He reminded them that the tour company hired security guards to sit on the floors and watch the rooms. "Please don't let me get any reports tomorrow morning. Please don't make that security guard knock on my door."

The bellman, who had gone in sauntering search for the missing suitcase, shocked everyone when he entered the lobby, pulling the suitcase behind him. Cries of joy filled the place and then a baffling silence as the bellman lifted his arm to display, dangling from his hand, some of Tracy's bras. Barbara snatched them and held them close to her stomach while Tracy knelt on the floor to open the suitcase and check what was missing.

"He was behind the hotel," the bellman was explaining to Elaine loudly enough for everyone else to hear. "In the back corner behind the benches. I figured that's where he would go. He was just starting to go through the bag when I shouted at him. I think he was looking through the underwear first because people sometimes hide their money in their underwear," he pondered out loud. "Or maybe he had a fetish."

Barbara cried out, "THANK YOU!"

Tracy was delighted. Her suitcase was open to the entire lobby, her bras revealed to all of her classmates, but from what she could tell, nothing was missing. She knew from what she'd read not to pack valuables in her checked luggage, so her camera, her money, her iPod, and her cell phone were all in her carry-on.

She suddenly froze. "Where's my carry-on?!"

Barbara froze with her. Don't tell me she lost her carry-on.

Lu said, "Right here, I have it."

Barbara leaned over and inconspicuously pressed Tracy's underwear into a corner of her suitcase, whispering, "You can buy some new underthings tomorrow if you need to." Barbara thought Elaine Caine or the hotel or the tour company should cover the cost to replace the underwear soiled by a pervert and a bellman. Tracy didn't seem to care. She was grinning.

"I can't believe I didn't lose anything."

Pete was passing out the hotel keys. Barbara's stepson, Cody, headed toward the elevator with his roommate.

"Promise me you won't be the trouble room."

"I promise." He kissed her on the cheek. "Good night. Don't let the bed bugs bite."

Dreading the room her card key would open, Barbara hoped she would have the choice.

"OH, YEAH! OH, YEAH!" Wally's ten-year-old shouted when they opened the door to their room. "This is amazing!" Clint ran inside.

"Boy, come back and get your things."

"They got a picture on the wall and everything."

"Son, your suitcase." Clint raced back, grabbed his suitcase and backpack, and pulled them into the room. Wally and Clint were sharing the room with Zach, their prodigy, who Wally liked to think of as their secret weapon if their tour turned into a Starburst War. The three Brandons and Lash with his sorry, old, beat-up suitcase were next door. Wally could hear them through the wall. Clint was trying to see if the door connecting the rooms would open. "Wouldn't that be fun if we could have one big giant room?" Clint asked and then squealed, "Look at the view! We're so high up." Zach and Wally both approached the window and looked down onto the traffic from the seventh floor. "I don't think I've ever been this high up."

Zach said, "We were just on the top of the Empire State Building."

"Oh, yeah. I mean I've never been this high up to *sleep*." He turned away from the window and jumped on the closest bed, "I call this one!"

"Let Zach choose."

"Hey, which bed am I sleepin' in?" Clint asked. "We can make one bed the kids' bed or we can make one bed the Williams' bed. Zach is smaller than you are, so I'd have more room, but you're family."

"Let Zach choose."

"I don't mind either way," Zach said.

"Zach might elbow you if you're in that bed, he plays the violin in his sleep."

"No, I don't."

"That's what your mama told me."

"She did?" Zach looked puzzled, processing previously unheard information.

Clint said, "Zach, don't mind him. My dad's just cuttin' up." Clint bounced to the television and turned it on. "Hey, look at these news people. I never saw them before."

"It's a different market," Zach answered.

"But maybe on one of the channels…" Clint began changing channels. Wally, still standing at the window, saw a piece of paper slide beneath the door connecting the rooms. He bent over and picked it up.

He read a familiar eighth-grade hand, "Help me, I was kidnaped by my school and their holding me for hostage." In another eighth-grade hand, "We'll return Brandon Burns for 100 dollars." (50 was scratched out.)

Wally reached in his pocket and pulled out a nickel. He placed it on the carpet and used the ransom note to push it beneath the door. Laughter broke out. He called through the door that they had fifteen minutes to settle down and get to bed. Wally saw Zach's face agog on the bed near the wall. He followed his gaze to the television where a topless woman in a G-string was dancing in a television studio with orange lighting. Clint was frozen.

"We don't have nothin' like this at home."

"Did you buy a movie?" Wally rushed to the television and changed the channel.

"Naw, I didn't hit anything special. That was just the T.V. They have naked people on regular T.V. It's looks like they're in someone's garage."

Wally found ESPN and told them to leave the television alone.

"This city's crazy," Clint said. "Everything's different. We get the news, they get naked people dancin'." There was a roar outside the window and Clint scoped it out. "That was a truck."

"A very loud truck," Zach said.

"You think that was loud? You're in for a mess of trouble when my dad starts snorin'."

Another piece of paper, this time folded, slid under the door. Inside was a lock of Brandon Burns' hair—a sizeable lock actually, a whole curl—with the words, "This is all you get for five cents. For a doller you get an ear. For a hundred the hole boy." Wally told them through the door that they were crazy and to get ready for bed.

"And I know your mama ain't gonna be too happy to see a bald spot on her boy's head after only one night in New York." He told his own roommates that he was going to take a shower; they could take theirs in the morning. Zach went to the bathroom to change into pajamas and brush his teeth, and Wally started unpacking what he and Clint needed to turn in for the night.

"So, Son, how'd you like the city so far?"

"There's a whole mess of people here."

"Sure is."

"It's bigger than any place I've ever seen in my entire life."

"Your entire life?"

"How many people he say lived here?"

Wally wanted to answer his son, but he couldn't remember the answer. "There were a bunch of different categories."

"Well, how many live just in New York?"

"New York or Manhattan?"

"New York. In the five thingamajigs of New York."

"Several million."

"I know that, but just how many?"

"Where were *you*?" Wally asked.

"What do you mean?"

"Weren't you on the bus?"

"Sure I was, I was sittin' right next to you."

"How come you can't remember?"

Clint wondered at this before he answered, "I'm not a grown-up, I'm not a teacher."

"Son, I don't remember." Wally looked directly at Clint when he said this and saw just a hair of a twinge in his face.

Disappointment?

"Well, Jack knows a lot."

"He sure does."

"I mean he even knows how many people live in Atlanta. Did you know how many people live in Atlanta?"

Wally didn't reply because he still didn't know how many people lived in Atlanta. Around the same amount who walk through Grand Central every day, but what was that?

Zach was changed, his teeth brushed, and Wally carried his toiletry bag, his shorts, and tank top into the bathroom. Behind the closed door, he took off his clothes, stale and sour after fifteen hours of driving, flying, waiting in airports, and touring. He took a few minutes to figure out the shower levers and dials, conducted experiments with the hot and cold—did anything mean *home* like your own bathroom?—and climbed into the shower. He heard the television's volume lower, the sportscaster's voice growing quiet before disappearing altogether, and he knew exactly what was happening and who was pushing the buttons. He shouted for Clint to turn the channel back to the game and "leave them naked people alone."

"All right!"

"Turn the volume up so I know you're on ESPN." Clint obeyed, and the volume was restored. He heard Clint saying something about "my dad's ears," but he didn't disobey or pretend that the naked channel was ESPN. He didn't lie. For now. Traveling with Clint and the eighth graders, he kept imagining Clint three, four years older, seeing the naked ladies on television differently. Wally had seen Zach's wide eyes, noticed how he suddenly withdrew into himself while Clint was carrying on, cracking up, seeing it all as a hoot. But it wouldn't be long before Clint started locking his door and not telling his dad the truth. Like his other two kids.

More disturbing, though, were the thoughts he was having that Clint might be making comparisons, that he was at that age when he started seeing how his father held up against the rest of the dads and against the man from New York who "sure does know a lot." Like his other kids loved to do. It was natural, but Clint was Wally's youngest, and he didn't want his youngest to grow up. These weren't crippling anxieties for Wally, just thoughts percolating at the end of a long day, thoughts he couldn't really articulate and thoughts that disappeared for the night when he emerged from the bathroom and saw that Zach was in one bed, reading a book, and Clint was in the other.

Wally tossed his dirty clothes into a pile in the corner and then collapsed onto the family bed, missing Clint by deliberate inches, sending him briefly into the air and more than briefly into a fit of giggles. Wally asked Zach if he were almost done with his reading. Zach said, "Yes, sir. Thank you," and placed the book on the end table between the two beds.

"Lights out," Wally said.

He switched off the two lamps between the beds. Nothing changed.

"It's still bright," Clint said. "It's like them TV shows where they turn out the light but then it's just blue and you can still see everything." The three lay there in the well-lit dark. "Someone's going to have to close them curtains."

"You're closest," Wally said and laughed when Clint let out a fake groan, as if he didn't have the energy he obviously did. He hopped out of bed and to the window. Wally smiled as he watched his son, on his skinny legs in a city far from home, tug and pull first one drape closed and then the other.

Right before Wally officially conked out, Clint observed: "It's almost midnight, and there are taxis and horn honkin'. I wonder how you go to bed here. Is that why they call it the City That Never Sleeps?"

"We'll have to ask Jack tomorrow," Wally said. "I always figured it was a kind of a compliment, but maybe not."

DAY TWO

7:15   Guide Meets Group at Hotel

7:30   Breakfast

8:30   Subway to Central Park

8:45   Central Park

10:00 Metropolitan Museum of Art

12:00 City Bus to Rockefeller Center

12:30 Rockefeller Center and Lunch

1:30   Radio City Music Hall

2:30   Fifth Avenue

5:00   Return to Hotel

5:45   Meet in Lobby for Dinner and Theater

6:15   Dinner

8:00   Theater

10:45 Group Photo

"GOOD MORNING! THIS is your wake-up call. We hope you have a *great* day!"

Kelly, the lead teacher from Georgia, hung up the phone and asked her second-in-command, "Ramona, are you up?"

"I've *been* up. Ever since those damn fire trucks."

"What fire trucks?"

"What fire trucks?!" Ramona rolled over and propped herself up, staring across the aisle that separated their beds to see if Kelly, honestly, had slept through the screaming sirens that rattled the windows and made their walls throb. "Were you having sweet dreams, darlin'? Were you dreaming of your precious little Hunter?"

"I don't know what I was dreaming about, but I am full of energy and ready to go."

"You and your twenty-something self."

"Do you want the first shower?"

Ramona fell back onto her pillow and moaned, "Oh, pleeeeaaase don't make me go out there again. One day was enough. Pleeeeaaase don't make me go out into the greatest, most fantastic, absolutely wonderful, unbelievably terrific, splendiferous city on earth."

"Mrs. Harrison!" It was Kelly's turn to prop herself up and stare across the aisle. "Would you seriously prefer a tour guide who hated his city? Someone who said, 'There's another ugly building, and why'd you people spend all your money to come to this dump?'"

"I just want them to tell it like it is. That's all I'm asking. Spare me the postcard propaganda. Their city smells like urine. Every five minutes I want to shout at all the New Yorkers, 'You people do know it smells like pee, right? You are aware of this odor, are you not? Please tell me you can smell this!'"

"I only smelled it once."

"Then you've got a sinus infection."

"I do not."

"And you can smell the garbage on the sidewalks. You can see the wet, slimy tracks from the garbage bags they draaaaaag to the curb. You can smell the dog poop they drop in the trashcans, the sour beer, the cigars, underarms, the nasty things cooking in the carts, bad breath, unwashed hair…"

"It's like you have a superpower nose."

"Just tell it like it is. That's all I'm asking."

"It's his tour," Kelly said and then decided to tease Ramona. "You remind me of Nancy telling you how to teach your own class." One second the pillow was beneath Ramona's head, the next it was colliding with Kelly's face.

She laughed as Ramona said, "I think I will take that first shower and use up all the hot water."

"I'm sure they have enough hot water for both of us."

Standing up, Ramona threw her arms in the air, did a dance and said, "Ooo, that's right, because this is Neeewww Yoooooork City!" Kelly laughed some more as Ramona continued on her way into the bathroom, "And the city of New York has more hot water than forty-two states and one hundred sixty-six countries…"

7:15 GUIDE MEETS GROUP AT HOTEL

DAY TWO. I COULDN'T even remember what the group looked like. I came out of the subway and bought a coffee from a cart on the corner.

Deliberate amnesia is crucial when you're doing back-to-back jobs; otherwise, the next tour becomes a refrain of *Did I tell you about the Dutch yet?* or *Didn't we already talk about Macy's?* It's a necessary part of the job to scour and scrub the brain clean and start fresh with each group, but there was something mildly upsetting—frightening, actually, as I approached yet another birthday and Day Two of a tour that was taking me four days closer to my death—that my brain had so efficiently dumped out its contents.

Where was this group from? Colorado? No. Kelly was on this trip, the teacher from Georgia. I liked her. We had had a fun conversation at dinner which helped me recall more and more of her previous trip.

This tour, the one I was on now, was comprised of two groups, one from Seattle and one from rural, and I mean rural, Georgia. I used my free hand to tick off the players I remembered. On the Georgian side, besides Kelly, there was the African American woman who didn't seem to like me except when I talked about the criminal underworld in Chinatown; their vice principal, who seemed sweet to me, but that fake sweet, the sugar substitute bound to give someone cancer; there was that eighth-grade boy prodigy whose parents taught at the college and who was going to force me to buy a bag of Starbursts just for him; the giant with the jokes and his ten-year-old who never stopped bouncing; the three Brandons who apparently became best friends because they had the same first name; the funny, cartoonishly racist grandmother who was disappointed by the Golden Gate Bridge because it was red; and her son, the ironworker, who was missing several teeth but was always smiling despite that fact.

On the Seattle side, there was Pete, the teacher who had some fantastic stories about 1970s New York, which I mentally added to my collection. Sometimes I felt guilt for not living in New York in the Seventies, that my absence deprived me of being a real New Yorker, but I'd lived in New York long enough to see the seedier side. I arrived in 1990 when the murder rates were breaking records, above two thousand per year, thank you very much. One night, a bullet from Morningside

Drive shot through the window of my dorm room and hit the ceiling directly above my head. That had to count for something.

Who else? There was the blue-haired girl who kept to herself and showed up late twice already; the shopping bubbleheads; the father who spent most of his time in Chinatown standing on the corner; the energetic drama teacher with her four student council officers who kept in a tight group and behaved as if their official terms carried past graduation into the real world where, in fact, when it comes to a graduated student council official, there is no lamer duck.

I was early. I planned to enjoy my coffee in solitude until the last minute, to rest my voice and conserve my smiles, when I saw a short pinch-faced woman waving to me. It was the nasty, complaining mother from Georgia. Dina. How did I remember that name? Dina the Dour. She was smoking in front of the hotel. As she was absolutely my least favorite person on the trip, I wanted to point at my watch and shout, "I'M NOT ON FOR ANOTHER TEN!" But she was already moving toward me. It would have been awkward to run.

"Did you hear what happened last night?" she asked, each syllable punctuated with cigarette smoke. She went on to tell me that some "New Yorker" just "walked on by" the bus and stole one of "our" suitcases when we were still "trapped inside." I figured this must have happened immediately after I left the group and that Dina was telling me this because I was somehow at fault. I should have alerted the New York media that K.C. Crown Middle School was in town for four days, so the residents of the city needed to be on their best behavior. Although I was concerned about the suitcase, I knew Dina wasn't going to be an objective reporter, so I decided to play an old game of mine.

Overacting, my hand on my heart, I cried, "You were *trapped*?! On the bus?!"

"Yes."

"How? Did the door lock?"

"Well…"

"Because sometimes the circuits short…"

"No, no…"

"Or the door is blocked by something at the curb."

"We were just listening to Elaine…"

"So you weren't trapped?" I clarified.

"No, I mean…"

"You weren't trapped on the bus?"

"No, but…"

"You mean you were still on the bus but you weren't at all trapped?"

"Yes."

"Not at all?"

"No."

Your witness.

I feigned relief, touched her arm, and said, "That would have been horrible, could you imagine? After all day traveling and touring and we finally make it back to the hotel and you're trapped inside the bus and need to be rescued by the New York Fire Department?" I knew Dina wanted me to address the subject of the suitcase, but I couldn't resist evading her topic and pulled out one of the four thousand anecdotes I always have at my disposal: "One of my groups from Minnesota went to the Apple Store on Fifth Avenue when it first opened and they went late at night because the store doesn't close. It's open twenty-four hours. Well, the entrance is a glass cube and you have the option to take the staircase or the glass elevator and they took the elevator and it got stuck. I mean, they were *literally* trapped and had to be rescued by the NYPD after forty-five minutes of people gawking at them. And when they finally were rescued—it's a hydraulic elevator so the fluid had to be drained so that the elevator would descend—they had to jump out through the doors before it sank even farther and a couple actually got burns on their hands from the lamps. It might have been the FDNY that rescued them, I can't remember. Anyway!" I patted her shoulder as I broke for the hotel's front door, "I better get inside; it was wonderful talking with you."

Inside, I saw that the lobby was self-segregated. Filling the couches on one side were most of the people from Georgia, and filling the couches on the other were most of the people from Washington. This wasn't unusual—it's hard enough for eighteen people traveling together to cohere, and doubly, or maybe exponentially, harder for two groups.

Pete, the leader from Seattle, greeted me and told me they were only waiting on four more. As he was filling me in about the suitcase, we were accosted by two of the shopping girls who asked if we could do anything to increase the time allotted for Fifth Avenue.

"No," Pete said, "but it's possible we could *decrease* the time."

They smiled weakly and walked away. One said that he had to be joking; the other told her that he would do it. "In a heartbeat."

Just then Kelly, the leader from Georgia, came up to us and said she needed to figure out a way to get more time shopping on Fifth. I caught a flicker of disbelief cross Pete's face. He pretended someone in his group needed him and excused himself. Kelly explained that she and her boyfriend were going to his brother's formal wedding and she needed the perfect black dress. Since Kelly had gone on the Radio City Music Hall tour the year before, I suggested she skip that and start shopping as soon as we finished lunch.

Problem solved, I looked at my watch for the fourteenth time that morning. 7:25. I handed out everyone's meal ticket which listed the choices for breakfast and had two remaining—one for the Seattle boy who couldn't make the trip and one for someone else. The teachers scanned their groups for the one who was missing. It was the girl with the blue hair. Big surprise! And not because she had blue hair (some of my best friends have blue hair) but because the person who is late once is usually the person who is late consistently. So far, the Georgians had a perfect record and it wouldn't be long now before they started resenting the Washingtonians, not long before they started meeting in their corner of the lobby, whispering, conspiring, and eventually escalating the tension from segregation to all-out hostility, a war, if you will, of

Southern Aggression. But that generally happened on Day Three. The girl with the blue hair came off the elevator at last, and I led the group out of the hotel.

7:30 BREAKFAST

SEVEN YEARS AGO: A welcome breakfast was sponsored by Lexus in the Empire room at the Waldorf Astoria on Park Avenue. Barbara remembered a buffet with silver trays and chafing dishes, two tall chefs behind the table serving eggs to order, quiche, omelets. Lobster, the ingredient du jour. Mimosas in flutes and coffee in urns and the guests all politely waiting their turns. The men were freshly shaven; the women wore pearls or simple gold chains, their clothing spotless, not a wisp of lint! There was no lint at the Waldorf Astoria. There were no odors either. The food smelled fresh, as did the guests with just a trace of perfume or after shave, all of which complemented one another. Nothing clashed.

Today: Barbara was crammed into an undersized booth in a crowded Greek diner on Eighth Avenue, shoulder to shoulder with Dennis, who was wearing frayed black jeans and a *Battleship Galactica* t-shirt, and knee to knee with Grandma Kettle, who was flossing her teeth with her meal ticket. Her son, the ironworker, made the fourth at the table, and he was regaling them with tales of his morning's hunt. His accent was thick, Barbara only caught every other sentence, but she gathered that he had jumped out of bed at five thirty and set off into Times Square "to get the lay of the land." Unfortunately, he went in the wrong direction and "ended up at a river." During his roundabout way back, he saw a horse stable, a garage for hot dog carts, television studios, and he found an Ironworker's Local where they "got to talking" and then gave him a hat he was now proudly wearing. "And I only found them cuz I got lost."

"That's right," Grandma Penny agreed. "When we're lost, we find the most important things."

In China, that might have been ancient wisdom; in California, New Age babble; and in New York, coming from a Southerner trying to make small talk in a Greek diner, it was a folksy homespun latch hook placemat, with vaguely religious undertones, that sat on the table without comment; that was, until Dennis finished stirring his coffee, tapped the spoon on the rim of the porcelain mug, and said, "And sometimes we find the most important things when we're *not* lost."

Grandma Penny considered this and said, "True, true, that's right."

"Seventy-nine degrees," Travis said. "A great day for the park."

"But not a great one to spend inside a museum," Dennis said.

Barbara could only add, "Mmm."

The waitress, a round middle-aged woman, slid down the narrow aisle to their table and asked, "Goodmorningwhatyouliketodrink?"

"What now?" Penny asked.

"Pancakes," Travis said.

Barbara told them the waitress was taking their orders for drinks. They handed her their tickets with their choices marked. Then, even though it was obvious Penny couldn't understand the waitress, she started a conversation by telling the waitress that she spoke very fast and that they were from the South where "we speak at a stroll." Barbara quickly interjected that she and Dennis were from Seattle. Penny asked where the waitress was from. She may or may not have understood "Puerto Rico," but she made an impressed sound as if she did and told the waitress that they were from Georgia, about an hour outside of Savannah.

"Have you ever been there?"

"Oh, no!" The waitress laughed. "I been to Myrtle Beach once and twice to Miami."

"Okay, okay, well, we're in between those places. You're just gonna have to come on down, and we'll make *you* breakfast. Have you ever had grits?"

"Greets? No, Idonteenkso."

"Aaall right, we'll make you some grits."

"Si, we do that."

They squeezed each other's hands, and after the waitress went to the kitchen to put in the orders, Penny said, "Do they got any restaurants where the waiters speak English?"

Dennis pointed out, "That *was* English."

"Oh, you know what I mean. I. Am. Famished."

Barbara could not do this. She could not sit through a breakfast with these three, at this table, in this diner. The morning sun was hitting the windows and coating them with a glare like some kind of sealant, a glue that choked her throat. She couldn't breathe. Someone asked her if she were all right. She placed the back of her hand on her own forehead.

"I just need some air," she murmured. Dennis, afraid she was going to throw up on him, practically jumped out of the booth. She bumped the table as she tried to stand. Minimal clattering. She took deliberate steps toward the front, concentrating on the exit.

From the counter where I was sitting with Kelly and Pete, I saw Barbara stumble out of the restaurant. I had just taken a CPR skills class and learned that many choking victims die away from the dining room. Too embarrassed to cause a scene, they quietly remove themselves, and then, when they can't dislodge the food on their own, oxygen depleted, with no one to witness, they faint, fall to the floor, and die. So I followed Barbara out of the restaurant. I expected to find her sprawled, unbreathing, on the sidewalk. But she wasn't choking. She was taking deep breaths, leaning against the wall of the store next door. I asked how she felt. She nodded, hands on her hips. She looked healthy—flushed cheeks, yoga shoulders.

"I'm fine." She straightened up and looked at me. "It's just. I've been here before. I was in New York one time before." She suddenly broke down. Actual tears. Bringing one hand up to her mouth, the other hand to her stomach, she was reliving something awful. 9/11? 9/11. She was in the towers seven years ago. She was in the towers and she hasn't been back since…

"It's stupid, I'm being stupid. I can't explain it."

"Do you want me to bring you your breakfast? To go?" She shook her head. "A bagel?"

"I saw a Starbucks." You'd have to be blind if you didn't. "I think I should go there."

I assumed her need for Starbucks was some form of homesickness, serious Seattle withdrawal. There wasn't a cloud in the sky and maybe that was flipping her out. I told her that there were two Starbucks in the same building across the street, and I walked her there. I kept up my end of the conversation, telling her that Worldwide Plaza, where we were headed, stood on the site of the third Madison Square Garden, the arena that John Steinbeck helped construct, where Muhammad Ali boxed under the name Cassius Clay, where Marilyn Monroe sang "Happy Birthday" to JFK, where they set the original *Manchurian Candidate*…and so on and so forth. We reached the door, and I told her I would lead the group past the window on our way to the subway.

I returned to the diner, thinking Pete could fill in the details, but it wasn't until later, after further observation, that I changed my diagnosis: she was suffering from *Split City Disorientation*, something many New Yorkers experience, especially as we age. There was a city that Barbara remembered from several years ago and a new one she didn't recognize. It was as though after months of anticipating a trip to a city she loved, she was dropped into another city entirely. How was she to know she wasn't in Cleveland or Pittsburgh? There were yellow cabs and hot dog stands and the Empire State Building, but nothing else said New York to her. Even Times Square, briefly seen the previous night from the bus through the eyes of a student group, was not how she remembered it. Her Times Square had been larger, brighter, more chic. They had driven through it in a limo from dinner at Sparks Steakhouse on their way to a sold-out Broadway musical.

Barbara entered Starbucks, a comfort zone of beige and taupe just like it was at home. She approached the counter and ordered her usual. She was going to take thirty minutes off to sit in Seattle before venturing back out into this city they kept saying was New York. Central Park and the Metropolitan Museum were on the day's itinerary. These were two places she remembered, and she hoped they would live up to the demanding expectation of her memory.

8:30 SUBWAY TO CENTRAL PARK

FORTY-FIVE MINUTES LATER, after thirty-five plates of breakfast were consumed, after the pancakes were praised by the pickiest and least experimental of diners, after Kelly scolded the Brandons for wasting ketchup (you really only had about five minutes from the time the Brandons finished their food before you needed to clear their table), after I made the rounds to recommend restrooms, after ten of them who couldn't wait in the long line for the miniature bathrooms at the back of the diner returned from using the bathrooms back at the hotel (after promising me, because of our tight schedule, that they would use the ones in the lobby and not go all the way up to their rooms), after two of the Seattle girls yelled "SHOPPING!" and Pete gave them a teacherly look, after the two groups were counted and the drama teacher had to go back into the diner where she found their eighteenth (guess who!) in a corner with her iPod and camera, after the ten-year-old asked why toast "in breakfast places" always tasted better than toast at home, after Dina the Disgruntled complained that they didn't refill the coffee fast enough, after I pushed Dina in front of a speeding UPS truck (just kidding), and after we picked up our one fugitive at Starbucks, I led the group up to Fiftieth Street where we took the stairs below ground for our first subway ride.

"STAY TO THE RIGHT, STAY TO THE RIGHT!"

The warning became a chorus behind me as I pulled a thick stack of Metrocards out of a pocket of my shorts and claimed a turnstile. Because of how long it can take tourists to figure out how to use the card—*Yellow facing you…that's upside down…no, the other way…the M in the front…not too fast…but faster than that…a little slower…one at a time…no, the yellow facing you*—I often swipe all the cards myself, sliding them through the sensor's track, shouting GO with every beep and achieving a rhythm of such fluency and beauty I can often hear an Olympic commentator praising my efforts with increasing excitement: *Jack Cort is so smooth, he makes it look so easy, effortless, but it's years of training, and wait!, he's going to do it, he's going to win the gold medal for his country and set a NEW… WORLD…RECORD!* The tourists always get into it, practically leaping through the turnstile to get inside the station, wrongly believing that they have only one second before the turnstile locks up and their ride is forever lost.

"Why do I have an extra ride?" I called to the teachers after all had passed through. "Who are we missing?"

Lu reminded me about Tommy, the Seattle boy who "didn't make it." There was a slight awkwardness. I really would have to ask about him. I swiped myself through and then hurried to the front of the group where I knew most of the students would be leaning over the edge of the platform looking into the tunnel.

"STEP BACK, STEP BACK!" I walked down the line, pretending to swat at anyone less than a yard from the edge. Clint pretended to swat back. Then I led them farther up the platform and jumped into a spiel recited so often that I let my mouth do the talking while my mind worked on the timing of the itinerary.

My mouth: "When the train pulls up, look to me and I'll point to the car we're going to take. Don't use just one door, spread down the length of that car, and use every door of that car. Let people off first, they're going to work, and then quickly move into the middle of the train. But don't RUN! It scares the New Yorkers. Take a seat if you can or hold onto a bar. If you don't, you'll fall to the floor when the train starts."

My mind: "8:41, we're on schedule. A five-minute train ride, we'll still be to the park before nine. The C, one of the lamer local trains, will take a few minutes to get here, so when I'm done with these instructions, I'll move right into subway trivia."

"Starburst for the person who can name the city that built the world's first subway system!"

"NEW YORK!" shouted Tracy, the excitable, nose-squealing, *Great Gatsby*-loving tourist from Seattle.

"Nope."

—PARIS!

—ITALY!

—LONDON!

"London it is!" Zach, the prodigy from Georgia, added another Starburst to his collection. "Now, the first in the U.S.?"

"NEW YORK!" Tracy again.

"Nope."

—WASHINGTON, D.C.!

"That's not even forty years old."

—CHICAGO!

—SAN FRANCISCO!

—LOS ANGELES!

"Los Angeles? Are you kidding? No, this city is a major American city, but no one ever seems to think of it unless you're talking phenomenal sports teams or colonial tea parties."

"BOSTON!" Wally screamed. People on the sidewalk above must have heard. I threw him a Starburst. Clint cheered and hugged his dad. Wally smiled proudly before he passed the candy to his son.

While waiting for our train, my mouth addressed daily ridership numbers, the people who operated each train, what powered the system, and the merits of the four-track system—the local and express tracks—devised more than a century ago. As if on cue, an express A train began making rumbling sounds south of the station. The group looked up and down the tunnel, their vision of the train blocked by the screen of vertical steel supports dividing the local and express tracks, so they jumped when the A suddenly appeared out of nowhere, screamed through the station and, without stopping, disappeared on its way uptown.

Wally asked, "How do those people get off?"

"They don't," I joked. "They never get off. They made one mistake and now they're stuck."

"Really?" Wally said, and the rest laughed.

Clint said, "He's messin' with ya, doncha know that?"

Our train was approaching, so I quickly explained, "That was an express train and this is a local station."

"Oh, okay," Wally smiled weakly. His "Boston Triumph" was already history, and Clint hadn't even swallowed his Starburst.

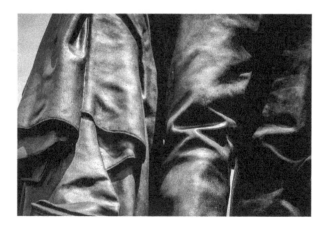

8:45 CENTRAL PARK

AFTER MY INTRODUCTION to the park at Seventy-second Street, Clint reached over a stone wall and snapped a gingko leaf from a branch. He examined the stem, twirled it around between his fingers, waved the leaf like the fan it resembled, and then looked up at his dad.

"This ain't real?" he asked. Wally was waiting on two John Lennon groupies from Seattle, who were taking multiple pictures of the Dakota, as the rest of us disappeared into the trees. Wally was trying to bring up the rear, to make sure no straggler was left behind, but he had no clue where we were going and hated losing sight of the group. When Wally didn't respond, Clint said, "What does he mean, it's not real?"

"Well, go up and ask him what he meant," Wally said, and Clint took off toward the front of the group.

What I meant was that the park we were entering was not a green rectangle preserved by the city before the developers could spoil it. The green rectangle was, in fact, completely developed. I had told them it was one of the greatest examples of nineteenth-century art in America, a massive earthwork: a billion cubic feet of soil was removed, carted in, shifted around; rock was blasted with more gunpowder than was used at the Battle of Gettysburg; swamps were drained and tunnels carved through stone; lakes were created with concrete, lined with vegetation and filled with New York City drinking water.

"This is fake?" Clint asked when he caught up with me, handing me his leaf, near the *Imagine* mosaic embedded in the asphalt trivium of Strawberry Fields.

"That's right," I said. "Made of a high grade polyurethane plastic."

"Wow!"

"And do you hear those birds? They're actually recordings played through speakers strategically placed in trees throughout the park."

"But I see a bird right there."

"Robot. Remote-controlled." Clint was mystified. Laughing, I repeated Clint's own line, "I'm messin' with ya, doncha know that?"

"I don't get it," Clint said.

That morning my mind-mouth disconnect might have been making things murky. I concentrated on explaining myself as clearly as I could to the boy who was avidly listening. I told him that the trees were real, though they were planted as part of a plan, that the water was real, but that it was pumped through pipes. I described a walk through the park as "a stroll through a series of landscape paintings made from grass, flowers, rock, and trees, positioned to create pictures, so that you turn a corner and the trees that were blocking your view suddenly open up on a body of water and then you cross a bridge and you're in the middle of a forest and then you're standing on top of a castle and then you're descending through a garden and past a lawn and through a tunnel into another different part of the park. It's just like the art you're going to see in the museum today, materials manipulated to guide your eye."

"Got it!" Clint clapped his hands and raced back to his father to relay the information.

Wally nodded when Clint finished and said, "How 'bout that?"

"I'm goin' back up there to see what else I can get!" Clint said and bounced away.

Wally stayed in the back, playing the role of shepherd, the protector and the man who kept everyone moving, an eye out for the strays who wandered off to photograph a flower or to buy a bottle of water. That was his role on this trip. Because Wally was slowly bringing up the rear, however, he kept missing pieces of the tour, coming in as the commentary was wrapping up, so he had no idea why the three Brandons were pointing to a rock and calling it a giant pile of "shist" and warning each other not to step in that "shist."

After leisurely descending a hill along a curved path with shrubbery and trees on either side—now this was nice, this was more his pace—Wally watched as the group rushed across a street, dodging cyclists who almost took three of them down. So much for strolling. He and the Brandons were on one side of the road as the tour convened in front of a tall statue down a path on the other side.

A Brandon said, "It's like a river of bicycles."

"Boys," Wally said, "we gotta cross this crick." They grinned as he took each of them by the arms and lined them up one behind the other. He waited for gaps in the traffic, then tossed them, one by one, into the road, and told them to swim for it. Giddy with the game, they sprinted safely to the other side and turned to help Wally.

With a better view around the bend of the drive, they shouted, "YOU'RE GOOD, MR. WILLIAMS, NOTHIN'S COMIN'!" Wally reached down and removed his shoes, Merrells that slipped on and off without laces, and held them in either hand. Then he mimed the crossing of a hazardous rapid, his arms above his head. He skipped nimbly to his left and right, dodging imaginary cyclists. When four real racers suddenly appeared, he quickly scampered the rest of the way and "jumped" to shore, eliciting howls of laughter from the boys as they scurried to rejoin the group.

Physical comedy was still the purest of them all, timeless, classic, though at age forty-two, Wally wished he could shed some of the weight that made his physical comedy so effective—for the sake of his wife and kids, for the sake of his knees as he walked through Central Park, wondering just how many of the "fifty-eight miles of pedestrian path" the group would be covering today. Fifty-eight miles of pedestrian path: he had heard that number. That was a number that stuck.

Wally was brushing his socks clean and replacing his Merrells, when Clint popped up in front of him and asked, "What're you doin' with your shoes off?"

"Just crossin' the road."

"Hm," Clint took that in stride and pointed up to the statue the group had just abandoned. "Do you know who that man in metal is?"

"No, Son. Why don't you tell me?"

"Daniel Webster."

"The fella who did the dictionary?"

"Jack said he was a senator."

"Oh, that's right, the fella with the dictionary was *Merriam* Webster."

"I don't know about that. I wish we had statues in our woods. That would make it fun if you just kept comin' up to statues in the middle of the woods."

Shoes on, Wally started walking as Clint hopped from side to side.

"We better hurry up, Dad. We don't wanna get lost. We'd never find our way home."

"We'd figure it out," Wally said.

"How many statues do we have in Sherrod County? The sign back there said there are fifty-some statues just in this park! If we had a mess of statues near us, d'you reckon you could talk about 'em?"

"How so?"

"Like Jack. Dad, if Jack came down to Sherrod County, you could probably show him around, couldn't you?"

"Of course. We both could."

"You could tell him all about the secret trails and every tree in the woods. You're good with trees."

"I know my trees."

Clint pointed to the row of trees along the path and asked, "What're those trees, you think? I never seen them before."

Wally looked up into the branches. The leaves looked like maple leaves, but the bark he didn't recognize at all. The bark was dappled and sick-looking, but these trees were everywhere and obviously healthy. They were thick, flush and tall.

Clint waited patiently for about twenty seconds until Wally admitted, "I can't tell."

"Jack'll know!" Clint said and was gone.

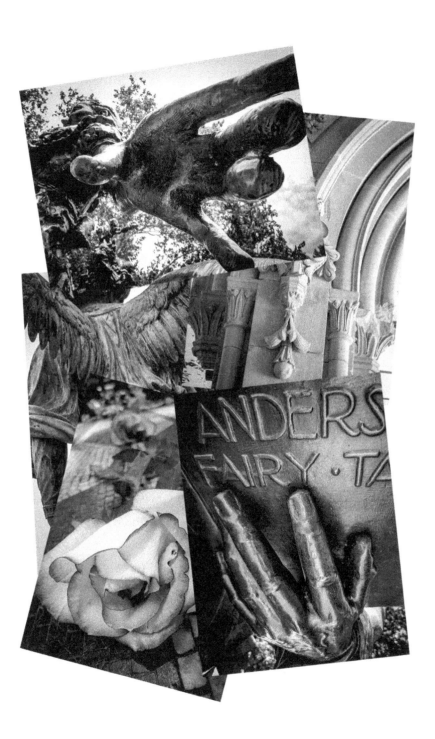

ALONG WITH THE TEN-YEAR-OLD, there were two others who kept me company as we walked through the park: Tracy from Seattle and Zach, the Georgia prodigy. Kelly mentioned to Zach that I worked in the theater and loved Shakespeare, so the eighth grader worked his way up to the front to have an "adult conversation about the Bard." He would ask a question—"What do you think was his most successful comedy?"; "His weakest tragedy?"; "Do you agree with Harold Bloom of Yale that Falstaff was Shakespeare's greatest creation?"—and then he would mull over my answer while Clint begged me for a Starburst trivia question, for which only he was eligible, and Tracy read me more from her to-do list to make sure that we didn't pass something without her knowing it.

I let the three of them choose our way—either a stroll along the lake, past the Bow Bridge to approach the Angel from behind OR a stroll south to see the Mall and approach the Angel as intended. I told them the area around the Mall was where you could find a statue of Shakespeare (for Zach) and Balto (for Tracy's to-do). They chose the latter and we set off toward the Mall. Clint asked me if I thought they made the right choice. I told them there was no wrong choice in Central Park and then, after looking at my watch, confessed that we really didn't have time to walk all the way down to either Shakespeare or Balto. Tracy checked the statue off her list anyway. Close enough.

The group was excited to see the Mall, because they recognized it from so many movies, which meant we had to wait until almost everyone had gotten a picture in front of the famous backdrop. While they snapped away, I showed them how the Mall resembled a cathedral, formed from nature, with four rows of elms that created two side aisles and a nave, the tree branches interlocking above to create a vaulted ceiling of sorts, the promenade forming a cross where we were standing. I then pointed everyone toward the "church's altar," better known as the Bethesda Fountain. I led them down the staircase and into the arcade, its ceiling of blue and white encaustic tile recently restored. When the Bethesda Angel, or the *Angel of the Waters*, appeared at the end of the tunnel, framed in an arch, water cascading below her bare feet, cameras were powered on once again.

As the tourists tried to capture one of the most photographed sculptures in the city, I provided the context for those near me. This was the park's most important statue, I told them, the first statue in New York sculpted by a woman and, as a result, a statue heavily criticized.

Clint was shocked: "How can anybody criticize that?" Heart on his sleeve, he added, "That's the most beautiful thing I've ever seen." While I spoke of the significance of the Angel, the metaphor for the park itself—nature as a means of healing and restoration—I was interrupted by a religious eighth grader named Ashley.

After I said the Bethesda Angel appeared "somewhere in the New Testament," she piped up, "It's actually John, Chapter Five."

"Really?" I asked, impressed.

"Yes, I'm a Bible Bee champion."

I was confused: "A what?"

A friend of hers said, "Let's just say she would get all the *Bible* Starbursts."

I asked, "Do they come in that flavor?" Ashley screwed up her face, so I had to say, "Just kidding. That's very cool. John, Chapter Five, thank you, I'll remember that."

Most didn't hear this exchange; they were busy with their cameras. I looked at my watch and suggested we take a group picture. Unfortunately, they did not congeal as one. The two groups naturally divided into their own Washington and Georgia subgroups, not interested in documenting the other state's existence on their tour. The K.C. Crown Middle School was the first to stand and sit along the stone rim of the fountain. I was recruited as photographer. Despite the majority of digital cameras, each of the Georgians wanted a photo taken with his or her camera, so eight hung from my forearms like ornaments from a Christmas tree, and volunteers from Washington helped take up the slack, taking pictures with whatever cameras had been lined up on the bricks of the Terrace. Then they switched, and the Washingtonians posed for the Georgian paparazzi. Tracy, who had been the only one to lose her balance and fall on the subway ride, was standing in the back row, on the bowed edge of the fountain when she stepped back and dunked her foot in the water but was able to catch herself before her whole body made a splash.

Then the photo shoot broke into even smaller groups—families and individuals—and Wally approached me to "get a few things straight." He asked me about the rock (Manhattan schist), about the tree with the maple leaves (London planes), to go over the cathedral again, and to finish what I was saying about the woman who modeled for the Angel.

I told the few gathered that the Angel was modeled on Charlotte Cushman, a very famous actress, the Meryl Streep of her day, who was diagnosed with breast cancer and underwent multiple water treatments.

"What happened to her?" one of the girls from Georgia asked.

"Did she make it?" asked a Brandon.

"No, sadly. She died of breast cancer." The two of them seemed mildly crushed. I should have followed up, asked if they knew someone with cancer, but we were running short on time, so I didn't say anything else, nor did I tell the Bible Bee champion that Charlotte Cushman, the actress, the Angel with whom she was posing and taking multiple pictures was a lesbian and shared a Boston marriage with the sculptor, Emma Stebbins.

I looked at my watch for the thirtieth time that morning and called everyone together. We counted and then soldiered on. We passed the Boathouse ("We won't have time to row a boat, huh?" Tracy scratched it from her list), down a staircase and through a tunnel beneath another bridge ("Is that the *Home Alone 2* bridge?" "Where's the one from *Cloverfield*?"), up a tree-lined path (where Zach wondered: "What's your opinion on Hamlet's delay?"), and over into one of the children's sections of the park where Stuart Little, E.B. White's mouse, sailed his miniature boat and where stories were read to children at the foot of yet another bronze statue, this one of a man with an open book.

"Starburst Trivia: What author of fairy tales sits there? See the duck, he wrote 'The Ugly Duckling,' 'The Little Mermaid,' 'Thumbelina?'"

A Brandon: "Hans Christian Anderson!"

"Very good!"

A Brandon, with Starburst in hand: "I READ IT ON THE GROUND! I READ IT ON THE GROUND! IT SAYS SO RIGHT THERE! HAHAHA!"

We took a minute to peek through the telescopes at the nest where the baby red-tailed hawks were hiding and then stopped for another photo shoot at the bronze statue of *Alice in Wonderland.* This time, I forced both schools to pose, all the students together, so that we could move on; however, afterward, the Georgians told their kids to stay put for an exclusive photo, which was then, of course, followed by the Seattle kids in an exclusive photo, which was then followed by the drama teacher posing with her student council who had all appeared that winter in her children's production of *Alice in Wonderland.*

"Okay, we really have to go now," I called, regretting the stop.

My life was becoming a prolonged wait for people taking pictures.

I was perpetually on a vacation that wasn't mine.

I looked at my watch.

10:00 THE METROPOLITAN MUSEUM OF ART

FIFTEEN MINUTES LATER, my thirty-five were sitting together on the staircase in front of the museum and its grand, stone façade of columns and arches that stretched almost four city blocks along Fifth Avenue. A few of the women patted sweat from their foreheads with folded tissue, and I noticed Pete talking to a stranger, a young man the Seattle kids seemed to recognize, a former student, I guessed correctly. Clint and Tracy were passing out floor plans, and I was distributing the admission buttons, today's featuring the white M on a background of brown.

—Hey, it's Rectal Awareness Day!

—Brandon!

As I watched them all bend and squeeze the metallic tags onto their shirts, I tried to figure out the best way to introduce the Met. I wondered which of my standards to use for this group, some of whom were regular museum members, many of whom had never been inside a museum in their lives. I mentally dismissed #14 (the cubiculum-above-Pompeii speech) and #5 (the *Perseus with Head of Medusa* intro) and opted against #4 (the monetary value of the collection) as well as #12 (the history of the architecture) and #8 (the story of *Aristotle Contemplating Bust of Homer*). Sensing that several were intimidated by the imposing building and had no idea where to begin, I chose to go with a mix of #9 (the personalized playlist) and #2 (the Hall of Mirrors). It seemed to work: When I told them to meet back in two hours, they rose in a flurry, some with their maps pressed toward me, others running up the stairs, and almost all chattering with their museum buddies about what they wanted to see first.

And then there was Dina the Dismal. She stayed seated on the front steps. She needed "to give her dogs a rest." She let me know that art wasn't really her "thing." I asked if she planned to sit outside for two hours and she said she'd "meander in eventually." I told her about the roof garden and said she would probably enjoy the view of the city.

"I might go up there at some point," Dina said. I felt her trying to drag me down into the dark recesses of her miserable soul, so I said, "Great! Have fun!" and bounded up the stairs away from her.

PETE, THE TEACHER who pictured easels and masterpieces lining the runways of LaGuardia, was the reason both groups were spending a full two hours at the Met—this was one of the demands he made of his account manager—so he was the last person who should have been sitting in the basement cafeteria where there wasn't a single item of beauty or truth to contemplate. Not a statue, not a photo, not a shard of stained glass. But the student from the staircase, David, or Dave, which was the collegiate name he was trying out, had rolled out of bed too late and needed breakfast. "A quick bite and I'll be good to go." This would also give them a chance to catch up face to face, instead of ear to ear, which was how you conversed at a museum. But the room depressed Pete. That spring, the café in the sculpture court had closed for a relocation that was still pending, and the café on the balcony above the Great Hall didn't open until eleven, so they were directed to the new cafeteria located in the bowels of the museum, with no views of Central Park, no sculpture garden, just the choking smell of grilled food caught in the wall-to-wall carpeting.

There was a chance that David, or Dave, would never finish his breakfast because he kept talking. He reminded Pete of himself that first year in New York. Pete wore a trench coat and Yankees cap with the same pride that Dave exuded as he carried his *New Yorker* magazine up the museum stairs, trying a bit hard to impress. Dave was done with his first year of school but was spending the summer in the city taking accelerated German and working an internship with CBS.

"So, all in all, the grades were good except for that C+ he gave me because I never talked in class. That doesn't sound like me, I know, but everyone in my class was a sophomore. I think it was a bad decision taking CC the first year instead of Lit. Hum."

Five more minutes at most and then Pete would insist they go upstairs.

"…back in the dorm, all the other first-years were reading Homer and Virgil. There weren't that many reading Hegel or Kant."

He should have met with David later this afternoon (he could have sat down with David during the two-hour shopping spree), but when he had emailed David the itinerary, David came right back with "I'd love to go to the Met with you!" Understandable, but Pete never felt he had enough time here. He used to come to New York with his wife, and they would spend entire days at the Met, but though she loved the city, there were other destinations now pulling at her. There were trips to see her parents, who were growing older, needier; trips to visit his own mother; there were school events; and how much time did they have to travel anyway?

"So. Back home. How was everyone…you…how was graduation after Tommy's accident?" Pete didn't want to talk about this here, in this bland basement, but he yielded. He briefly described the graduation as difficult, mentioned the minute of silence, punctuated with whispers of kids who didn't know Tommy and whimpers of those who did. He didn't describe the funeral or the grief counselors that first Monday morning or the balloons, tied around the tree, that were left to deflate and sag above the melted candles. David commiserated with tilted head, he knitted his eyebrows, he finished his tart. He lived in New York now, almost three thousand miles from the tragedies of the Pacific Northwest. Dry from all the drizzle and tears.

Pete stood, made a gesture of opening the Met's map, a map he did not need. David took the cue from his teacher and obediently drank down his coffee, wiped his mouth, and picked up his tray. They left the cafeteria. Pete vowed never to return and was relieved that there was at least one room at the museum he could check off for good.

Crossing the threshold into the gallery spaces of the Met usually gave him the same joyful feeling of anticipation as when he entered a restaurant or a hotel lobby to reunite with an old friend. He looked forward to seeing how they'd both changed, how they had stayed the same.

When Pete came to New York, he was a Monet boy, having been introduced to Impressionism by his aunt, a Francophile whose Christmas presents were frequently wrapped in images of Paris or the surrounding countryside. As part of his Art Humanities class, he lectured on *La Grenouillere*, and in preparation for that, concentrated on how Monet conveyed water with dabs and dollops of only a few colors. That research brought him to Renoir, whose brush stroke fascinated him because he couldn't comprehend it—that swishy, swirly, smudgy pastel confection. Probably, in response to all that color, Pete moved next to Manet whose blacks led him to Rembrandt who opened the door to Velasquez and then Caravaggio whose every painting he sought out while in Rome where he was introduced to Bernini's sculptures and after Bernini to Michelangelo, Rodin, George Grey Barnard, and Augustus Saint Gaudens. Those were just the first five years (from the age of eighteen to twenty-three), the span between appreciating the colors on the parcels beneath the Christmas tree to standing in the rain beneath a statue of Lincoln in Chicago.

How many times since had he fallen in love with a new painter or sculptor or movement? There were two years when he didn't want to look at anything older than fifty years and a subsequent phase when the only thing that appealed to him had been pulled from the ground after centuries of muddy exile. A broken handle from a Greek urn would inspire ecstasy in a way that, once upon a time, only Van Gogh's olive trees could. He was an addict. These initial hits of a drug too wonderful to grasp only begged for more. He studied the artist until the artist no longer held the power for him. He could still appreciate the paintings for what they were, where they stood in time—in both their own artistic lineage and in his own development from a teenager to a man with a beard more gray than brown. Walking through a museum, where so many of his favorite artists were represented, where so many versions of himself haunted the hallways, gave him a thrill each time he visited.

On this day, though, he couldn't access that feeling. There was a pointlessness to what was framed, a meaninglessness to what stood on pedestals. Most of the artists had died generations ago, and so many who revered them were dead or dying as well. He felt an even deeper sense of emptiness when he observed the people walking by these once-admired objects of art. The evidence of the crowded staircase and front hall pointed against the conviction he was harboring that no one cared about these works; however, he decided today that all in attendance were part of a tour group and that this was their least favorite stop on the itinerary. There were probably ten, maybe twenty, teachers wandering these halls enraptured while all the students they dragged here were looking at their watches or stealing a nap on an out-of-the-way bench. He liked to blame the parents, but he couldn't. His own children hated museums. They had virtually no curiosity about the world around them. For his two teenagers, life was about pop music and video games, about eating cereal with milk at three in the afternoon and watching reality television while using their free hands to rub the moist, itchy spots between their toes.

David stopped in front of the Duccio, a small painting of the Madonna and Child on a gold background, in a room full of Madonnas and Children. It was the museum's costly record-breaking acquisition from a few years earlier, dubbed the "Mona Lisa of the Met," but unlike the hordes rushing through the Louvre for a snapshot of the Da Vinci, most Met visitors simply passed by this painting on their way to something flashier. Pete and David both absorbed the Duccio in silence. A private devotional piece…the bottom of the frame charred by some owner's candle…Mary's robes a color blue with a shade of green that didn't show up in reproductions… the robed baby, with the face of an older man, reaching up to lift his mother's veil from her face. There was emotion in it, a real connection between mother and son, and Pete felt a profound melancholy that, no matter what she does, her child will die. She has no control over it. He looked to other representations of Mary in the gallery and preferred the ones without the sadness, taking solace in the earlier paintings, pre-Renaissance, that lacked the emotional depth, when people were more geometry than feeling.

"Dave?" a voice spoke behind them. They turned. There was a young woman with two older adults, most likely her parents. David cried out a name Pete didn't catch. This was a friend from college, someone who called David Dave. This encounter was important for David, because nothing made you feel like you belonged in a city more than running into a fellow resident. While making the introductions, David said, "This is my high school teacher who helped me with all my college applications. He was my favorite. I probably mentioned him." It was in the *probably* where Pete picked up more trace inklings of futility.

Pete smiled politely and turned his attention across the room to study another painting. Then he stepped into the next room. He moved slowly to show David that he wasn't going far, but once he was in the next room, a gallery of monks and angels, he continued walking. Through a room of saints and horses. He was being drawn somewhere. There was something he was supposed to do. There was something nearby he was intending to see. It was slowly coming back to him. He let his feet lead.

And then he was standing in front of it.

Tommy Newman, the student-in-absentia, had been in several of Pete's classes, but he had also been his aide during fourth period when he was supposed to help him grade quizzes, make copies, reduce the chaos of the piles of paper on Pete's desk. In that respect, he was useless. Pete would give him the assignment, and Tommy would ask him a question about that morning's *Ethan Frome* discussion; or about the opening sequence in a movie he had Netflixed upon Pete's urging; or about the three greatest architectural treasures of downtown; or about a performance at Seattle Rep or a book he was reading. Even when grades were due or the piles on his desk threatened to carpet the floor, Pete never told Tommy to get to work. He would just fill his own mug from the small coffee maker on the book shelf and begin to talk.

Tommy was a lively student, unafraid to argue, with a rapacious curiosity and photographic memory, reminding Pete when he repeated himself, asking Pete to clarify when he couldn't follow. Tommy told him that this un-class was his favorite of the day and that he learned more there than in any room all year. Pete needed his planning period not only to catch up with his lessons but to keep abreast of all the deadlines the tour company set; however, he looked forward to his un-class with Tommy as much as his student did, even if it meant, and it frequently did, that he had to stay after school to stay atop the waves of paperwork.

It was immediately before prom weekend when they touched on the topic of subtlety. Tommy felt that if a book didn't make sure the reader understood the point, then the book was a pretentious failure. Pete argued that in non-fiction that was probably unassailable—for the moment, let's take that as a given—but in fiction, there were more rewards to allowing the readers to discover a surprise or ironic contradiction on their own. A work unexplained, less obvious, is the work that gets stuck in the forefront of the brain. A subtle work will guide the readers just so far and let them walk the rest of the way. It was far more satisfying to read a book that raised questions than one that spelled them out. Tommy groaned, and Pete recognized the strain of laziness he had occasionally detected in Tommy, an over-achiever who sometimes looked for the easy way in or out, the short cut, the fastest route to the answer which he could declare, and then check off and move on.

"But how do you know that the reader will get it?" Tommy asked. "That one writer of yours said a few good readers die every day."

"But he hasn't given up on the readers still living."

Tommy was unconvinced.

Pete went on to say, "The greatest art is the art created by the artist and the spectator, that engages your role in the experience. When we go to New York, I'm going to show you a painting at the Metropolitan."

Pete was now standing directly in front of it. There was an elderly couple behind him at a Rembrandt self-portrait, so he whispered. Audibly enough for Tommy.

"I was never very interested in this kind of painting. A young woman, dressed up in silks, sitting at a table, her head in her hand. I could appreciate the technique—the virtuosity it took to paint the tapestry on the table or the painting within the painting, the glass cask with reflected light—but the subject bored me. Then one day, waiting for a friend to finish taking notes on another painting, I started studying the details of this one, I pushed into this painting and found there was so much more going on. The cask itself and the almost empty glass.

Wine has been consumed, which might explain why she's nodding off. Then I noticed the cloak on the hook on the wall behind her and a man's walking stick on the table. There's more I discovered later—the lion finials on the chair that traditionally represent masculinity, and the fact that the painting within the painting is an earlier work by the artist himself on the subject of Love. *Eros.* So here we have a woman surrounded by a man who is nowhere to be seen. The door behind her, however, is open, leading to an interior room, a bedroom. He's inside. There's no doubt the more you stand in front of the painting that someone else is with her. She's not alone. You can imagine the woman opening her eyes and joining him. More I learned even later: I read an essay that an x-ray cardiograph was taken of this painting, and beneath these layers of paint, are the earlier drafts of Vermeer's painting. And who do you think is standing in the doorway, beneath the oil, leering at the tipsy lady? The man. The man who owns the cloak and the walking stick. The man who poured the wine. If the man were still there, in the finished product, there would be nothing for the mind to do, you would understand it all in the first glimpse, but Vermeer painted him out and left only the clues. Which invite you to push into the painting. Vermeer relocated his man and stimulated the viewer's mind—to help complete the story and to create a richer work of art."

Pete remained as still as he could and let Tommy have his own experience with the painting in front of them. An experience that could take hours, years, a lifetime. Minutes passed and then Pete thought he heard the boy's voice behind him.

"There you are." It was David, not Tommy. After a glance, David said, "That's beautiful. Wonderful light. The Flemish school, right?"

Pete was tempted to ask David what else he saw, to push him into the painting, through the door and into that next room, but David had other professors now, another life, and Pete seemed to be saving his lectures for his dead students.

THE BRANDONS AND LASH (who was still on the first of his two disposable cameras) had spent thirty minutes looking for the baseball card collection and the two million dollar Honus Wagner card, but "after getting lost a hundred times" as they later reported, "come to find out the baseball cards aren't even up! They're paintin' the walls or somethin'."

So the four aimlessly meandered some more, found the Arms and Armor collection. They cracked up over the codpiece that pointed north and the suit of armor for the fat king over in the corner. They loved the guns and the swords. Then they wound up in a whole other part of the museum.

BRANDON 1: This place is huge!

BRANDON 3: If this was a house, your whole family would have to carry walkie-talkies.

BRANDON 2: I *wish* this was my house. If this was my house, would I get to keep the art?

BRANDON 3: Yeah, it's all included.

BRANDON 2: Then I would charge friends to come over and visit. Ten bucks just to walk in the door.

BRANDON 1: And if someone really likes art, you can make 'em pay *fifty*.

Lash was listening, as impressed as they were, if not more so, by the number of rooms, and by how many walls had to be painted before they put the art up, and by how nice the floors were—just the floors!—and by how rich everything looked. He didn't think he had ever walked through as many doorways in a single building. He also thought it was funny that there were so many rooms with paintings on the walls but no furniture on the floor. (His family did it the other way around.) For the most part, he didn't know what to make of the art itself. He thought it was all nice and expensive looking. He wondered if the "people who did the stone statues got paid more than the people who did the metal statues." He also wondered why some artists painted animals and some did "woods and waterfalls" and some did people's faces. It was probably because they were better at one than the other. For example, he could draw a dog better than he could draw a real-looking horse. Snakes, he drew best. If he had to paint a painting for this place, he would probably paint a snake. Lash was most amazed by the pictures with a variety of things in them—like people *and* animals *and* nature *and* an interesting story.

There was one giant painting of a man stabbing a woman, which stopped all the boys in their tracks.

A mother and young son stood in front of the painting, and the little boy asked, "Why is the man stabbing the woman?"

Lash tried to listen in for the answer, but the mom was texting someone and not really paying attention, because all she said was, "Um, they used to do that."

Lash and the Brandons moved into another gallery and then raced each other for a bench they saw sitting empty in the middle of the room. They all fit on it.

BRANDON 1: There sure are a lot of naked people here.

BRANDON 2: Where?

BRANDON 1: Not real people! Naked people in the pictures.

BRANDON 2: And naked statues.

BRANDON 3: A lot of naked statues. Why do you think?

BRANDON 1: It's hard to carve clothes. With all the folds and buttons. It's easier to carve a chest without a shirt.

BRANDON 3: But it's not easy when you get down below, you know what I mean? It'd be easier if the man was wearin' a bathin' suit or one of them toga things. It's hard to carve, you know, a man's junk.

BRANDON 2: That's why there are more naked women. They're easier to carve.

BRANDON 1: And they're nicer to look at.

BRANDON 3: Why do you think the guys are so small?

BRANDON 2: What do you mean?

BRANDON 3: Maybe if they made the dicks too big, they'd fall off. They'd be too heavy.

BRANDON 1: It'd be easier to carve if the dick was bigger.

BRANDON 3: Maybe the artists are showing off how good they are by carving it real small with a lot of detail.

BRANDON 1: Could be.

BRANDON 2: You, you think these are small?

BRANDON 3: You know what we should do? Let's play spy.

BRANDON 2: Okay.

BRANDON 3: Pick someone out and follow 'em.

BRANDON 2: But they're not doing anything. Everyone's just looking at art.

BRANDON 3: But we could see…

BRANDON 1: BOOORING.

BRANDON 2: We could pick someone we think is here for naked art and count how long they look at art with clothes and then how long they look at art without clothes…

BRANDON 3: And then we can tell them their times! "Sir, you've been lookin' at that naked lady for ten minutes!"

BRANDON 2: Or naked man. I bet we can find a man looking at a naked man painting. My dad says there's lots of homos at museums.

BRANDON 3: Why?

BRANDON 2: I don't know. This could be where they come to look at naked pictures.

BRANDON 1: You're a dumb ass. You go on the computer for that. Your dad's a retard.

BRANDON 2: My dad wasn't sayin'…

BRANDON 1: It would be more fun to follow someone we know.

BRANDON 2: And we can see what naked pictures they're lookin' at.

BRANDON 1: Forget the naked pictures!

BRANDON 3: We could split up into two teams and see who finds the most people from our tour. You get points and we should have higher points for different people. Like someone from our group is worth one point and someone from Seattle is worth two.

BRANDON 2: Why are they worth two points and we're only worth one? That's racist.

BRANDON 1: Cuz we don't know them. It's trackin' someone we don't know. We know where to find the people we know. Like if your mom was here, we'd know just to go to the cafeteria and there she'd be stuffing her face with a cake.

BRANDON 3: Man, that's cold.

BRANDON 1: Someone from Seattle could be anywhere.

BRANDON 3: Okay, one point for our group, two points for their group.

BRANDON 2: And five extra points if you get them looking at a naked picture.

BRANDON 1: FORGET THE NAKED PICTURES!

BRANDON 3: And the tour guide is three points. Anybody else special?

It was then that Lash spoke up for the first time, and they liked his suggestion. It was agreed: four points would go to the team that located the "real pretty girl from Seattle."

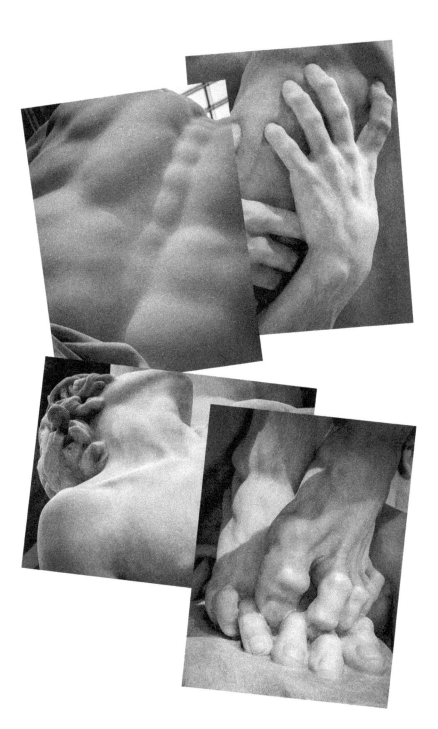

RAMONA, THE TEACHER from Georgia who wanted me to "tell like it is," had not been able to take her own advice. Although she wanted to tell Nancy (her Civil-War-didn't-have-as-much-to-do-with-slavery-as-people-think-it-did bitch of a vice principal) that she preferred to be alone, she knew that, to avoid drama, she needed to trick Nancy into thinking it was her own idea. It was easy. As several of them pored over their museum maps in the main lobby, Ramona announced that she planned to spend her entire time in the department of African Art.

Nancy faked interest with a disingenuous, "Oooo, I bet that would be wonderful."

Ramona said, "Oh, good, join me."

"Maaayyybe. But you know what? I'm supposed to pick up something from the gift shop for a friend. I better do that first. Then I need to get to that roof garden."

Ramona faked her own disappointment, "Aawwww." Kelly, concealing a smile, expressed her curiosity about art from the Middle East, which gave her a free pass as well.

Then Faith, one of the girls, said she really wanted to see the African Art and asked Ramona if she could walk with her. This meant that Ramona had to spend a substantial amount of time in African Art, which was really not part of her plan. She had been hoping to find a seat and rest her feet after that hellish hike through Central Park. But this kept her honest, and she appreciated that.

Ramona and Faith found their way to African Art, which had more oversized phallic pieces than Ramona cared to study with one of her thirteen-year-old students. They stopped in front of shields and stools and a Reliquary Guardian Head before finding themselves in Oceania. The African Art section blended quickly into Aztec art and art of the South Pacific, but Faith didn't notice; in front of an Aztec jaguar, she announced, "I love Africa so much." Ramona wondered what the white girl expected her black teacher to say in response, but before she could say anything, Faith went on, "I like learning about other cultures. It's crazy how different they are." When they turned into a hallway lined with contemporary photographs, Faith asked, "Could we stick with the civilizations instead of the paintings and stuff?"

To get to Africa, they had passed through the Greek and Roman wing, where Ramona had seen benches, so she asked if Faith wanted to spend more time there.

Faith nixed it: "Too white."

Ramona laughed, "You're white."

"I know, so I don't need to see white stuff." Faith ran her finger over the folds of her map. "Let's go see the Asian Art!" That was unfortunate for Ramona's feet, because that department was up the stairs on the opposite side of the museum. On their long walk there, somewhere along the balcony on the second floor, a pair of Brandons passed them by with the words, "Two points!"

Ramona later admitted that she was impressed by the Asian wing. She enjoyed the painted scrolls, porcelain jars, silk robes, altar sets, Standing Statues of Vishnu, Buddha, Parvati, and Ganesha, and an elaborately carved roof of a meeting hall from India that took years to create. After passing through a small round door, a moon door, they discovered themselves in the Chinese Scholar's Garden, consisting of a covered walkway constructed with bamboo and a courtyard with a rock garden. This was a room that practically asked you to stop and sit and just be. Ramona and Faith sat together on a stone bench.

For a minute or two, sitting in the warmth of the sun coming through the skylight, they listened to the sound of water trickling into a pond in the far corner.

Then Faith said, "Isn't it funny what people think is God?"

"How so?"

"Like that elephant thing in India? Don't you think you'd feel pretty stupid when you found out that nobody else was praying to an elephant except for you?"

"Well, entire communities pray to that."

"*Funny*, huh?" Faith said looking directly at Ramona. "Sometimes I think…" she began but abruptly halted.

"What do you think?" Ramona asked.

"Ashley's pretty religious," Faith said, referring to one of her roommates, the Bible Bee champ. "She prayed last night. On her knees in the hotel. At first, I thought she was joking, but then I knew she was serious. But then she kept it up for so long I thought she was joking again, and just when I was about to say something, she got off her knees and got into bed. So she must have been serious."

Ramona had been teaching long enough to know that when a quiet student like Faith began to express what she was thinking, it was best to shut up and listen. With an occasional murmur to show she was paying attention, Ramona let Faith ramble.

"But I don't know why I thought she was joking. She prays before she eats. I do too. At home. I wonder why I don't when I'm on vacation. There's a lot of things people do just to do 'em, you know." Faith's eyes wandered along the carved windows. "There are good people everywhere and some have never heard of Jesus."

"Mm."

"It's not their fault they're praying to someone else, not if their whole village does it. What if *we* have the wrong God anyway? How would *we* know?"

"Mm."

"Some of the people who quote the Bible all the time…they're not very good in anything else. They're kind of dumb. So why are they telling me…how to think?"

"Mm."

"My pastor. I don't think he could get a job doing anything else. I can't figure out where he'd go. My dad had to help him change a tire once. And help him when his basement got flooded. Who'd hire him?"

Ramona wanted to interrupt and tell Faith that there was something to be said for a pastor who fostered an environment where her father was so willing to help. As far as she was concerned, charity and loving thy neighbor were two of the most important virtues in a church family. She also wanted to commend Ashley for kneeling to pray in her hotel room, for keeping her prayer a part of her daily practice, but just then Faith asked a crucial question.

"Do you know I was with Brandon Ellerbe?"

"Really? No." Brandon Ellerbe was the black Brandon. (#3.)

"We were going together. In April. Then Mrs. Davis brought me in her office and said that it wasn't good for me or him. But she never talked to *him* about it. She said it would ruin my reputation, but she didn't tell him it would ruin *his* reputation. She said she was gonna tell my parents, and I'm not allowed to be with anyone until I get to high school, so I said I wouldn't see him anymore. It wasn't like we were getting married. He's just funny, that's all. She goes to my church, but I don't think she was being a good Christian. Aren't we all supposed to be the same in God's eyes? Everybody has a different God, I think. Every single person."

"Mm," Ramona repeated, but this *mm* was angry. Back in April, when Nancy was calling Ramona into her office to talk about slavery and cupcakes, Nancy was also calling Faith into her office to tell her that dating a black boy would ruin her reputation. Ramona was livid and didn't know how she was going to face Nancy without bringing it up, which would only add tension to a work relationship already fraught with it. Ramona also knew that once she started talking, she wouldn't be able to stop. She would have to hold it all inside. If Nancy were not going to be completely honest, upfront, or direct with Ramona, then Ramona would not be honest, upfront, or direct with Nancy, and they would both stand facing each other with fake smiles as they choked on what they really wanted to say.

Ramona wanted to charge Nancy rent for the amount of space she was taking up in her head. She had gotten out of walking the museum with her vice principal, but here she was anyway, stinking up the air.

When Ramona tuned back in, she heard Faith say, "I hate my first name."

"Why? It's beautiful."

"I have a cousin who always calls me *Blind*."

"I see."

"I would go with my middle name, but it's an old lady name."

Ramona laughed and then suggested, "You could go by your initials."

"No, I can't, Mrs. Harrison. My initials are F.U. F.U. Hutsell."

Ramona laughed again, "No, that won't do."

"So I'm stuck with Faith."

12:00 CITY BUS TO ROCKEFELLER CENTER

FIVE MINUTES BEFORE our designated meeting time, I found the two groups sitting on opposite sides of the vast staircase in various degrees of readiness. Some had just sat down and were showing their purchases from the gift shop—postcards or posters of their favorite paintings, a book of historical perfumes, Christmas ornaments in the shape of shoes from the Costume Institute; others, like Dina, looked as if they had been sitting on the warm stone for days, missing only a sleeping bag and a cooler. I had the Georgians follow me over to where the Seattleites were gathered, and while we crossed, I listened to the Brandons argue over a complicated scoring system in which someone looking at a naked painting put one team over the edge.

The Seattle group wasn't all there. Grandma Penny announced that *they* were all ready to go, and I reminded her that it wasn't yet noon. At 11:59, Lu and her student council appeared, racing out the front doors, shouting, "We made it! We're here, we're here!" and holding their brightly colored paper bags. But we were still waiting on, you guessed it, Melanie, the girl with the blue hair. Pete stormed into the museum to see if he could find her in the lobby or the gift shop, and as soon as he left, our ten-year-old spotted her sitting at the bottom of the staircase, playing with her camera. Lu then went inside to look for Pete. Pete emerged from another door seconds after Lu entered, and

I had to catch one of the student council kids before *he* went inside to look for *her*. A call was made instead, and soon we were all together again.

As we were walking down the staircase, Barbara noticed that we were still missing one. People cried out that couldn't be.

—Melanie's here.

—Are you counting Tommy?

—It's Brittany's dad!"

We all looked up and down the staircase for a man sitting alone. Nowhere to be seen.

I asked Brittany, "Where's your dad?"

She answered, "How do I know?" Her face reddened. I asked her to call him, and several of the group sat back down in despair.

Both Laurie and Jenny, the shoppers, threatened Brittany: "This better not cut into Fifth Avenue!" Laurie and Jenny, a year older, were often cruel to Brittany, like cheerleaders taunting the girl trying out for the squad. I sensed Brittany was recruited into the posse by the two guys.

Brittany turned to me, "He says he's near the blue whale."

"The blue whale!?" I tried to think of the department that would have a blue whale. Maybe there was a South Pacific tribe that worshipped the whale and there was a statuette or a robe…

Brittany elaborated, "He says he's in the History Museum."

Oh, *that* blue whale, the most famous blue whale in the city, the twenty-one-thousand-pound foam-and-fiberglass model hung from the ceiling, stretching ninety-four feet in a cavernous room situated more than half a mile from where we were waiting, THAT blue whale.

I said to Pete, "I think we should go on without him." Dennis had not told anyone he was switching museums, which was annoying, but despite all the mumbling and some of the more audible denunciations on our way to the bus stop, we were still only ten minutes behind schedule. There were several buses heading down Fifth, and I quickly passed out the Metrocards and shouted instructions.

I chose the emptier second bus to the relief of the New Yorkers boarding the first one, but my people were fast, hungry for lunch, and afraid they would miss out on shopping. They worked so quickly that our bus pulled out first, while the bus of New Yorkers who had given us nasty looks was still coping with a folding stroller.

12:30 ROCKEFELLER CENTER AND LUNCH

WHEN THE CITY BUS neared the southern end of Central Park, Wally actually recognized a part of town. The group had been down this stretch here the day before, and New York suddenly shrank, felt a little more manageable. There was the Sherman statue with that devil angel, the big hotel, one of the famous ones, the name escaped him. There was something around here about *keeping up with the Joneses*, but he missed that the first time around and forgot to ask about it. Most on the bus were peering through the windows, memorizing where the stores were for later, and Clint was listing all the places he wanted to go. Wally just nodded and said, "Sure, Son." Clint had the energy of a ten-year-old and Wally the fatigue of a forty-two-year-old fat man. Back at the museum, Clint had not stopped, especially in that Egyptian wing. Wally was glad to be sitting down on this bus, though it had taken a while to get a seat. He had to make sure that every woman had one before he kicked out two Brandons and got his own. He might have been the sole passenger praying for red lights or a traffic jam just so that he could rest.

"NEXT STOP!" I called out, "NEXT STOP!" Wally groaned.

By 12:30, seventy legs hopped off the bus. The sidewalks were crowded with shoppers and office workers taking their lunch break, so everyone had to be herded into a corner beneath a giant man holding up the earth. Wally's ankles were never very flexible, but now there was absolutely no bending between heel and knee, so by the time he made it to the group, the tour of that statue was over. All that Wally heard was: *...the Roosevelt head on the dime, which is technically better* *known but not recognized as his.* Now that could be about anything, he thought, as the group walked into the building behind the statue.

Wally was committed to getting as much information from this tour as possible so that when Clint asked a question, he would have an answer, just like he did at home, but there were still too many photographers and stragglers he had to wrangle in the back, and by the time he had them with the group, the tour had already started. This was the tour Wally was on: Inside the lobby of the International Building, he heard *got his license to kill by working in this building and shooting someone in the RCA Building*; as they exited, he heard, *note how the floors slope*; and at the ice skating rink, he heard *as if it were the doorway to hell, so it was created to lure them downstairs* and *the green flag is Libya!* (Starburst question) and *Leapin' Louie!* Then Wally figured he was too hungry, because though he made sure he was standing in the middle of the group when the next part began, he only followed bits of the story. *Oil man, philanthropist, Metropolitan Opera, the Great Depression, long lease, expensive rent, business and entertainment district, Radio City, nineteen buildings, most important lobby, not Picasso, not Matisse, Diego Rivera, Communist Party, Lenin on the wall, sledgehammers. Jose Maria Sert, ceiling paintings, fascist, problem, kept hush-hush, over here, see there, at the top, fascist salute, how we used to say the Pledge of Allegiance.*

Wally followed the group as they passed beneath the ceiling paintings, from one side to the other, his eyes on the man in the middle, as instructed, and he did see that the man appeared to follow them, swiveling, turning his hips and twisting, but Wally was not impressed. Everything around him looked like it was swiveling, turning, and twisting. These were called hunger hallucinations. Lunchtime. The group walked down the stairs into the Concourse with two corridors lined with restaurants and five sections with tables and chairs. They had only thirty-six minutes to eat. Where to go? Wally craved something simple, a McDonald's or Taco Bell. He would enter, he would order, he would sit—he would sit!—and he would eat. Clint wanted pizza, but that was at the end of the long hallway. Instead, Wally pulled him into the first place he saw, which was crowded with people who looked like they worked in the building. There were salad bars, grills, a coffee station, refrigerated units filled with food in plastic containers, and all kinds of bottled drinks.

Trying to read a sign in front of the sandwiches, Clint asked, "What's foc, foc, foc…?"

"Clint!"

"Well, I can't read it. What does this say?"

"Focaseeyah." Wally was floored. Everything was a trial! Even sandwiches. During other vacations, when Wally took their family to the beach, none of the restaurants were crossword puzzles.

"What is focaseeyah?" Clint asked.

Wally made a guess, "It's a kind of meat the Spanish people eat."

Clint looked up at this dad and said, "I'm thinkin' we go for pizza."

"You're always thinkin' we go for pizza. Try something new."

"This is all fancy food," Clint whined, but he was right. And the portions looked small. This was the kind of place where Wally would pay thirty dollars and then have to be on the lookout for a hot dog cart.

Clint was watching his father carefully, and after another critical minute of the allotted lunch time passed, Clint declared: "We both know this ain't gonna work."

They went in search of pizza.

1:30 RADIO CITY MUSIC HALL

FIVE MINUTES AHEAD of schedule, all in the group presented their tickets and filed out of the holding pen and through the front door of the entrance to Radio City Music Hall; that is, all except for Kelly Mitchell who, after seeing her Georgians off, turned away and stepped forward. It was a move, which reminded me of the moment in many an opera when a giant party scene ends and the plodding chorus makes its way through the various exits to leave the young lyric soprano alone onstage for her aria, and I would not have been a bit surprised if Kelly had opened her mouth and trilled a high C. Since watching Ruiz reunite with his family in the magical land of LaGuardia, she had been pirouetting through a romantic city, drawn to any gesture of love. She had witnessed a proposal on the top of the Empire State Building, which wasn't the most unusual setting, but only two others in the group even spotted it.

The ghost of Heidi Hubbard, her predecessor who got engaged on the last day of her tour, was still haunting the streets of Manhattan. Kelly had half-expected her Hunter to be sitting in the diner that morning, which was the reason she woke up so perky and ready to go. Every time she turned a corner, she could almost picture Hunter there holding a bouquet—in every other gallery at the museum, on every other bench in the park. Kelly also knew, however, that it would not have been Hunter's style to appear in a tuxedo at Rockefeller Center holding flowers and an engagement ring from Tiffany's. Hunter's idea of romance was giving her a two-point lead during their weekly game of air hockey at McHale's, a roadside bar near their house. He gave her four points on Valentine's Day.

On the other hand, many a man, even those violently opposed to any movie that could be construed as a *chick flick*, stepped willingly into a girlfriend's fantasy proposal if it meant securing the engagement. And the time felt right. Kelly and Hunter had been a couple for two years, living together for six idyllic months, and they were about to attend his brother's wedding in Charleston. The wedding was a formal affair at a yacht club, and Hunter was more interested in what Kelly was going to wear than at any other time since she had known him. He had given her five hundred dollars to help pick out something "real modern." He wanted them to look "smokin' hot, Hollywood carpet hot," and when he painted the picture of how they would appear at the ceremony, she felt he was omitting one detail: a diamond ring she would be sporting on her left hand. His brother's wedding would be a prequel to their own. He would want everyone at his brother's reception begging to be invited to theirs.

So the dress was very important.

What was not important was the retail history of Fifth Avenue that I was sharing as I walked her east on Fiftieth toward Saks (whose shoe store had its own zip code): "A piece of trivia I love about Saks is that they were the ones that blocked the plan to connect the pedestrian tunnels of Rockefeller Center with those of Grand Central, which would have permitted a commuter to stay completely dry during a rain storm on a walk from Lexington and Forty-second all the way to Seventh Avenue and Forty-ninth."

"Interesting," Kelly said as we entered the department store. "But it's time to get down to business." She scoped out the marble floors, the plants, and the glass counters filled with cosmetics and fragrances. "Dresses won't be on this floor," she determined. "Elevators."

"This way," I answered, having used those elevators dozens of times, whenever I needed a restroom. My comprehensive knowledge of restrooms throughout the city, not only free but luxurious, is rivaled by few. It is a knowledge I rarely divulge since part of the luxury is the solitude some of the finer restrooms afford. There are some secret lavatory gems in Midtown, facilities far larger than my apartment, where I have seriously considered spending full afternoons with a cup of coffee and a good book, and as willing as I am to share as much as I can about the city, this is a topic I keep buried in my notes.

"Interesting," Kelly said when we reached the third floor. She made a beeline for a rack off to the right, and I followed. It became clear to me that Kelly didn't need my navigational skills; she really just wanted a second pair of eyes and someone to carry her purse while she used her free hands to test fabric and hold the dresses up to her body. After she picked up her first dress, I asked her if she wanted a dressing room, and she said, "Of course not." She actually laughed. "I need at least four other dresses before I waste a trip to the dressing room." I was impressed. Very clever. I could see how employing such time-saving tactics might make shopping for clothes much more enjoyable.

Another component that might enhance the experience would be to look as good in clothing as Kelly did. After a saleswoman arrived to assist, the possibilities chosen and the dressing room secured, Kelly began her fashion show. I had to restrain myself. I wanted to wave other shoppers over to watch. Pump up the volume for the music playing over the speakers, and this could be a cinematic montage. She made it look so easy, disappearing around the corner and emerging mere minutes later wearing the newest fashion gripping and hanging from all the right places.

I was of no help in choosing what she should wear to the wedding in Charleston. I liked everything she tried on, despite the variety of styles and degrees of formality. But she didn't need my help. She was determined. What looked beautiful to me was second rate or ill-fitting to her. What did she see that I didn't? She was looking so much further into these dresses than I was. She saw how the hem responded to the breeze of the South Carolina shore, how the shade of black corresponded to the deeper tan she would have by mid-July, how the shoulder straps in one instance would only do if she wore her hair in curls, and what jewelry she would need with that neckline.

I needed to get back to Radio City to pick up the thirty-three (minus Kelly, minus Dennis). I asked her if she needed any recommendations for other stores. She rattled off seven or eight others in the vicinity that were on her list, and I bowed to her wisdom.

"All right, then," I said. "Two hours to go."

"Two hours and counting," she mumbled from a dance floor in Charleston.

2:30 FIFTH AVENUE

TIME TO SHOP. You can guess who were the first to burst through the bronze doors of Radio City Music Hall. As soon as they saw me, they smiled broadly and hurried down the ramp.

"Note the sloped floor," I pointed out.

"Yeah, yeah," they muttered.

Right behind Laurie and Jenny were Barbara's son, Cody, the star quarterback, and his sidekick, Ryan, whose parents made a lot of money and who made sure that we all knew that his parents made a lot of money. This clump of consumerism also contained Brittany, daughter of Dennis, and Dana, Seattle's version of Kelly. She was the one who would garner the applause from the dressing rooms on their shopping spree. Lash, the eighth-grade sharecropper, was right behind them, keeping close to Miss Teen Seattle without being too obvious.

We walked the block to St. Patrick's, and I had everyone sit on the steps to give them their Fifth Avenue instructions. They huddled tightly together and told each other to be quiet. The fewer interruptions, the faster I finished talking, the sooner they would be released. There was a part of me desperate to take this opportunity to lecture for thirty minutes, to point to Fifty-second and Fifth where Richard Morris Hunt built one of the greatest Vanderbilt mansions in the neighborhood, lit with electricity!, to tell of the enormous costume party that was thrown there, how society was turned on its head when the hostess, Mrs. Vanderbilt, forced the doyenne of the old guard, Mrs. Astor, to invite her to tea so that Mrs. Astor's *daughter* would be invited to the biggest social event of the era. (And wasn't it funny that Thomas ALVA Edison installed the electricity in the home of Mrs. ALVA Vanderbilt? I haven't seen that name anywhere else.) I wanted to tell them of other bygone mansions like the one a block north of St. Patrick's, home in the 1870s to Madame Restell, who made a fortune as the nation's most famous abortionist and who was found in a bathtub with her throat slit the year before the cathedral opened. There was also the University Club on Fifty-fourth, which would have provided a boring digression about all the social clubs in the city, as well as the St. Regis Hotel with its famous Maxfield Parrish mural, depicting a king passing gas and his courtiers muffling their discontent, which used to hang in Times Square at the Knickerbocker...

But I knew that if they weren't free within three minutes, at least one of them would go for my eyes.

I reminded them of the stores we had passed twice already and told them about a few they might not know were inexpensive. Right before I let them go, I mentioned the Museum of Modern Art and told anyone interested that, as a member, I could get up to four people inside for only five dollars instead of the usual twenty. The shoppers from Seattle and the Miserable Mother from Georgia scoffed at this preposterous idea. The girls rolled their eyes; Dina farted at me with her lips.

Only Pete, who wanted to "push into more paintings," took me up on my offer.

And then it was time. I had the entire group line up in their starting blocks in front of the cathedral, and I shot my pistol into the air. In an explosive blast of energy that shredded the concrete, they vanished into the crowds.

BARBARA SWOPE, THE STEPMOM from Seattle, was doing much better: she had not shed a tear or run screaming out of any building since the morning. Walking through Central Park and exploring the Metropolitan reminded her of the city she had visited years earlier.

She remembered Fifth Avenue too. Lexus had given a gift card (five thousand dollars) to her fiancé (who did not become her husband), and the two of them had gone shopping at Tiffany's and Bergdorf's. She did not want to go into those stores now. Without the thousands of free dollars, she suspected they would not be nearly as much fun. Instead, she wandered into the lobbies of the St. Regis, the Peninsula, and the Plaza, with their swirling marble, fresh flowers, and sparkling chandeliers. If she had married Christopher, how many times would they have returned to New York? Would they have tried these other hotels or would they have always stayed at the Waldorf Astoria? On her way out of the Plaza, she asked a limo driver for walking directions to the Waldorf.

Barbara broke off the engagement with Christopher because he did not want kids. He only wanted to have fabulous dinner parties with a scintillating social set in San Francisco and travel the world with the love of his life. That was all. She asked now, *Would that have been so goddamn bad?* But she was being facetious: Barbara had always wanted a family, and six years post-Christopher, she had one, and she genuinely loved them. She had a stepson and two boys of her own with Michael, the man who did become her husband. The twins were four years old. They loved to travel as much as she did, so she felt she had to tell them a small fib in order to spend the four days with their half-brother in New York. She told them she was going with Cody on a field trip for school. She had made it sound like they were traveling down to Olympia or maybe Portland, somewhere on a bus. They would have cried had they known she was taking an *airplane* without them. It was the first time she had ever been away from them. The day before she and Cody left, she took the twins to a nearby store and bought them each a stuffed animal. A monkey. As she tucked them in that night, she told them to remember how much she loved them and to give their stuffed monkeys a big hug whenever they missed their mommy.

She recognized the hotel as soon as she made the turn on Park Avenue. She remembered the French church that stood across the street, as well as the graceful stone building at the end of the avenue and the out-of-place gray monster that rose above it. She crossed Park and entered the Waldorf. She almost burst into tears when a doorman smiled at her and again when she climbed the steps and saw the mosaic in the lobby. She had a photograph of that floor hung in their foyer at home. She made a round through the public rooms on that level, her head lowering when passing real guests, and ended up in the other lobby. She looked for her ex-fiancé, almost expecting to see him sitting in one of the chairs near the ornate historic clock from Chicago's Columbian Exposition, talking with other Lexus dealers and their significant others. She recalled kissing Christopher and walking with the well-dressed crowd out to Forty-ninth Street and the limos that would take them to dinner.

Suddenly, inexplicably, she experienced crippling guilt. She had lied to her twins about where she was going, and now she was reliving, if only in her mind, a romantic weekend with a man who was not her husband. She looked back at the clock and took her cell phone from her purse. It was naptime for the boys. She called home, thousands of miles away. She actually felt nervous, which was ridiculous. She was alone calling from the lobby of a hotel. She wasn't calling from a bedroom tangled in sheets after a sweaty afternoon tryst. Get ahold of yourself.

Her husband picked up, "Hey, Barb, you should be on Fifth Avenue right now."

How did he know she wasn't? She nervously asked what he meant by that.

"Your itinerary. Shouldn't you be on Fifth Avenue?"

"We are, yes. We have another thirty minutes. How are the twins? Are they down?"

"One is down," he said. "The other is here with me in the kitchen. One of the boys misses you *very* much. He's sleeping in his bed, curled up in your robe, and he hasn't let go of that stuffed animal since you left. The other one won't take his nap, will he? He's taking a long time eating half a grilled cheese. Yes, we're talking about you, Squirrely. You can figure out which is who. Our guy here found out that you took a plane without him."

"Michael!"

"I know, my fault, I'm sorry. It slipped. I stuck the itinerary on the fridge, the boys asked about it, I broke during interrogation."

"And he's not taking it well?"

"I'll let him tell you."

When Barbara thought she could hear her son breathing into the phone, she asked him how he was, and he answered directly, "I know where you are."

"Oh?"

"And I'm *not* hugging the monkey!"

The phone was returned to her husband before she could reply.

"Did you hear that?" Michael asked. "What does that mean?"

"He's not pleased."

"No, he is not. How are you?"

"Fine."

"Just fine? That trip cost a lot of money for just *fine*."

"No, great, great." Barbara started to panic, afraid she would spill where she was and have to explain what she was going through to her husband who wouldn't understand, not that there was anything to understand, but she didn't like talking to her husband while in the lobby of the Waldorf. She wrapped up the phone call by promising that she and Cody would call around dinnertime.

Christopher, the man who did not want to have a family, was, of course, now married with two kids. Barbara was in no way attracted to him or the life he had now, but she was still enamored with the man he had been, even though she loved her children, even though she loved her husband. She was also in love with the Waldorf, the trip, the life that was not hers anymore. Michael worked in marketing for a sporting goods store, which was perfect for three boys who could take advantage of the free and discounted camping, hiking, and fishing equipment he brought home, but Barbara did not like to camp, hike, or fish. She was not someone who wanted to sleep on the ground with three boys and a man who were loved ones at home but smelly strangers out in the wild.

"Taxi, ma'am?" Back outside on Park Avenue, Barbara enjoyed being mistaken for a guest by the doorman. She would not tell him that she had been a guest only once and was now spending three nights in a dump on Eighth Avenue in a room with a broken air conditioner, scabies, and hookers in the hallway. (He could have told her that the Waldorf had more than its share of hookers but that they were just better dressed.)

Then she saw one of the Georgians, one of the boys, on the corner. He was holding a can of Coke up to his mouth, but his hand was
shaking. She looked around for one of his kin—to Barbara, they were
all related—but there was no one else. She could tell something was
wrong and caught up to him as he tried to cross the street behind a few
businessmen. She came up from behind him, touched his shoulder. He
jumped. He was spooked.

"Hi, I'm on your tour," she introduced herself. He recognized her.
"Are you all right?"

"I don't know where I am," he said. "I can't find all the stores."

"You're a few blocks away."

"But I was right on Fifth," he began. "Then I looked up. All the
signs are wrong."

"Calm down. What's your name?" He mumbled. "Lash?" she asked.
He nodded. Southerners had the strangest names. "Lash, you're with
me now. We'll go back together. Where are your friends? Where are
your teachers?" He just shook his head, which was hunched between
his shoulders. Overwhelmed. Barbara couldn't picture her stepson ever
trembling like this. Nor could she picture Cody ever getting lost. Star
quarterbacks never got lost: the world simply shifted positions of play
in order to put them back at the center. Barbara and Lash walked in
silence for a block before he mumbled something she couldn't make
out. She touched his shoulder and asked him to repeat himself.

"I got robbed," he said.

"What? Where?" Lash pointed over his shoulder and Barbara
stopped him. "What did they take?"

"Twenty dollars," Lash got out. "Just one man. He wouldn't give
it back." Barbara was confused. Of course, he wouldn't give the money
back. If someone stole it from you, chances were they were going to
keep it. "He said I only gave him a ten, but I know I gave him a twenty,
because that's all the money I have. Two twenty-dollar bills."

"Lash. Listen to me. Who took it?"

He held up his soda and said, "The man on the street."

"The man who sold you the Coke? Someone working at a cart?" He nodded. "I see. So you gave him a twenty for a can of Coke, and he gave you what?"

"Eight dollars."

"He gave you change for a ten?" Lash nodded. "You gave a twenty, and he gave you change for a ten?" Barbara wanted to make sure this wasn't a case of an eighth grader with poor math skills. "Are you sure you gave him a *twenty*-dollar bill?"

"I only had two twenties. That's all my dad gave me. I didn't use any of it, but I walked so far and got thirsty, so I bought a Coke for two dollars and…" His eyes filled with tears, he bit his lower lip, and he stopped talking.

Barbara wanted to give the kid ten bucks and walk him back to Fifth, but then she felt angry, ashamed, and compromised. This was her part of New York City, the glamorous, golden Manhattan, where there were no con jobs, muggings, short changers, vandals, or tag artists. She told Lash to take her back to where he bought the Coke. He resisted, but she was already walking east. The cart was past the Waldorf. Barbara wondered how far this boy had walked before realizing he was no longer on Fifth Avenue. Half a block away, Lash pointed out the cart. The vendor behind it was sitting on the side of a lamp post, his hands on the knees of his pants. Barbara walked directly up to the man, who straightened with a jerk as soon as he saw the boy behind her, and it was his reaction that answered Barbara's first question. This had not been an innocent mistake.

She told the vendor, "Give the boy his money back."

"What money?" he asked, unconvincingly.

"You pretended he gave you that ten, when he gave you a twenty. I'm sure that works all day long, but this boy only had a twenty-dollar bill, so he knows for sure what he gave you."

"I don't know what…he gave me a ten…"

"He gave you a twenty. You gave him eight dollars, you owe him another ten. I'm not leaving here without the rest of his change. I'll call the police," Barbara threatened, though she had no idea how long that would take and they were already pushing the deadline.

The man held his hands in front of him, pleading with her to be reasonable, but when Barbara opened her mouth to rail at him again, loudly enough for passersby to hear, he quickly handed her a ten.

"This is horrible," she told him. "It's people like you…that. People like you!" She walked to Lash and gave him the money. The boy muttered, *thank you, thank you, thank you* as they started to walk, but his hands were still shaking. Barbara reached down and took one of them in hers. It was moist. She squeezed it. She told him to calm down, that it was all over, to let it go, forget it. She was somewhat embarrassed. He was nothing like her stepson, the confident and independent athlete. They were next to the Waldorf when she noted, bewildered, that seven years earlier, she had taken a romantic stroll with her fiancé on this very block. She released Lash's hand to keep the worlds from colliding.

BACK ON FIFTH AVENUE, there was total chaos. As far as I was concerned, both groups were now officially annoying. The sooner they met back, the sooner I could get them to their hotel, the sooner I could go home. Kelly was at Bloomingdale's and was going to take a taxi to the hotel, so Ramona was in charge, but Nancy, the vice principal, was not happy, because one of their boys was missing. Every student was supposed to be with an adult. The Seattle group was missing two people—the stepmom and the girl who was traditionally late. To their credit, the shoppers were right on time, but now their priorities had shifted: they were demanding as much time as possible back at the hotel to dress up for the theater.

"What are we waiting for?" they asked. "Can't we just go?"

"Now you know how *we* always feel," said Grandma Penny who was morphing quickly into Mother Tucker.

Laurie ignored the weird old lady: "We can leave Cody's mom. She's an adult."

"We're missing two *students*," I told them.

"Cody, call your mom and find out where she is. I have to do my hair! This is crazy! CRAZY!"

Pete was calling Melanie's cell phone. He was livid. She was not supposed to be alone, and she was not supposed to be late, but every single time she was both of these things. Pete was brandishing a poster box from the MoMA like a deadly weapon. The Georgians were arguing among themselves and were very concerned, because Lash didn't have a cell phone and was not the most sophisticated boy in the group.

"I thought he went with y'all!" brayed Dina.

"I thought he wanted to go with Zach," said Wally.

"There's Melanie!" someone shouted. "MELANIE!!" Melanie was coming out of the cathedral right behind them. "OVER HERE!" Pete wanted to know why she was always late. Everyone watched as he waved his arms and she calmly listened.

Mother Tucker said, "Somebody needs to buy Blue Hair a watch." There were murmurs of agreement, with the idea and the nickname.

Clint was next to me, shifting from foot to foot. "Maybe someone took Lash," his voice quivered, "like for ransom."

"I doubt that, Clint."

Cody, with his phone to his ear, reported, "She's almost here. And she has your kid with her."

After another minute, Barbara and Lash came around the corner, her hand on his shoulder. They made an odd couple. Some of the adults cheered. The Brandons and Clint clapped. The shoppers sprang to their feet and snapped their fingers at me as if to say, *Okay, they're here, let's go, let's go.*

5:00 RETURN TO HOTEL

"I CALL FIRST SHOWER!" Tracy cried out as she opened the door.

Melanie, her blue-haired roommate, already sitting on her bed and leaning forward to stretch her legs, looked up to say, "Knock yourself out."

"Everybody in the lobby was calling first shower," Tracy explained. "That's why I said it, but if you want to go first, I don't mind."

"You go first," Melanie said. "I'm not taking a shower."

Tracy lined up her purchases on her bed and rubbed her strained biceps. "I bought so much stuff. Did you get anything today?" Melanie didn't respond. "I bought twelve postcards and two posters at the museum, which I thought was one of my favorite places on the trip so far. Did you like it? I loved it. I fell down the big staircase inside. The stone one behind the flowers. But a very cute Italian helped me up, so it was worth it, and on Fifth Avenue (he could have been Spanish) I went into like ten stores (or Portuguese), and I didn't buy anything in most of them, but at H&M and the Gap I did. You know, there are Gaps in Seattle, but there were some things here that I've never seen in Seattle. I wonder if they'll come next season. Have you been to the Gap this season?"

Melanie looked at Tracy as if she'd never heard a stupider question in her life. Melanie, Tracy was certain, didn't shop at the Gap, although black t-shirts were reasonably priced and that's all Melanie wore. Her facial expression might have had more to do with Tracy's use of the word "season," but Tracy felt you had to start using the term at some point.

"Maybe they don't carry certain things in the Northwest. I don't know. But I bought some really cute shirts here, and I think it's nice that I can say, 'I bought this outfit in New York.' I love the smell of new clothes. I think it's better than the smell of new cars, which sometimes gives me a headache." She held a skirt up to her mouth and tugged at the price tag with her free hand. She clamped her mouth on the plastic gristle and ground her teeth until it broke. "Where did *you* go?"

Melanie was sitting cross-legged now and leaning forward again to stretch her lower back, rocking to the sides to stretch her hips. She didn't answer.

Tracy turned on her own camera and found the picture of herself with the Abercrombie and Fitch model. They plucked them right out of a catalog and had them stand in the doorway, shirtless with their jeans worn as low as they could possibly go. Tracy had waited in line, and when it was her turn, she handed her camera to one of the guys whose turn it was to wear his shirt, and she stepped right into the outstretched arm of the half-naked model. She wrapped her arm around his warm, smooth, muscular torso and leaned her head into his armpit. The smile in the picture was her biggest yet. Her sister was going to be so envious.

Melanie was not envious; she asked, "Do those guys know how to work the cash register, or do they just stand in the door all day?"

"I don't know," Tracy said. "I wish we could go back on *Saturday*. Do you know who's going to be there on Saturday?" Melanie didn't. "The guy on the bag! The guy on the Abercrombie *bag* is going to be there in *person*! Can you believe it?"

Melanie believed it.

Tracy asked, "What are you wearing to Broadway? Did you buy something new, or did you bring your dress-up clothes from home? I packed dress-up clothes because I didn't know if I'd be able to find something here and in case something changed on the itinerary and we couldn't shop, I wouldn't have anything to wear. But I just bought these. For the theater. I'm going to wear this skirt and this shirt." She held them in front of her, shirt on top, skirt on bottom, careful not to let them touch her body before her shower. She held them there for several seconds until it was clear that Melanie was not going to look over or partake in any conversation about clothes. There wouldn't be any gossip or pillow fights either, Tracy thought, as Melanie flopped back on the bed and stretched out. She wasn't that kind of roommate.

Melanie asked, "Could you wake me when it's time to go down?"

"Definitely! I can definitely do that." Do you want me to give you time to get ready?"

"I'm ready. I'm dressed. I just need a nap."

At home, Tracy had to share a bathroom with her sister, but here in New York, the entire thing was hers. She could envision the other

girls on the trip, shoulder to shoulder in front of the mirror, borrow-
ing each other's mascara, jostling for better light, sharing compliments
and moisturizer. Passing on beauty tips. Dana, the model, could teach
a class. She pictured Ms. Takahashi, the drama teacher, helping her
student council, braiding Michele's hair or holding Jennifer's chin and
painting on a beauty spot or something theatrical. Actually, Tracy envied that a little. A lot. Look on the bright side, she told herself: you
have the room all to yourself, you don't have to rush, and you can enjoy
this.

When she emerged from the bathroom, after a forty-minute ceremony, she hoped that Melanie would notice her transformation. She
pretended, of course, not to expect any compliment, but she prepared
in case one came: "Oh, yes, I just put a little makeup on." Tracy had
read that too little makeup was superior to too much makeup. Tasteful,
bare. Like Dana, their supermodel. Or like the teacher from Georgia.
Tracy only used a small amount of eye makeup and some lipstick, usually lip gloss, but tonight was the thee-ay-ter. She had methodically
applied the shades to her lids, lips, and lashes and admired her hand-
iwork in the mirror. Beauty was a chore, but a chore closer to setting
the table than vacuuming or taking out the trash. She avoided looking toward Melanie, but she could still tell that Melanie was asleep.
She deliberately bumped her hip against the dresser in hopes that the
items rattling on top would wake her up. But there was no sound. She
bumped it again, but it was solid, unlike her dresser at home. If she
bumped it any harder, she'd bruise. She slid some coins into her palm
and noisily dropped them onto the piece of sturdy furniture.

Finally, she just said, "The bathroom's all yours!" That woke her.
Melanie took a deep breath and sighed. She made fists, stretched her
arms, and bent her knees, but did not open her eyes. Tracy gave up.
Melanie was not into clothes or make-up, with the exception of black
eyeliner, which Tracy thought she probably bought in bulk at Costco.

Tracy looked at the clock. They had ten minutes. She sat on her
bed and looked to footwear. She had painted her toenails a fire engine

red for the trip, but unfortunately she had to hide them in socks, because she insisted on comfortable shoes. Even for the theater. She might wear her heels tomorrow, but tonight her school was taking the subway to Lincoln Center, which was not in Times Square or near their hotel, and she didn't do well in heels, and she didn't want to be distracted. At least her shoes were spotless white, brand new and clean. She tied her laces and stood up. She gave Melanie one last opportunity. And was met with silence.

"I'm going downstairs now," was all Tracy said as she transferred her belongings from her "Louis Vuitton" to the brand new white purse she had bought from a man behind a table on Fifth Avenue. She exited, running her free hand over the back of her head and down her shiny, apple-ly smelling hair. At the elevator, she gazed at herself in the mirror. The lighting was different. Her eyelids jumped out at her. Maybe she was wearing too much shadow. Well, it was a formal night. The elevator opened and she walked into it, swishing her hips a little more than necessary.

5:45 MEET IN LOBBY FOR DINNER AND THEATER

BARBARA ENTERED THE LOBBY with ten minutes to spare. Almost everyone was down. Another tour group arriving by bus took up one side of the lobby, so both Georgia and Seattle were forced to mix on the other.

Her first thought, as she looked her fellow theatergoers over: *What would the American male, as a species, do without khaki pants?* The Georgians must have insisted on a no-jeans policy as well, because there was no denim anywhere in their midst, but every male—the boys and the men, from Clint to Cody, from ironworker to teacher—was wearing different shades of khaki pants, the uniform for an awards ceremony at the school or for your first Broadway show. She thought at least Pete would be wearing a suit, but it was summertime. She also assumed that Ryan, Cody's friend, would be wearing the latest fashion out of

Milan, always doing his best to show how much money his family spent on their only child, but even Ryan was in khakis. The younger boys, most of whom were unused to dressing up, were tugging at their ties or fussing with buttons, still deciding whether to wear their shirts tucked in or out. She heard Kelly telling her boys that everyone was tucking. Kelly looked beautiful, Barbara thought, and so did the black teacher (Rhonda? Rona?), who wore a canary yellow shawl over her bare shoulders.

The shopping roomies were already down, surprising since they had claimed they needed "at least two hours." As Barbara expected, most of the girls were dressed to look like they were well into their twenties. Dana, the model, pulled it off effortlessly and with a little class. Laurie and Jenny, no surprise, looked like escorts. The high schoolers were making a fuss, posing for each other, squealing with admiration.

—Oh my God!

—Where did you get that?

—So CUTE!

—SO cute!

Then Barbara saw one of their girls standing in the corner. The chubby, freckled one. She was wearing brand new white sneakers, a white knee-length skirt, a blue cotton short-sleeved shirt, and a blue velvet headband that didn't quite match the shirt (or her overpainted eyelids). She clutched a small white purse in front of her and was watching her classmates who were taking photos in various combinations as if reliving prom.

No one was saying anything to her.

No one was asking her to pose for a picture.

Barbara caught her stepson's eye. She waved him over.

"You look nice," Cody told her.

"Thank you," Barbara said. "Now I need you to go over to that girl and tell her the same thing."

"What do you mean?" he asked. "Who?"

"The girl in the corner."

"The sophomore chick?"

"No one is saying anything to her."

"What are we supposed to say?" he asked. "Nice headband?" He laughed at his own joke and was surprised that his stepmom didn't. She was mildly surprised herself. "What's the matter with you?"

"She can't compete with your friends, but she tried. She tried very hard. Look at her."

He sighed, "But then she'll take it all wrong and start hanging out with us. No, seriously, if I say something, if it comes from me, she'll know I was put up to it, which would backfire on you, or else she'll think I really mean it, which will backfire on me."

"Just walk by her and say it quickly."

"Come on."

"As if you're noticing her in passing."

"What's the big deal?"

"Cody, please do this for me."

"Aw, man, you owe me." Barbara gave him a hug and then hid behind a couple Georgians just in case the girl did think Cody was put up to it and looked around for the one responsible. Cody performed well. He didn't overdo it. He just walked by, gave Tracy a look up and down, said something, and moved on.

But how her face lit up.

She thanked his back and held her smile.

She pressed her sad little purse to her heart.

A voice suddenly bellowed through the lobby: "Oh, OH, everyone looks so GREAT. You look like angels!" Elaine Caine.

"Damn it," Barbara said, dismayed at the changing of the guard.

"Okay, we're all here, let's go, we have to walk to dinner, but don't worry, don't worry, it's not very far. It's right in Times Square." Elaine pushed through the revolving door and waited out on the sidewalk for them all to join her. Barbara grimaced. Everything was harder with almost forty people. Moving from a lobby to the sidewalk, a distance

of eight feet, took almost a minute and a half. Once all were standing in front of the hotel, Elaine said, "Okay, great, let's do this!" and
then took off, barely waiting for them to follow. These westerners and
southerners, dressed up for a night at the theater, were not going to
walk as quickly as she wanted them to. Cody held out his arm and
Dana took it, and Laurie and Jenny each took one of Ryan's arms, as
if they were promenading along a red carpet instead of trekking over
dirty sidewalks through crowds of sweaty construction workers and
New Yorkers on their way to the gym.

Barbara held back. She learned that day that the farther behind
the group she walked, the less likely she would be called a "fucking
tourist." She hated being called a "fucking" anything, but a "fucking
tourist" was the worst. Wally, the giant from Georgia, however, was
trying to bring up the rear, and she didn't want to explain, *I'm sorry,
I don't want to be seen with you all,* so she started walking. Wally and
his son were soon beside her, and she wondered if people would think
this was her family, this father and son in their identical blue plaid
button-down short-sleeved shirts. As their well-khakied crew tried to
make their way elegantly around a pile of garbage bags, Wally thanked
Barbara again for finding Lash and for helping him get his money.

Clint said, "Lash wasn't even on Fifth Avenue. How'd you know
where to look?"

"I wasn't looking."

"So you got lost too?"

Barbara smiled, but before she could answer, a Hasidic Jew, one
of the hundreds in Midtown wearing the traditional attire—the black
suit, the hat, the long curls beside his cheeks—walked right in front of
them, and Clint frantically grabbed his father's wrist.

"Dad!" Clint whispered, "I have seen that same guy forty times
today!"

6:15 DINNER AT PLANET HOLLYWOOD

DENNIS BREWER, WHO RESOLVED not to embarrass his daughter but then wore a *Battleship Galactica* t-shirt to breakfast, had spent five hours at the American Museum of Natural History, where he wandered the long hallways and lost himself in fossils, meteorites, gems, and plants as well as totem poles, shells, head dresses, and countless animal habitat dioramas. The majority of the objects were preserved inside glass cases, so he regarded dinner at Planet Hollywood as a natural extension of his day and his research, because here was another series of glass cases and wall units. This time what was being preserved were costumes worn by Leonardo DiCaprio and Cameron Diaz, props used by Will Smith and Tommy Lee Jones, and models of spacecraft that were made to fly in the movies. Still under the influence of the anthropological exhibits at the museum, he couldn't help but conclude from the clothing on display that actors in Hollywood were a very small people, a population from an exotic island about whom Margaret Mead might have written.

Cutting out for the Natural History Museum had been a good judgment call on his part. The decision was impromptu, brought on by his daughter's treatment of him in Central Park and on the steps of the art museum. She completely ignored him, and he decided that if he had to be solo in New York, then he was going to do what he wanted to do. Dennis crossed back through the park and found a reason for this four-day trip that did not include his daughter. His feelings of rejection and self pity dissipated as soon as he climbed the stairs and entered the rotunda where a cast skeleton of a massive Barosaurus reared up on its hind legs to defend its baby from an Allosaurus predator, a reenactment of a Jurassic battle that might have taken place one hundred fifty million years ago. There was nothing like the time line of the American Museum of Natural History to take you out of yourself and put things in perspective.

However. He had something to share tonight with the people at his table (Elaine Caine and Jacob and Sun, the two budding computer scientists from Seattle). "So I'm reading the signs outside the Hall of Evolution when I hear a woman telling someone else not to look. Not to look at what? So I turn and see some lady with a girl of about six, seven? I guess she was looking for the bathroom or the Hall of Meteorites. I don't know why they had to go through the Hall of Evolution, but while they walked, she kept her hand over her daughter's eyes. She is literally holding one hand over her daughter's eyes and guiding her by the neck with the other hand and telling her not to look. Not to look at the Hall of Evolution. The girl asks why, and the ignorant wacko mother says, 'Because it's all lies.'"

He paused to let this absurdity sink in.

Jacob and Sun shook their heads.

Elaine asked, "What kind of accent did she have?"

"She sounded local to me. I don't know, New Jersey? There are bumpkins everywhere. Take a quick drive out of Seattle, and you've got Bible Thumpers and armed camps of white supremacists…"

"Horrible," Elaine said.

"One of the leading intelligent design morons lives in Seattle! Pathetic! How can evolution still be a hot button topic?" He turned to the boys. "How can it still be a hot button topic?"

Jacob and Sun shrugged their shoulders.

Dennis asked, "How long did it take for the Church to accept that the earth went around the sun?"

Elaine said, "I read somewhere that eighteen percent of Americans aren't sure it does."

Dennis was speechless, but only for three seconds, "These people demand that scientists prove their theories beyond certainty, with a barrage of experiments whose conclusions they intend to disregard anyway, and while these scientists are busy explaining how the earth is round and the sun is hot, the religious, the spiritual, who simply know it all, refer vaguely to energy and intuition and what the Bible tells them."

Just like the two women at the aphrodisiac party last February, the women who were so convinced that a miscarriage buried in the back yard needed a steady supply of rose quartz or that no, it didn't, because Jesus in heaven had all the rose quartz the baby's soul required. How could they live their lives with answers they were making up as they went along? How could someone be so certain without conducting any experiment, testing any hypothesis? And the biggest mystery of all: How could his wife have expected him *not* to ask the question that broke the camel's back and ended the party and his marriage?

Is it painful, or just physically draining, to be so fucking stupid?

"But here's the best part," Dennis resumed his story. "Get this: the mother with her hand over her daughter's eyes? Looking for the bathroom or the exit or whatever? She walked her daughter right into the wall. BAM! Covered her child's eyes and walked her child right into a wall. Says it all!" He gestured to Jacob and Sun. "We're walking our next generation right into the wall." They nodded, and Dennis looked beyond their table to their fellow diners. "I mean how many of these stupid bastards do you think are creationists? How many think the earth is only six thousand years old? Never mind that agriculture itself was introduced twelve thousand years ago! What do you study in school? You do study evolution, right?"

Elaine said, "Most schools do, don't they? Maybe Kansas…"

"Georgia has Bible classes now in their curriculum! Can you believe that? Their state passed that. In their curriculum in public schools! I'm going to ask everyone. Jacob, Sun, do you believe in evolution or creationism?" They said evolution, and Dennis made two marks on his paper napkin. "I'll be back." Like a waiter, Dennis walked to the first table.

"Good evening, ladies. I'm just taking an informal poll with a 5.4 percent margin of error," he chuckled at his own joke. "How many here, a show of hands is sufficient, believe that we are all products of evolution OR were we created out of nothing by some intelligent designer, a designer, who by their own argument would be so complex that the designer itself would require a designer?"

This was the table occupied by his daughter and her friends, and Brittany looked up at her father with an expression that might have been worn by a pedestrian watching a crane topple from a roof of a high rise.

RAMONA SPOKE FOR EVERYONE at her table—for Kelly, Nancy, Ashley, and Faith—when she answered the man from Seattle with the words, "We're eating our dinner."

Dennis replied, "Just a quick answer. A or B."

Ramona said, "We get people calling our homes in the middle of dinnertime asking all kinds of questions that *they* need answered…?"

"I'll put one down for creationism," he said.

Ashley, the Bible Bee champ, said, "TWO for creation."

"Two, thank you."

Ramona ordered, "No one else answer." Ramona wanted to put a stop to this on principle, but she also didn't want to hear anyone else voting for creationism. She didn't want to give this northwesterner data for whatever culturally biased project he was working on.

Dennis stood there for a few beats, looking at the girls and then at their chaperones before saying to the whole table, "And by the way, the Civil War *did* actually have as much to do with slavery as people might think." With that, he left a stunned table of Georgians.

This was a complicated moment.

Ramona avoided all eye contact.

This man was referencing the line that Nancy said to Ramona in her office, the very line that Ramona shared with Kelly and which had become an inside joke between them. How was this complete stranger able to quote it? Who would have told him? It did not occur to her that she herself was the one who whispered it across the ceiling and into his ear at Grand Central, and so she was completely baffled.

She heard Nancy stabbing her brownie with her fork. Surely her vice principal recognized her own words. Kelly was taking long sips of her iced tea, keeping her mouth full of liquid, so that she wouldn't have to answer any questions. Ramona wondered why Kelly would have talked with Dennis about her vice principal's ideas on the Civil War, and Ramona also wondered why Dennis had seemed to address the whole table instead of just Nancy. His spite was directed at her as much as at anyone else.

Faith broke the silence: "That is one weird man."

All three clearly thought it best to agree with Faith and for the moment pretend that they didn't catch the reference. Ramona knew that Nancy was going to be sticking close by for the rest of the evening, looking for an opportunity to ask her what the meaning of that exchange had been. Ramona would likely have no chance to talk with Kelly until they returned to the hotel.

"GEORGIA!" Elaine Caine came to the rescue with a firestorm of logistics, and Ramona was grateful. Elaine handed Kelly the Broadway tickets for *Phantom of the Opera* and impressed on her how crucial it was not to hand out the tickets until they reached the theater because they were non-refundable and very expensive, and Elaine didn't want anyone losing their ticket and missing the show. Since the other group needed to take the subway to Lincoln Center, Elaine was leaving with them. The Georgia group could wait another twenty minutes, because their theater was just around the corner. "And I signed the voucher, so dinner is TAKEN CARE OF!" Elaine shouted. "It's all taken care of so don't you worry about any of that! OKAY, SEATTLE! LET'S GO!" Elaine Caine took off like a bat out of hell, and Seattle chased her out of the room and down the stairs.

One of the Brandons asked why Elaine just up and left. "Ain't we goin' to a show?"

"*Aren't* we *going* to a show?" Nancy corrected but didn't answer.

Kelly told everyone they were leaving soon. "Use the bathroom."

The rest of the Georgians began to congregate around their table.

Dina, clutching a cigarette and her lighter, proposed they head to the theater early.

Grandma Penny asked, "Did that crazy Seattle man ask y'all about evolution or just us?"

"I think he was asking everyone," said Faith. Others mumbled their agreement.

Ashley asked, "Did he tell y'all the Civil War was all about slavery?"

Everyone was baffled by that, and no, no one else got that comment. Only their table. Ramona dreaded the rest of the evening, the remaining hours she would have to work to keep her face a placid, neutral mask, and she knew that no matter how great the Broadway show was, none of the performances were going to be able to compete with hers.

8:00 THEATER

IF YOU'RE THE ONE to choose the show for an entire group, you relinquish the freedom to enjoy that show. And if you're sitting in a theater like the Vivian Beaumont at Lincoln Center, where the audience sits in a semicircle around the stage, so that you see the other members of your group, then you, unfortunately, cannot lose yourself in Florence in the years following World War II. Pete was sitting on the side next to an empty seat, because after handing out tickets scattered throughout the house in groups of three, five, two, four, four, one, he was left in the lobby with two tickets, one for himself and one for Tommy. Once again, Pete had not been paying attention, so Dennis had to sit alone and Pete had to sit beside a ghost.

Pete had chosen this play because of a review that urged anyone interested in the future of musical theater to buy tickets now. Pete obediently asked his account manager to buy nineteen tickets. He liked to prepare his students for the musicals they were going to see; however, the last few weeks had been too distracting and overwhelming. He went so far as to purchase the cast recording for the show, but the CD was still wrapped in plastic on the passenger seat of his car. At their last meeting, he tried to read them the synopsis but was interrupted by insolent questions about flying monkeys and good witches, the relentless reminder that several of them had wanted to see *Wicked.*

Introducing them to the music would not have been a bad idea, since it was tricky—melodic, certainly, but with atonal nods—and the clear soprano voices, which he found glorious, were not delivering the high belts (i.e., shrieks) this *American Idol* generation loved and expected in their concerts and car commercials. The lyrics too were a bit challenging to the ear on first exposure, and it didn't help that one of the early scenes was spoken and sung in Italian.

Pete tried to concentrate and for several minutes at a time was able to follow the story of this American mother and daughter on vacation in Italy. The set had columns and statues that slid off and on and paintings that descended out of the fly space. Leaves blew across the stage, actors rode bicycles, and the lights and the costumes evoked an Italy more authentic than that Little Italy restaurant where the theme from *The Godfather* was played every five minutes. The young actors playing the daughter and her love interest were also attractive, which would, no doubt, please the hormone monsters. He was enamored with the mother, who for some reason was doing everything in her power to keep the two young lovers apart.

Something was wrong, Pete sensed, with the daughter, but as he was trying to guess what it was, to jump ahead of the script while still catching each lyric as it was spun into the air, his eye fell on Cody, the quarterback, whose head bobbed up and then fell again. Next to Cody, Laurie and Jenny were whispering to each other, and Ryan was looking at his phone. Pete prayed that one of the strangers behind them would roll up his or her program and slap it across their empty heads. He looked back at the stage, using his hand to block his view of that part of the audience, but then he feared that a student would see him and think that the one person who wanted to see this show was napping. He knew he could not afford that. There would be full-out

mutiny. The actress playing the mother was singing a beautiful, dev-
astating song about the acknowledgment that her marriage was pure
convention, devoid of love, and Pete listened carefully, pledging to call
his wife as soon as he got back to the hotel. They were happy, he and
Jean. Their teenagers were a handful, but he and his wife had grown
into a strong, invincible team.

His eyes wandered again. Dennis, though alone, had one of the
best seats, center and close to the stage. He could easily focus on the
performance; too bad Dennis had already voiced his disinterest in the
arts. Lu, the drama teacher, was loving it. She leaned forward with her
mouth slightly open. After each song, she was the first to clap and the
last to stop. Pete couldn't help but monitor the length and intensity of
the clapping from his group. Two of the boys, Jacob and Sun, the computer boys, didn't clap at all. They were watching the stage but didn't
seem to pick up from the rest of the hundreds of clapping hands that
applauding was part of the social contract. Oh, for Pete's sake, Pete!
Watch the show, watch the show.

The music was now making him nervous. The girl—something
was definitely off with her—was now lost in the streets of Florence,
and a rape scene seemed inevitable. Oh, brother. Why did he bring
them here? He should have read the synopsis himself, at the very least.
She was going to get assaulted onstage by one of the extras, and there
was still an entire act to go. Pete didn't even know if this show were a
comedy or a tragedy. He didn't remember anything from the review,
only that if you were interested in the future of musical theater, you
needed to buy a ticket. So he did. But why did he make *everyone* buy
a ticket? Who else in his group, besides Lu, was at all interested in the
future of musical theater?

The good news was that the daughter was not attacked. The bad
news was that Pete felt himself turning against the entire audience—
not only the kids he had been teaching for at least a year, the generation that didn't seem to value anything that he held close to his heart,
but now the rest of the audience as well, all of whom, he suspected,

would rather be at a show with more dancing, flashier scene changes, less ideas, less soul, more marketing money. Pointless, pointless the life he was leading. Why was he asking children to conjugate the Latin verb for *irrigate* or to stand in front of a seventeenth-century painting by Vermeer and push into the room when they were going to do only one of two things: roll their eyes when he turned his back or drink-and-drive into a tree?

And now the young couple was singing and embracing, kneeling on a bed. As their voices rose, their clothes fell. She pulled off his shirt, and now Pete was concerned there was going to be full nudity at the show he'd brought fifteen students to (fourteen, not counting Tommy). Big deal! Who cared? They sent each other more provocative streaming video on their cell phones, and the amount of hard-core pornography they downloaded from the Internet could crash a hard drive. Pete listened to the music, to the voices swirling through the auditorium, and then came the mother. She opened the door, stopped in her tracks, and the lights snapped out. Pete was lost in the story again, captivated by the music and the characters; that is, until the house lights came up for the intermission when he remembered Ryan, and he left his seat to confiscate his phone.

10:45 GROUP PHOTO

AT THE MAJESTIC THEATER on Forty-fourth where *Phantom of the Opera* had been playing to school groups and international tourists for over two decades, the reviews were in. Clint, who thought it was "really, really, really good," called it his favorite Broadway show. His father reminded Clint that it was his only Broadway show, but Clint said he saw "that one they made into a movie." "Which one?" "You know, they were singin' and all." One of the Brandons liked the special effects, especially "when the guy jumped off the bridge into that hole." Another Brandon didn't like when they sang foreign and thought sometimes even the English sounded foreign and thought it was "weird that they sang everything they wanted to talk about." The third Brandon slept through most of it except for the parts "when Mr. Wally kept whaling on me." Grandma Penny compared it favorably to the production she saw in Atlanta; Travis, the ironworker, said a show "can't get much better than that"; and his daughter, Alice, thought parts of it were scary. Zach, the eighth-grade Shakespeare scholar, "questioned the dramaturgy" and "the theft of Puccini," while Lash, sitting next to him, wondered how the actors remembered all their words and where to go. Lash also spent a lot of the time looking at the decoration in the theater and wondering if the people who came here went to the theater every night. How many times a week did the New Yorkers see *Phantom of the Opera*? There were a lot of shows, he figured, so they probably jumped around a lot. During intermission and after the curtain call, Dina said it was worth every penny as she bolted for the street, cigarette in one hand, lighter in the other. Dina's daughter, Pamela, said she cried at the end, Faith said she wished she could sing like that, and Ashley, the Bible Bee, felt the show was a little satanic.

Nancy and Ramona kept their opinions to themselves (the show had been a two-and-a-half hour hiatus from the Civil War that had less to do with slavery than people think it did), and now both were throwing themselves into the task of helping Kelly keep track of everyone as they moved their way through the crowds into the middle of Times Square on a busy Thursday night.

Kelly, leading the group with her playbill held high above her head as a makeshift shepherd's crook or tour guide umbrella, was transported. She hummed one of the songs. She did not know which. This was her third time seeing *Phantom of the Opera*, but never had she felt the romance as she did tonight. Could it be because of the chemistry of the three talented performers or because that afternoon she had found the perfect black dress, which was now hanging in the closet back at the hotel, where she would slip it on and help Ramona envision exactly how she was going to look in Charleston, South Carolina come the end of July? She led her flock through the throng, which was comprised almost entirely of couples holding hands. Everyone in Times Square was in love. She desperately missed Hunter. She pictured him at McHale's, their Thursday night ritual, sitting at the bar and gazing at the empty air hockey table, where she would have been, had she not been in Times Square, at the Crossroads of the World.

Kelly picked out Photo Island, an unofficial name of the concrete median between Forty-fifth and Forty-sixth. After crossing her sixteen safely, she lined them up behind several other school groups crowding together between a metallic art project and the busy downtown traffic. Then Kelly made her way up to the photographer at his stepladder to tell him that K.C. Crown had arrived. He was climbing up to take a picture of seventy middle schoolers, all wearing gray slacks and the same blue dress shirt. He paused and pointed to his assistant who gave Kelly a clipboard. She filled out a card confirming the order. When she was done, she stayed put, waiting near the stepladder until it was her group's turn. What a zoo! People everywhere, traffic still busy this late at night. The groups bobbed up and down, passersby stopped to watch the photo shoot, some accidentally walked in front of the posers, others deliberately waved over their heads. She checked her phone to see if she had any messages and realized she had shut it off before the show started. She powered it back on and tried to figure out where the group standing next to her was from. Based on their shoes and sunglasses, Colorado or maybe Nevada, somewhere out West. She had three texts and five voicemails. Her mother's sister was in the hospital, and she hoped that none of these pertained to her.

The first text was a picture. Of a man's genitals. She pulled the phone to her chest and looked behind her. No one else had seen her screen. She tipped her phone back and looked more closely. Hunter's. Hunter had texted her a picture of his semi-hard penis. This was not the kind of romantic gesture that inspired a Broadway musical. And what was he thinking? She was traveling with children, not to mention her vice principal who was always looking over her shoulder. He was out of his mind to send this.

She clicked to the second message. Another picture. This time of Hunter's upper body and face, his eyes closed, head on a pillow. The angle was wrong. She studied the shoulder. His own arm had not taken this picture. What was happening?

The third message was a text: *Your bboy is mighty fine bitch!*

For a few moments, Times Square became as quiet as her backyard at home. What was happening? Who was sending her these? They were from Hunter's phone; each of them came from Hunter's phone. She didn't get the joke. Kelly dialed her voicemail; the messages were all from Hunter, short and cryptic, asking her to call him back. In one message, he tried to pass the texts off as a joke, but by the next message it sounded like he had given up on that ploy. The photographer was saying something to her from the ladder. She looked up at him.

"Are you all right?" he asked. She didn't move. "Don't you want to be in the photo?" Kelly looked in front of her and saw her group stepping into the area in front of the stepladder. She joined them as they turned to face the photographer. She started to replay the last message. The boys were instructed to kneel in the front, the girls to stand behind them, and the adults to form a third row.

"Okay! Five pictures now! Keep looking up here!" After a pause, "Phones down!" Kelly held the phone behind her. Wally and Ramona both glanced at her. She faked a smile with a hole in her chest. She wanted to kneel with the boys, because keeping her balance was difficult. As the pictures were taken, Kelly just stared into the camera, a weird grin plastered on her face. The picture would have come out so differently if there had been no other groups before them, if they could have posed as soon as they arrived. Kelly's smile would have been vibrant, her eyes not as dazed; her shoulders would have been held back instead of collapsing forward. She would have been humming. There would have been music in the air. So many people were humming music in Midtown Manhattan when the theaters let out—it was a giant symphony—but the only thing she could hear now were Hunter's panicked messages and the frightening roar of bus engines.

Ramona came up with the idea that Wally should lead the group back to the hotel, because he was so tall and easier to make out. Kelly agreed and walked with Ramona in the back. As they made it out of Times Square, Ramona asked Kelly if everything were okay. She nodded as she replayed the messages she needed to hear one more time before she called Hunter back. But she did not call back. On Eighth Avenue, her cell rang, and as soon as she saw Hunter's name on the display, she threw the phone into the street where it bounced once on the ground and missed the back of a cab before sliding, like a puck in their game of air hockey, right into the sewer.

ON THE PLAZA, or *piazza*, at Lincoln Center, the sophomore, Tracy Powell, was trying to hum, but she couldn't remember any of the tunes and she wasn't particularly musical, so she was humming what she felt was the gist of the music, string instruments pleading in long strands. It was very pretty music. Tracy thought back on the opening when the mother and daughter arrived in the piazza. The locals walked about, someone rode a bicycle, and everyone sang. As they walked away, the daughter's hat blew off her head and slid across the stage before floating up into the air—Tracy could see the wire—and then dropping slowly into the hands of the young Italian. Love. *Amore*.

As she relived the beauty of that, a wind blew across the piazza where they were standing, and the beret their drama teacher was wearing flew off and rolled with the gust toward the street. Ms. Takahashi ran after it. It landed upside down in a puddle, and as she crossed the small street, she almost collided with a man on a bike with white plastic bags hanging from the handlebars. He maneuvered quickly around her and looked back long enough to shout, *Summabeach*! She held her hands up to him in apology and then bent over, pulling the beret out of the puddle, letting it drip as she returned to the group.

Tracy wasn't biting her lips to keep her excitement bottled in, so her words were out before she could stop them. "That's exactly like the show! Except no one caught your hat."

Several laughed.

Ms. Takahashi then shook her wet hat at the Lincoln Center buildings and shouted, "My life is not a musical!!" Everyone else laughed. She smiled briefly at Tracy, appreciating the graceful set-up. "Where's *my* Italian?" she cried, and then the others began offering their jokes.

—Your hat isn't lucky.

—No one loves a beret.

—You were almost killed by a bicycle.

—That's a short musical.

—*Death in the Piazza.*

But Ms. Takahashi was funnier than them all. At that moment, a pair of well-dressed young men approached on their way out of Lincoln Center. She looked into the sky and flung her hat directly into the chest of one of them.

"Oh, I'm so sorry," she said. "My hat."

Most in the group burst out laughing. The man who caught the hat handed it back to her and the two walked on. She feigned shock and outrage and then swiveled and pretended to hurl the beret at the back of her negligent lover's head.

Tracy asked aloud, "Wouldn't it be funny if we just threw our hats at people we liked?" No one laughed at this. A few looked at her as if to say, *That's what her joke was, that's what we were laughing at.* Tracy bit her lips again, but Ms. Takahashi, who owed Tracy this entire routine, was quick to help.

"I'll take flying hats over cheesy pickup lines any day. I think I'm going to start taking this hat with me whenever I go out. This is very aerodynamic." Once again, she threw her hat like a frisbee and it flew several yards into the plaza.

Pete was coming from the theater with the students who had to use the bathroom. He picked up his fellow chaperone's hat with a raised eyebrow.

—Drop the hat, Mr. T! Or you'll have to marry her.

He understood and smiled but didn't reply.

Elaine Caine didn't know what the heck was going on, "Okay, OKAY, here we go, EVERYONE. We have to go into the subway right here…"

"Hey, Lu," one of the student council kids sidled up to his teacher. "What's the worst pickup line you've ever heard?" Tracy was walking with them, watching her skirt and shoes as they went. They were both still gleaming white, but the entire evening had been a battle waged to keep them so. This was why so many New Yorkers wore black, she was now convinced, and she had stupidly worn so much white.

Lu thought back on all the pickup lines addressed to her and said, "I think the worst was 'I'm into Asian chicks, you into white guys?'"

—NO WAY!!

—Way.

They walked down the stairs into the subway.

—Hey, Lu?

—What?

—Let me swipe your Metrocard for you. All. Night. Long.

—Inappropriate.

Those in earshot snickered, swiping and pushing through the turnstiles. On the platform, Tracy stayed with the student council group and listened to them joke around.

—Hey, James?

—What?

—I see you're taking the downtown train.

—Hey, Michele? I'm always going downtown.

—Hey, Lu? I see you have a theater program.

—That's right.

—Well, let me buy you a drink and show you my credits.

—I don't get that one.

—Hey, Bobby? What credits?

—Ooooo!

—Busted!

—Burned!

The train squealed and rattled into the station. They concentrated on boarding and then stood in the middle of the train, holding on so they wouldn't fall.

—Hey, Michele?

—Whatcha got?

—You're squeezing that pole too tight.

—Don't be gross.

—Hey, Jennifer? You take this train a lot?

—Third time today.

—Well…No, I messed up. Void that one.

Tracy knew better than to join in—somehow the seniors could flub a joke and keep moving on; she would only humiliate herself and regret it all night—but she stood in their circle. She might have Ms. Takahashi for a teacher next year, and this would be a good way to start to bond.

After only one stop, Elaine was already shouting, "Okay, WE'RE ALMOST THERE! The next stop is where we get off! Make sure you're near a door…"

When the doors opened, their school leapt from the car to the platform. Pete and Elaine made sure that none of theirs had been left on the train, and they then led the way through the turnstiles and up the stairs. Tracy was in the back, eavesdropping on that quintet and making sure no one stepped on her white shoes, so she didn't know what had happened, why after climbing the stairs, they were all being forced to gather out of the way. Elaine Caine stood waiting on the corner, and their teacher was livid.

"I've had it! We didn't see *Wicked*. Deal with it! We met six times about this trip, and you've known we weren't seeing *Wicked* for four months. I'm so tired of listening to you gripe and bitch about wanting to see something else, wanting to do something else, wanting to be somewhere else. You're part of a group! If you want to come here and shop from morning till night, then ask your parents to bring you. That's not why I arrange these trips, and you've known that since you signed up! We were at a world class theater tonight, and most of you didn't even get it. You were playing with your goddamn phone during the show, and you two were talking. Yes, I'm swearing. You want to pretend you're grown-ups? Then I'll treat you like grown-ups. I don't put this much time and energy into these four days to be treated like this. I don't need to be here, or I don't need to be here with *you*. I could be home with my family. I could be here with my wife. I do it because I want students to see another part of the country. I want to share with them the city I love, and I don't know anymore why I bother." He stood there trying to get his breath. "I should have canceled this trip after Tommy died." No one said anything. "Just show a little fucking respect." He waved at them to follow. And they did so in complete silence. Ms. Takahashi caught up to him and patted his back. Now, after being denounced publicly, they were off to get their photo taken in the middle of Times Square like all of the students before them who had gone on this trip.

So both schools had challenges with their photo that night.

And I had no idea.

I was at home, enjoying an evening to myself, resting my voice, watching a DVD, unaware of all that had happened after I dropped my two groups off at the hotel. I had no idea a grief-stricken teacher was cursing at teenagers on Fiftieth Street or that a cell phone was ringing in a sewer below Forty-sixth, no clue about the evolution poll conducted at Planet Hollywood or the tension building between a history teacher and her vice principal. I only had two more days with them, one and a half really, but if I had known all of this and reminded myself that Day Three is the day when things blow up, I probably would have turned off the TV and gone straight to bed or even called Carol, who had assigned me this job, to tell her I was sick.

DAY THREE

7:00   Guide Meets Group at Hotel

7:30   Breakfast

8:00   Subway to Battery Park

9:00   Ferry to the Statue of Liberty and Ellis Island
           (*Stops and Timing TBD*)

12:30 Return to Battery Park

12:45 Lunch

1:30   Tour of Wall Street

2:30   Ground Zero

4:45   Return to Hotel

5:45   Meet in Lobby for Dinner and Theater

8:00   Theater

10:45 Return to Hotel

7:00 GUIDE MEETS GROUP AT HOTEL

BY THE THIRD DAY, you know the ones you like, the ones you loathe. You've figured out how to discuss history and to touch on politics, which movies to reference, whether they read books. You know how quickly your people move from place to place, how punctual they are, how much time they like for lunch. On the other hand, you need to be careful, because, of course, you don't know these people at all, and as they relax into the trip, or as they become more tired, sleep-deprived and sore, they can turn on each other and on you like the Irish at an 1863 draft office. If you are going to be stripped naked, stoned, or dismembered, it's going to happen on Day Three. On the last day, they tend to hold their tongues, knowing the trip is winding down, but if there's something that can be construed as a problem, and that problem hasn't evaporated by the end of the second day, it will be addressed on Day Three when their vacation can still be salvaged.

Like a detective called to a crime scene, I walked into the hotel, senses fully engaged, looking for clues as to what might have transpired since last I left my thirty-five. Fortunately, like a medical examiner who had already inspected the body behind the yellow tape, Dina greeted me with her report: her burger at Planet Hollywood was undercooked; her seat at the theater was way off to the side; the play was very good, but a lot of the kids slept "cuz they were just too dang tired"; and Kelly threw her cell phone into a gutter, so there was no way of communicating with her in case I needed something.

Ten-year-old Clint ran up to me, thrilled and surprised to see me: "Hey! You with us again?" Clint was having a hard time grasping that this was my job. He had asked on Day One if I got paid for what I was doing. "Look, Dad. He's back!"

"Hi, Wally," I said.

"I got a question for you," Wally said. "Part one: How did New York become the theater capital? Part two: Why are there tanks of liquid nitrogen on the sidewalks here?"

Grandma Penny stepped up, "We're all here. Let's get to breakfast."

"We're all here?" I asked, looking for someone actually in charge. I saw Kelly sitting on a sofa with the Brandons. She was wearing a Yankees baseball cap with sunglasses and looked like a celebrity traveling incognito, someone who didn't want to be approached.

"Well, *we're* here." Grandma said with a tilt of her head, "Don't know about *them*."

On the other side of the lobby, most of Seattle was slouched on the sofas, leaning into each other with eyes closed. Some of them looked like they had rolled right out of bed, hair unbrushed. The shoppers, though, were showered, makeup applied. I didn't see Pete anywhere, but his second-in-command was suddenly standing beside me. Lu's arms were down to her side, her fists clenched. She was staring straight into my ear. I turned to face her. I was scared that I'd forgotten to do something. (There was a guide earlier in the season who left his group at dinner without giving them their *Lion King* tickets. He was on the subway when they got to the theater and figured it out. They called and called, left multiple messages. He was under the East River blithely skimming *New York Magazine* with four thousand dollars worth of Broadway in his jacket pocket. Imagine his surprise when he resurfaced in Brooklyn to find forty tickets and twenty-three missed calls. Imagine his sleepless night and the glares that met him in the morning. Day Three, by the way. That guide has since disappeared. A garbage dumpster in the West Thirties, that's where I would start looking.)

I ventured a very neutral, "Hey."

"The show was..." Lu began. "AMAZING!" I told her I knew she'd love it. She started waxing rhapsodic about the scenery, the story, the lush orchestration, telling me how many times she cried. Grandma Penny, standing a few yards behind Lu, was holding her left arm up, fist clenched—which seemed to be the gesture of the day—and using the manicured nail of her right index finger to tap on the face of her watch. I was surprised I could hear the sound so far away.

Since when were Southerners so punctual?

When traveling with people from the West Coast.

I asked Lu how close their group was to leaving. She told me they were ready, that Pete would meet us at breakfast.

7:30 BREAKFAST

PETE'S TEMPER HAD DIED down after his tirade on Fiftieth Street. After the students were safe in their rooms, he sat in the bar downstairs, nursed a ginger ale, and flipped through a complimentary tourist magazine. He read the synopses of the other shows currently playing, surprised by how many he had already seen in Seattle. He read an interview with the star of *Light in the Piazza* and wished he could share a drink with her. What he wouldn't give to talk about the play, her character's arc, the leitmotifs he missed owing to his tin ear and distracted attention. This was becoming a chronic condition—yearning to speak with people who were unattainable, be it Broadway star or the deceased.

Afterward, Pete slept well, still immune from his student days to the noise of traffic, so it wasn't until morning, when he was in the lobby counting heads just before I arrived, that he felt his blood pressure rise again. No matter how many times he lectured, how many words and arguments he wasted, nothing was changing. Pete told Lu to take the group without him. He went upstairs for something blue.

Pete clenched his fist and knocked on the door. Melanie opened it. She was dressed but shoeless. There was no apology, just a polite look of bewilderment as if he were room service wielding a tray she hadn't ordered. Pete refused to state the obvious. Exasperated, he was not going to repeat everything he had already repeated. But Melanie didn't move. She stood there waiting for him to say something. To explain why he was there. Was she mentally ill?

He stated the obvious, "Everyone was waiting on you. I sent them to breakfast."

"That's fine. I don't want to eat at McDonald's."

Apoplectic. Pete was beside himself. He was going to require a medical team with a crash cart to get him through the rest of this trip.

"It doesn't matter what you want," he said. "It's on the itinerary. It's what everyone is doing. The group. We are part…of…a…group. This isn't about you or what you want; it's about enjoying the trip as part of a larger body of people. We're eating at McDonald's because it's fast and we need to get down to the ferry. We have an appointment."

"I thought everyone was coming back here before we left."

"Why would you think that?"

"Yesterday some people came back to the hotel after breakfast."

"That's because we were eating across the street and the bathroom there was too small."

"Oh. Well, I'm ready. I just need to get my shoes and camera." Melanie let the door close. It immediately reopened. "Do you want me to meet you there?"

"No, Melanie. I will walk you to breakfast."

"Okay." She let the door close again. He thought that, after more than twenty years of working with teenagers and having two of his own, he would have become some kind of authority, able to serve on some kind of cabinet in an advisory position, but he felt he knew less now than when he started. Maybe teenagers had changed. Today's teens could be members of a genuinely new, radically transformed generation, with their cell phones, cyber-social networks, and Googled research papers. In the olden days, there was a debate about whether or not to allow calculators in the classroom. Teachers wanted students to be able to do the math in their heads. Ha! Now nothing had to be done in their heads. Their brains were being relocated from the cranium to the palm of the hand. That organ transfer had to have some costs.

Or he was just too old and couldn't remember what it was like to be their age.

Melanie opened the door, shoes on her feet, camera around her neck. She gave Pete the double thumbs-up. Through the hallway and down the elevator, Pete attempted to work something out. He told her she needed to connect with someone in the group, to walk with that person, eat with that person, and show up on time with that person. Melanie said she didn't really know anyone. She didn't like the shoppers. Pete felt closer to her in that moment, but he would not be swayed. He told her that her roommate, Tracy, who was also often on her own, was a solid candidate and that was the end of that discussion. He tried to hand her one of the meal tickets for McDonald's, but she declined.

"I can't eat there."

"You need food. There's lots of walking today and you need to keep up." They exited the lobby, turned the corner, and began walking toward Times Square in silence. Halfway down the block, they encountered teams of men stripping a theater of a production recently shuttered. The men were removing pieces of the set and loading them into trucks, and Pete and Melanie simultaneously stopped to watch the activity. From across the street, they peered through the doors and onto the bare Broadway stage. Melanie took a picture.

Behind them, a man sitting against a wall said, "Hey, Blue Hair!" Pete looked over his shoulder at the man. Homeless. Harmless. They had homeless in Seattle. They resumed their walk. "Hey, Blue Hair! I like your look!" Neither acknowledged the compliment. "I got a question for you! Do the carpet match the drapes?" Pete picked up his pace, and Melanie kept up with him. "WHERE YOU RUNNIN', YOU BLUE-HAIRED PUSSY?!" Pete looked down at Melanie. She wore a blank expression. She gazed off in front of her.

To be honest, Pete didn't want to eat at McDonald's either. At the corner, there was a food cart with bagels, doughnuts, glazed pastries, and coffee. A handwritten sign in the window also promised hard-boiled eggs.

"Why don't we grab something from here?" Pete suggested. "My treat."

Melanie didn't say thank you. She just leaned over to study the contents behind the glass, hands on her knees, camera dangling from her neck. She was quiet to begin with, but the silent treatment now could have something to do with his failure to stand up for her. A free breakfast was the least he could offer after having said nothing to the foul-mouthed homeless man. A "pussy"? He called his teenaged companion, who could have been his daughter, a "pussy," and the only thing he did was walk a little faster? Well, he wanted to avoid a scene. He didn't want to make matters worse. When he was at college here in the Seventies, he quickly learned not to provoke anyone. You never knew what they carried, how close they were to the edge. Wasn't the most reasonable strategy to avoid eye contact and walk on?

He was probably wrong. Pete did a lousy job protecting his students, he wanted to explain. There were balloons tied around a tree in West Seattle that testified to that.

8:00 SUBWAY TO BATTERY PARK

BOTH GROUPS WERE WAITING on the sidewalk in front of McDonald's for Grandma Penny and Granddaughter Alice to come back from the "powder room." Lash unwrapped his second disposable camera from its silver foil packaging.

"Good budgeting," I complimented him. "One camera for every two days."

"Yes, sir."

Throughout the previous day, I had noticed Lash taking several pictures of Miss Teen Seattle, positioning himself so that she was always between his camera and whatever New York scene everyone else was photographing. I could imagine the photographs that would be developed at Walmart: *The Dakota and Miss Teen Seattle; The Met and Miss Teen Seattle; Prometheus and Miss Teen Seattle.*

Lash was still shaken from yesterday's misadventure. First, he had been abandoned in H&M, so easily forgotten by his friends and chaperones—both teams thought he was shopping with the other. Second, he had gotten completely turned around in the forest of skyscrapers and still didn't understand how. Third, the man who sold him the Coke tried to steal his money, and he couldn't get it back without the help of a grown-up. And last, he was forced to walk up to the group late. Everyone had stared at him. He could tell some were angry. Then people kept asking what went wrong, and he couldn't find his voice. If he talked, he would cry, so he just nodded or shook his head at their questions, concentrated on the sidewalk, and prayed that everyone would stop staring. He wasn't used to so many eyes. People didn't usually pay him much attention, which was why it was so easy to leave him at that store. "They just up and left!" And then he got lost, and then someone tried to steal his money, and then he was late showing up to the meeting place. A vicious circle, and he couldn't stop thinking about it.

Since then, he had made sure to stay close to an adult—on the way to dinner, *at* dinner, to the theater, *in* the theater, to the photo, *at* the photo, to the hotel, to the elevators, to breakfast and *at* breakfast. He was the first to jump from his seat when the groups were called to leave, and now he was attached to my hip. His reasoning: You couldn't get lost if you were with the guide.

A couple of the Seattle girls were upset, rankled by their teacher who wouldn't let them go to Starbucks, even though he and Melanie were eating food from somewhere else.

"We had to eat at McDonald's!" one of them said.

Then they turned on me, because I was holding a cup from a deli.

"I don't like McDonald's."

—None of us do!

—Why did you bring us here?

"I don't choose these places! I follow the itinerary I'm given."

Wally called their group over to him, and while he counted them, Lash marveled at all the people who did not like McDonald's. At home, he and his siblings were thrilled to go to McDonald's. It was a treat, something to look forward to if you got good grades or it was your birthday. Maybe they didn't like *this* McDonald's. There had to be super nice McDonald's where they were from.

Someone passing by in a suit said to Lash, "Get the fuck out of the way." Lash didn't know where to get to. They were supposed to stand in front of McDonald's. His whole group was there. Why did the man pick on him? Lash always seemed to be standing in the wrong place. The New Yorkers didn't like tourists, and Lash, who was constantly in their way, felt that he was probably the tourist New Yorkers hated most.

On the walk to the subway, Lash did his best to stay "the fuck out of the way." He caught up to me and kept close to my back as the group made its way down below ground, hugging the right side of the staircase as a flood of commuters came up, no one smiling, many of them with wires hanging out of their ears. Once through the turnstiles, the group had to wait for a long time before a train came into the station, so when it did, the cars were too crowded. The next train was almost as bad. Everyone quickly positioned themselves at one of the four doors of the second car. Lash held on to the shirts of two of the Brandons. For dear life. There was no way he was going to be left behind again. The doors slid open, and New Yorkers began spilling among them onto the platform. He hoped the whole train would empty out and he could get a seat, but when the flow appeared to stop, he heard, *GO, GO, GO,* and his team entered the car, pushing in just as one last woman was pushing out. He held tight to the shirts bunched in his fists. As she made her escape, she cursed at him. She probably cursed at them all, but Lash took it personally since her elbow jabbed *his* rib. The doors immediately closed behind him.

This was a different kind of train than yesterday's. Instead of benches that ran along the sides, there were seats aimed in different directions and every seat was full. Most in the car were standing, Lash noticed, including women, even though lots of men were sitting down. The train jolted forward, and Lash lost his footing. He fell into a tall black man with wires in his ears who, without turning his head, just rolled his eyes to stare Lash down. Lash muttered *sorry* and stared at the label sticking out of the top of Brandon's t-shirt. There was nowhere to hang on. He would have to reach through people to grab one of the bars or lean against the door, but he was afraid the door would fly open and he would fall into the dark tunnel. The more he thought about that, the more he wanted to get away from the door. He cringed every time he lost his balance and fell against it. At the next station, the door on the other side opened up, and he had breathing room as people got off. There was air again, but before he could move to seek out a seat, the train filled up and he was back against the door. The Brandons were laughing.

Brandon 1: There must be over a thousand people on this train.
Brandon 3: More. There are like two hundred just in this part.
Brandon 1: Do you know how big the parking lot would have to be to fit all these people if they all had their own cars?
Brandon 2: Some would carpool.
Brandon 3: They're carpooling now. This is a big ol' carpool.
Brandon 2: Did our tour guide get off? When are we supposed to get off?"
Brandon 1: He said it was going to be like ten or twelve stops.
Brandon 2: Are we supposed to count them? How can he tell us all to get off when it's this crowded?

The train was moving again. Lash slid his arm through two Brandons to clutch a bar. His footing didn't feel stable, but if the door behind him opened, he could at least keep from falling out by holding onto that pole. At the next station, the door behind him opened, and he and his friends felt a mass of people press against them in both directions. Lash was standing in the middle of the doorway. A man told him to move and called him an "asshole" for good measure. Lash had been cursed at by three different people within the last thirty minutes. He tried to move to the side, but the Brandons were there, and he was still in the way.

"Get off and step back on!" the man ordered. "Let us off!"

Lash could not, would not, step off this train. *Call me what you want*, he thought. People were shoving now. He lowered his head and charged against them, squeezing through and to the right as the flood of human bodies poured off the car and another wave of humanity splashed back onto it. He was now in the middle, but the newly arrived commuters from two different doorways were pressing in on either side of him. A man with some kind of hand truck was standing between two sets of seats, and Lash found himself crammed into place between him and a couple of the Seattle girls who had somehow, miraculously, been able to sit down. The doors tried to close but kept popping back open. A loudspeaker said something Lash couldn't hope to understand. Why were people still trying to push on? Was this the last train of the day? The man next to Lash pulled his hand truck toward him, and a box knocked against Lash's calf. Lash was forced to make another maneuver, to stake his claim, and hold his ground.

There was some guy with a bicycle trying to get on. *Sonofabee*, Lash almost swore. It was New York doing this to him. Give him one more day, and he'd be telling people to get the fuck out of *his* way. People near the door told the bicycle man to wait for the next train. Someone kicked at the wheel. The train was full. Obviously. You couldn't squeeze one more person on board. Just then, three more people made it.

Before the train started, the man behind him repositioned himself, and his butt pushed into Lash's back and pressed Lash's crotch up against the shoulder blade of one of the seated Seattle girls who didn't budge. She was turned to face her friend, and they were taking the opportunity of solitude—no one else from Seattle was nearby—to gossip about someone in their group.

The train moved; Lash didn't. Lash couldn't. He was perfectly sandwiched between the hand truck man's butt and the shoulder of… of Miss Teen Seattle!

Miss Teen Seattle, the model, his favorite fellow traveler, his former seatmate, the future Miss Washington State.

He was smushed right up against her shoulder blade.

And her shoulder blade was moving up and down.

And the train was vibrating.

And he felt it happen.

He couldn't do anything to stop it.

And the more it happened, the better it felt, so the more it kept happening.

He started praying that she wouldn't notice, but his prayers got lost in the crowds of people underground—there was no prayer reception down here—and soon Dana's head turned to look over her shoulder with an expression of confusion. What was that pressing against her? Her face, startled, disturbed, turned upwards and recognized Lash. She didn't say a word, just slid away in her seat and leaned toward her friend.

Using his feet against the floor and one knee against the side of her back rest, Lash remained where he was, plastered up along the man behind him and keeping a few inches of space between himself and Seattle. He heard her say something, and the other girl looked up at him with disgust. He avoided her eyes. There was nothing Lash could do but continue pressing backwards until his kneecap cracked. He wished he'd never moved to this part of the car. He wanted to be back against the door. He would throw himself against it with all his might and plunge into the dark tunnel on the other side.

9:00 FERRY TO LIBERTY ISLAND

KELLY, WHO SPENT the day before in search of the perfect dress to turn heads in Charleston, now wanted all heads turned away. She was happy for the crowded subway, because she could disappear. None of these commuters knew her boyfriend, none of them cared about Hunter—why should she? She joined them in the present, in the task of getting from one subway station to another. When the group resurfaced at the bottom of Manhattan, she was grateful to be traveling in a pack, because she could conceal herself in the middle of it, and she was probably the only one who welcomed the sight of all the tourists queuing up along the waterfront in Battery Park. She could make it through the day as part of a mob, one of the millions.

But inside the first security tent, the millions were broken up into smaller groups of ten. Each individual was scrutinized, their belongings examined, their bodies inspected. Against her will, she removed her sunglasses, her baseball cap, took off her belt. She felt exposed and fully expected an alarm to sound when she passed through the machine and the security agent to declare loudly enough for all to hear: "HER BOYFRIEND SCREWED ANOTHER WOMAN!" She was surprised when neither of these things happened. She quickly located the plastic bin with her possessions and began to cover up. Sunglasses first to shield her tired eyes.

She had not slept well. At around one thirty, as Ramona lightly snored, Kelly realized exactly who the malicious text-sending slut was: that flirty white trash waitress at McHale's who made it a point to touch Hunter's bicep so often that Kelly finally had to say something. The waitress pleaded innocent but had kept her hands to herself ever since. Until last night. Until Hunter went to McHale's unchaperoned. Was it prearranged? Or did it just happen?

Lying in bed, wondering how easy it had been for the vengeful little whore to seduce Hunter, Kelly caught herself shivering. She got out of bed. She turned off the air conditioner and opened the window, but the noise of the traffic below turned their room into a subway station. She shut the window. She wanted to go for a walk but didn't know how prudent it would be to walk alone this late. There were people down on the sidewalks. But what kind of people? Suitcase thieves, but anything worse? Across Eighth, someone walked into a diner that was open twenty-four hours. She threw on her jeans and a t-shirt and left the room for some cheesecake. Within ten minutes of hatching the idea, she was sitting in a booth with a giant slice in front of her. She let the first bite of cake melt in her mouth, and she looked around the sparsely populated diner. Heidi Hubbard's boyfriend had surprised her with a rose; Hunter had surprised her with something else and turned her into one of those sad, lonely Edward Hopper people who sat in brightly lit restaurants in the middle of the night.

Entering Battery Park's second security tent, packed almost to capacity with people waiting to board the ferry, Kelly wondered if her fellow diner exiles were as fortunate as she was in finding crowds large enough to absorb their concerns. She rejoined her group, off to the side of the entrance ramp. Ramona had taken over Kelly's responsibilities, counting the group and making sure everyone knew to get off at the ferry's first stop. The group dispersed, melting into the crush, and Kelly hid herself inside a grove of tall Eastern Europeans.

She was grateful that Ramona had come on the trip. What would she have done without her? When she had gotten back to the room after her cheesecake, at almost three in the morning, Ramona murmured that Hunter had called.

Kelly asked, "What did you say?"

"I said I didn't know where you were," answered the voice from the pillow. "That was the truth. I also told him not to call here and wake me up again, or I'd castrate him. I'm assuming that's what he deserves. Am I right?" Kelly didn't answer. Ramona told Kelly to get some sleep, and Kelly burrowed beneath the sheets. The air conditioner had been turned back on. Eventually, Kelly did fall off to sleep, but when the phone rang again, her heart jumped and kicked her wide awake.

"You have to answer," she begged Ramona.

Ramona furiously turned over, picked up the phone, and seethed, "I'm gonna pop your balls with a fork!"

But it was only their wake-up call.

The crowd was moving now. Hundreds and hundreds of feet shuffled toward the small door at the far end of the tent. Kelly stared at the back of a tall woman in front of her. On her t-shirt, between the shoulder blades, a bear winked and said the word, *Exactly!* Kelly wondered if she would ever see the front of the woman's t-shirt. What was the set-up? She only knew the punch line. She resigned herself to the fact that everyone in the world was wearing two-sided t-shirts and that she didn't have the time or energy to walk around them all. She followed *Exactly!* out of the tent. The large, three-story ship was rocking on waves from a passing boat, and the gangplank was rising and falling, sliding back and forth along the sloped cement.

A few of the longshoremen were keeping the crowd back, warning them with the kind of New York accent tourists love: "Hold onto da rail, pick yuh feet up." They gave the go-ahead, and one of the men unnecessarily placed his right hand on the small of Kelly's back. To help her aboard. Men. In a futile form of protest, she refused to hold onto the rail. Instead, she held her arms crossed in front of her. This gave the crew member at the top of the ramp, the one counting passengers with his thumb and a clicker, a better view of her cleavage. He smiled at Kelly as she stepped on deck. She rolled her eyes behind her dark sunglasses. She entered the main cabin and started to scope out a seat.

Some of the Seattleites were directly behind her, and one of the girls was complaining about how exhausted she was. Kelly wasn't the only one who didn't get much sleep.

Dennis, the father of the exhausted girl, apologized and said, "But you can always stay with me," he told her. "I gave you a key."

"Daa-AAD."

"I'm just saying, Brittany, if you're so tired, there's an extra bed in my room that would be all yours. You won't have to wrestle for sheets or listen to catty teenage girls."

"But *I'm* a teenage girl!" she reminded him. "I like it! It's tiring, but it's fun."

"Well, make up your mind."

"It is made up! I was just saying I was tired."

"And I was just offering you a solution."

Kelly heard Brittany make a whining grunt—the kind of sound only teenaged girls can properly produce—and then felt her brush by to climb the stairs for a higher deck.

"I could never be a teacher," Dennis said. "I don't know how you deal with them." Kelly realized he was speaking to her. She offered a short laugh so as not to be rude, but Kelly didn't want to talk. She was grateful that all in her group were keeping their distance and giving her space. She didn't think anyone from Seattle would take up the slack. He climbed the stairs with her and followed her to an open stretch of a bench.

"Do you mind if I join you?" he asked but didn't wait for an answer. "I can't wait to get home."

Kelly felt the complete opposite. She wished the trip lasted a month longer. She was all too aware that she would be landing in Savannah the following night. Thirty-six hours and she would have to face Hunter in baggage claim. And what kind of Hunter would be there? Contrite with flowers and a prepared speech or…she didn't want to think of Hunter. She turned to Dennis and noticed the front of his t-shirt.

Kelly asked, "If you're not having fun, why are you hearting NY?"

"This? Because my daughter bought it for me to wear over the shirt I have on." Dennis looked at a pair of Japanese tourists on his right, scratched his shoulder, and then suddenly pulled the top shirt over his head. He was wearing a dinosaur t-shirt from the American Museum of Natural History. He folded his discard and handed it to the Japanese couple, saying, "Welcome to America." They declined at first, but he pressed the shirt into the man's hands and told him it was considered an insult to reject a gift. Dennis turned back to Kelly while the small middle-aged man held up the oversized curtain of cotton. "Unless you want it," he said to Kelly.

"No!" She stopped him before he could turn back around and whip the unsolicited gift out of the bewildered man's hands.

"Why did your daughter want you to cover up your museum shirt?"

"I guess dinosaurs are nerdy now." Dennis told Kelly about the several unforgiveable incidents: his use of the Star Wars baggage tag; his leaving the Metropolitan Museum "without notifying the world in triplicate"; and daring to offer Brittany her own bed in his room.

"Do you have any kids?" he asked.

"Just my students," Kelly said and realized for the first time that the babies she imagined having with Hunter were now mentally miscarried. On the second floor of a boat off Battery Park, their hopeful little faces gasped for air and expired.

"You're lucky. Having children is like…" He shook his head, wiped the corners of his mouth. "Of course, I don't really believe that. I love my daughter." They sat for a few minutes in welcome silence.

The ferry backed away from the dock, and the engines roared to propel it into the bay. Over the intercom came a prerecorded safety announcement intended to sound like the captain speaking. That was followed by a recording of a woman's voice, which provided context for a few geographical highlights of the harbor.

"…originally intended to celebrate the Centennial as well as the friendship between France and the United States. The Statue of Liberty has since become a universal symbol of our nation's freedom, opportunity, security, and future."

"What?!" Dennis abruptly sat up. "Did you hear that? Did you catch that?" The recording did not pause or repeat itself, but Dennis was uninterested in anything else it now had to say. "Did you hear that third word? Security? A universal symbol? This Park Service now claims that the sculpture of a woman holding a tablet and bearing a torch is somehow a symbol of *security*. Security!? I should take a poll."

Kelly thought, not another poll.

Several tourists were listening as Dennis's volume increased: "I should take a poll and see if anyone, ANYONE, here sees the statue as a symbol of *security*. I wonder if anyone would say she represented the *future*." Now he was directly addressing some of the faces turned to him. "What else did they say? Freedom? Well, of course, that's in the name. And opportunity? I'll buy *opportunity*."

Kelly was beginning to understand keenly Brittany's propensity for embarrassment. She pulled down the visor of her cap.

"I'd also say she represents the United States, New York City, the East Coast. Maybe the melting pot. She's *supposed* to stand for immigration, a welcome beacon…but security? Security? How? Where? In the points of her crown? In her torch? That's the National Park Service being…they're being very lazy or they're being sly. Political. Think of all the soldiers shipping out of New York Harbor during the World Wars, who looked at the Statue of Liberty and left for conflict overseas with the conviction that they were risking their lives to protect what she represented, understanding, AS THE PARK SERVICE DOES NOT, that liberty was something to fight FOR, a treasure that needed to be *secured*, and not one that did the *securing*."

A couple people applauded the passion of the argument, but then he added, "This is George W. Bush bullshit!"

"Please!" a stocky older woman said. "There are kids on this boat."

A college athlete wearing an SMU shirt said to her, "Liberals don't care about kids."

"Oh, a frat boy from Texas who's a Bushie!" Dennis exclaimed. "What a surprise! Where's Tom, Jerry, and all the other cartoons?"

"What's wrong with you, dude?"

Kelly's hat was now pulled down as far as it could go. She wanted to distance herself from Dennis, but she felt someone needed to hold him back. Was Dennis a fighter? Was he trying to provoke this broad-shouldered jock? The Texan's girlfriend was holding onto his arm and whispering something into his ear. Kelly did the same with Dennis, but there was still tension in the air. Suddenly, dozens of people stood up simultaneously and rushed to the starboard side of the cabin. The boat was approaching the Statue of Liberty. Kelly took advantage of the distraction and pulled Dennis toward the rear of the boat. He muttered invective under his breath. Outside, they stepped to the empty side of the middle deck and saw a motorized Coast Guard raft equipped with machine guns skipping the waves alongside the ferry.

"They've come to get me," Dennis said. "The National Park Service heard me, and they've come to put me down." Several Seattle students hurried down the stairs, looking behind them, rushing from something. Brittany was one of them, but she nearly froze when she saw her father no longer wearing the shirt she bought for him. Her eyes widened so dramatically that even Kelly had to wonder what was so wrong with dinosaurs.

Dennis called out, "Hello, Daughter!" He gestured to the ferry and asked, "How are you liking your voyage aboard the *Starship Enterprise*?" The high schoolers kept moving. After they disappeared down the second flight of stairs, Dennis looked back at the Manhattan skyline shrinking in the wake of the ferry and said to Kelly, "I would wear whatever she wanted me to wear if she sat with me for one meal."

9:20 THE STATUE OF LIBERTY

TRACY WAS ONE of the several hundred who added her weight to the starboard side of the boat as it got closer to Liberty Island. Nearly on its side, the ferry glided by the front of the Statue, and Tracy and the several hundred took the exact same photograph. But this one was hers. When Tracy returned home, she was going to sit down at the table with her grandmother and sister and go through every picture she took. She did worry that, somewhere in this chronology, by the portfolio of Day Three, her grandmother and sister would ask where her friends were. "Why aren't there any pictures of you *with* anybody?" She could fake it. She could tell them that those pictures were taken with another camera. "Isn't it funny that none of the group pictures were taken on mine? Well, so-and-so had a better camera, and I'll have to get copies when I see her next." But her grandmother would see through that.

Tracy thought this was the perfect opportunity to ask a few of her new friends to pose for one group photo with the Statue, but when she turned, none of her friends were there. Not Brittany or the shoppers or Dana or Cody, who complimented her on her outfit the night before. Tracy really wanted a picture of herself with him. If she could show her grandmother and sister that image—*Oh, that's just Cody*—she wouldn't need to say anything else.

But they had all vanished. She moved away from the railing through the hordes of picture takers. She saw several Georgians. She saw her teacher and Cody's stepmom talking, but none of the others in her group. She walked toward the front of the upper deck and came across Ms. Takahashi and her student council, who were spread out on benches vacated by Liberty's paparazzi.

—Hey, Lu?

—Whatchagot?

—Do they have security at the Metropolitan Museum?

—Of course.

—Then how did they let a pretty piece of art like you get outside?

They were all impressed with that one. That line could even be used on a real quarry. When the laughing died down, Tracy asked if they had seen Cody and the girls. They shook their heads, but one of them mentioned seeing a souvenir shop on the bottom deck. That made sense, so she went below but found no trace of them anywhere.

The boat slowed and sidled up to the dock on Liberty Island. Ropes were thrown to men leaning over the water; the nooses were flung over wooden pylons partially shredded by thousands of such stops every year. The masses descended from the decks above, and the capacity on the lowest deck was called into question. The gangplank was thrust out of the side of the ship by men running alongside it, and with a loud bang, it hit the dock, crashed the serenity of the island like a battering ram. *The tourists are coming, the tourists are coming.* The invasion force spilled out of its transport craft.

I met my troops at the end of the dock and gathered them along the asphalt walk that would lead them to the front of the statue. People were surprised. They always expect her to be so much larger. On television and movies, she appears taller than the skyscrapers. The cameras next to her face give the impression that the distant office towers would barely reach her hip. Some have even planned on reading the paper and enjoying a cup of coffee in the non-existent restaurant in her head.

"She is, though, one of the largest women in the world," I told them. "From heel to crown, she is a hundred eleven feet and one inch tall; her right arm is forty-two feet long…"

Tracy, faithful Tracy, nose-squealing, Gatsby-reading, tell-me-more Tracy, stopped listening in the middle of the measurements, before I discussed the symbolism of *Liberty Enlightening the World*, long before I reached my rousing finale about Emma Lazarus, immigration, the American Dream, the huddled masses, tired and poor. She was positioning herself near Cody who was flanked by two shoppers and a model. By this time, Tracy suspected that they had deliberately abandoned her on the top deck. Cody wouldn't have done that on his own, Tracy thought, at least not consciously. He was so nice when those girls weren't around. He had walked right up to her the previous evening and told her how great she looked. "That's a nice outfit." But all morning, he seemed to be avoiding her. He must have been pressured. But she was going to stay with the entourage this time. She had a plan. She was going to tell them that their teacher wanted it that way. They wouldn't doubt it; they believed he was out to get them. And they wouldn't object, out of fear he would turn and scream at them again.

When the tour ended and the time and meeting place announced, the six of them took off at a literal sprint. That was unforeseen. Tracy couldn't run that fast, but she hunched her shoulders and bent her knees to try before Pete called her name. He wanted Tracy and Melanie to stay together. He asked Melanie if she understood the rules, and Melanie nodded. He asked Tracy if she could promise to bring her back on time. Tracy said, yes, she would, but she didn't divulge what was really on her mind: that by chaining her to her blue-haired, anti-social, ever-late roommate, her teacher was effectively murdering the chances for social mobility she felt open to her ever since Cody's compliment.

Everyone else dispersed, but Melanie didn't move. Melanie stood her ground and aimed her camera toward the statue. From where they were, the trees were blocking most of Lady Liberty. The only parts visible were her forearm, hand and torch.

Tracy said, "There are better pictures around the front."

Melanie checked her results on the screen. "These are good shots."

"But you can see the *whole* statue if…"

"I'd really like to get a few shots of her feet, but where would you stand to get that?" Tracy didn't answer, because Melanie was talking to herself. Melanie started walking; Tracy followed. Tracy wondered how she was going to coordinate this visit. Melanie wasn't going to obey her. Melanie wouldn't do any of the things Tracy wanted.

Tracy said, "I was hoping we could get to the gift shop before we meet back."

"I need to take some pictures."

"Oh, no, I know. Me too. But after, I thought, maybe we could stop in the gift shop…"

"Do we have time?" Melanie asked as she squatted along a short wall and aimed her camera over the lawn. Tracy wanted to say that it depended on the amount of time they spent taking pictures of grass. Melanie stood back up, and they resumed walking. The trees were soon behind them, and the torch rose twenty-two stories above them.

People from all around the world were taking pictures of the statue and of each other with the statue.

Melanie hopped up onto the lawn and strode to the wall of the base that held up the pedestal that showcased the statue. Tracy watched and waited. She expected Melanie to take a perfectly vertical photo to capture the hem of the robe or even the statue's nostrils and was surprised—and then again, not so surprised—when Melanie started taking pictures of the blocks of stone directly in front of her. The blocks at the very base, below the statue, below the pedestal! Tracy checked her watch. This was a nightmare. She stepped up onto the lawn and walked to Melanie.

"Do you want me to take a picture of you?" Tracy offered.

"No, thanks." Tracy leaned against the wall and then suddenly jumped away when she remembered that the Statue of Liberty was a piece of art. She was yelled at by several guards at the museum yesterday for getting too close to the paintings, and an alarm actually rang when she touched a frame. She didn't think the frame counted, she explained, but the guard said that it was all part of the art. Then he lectured her on the philosophical question of where art stopped—at the piece itself, at the frame, at the eye of the spectator? He was a very eloquent guard. Today he would probably claim that the base and the pedestal were as much a part of the statue as the finger or the crown. Then Tracy reminded herself that people were walking on top of the pedestal and that there was even a staircase inside to take people all the way to the crown. Tracy wouldn't get in trouble for leaning against the stone of the wall at the very bottom!

Melanie suddenly asked, "Do you want me to take a picture of you?"

"Yes! Yes!" Tracy sputtered. "Thank you!" Tracy walked in circles looking for the ideal spot. She wanted to recreate the image of John Lennon, taken somewhere around here. She was grateful that she would have another picture of herself to show her grandmother and sister. While no one else would be in the shot, they would infer that someone else had taken it, and if they asked, Tracy could always answer, "Oh, let me see if I can remember. That might have been Cody or Dana…or, no, I think that one was taken by Melanie."

THE STUDENTS FROM GEORGIA were currently divided among other chaperones, so Ramona was at last free, after the packed subway and ferry rides, to sit blissfully by herself on a bench at the edge of Liberty Island. It was a beautiful day. A storm was coming later in the afternoon, but for now the sky was cloudless and blue. There was a breeze off the water. There was very little humidity.

She admired the skyline of Manhattan in the distance. The city was pretty from across the harbor. From the outside, the buildings were gleaming sculptures. From here, it was not a city full of closed doors and secret meetings, of back room deals and duplicity, aliases and alibis, false compliments, hidden agendas, whispers and scams. New York was best seen from a distance. There was a reason so many of the city's postcards were of its skyline.

"Well, *there* you are!" her vice principal's voice sounded behind her, and an anguished scream immediately sounded within. Ramona glanced over to Governor's Island, a few hundred yards away, and thought of swimming for it. "What are you doing over here?" Nancy asked and, without invitation, sat down on Ramona's bench, like bosses do, convinced they're honoring their underlings with their presence.

"Just thinking."

"Penny for your thoughts."

A penny. It was a relief to hear Nancy admit how little she valued her ideas, and Ramona held out her hand for the coin. Nancy looked confused, almost slapped Ramona's palm—almost "gave her five"—but then she understood the context.

"Oh, Ramona," Nancy laughed. "So what were you thinking about?"

"The Statue of Liberty," she replied. Then she mischievously added, "There's a story that the first draft was an African slave stepping out of bondage. Did you know that?" Ramona could feel Nancy tense up. "It's true. A freed slave was the original symbol. But then, as you can imagine, it was the nineteenth century, and the idea of a giant black woman standing above an American city…"

"Yes."

"There would have been historical resonances, though. One last sea voyage of an African slave. Cut up in France and shipped in boxes across the ocean to America. Alas, not to be."

"Mm, terrible," Nancy murmured. "How are your feet? Mine are sore." Ramona knew Nancy tracked her down to talk about something other than her feet, because if her feet were sore, she wouldn't traipse all over the island to complain about them. "It's like I've lost all cushion on the soles of my feet. Over the years. Where did it go?"

Feigning sympathy, Ramona shook her head and hummed a descending mm-mm-mm.

"How is Kelly?" Nancy asked.

"I think she was getting some coffee."

"Not *where*, I mean *how* is she?"

Ramona knew what Nancy asked, but she wasn't going to make it easy. "She's fine."

"She seems very unlike herself. I never saw her go this long without smiling."

"Well, it's hard to smile so much every day."

"And I heard she threw her phone in the trash?"

"A sewer," Ramona corrected her but added nothing.

"In the sewer? Why on earth?"

"I have no idea."

"You don't? Weren't you there?"

"I was right next to her."

"So why do you think she threw her phone?"

"I guess she didn't want it anymore."

"And you didn't ask her? Honestly? Back in your room? What did you talk about?"

"Nothing." Kelly had not been talkative. After making sure there were no deaths in the family, Ramona assumed her silence was Hunter-related. This was confirmed when Kelly declined to model the mythically-important black dress and, of course, when Hunter called their room in the middle of the night. "We were tired," she said to Nancy. "We went to sleep."

"If you don't want to tell me, I respect that. I'm just concerned for the children."

"I think they're having a wonderful time."

"Oh, absolutely. I think they're behaving wonderfully too. Much better than the high school group. With that child who is always late. The teacher is ineffectual, has no control whatsoever over her or over those rude girls who just want to shop, shop, shop. There's a name for them—*fashionazis*."

"*Fashionistas*."

"Mm. I don't think that's it."

"It is," Ramona said.

"There you go again," Nancy laughed impatiently. "Disagreeing with me just for the sake of it."

"I'm disagreeing with you because you used the wrong word."

Nancy pushed on, "That other teacher of theirs, the young one, well, she just wants to be buddy-buddy with her students. No professional boundaries whatsoever."

"She's very nice," Ramona said.

"Oh, absolutely. But, bless her heart, she has some issues, doesn't she? Have you ever seen an overweight Japanese person?" Nancy laughed. Was she thinking she and Ramona would bond over this? "Such a thing doesn't exist in Japan. It's their diet. High protein, lots of fish. They eat very sensibly in Japan. They're all a size zero."

"Except for the sumo wrestlers," Ramona said.

"I forgot about them." Nancy went mute, forced to reevaluate her entire theory. Then she was back: "And that man? That father who came to our table to ask about evolution? Can you believe such a thing?"

"Evolution or the man who asked about it?"

"Exactly," Nancy laughed. "And what on earth did he mean about slavery and the Civil War?" Here it was, Ramona thought. "Wasn't that peculiar?" Ramona felt Nancy scrutinizing her face for any tic. Ramona nodded. It was extremely peculiar, and Ramona still had no explanation. Ramona had been able to broach that subject with Kelly while in line for the restroom at the theater, but Kelly said she was as baffled as Ramona was. Kelly claimed not to have spoken to the Seattle dad at all. But this morning on the ferry, there they were, sitting close together and engaged in a passionate discussion. It *could* have been their first conversation, but they appeared closer than they should have been. Ramona tried to remember if the two of them had crossed paths on Day One. She was convinced they had to have talked. Kelly *must* have somehow told him about Nancy. How else would he have been able to quote her?

A long silence followed; Nancy had to break it: "Because we talked about that, didn't we? The Civil War? You and I? In my office?"

"I vaguely recall," she said. "We talked a lot about cupcakes for some reason."

"Did you talk with him about our conversation?"

"Nancy, I don't know that man. We have never spoken."

"Because I'd hate our conversation to be taken out of context. It wasn't an especially successful conversation *in* context, but *out* of context…well, no one could understand that."

"No, they couldn't."

"It doesn't make any sense. Obviously, you and Kelly talked about it. That's fine. I get that. It's natural for fellow teachers to complain about their boss, even though that boss has never meant any harm and she's just doing the best job…"

Ramona thought this would the perfect opportunity, as Nancy moisturized with self-pity, to bring up what Faith had shared with her at the museum: *You called Faith into your office and told her not to date Brandon Ellerbe because of the color of his skin.*

Call her out. Tell it like it is. Put her on the defensive.

Instead, Ramona took another tack: "Though I do agree with him on that issue."

"What issue?" Nancy asked.

"That slavery was a major component of the Civil War."

"Oh, well, well, we don't need to get into all that again. And I think it's time to start moving back toward the boat."

BRANDON 3: What'd you get?

BRANDON 1: This is that coin that shows you how skinny the copper is in the Statue of Liberty.

BRANDON 3: That's all?

BRANDON 1: It's all I wanted.

BRANDON 3: No, I mean that's all the copper? It's mad skinny.

BRANDON 1: That's the point of it. What'd you get?

BRANDON 3: I got a souvenir cup that came with the drink, two t-shirts, and a keychain. What'd you get, Lash?

LASH: I got some brochures from that building over there.

BRANDON 3: That's not the gift shop.

LASH: It's the ranger center. I know.

BRANDON 3: Are you gonna give your family a brochure?

LASH: Well, I was gonna get some postcards too.

BRANDON 1: Well, you better hurry up.

BRANDON 3: Where's Brandon?

LASH: The postcards are cheaper back near the hotel.

BRANDON 1: There he is! Look at him.

BRANDON 3: That's like four bags.

BRANDON 2: I just spent over two hundred dollars.

BRANDON 3: What'd you get?

BRANDON 2: Statue of Liberties.

BRANDON 3: The foot-high ones?

BRANDON 2: Yep.

BRANDON 3: What else?

BRANDON 2: That's it.

BRANDON 3: How many you buy?

BRANDON 2: Twelve.

BRANDON 1: Dang. For who?

BRANDON 2: I got one for my mom, for my dad, for my two sisters, for my brother, for my grandparents, for my aunt, for my uncle, for my cousins.

BRANDON 3: You got everybody the same thing?

BRANDON 2: Everybody loves the Statue of Liberty.

BRANDON 3: But you got like seven for people who live in the same house with you.

BRANDON 2: So?

BRANDON 1: A family only needs so many Statue of Liberties.

BRANDON 2: Well, they're not gonna put 'em all on one shelf, dummy. My mom will put hers on her dresser, my dad will put his on his desk, my sisters will put theirs in their…

BRANDON 1: Did you get one for your grandparents or one for each grandparent?

BRANDON 2: Everybody should have their own Statue of Liberty! Stop laughin'. Man, shut up, y'all don't know what you're talkin' about.

10:50 FERRY TO ELLIS ISLAND

NO ONE WAS LATE. We gathered, we counted, we boarded the next boat, and when we did, we instantly broke apart as if we had tickets for different seats throughout a multi-level opera house. I sought out fellow tour guides. This was where we usually ran into each other, compared groups by sharing stories and the most egregious comments. I had a few winning lines from my group but found no familiar face. My itinerary was out of sync with the rest of the industry today. I felt like the only loser having a Statue Day.

On the upper deck, the balcony of the floating opera house, I found Lu and her student council. They had taken over two benches and were playing some kind of improv theater game that involved blinking and double consonants. I didn't grasp it. I saw Dina the Disappointed sitting nearby, looking off the side of the boat and flexing her upper lip into a sneer. These were her daily exercises, fifty reps on the right side and fifty on the left. She wanted her disapproval registered from every direction. Her mouth, though, really did favor the right side. She needed to start smoking with her left hand. Her daughter, Pamela, sat a row away with Faith, who hated her name, and Ashley, the Bible Bee. From the look of things, they were either discussing the books of the Old Testament or wondering how New York got the cheese *inside* the pretzel. I didn't approach.

On the mezzanine level of the boat, near the back staircase, I ran into Grandma Penny and her son. They both waved me over. Travis had taken off the ironworker hat and replaced it with a green, seven-pointed foam Liberty crown. Penny had one too, but she was wearing it wrong. Instead of putting the foam ring over her head like the crown it was, she had pushed her face through it so that she looked like a demented seven-year-old dressed like a flower for a school pageant. They were both exuberant. They asked me to take their picture with the statue behind them—Penny kept the hat on exactly the way it was—and then they asked someone standing nearby to take a picture of the three of us. They pulled me into the middle, and we all threw our arms around the closest set of shoulders.

How many of these had I taken? I was in photo albums around the world.

Afterward, Travis told me where they went on the island, but it was hard to make out most of his words. His accent was thick, and I couldn't tell if his words were coming out too quickly or too slowly. Were my ears ahead or behind the story? Was he adding syllables or swallowing them? Were the four he had just uttered one word or three?

I told them I was glad they were having a good time and returned to the orchestra level of the boat where several of the Seattle girls were quibbling near the bathroom. I kept moving. It was Day Three, after all, and this was the day the girls would argue. BFFs would clash; they would lose their top friend status. Pete was scolding Melanie, but I didn't know why since she had been on time back at Liberty. Maybe he just couldn't break the habit. I kept moving. Dennis was talking heatedly with a few college kids from Texas. I kept moving. Cody the Quarterback was blaming Barbara for something. She asked what he wanted her to do. I kept moving.

Zach, the prodigy from Georgia, appeared and greeted me with a Shakespeare quote: "A traveler! By my faith, you have great reason to be sad: I fear you have sold your own lands to see other men's; then, to have seen much and to have nothing, is to have rich eyes and poor hands." It was as though the boy carried a quotation book in his pocket.

I countered with stage directions: "Enter Lear, Cordelia in his arms. Exit, pursued by a bear."

"A bear chases King Lear?"

"Sorry, no. I jumped around. The second one was *Winter's Tale*."

"Do you know where mine is from?"

"*As You Like It*."

Zach nodded and extended his arm. In the middle of his palm was one of the several Starbursts he'd won. He was rewarding me now. Before I could thank him, a familiar ten-year-old appeared to snatch the Starburst. Zach clenched his fist. There was a protocol, after all. You had to earn the candy, you couldn't simply grab it. Clint asked for a question. I asked him to give me one measurement of the Statue of Liberty.

"Her eye is three feet."

"Nope. That's her mouth."

"Her nose is four feet."

"Four-and-a-half."

"Okay the eye is eight feet."

"Whoa!" I cried out. "With a three-foot mouth? Maybe if *Picasso* sculpted her."

"Well, something's eight feet long," Clint pinched his lower lip. "Her finger!"

Before I could even tell him he was right, Zach passed Clint his Starburst.

The boat hit the dock at Ellis Island a little harder than usual.

Senior citizens lost their balance; a number of them fell into the water and drowned. Just kidding. But I needed something like that to wake me up as I positioned myself near the front door. This was my twenty-fifth trip to the island since the beginning of March, and I had four more to go until the season ended. Several of my New York friends had never been out on these boats at all—too touristy—but I had been here well over five hundred times. I could boast to my friends that while they were sitting in their stuffy offices on a day like today, I was strolling beneath a row of trees in the middle of the harbor. But I would have to admit I was also here during freezing rains and heat advisories.

I took a lozenge from my non-Starburst pocket, unwrapped it, and popped it into my mouth. Five minutes till show time. Once the gangplank was secured, I led the refugees from Battery Park down the ramp to shore.

11:10 ELLIS ISLAND

ONE HUNDRED YEARS AGO, when you arrived here at Ellis Island after crossing the ocean in steerage, and after taking a packed ferry here to this facility, when you were tired, maybe even sick, you presented yourself as best you could.

Seven years ago, when you arrived here at Ellis Island, after meeting the coaches on the south side of the Waldorf Astoria, and after taking an early evening cruise aboard a ferry hired exclusively for the Lexus dealers, when you were rested, maybe even slightly buzzed, you presented yourself the best you could. You wore a red Donna Karan dress with a beaded clutch and diamonds around the neck, the wrist, and a new one on the finger. Christopher wore a tuxedo. This was the gala evening.

You didn't even notice the six-second specialists…

There were no six-second specialists…

But you did remember the people who confronted you next. Men, with fingers dipped in solution or holding metal button hooks, would turn your eyelids inside out looking for a highly contagious disease called trachoma…

You were confronted by waiters in their own tuxedos bearing silver trays with glasses of white wine, champagne, and sparkling water. Always silver trays with glasses of wine, champagne, and sparkling water. By the gala, Barbara expected the trays upon her arrival anywhere in the city. She expected to hand her theater ticket to an usher who would hand her a glass of Chardonnay. She expected to find a waiter standing inside their room at the end of the evening with cold champagne bubbling furiously, a freshly poured froth.

During many years you weren't allowed into the country without a sponsor if you were a single woman…

You wouldn't have been allowed into the party either. Each woman entering the building held an arm of a car dealer. Were there any women dealers that year? None that she could remember. The men had won the trip, the women were now earning theirs—they dressed up to flatter their companions and make the other men jealous.

…so they sent her back to the United States where her fiancé waited, but this time there came a piece of paper: "Death in steerage: Christina Jansen."

Death? No death. Delicious hors d'oeuvres were passed, some were easy to pick up and eat, which she did, and some were difficult to handle, which she avoided. There were three other couples with whom she and Christopher always socialized during the outings. They had so much in common, except that the three couples had kids and she and Christopher were still planning the wedding. She and Christopher were then, on occasion, still discussing the idea of raising a family or the idea not to. He wanted the life they were leading with the travel and the parties. She reminded him that these other couples were enjoying the same life—they were on this trip, they were drinking wine and sharing toasts, *and* they were going home to a family. He argued that these couples hadn't just come back from Maui or spent Thanksgiving in Mexico.

Cocktail tables were arranged throughout the room and draped with long navy blue cloths and votive candles. Empty glasses or crumpled napkins with shrimp tails or wooden skewers disappeared as soon as they were discarded, snatched by waiters floating by like ghosts of immigrants past. There was a speech, and then there was movement toward a staircase that brought them up in three quarter-turns to the vast theatrically-lit dining room, better known as the Registry Room. The Lexus logo was projected onto the tile ceiling amid stars. On the floor were twenty tables with more blue cloth, votive candles, flowers, multiple glasses, and pre-set salads. The waiters stood holding bottles of wine in white service napkins. As soon as Barbara and Christopher sat at their table, Christopher gave their waiter a preemptive tip to keep his fiancée's water filled all night long. From certain angles, the skyline of Manhattan could be made out through the windows. Perfume, wine, steak. Silverware, laughter, conversation.

…as you walk, realize that so much was being seen or heard or experienced for the very first time—new skin color, new languages, Jell-O, chewing gum, and flush toilets. Put yourself in their shoes; try to imagine what it was like. Okay, 11:40 on the front steps outside.

11:40? After dancing and dessert? So disorienting. No. Still the morning. Seven years later. Today the room was bright, filled with field school groups. Teenagers ran along the balcony above the floor, younger children screamed to hear their voices echo. Everyone was standing, regrouping, preparing to break off. Her stepson was standing beside her.

"Guess who's still following me?" he asked. "Like a puppy?"

"Cody," Barbara groaned, "let it go."

"I knew what I was talking about. I knew that as soon as I complimented her, she'd be all over me." Barbara looked over towards Cody's posse. They were deliberately standing in a tight circle. Tracy stood behind, waiting to be noticed.

"Well, it was the right thing to do."

"For you to do. Not me. Because now someone's going to say something that's going to hurt her feelings more than if we ignored her last night."

"Don't you dare."

"Not me. Jenny or Laurie. Maybe Ryan."

"Then bring Jenny, Laurie, and Ryan over. I'll talk to them."

Cody took a moment and then said, "All right." He walked over to his little gang. Barbara looked up at the large American flags that hung over the floor from the balconies. The flags were there that night seven years ago. Lit by invisible lamps. Set to fluttering by the smallest movement of waiters serving, of guests dancing. Barbara felt someone at her arm.

It was Tracy. "You wanted gum?" Barbara looked past Tracy and saw the heads of her stepson and his cohorts disappearing down the Staircase of Separation.

"Yes, please. My mouth is dry."

Tracy held out two packs of Hubba Bubba, "Watermelon or Seriously Strawberry?"

Chardonnay or champagne?

"Um. Watermelon please."

Tracy handed Barbara a wrapped cube of watermelon and said, "I had no idea that chewing gum was invented in Brooklyn!"

"It was?"

"Jack just said so." Barbara was still holding the wrapped gum. Tracy looked like she was waiting for Barbara to open it. "You might want two."

"Oh. No, I won't," Barbara said. She unwrapped the gum and brought it to her mouth. Barbara hated chewing gum. It gave her ear aches. And Cody knew that! And he also knew she would be obliged to take the gum. She began to press it flat with her tongue as Tracy watched. Tracy looked so happy to be making this connection. Barbara could see in her eyes that Tracy thought the two of them would be great friends, that they would get along better than most girlfriends and mothers-in-law. "Mmm, perfect. Tank oo."

"Glad to help," Tracy replied and finally turned. "Where'd they go?" Just then, Pete waved to Tracy and pointed to Melanie. "Darn it."

Barbara took off in the opposite direction. She held the gum, its artificial watermelon flavoring intensifying with the increased saliva flooding her mouth. She held her tongue at the back of her mouth, protecting her throat, keeping the juice from choking her. The taste of her stepson's chicanery. She crossed the vast floor where she once ate a catered meal and found a garbage can where she bent over and blew. She spat six times and then laughed to herself. This was her life now.

For the next twenty minutes, she wandered through some of the exhibit halls that flanked the main room. She and Christopher had walked through a couple of these exhibits before dessert, and she recognized a statue of a woman, her right hand holding a suitcase, her left hand holding her hat to her head. She and Christopher had stood in front of her and tried to figure out who she was supposed to be. Today, Barbara saw a sign mounted at the base. Had that always been there? Couldn't she and Christopher have read that? Why would they have made such a fuss over not knowing who this woman was? Because, by the gala, the two of them were used to having everything done for them. Let me take your shrimp tail, let me refill your glass, let me tell you about this sculpture.

Downstairs, Barbara found herself in the gift shop, surrounded by t-shirts, books, miniature flags, and souvenirs from the various homelands that had sent their huddled masses yearning to breathe free. She saw Lash, the boy she had rescued yesterday, standing at a computer with the same flustered expression he had worn on Park Avenue. An employee, a twenty-something, had her arms crossed in front of her.

She asked, "Are you gonna buy it?" Lash mumbled, and she said, "Can't HEAR YOU."

Barbara put her hand on Lash's shoulder and asked if he were having a problem. This was a computer with a database of surnames. Here, you could find out what your name meant, where it came from, and a reference to the immigrant who first brought that name to the United States. The information, printed up on cardstock, made for a nice personalized souvenir from Ellis Island.

The cashier explained, "A lot of people come up in here just to see what their name means and then walk away, and paying customers don't get a chance cuz the line's so long."

Barbara said, "But there is no line." Then she added, inexplicably, "And my son is very interested in seeing whether or not this will make a good Father's Day gift."

"All right. What's your last name?" she asked Barbara.

Barbara didn't know Lash's last name. She didn't know the last name of the boy she just claimed was her son. Her son with the strong southern accent. She squeezed Lash's shoulder, and he gave it. Then he had to spell it. D-A-U-T-E-N-H-A-H-N. The computer searched, and the name's entry popped up on the screen.

Dead rooster. That's what his name meant.

Lash thought it was interesting, Barbara thought it was weird, and the girl at the computer said, "I'll print it up, twenty dollars."

"He's still reading."

"I thought you said he wanted it as a gift?"

"I said he was interested in seeing whether it would make a good gift."

Lash said, "I like it."

"Great." The girl started to process the order.

"But," Lash mumbled. Barbara could tell he thought the price was too high. For a piece of paper. There was probably a way to print something similar from a home computer. She wondered if he had a home computer. Didn't everyone? "But I don't have that much. Thank you, ma'am." Hands in his pockets, he nodded, slouched, and walked away.

The cashier looked at Barbara, "Then you'll be buying it?"

"Why?"

"For your son."

"He's not my son," she said, ashamed. And ashamed she was ashamed, because she felt her impulse to put distance between herself and Lash was no different from the one that sent Cody hurrying down a staircase from Tracy.

"I SAW WHAT YOU did," Wally said through a mouthful of the peanut butter fudge he had just bought with Clint at a stand near the gift shop. Comfort food, fudge. He didn't know if there was any Ellis Island significance. "You're takin' care of Lash like his own mama."

Barbara looked frazzled and embarrassed. "A maternal instinct, I guess."

Clint swallowed his fudge and said, "Show her the mother in that picture."

"Son, you can't just swallow whole chunks of fudge."

"Show her the picture." Clint pulled at Barbara's arm. They led her out of the store, past the food counter, and into the dining room. One of the walls was papered with vintage Ellis Island photos, and Wally pointed to a photo near the ceiling.

"See that family there?" There were two parents and a young boy with their backs to the camera, gazing at the Statue of Liberty in the distance. "That family there got broken up. The mother was sent back to Europe."

Clint added, "They didn't let her in, they didn't let her in. Do you know why?"

Barbara said, "I don't have any idea." Wally let her stare at the picture a little longer. Clint was giggling. Barbara slowly shook her head. She wasn't looking at the picture closely enough. The picture was part of the wall, and so was an electrical outlet, a silver plate positioned in the middle of the mother's right shoulder blade.

"You tell her, Clint."

Clint shouted, "She couldn't get through the metal detector!"

"Metal detect…?" Barbara stopped herself when she got the joke.

Wally said, "They weren't gonna let people through who had metal rectangles stuck on their backs."

She laughed, "Obviously."

Clint said, "We're fixin' to find Jack and see if he can get it."

Barbara said, "I bet he won't."

Wally was beaming, relishing a post-joke high. Barbara headed off to use the restroom, and he and Clint walked outside to take a scenic route back to the meeting spot on the front steps. Ellis Island had redeemed itself. He had his son cracking up—Clint wasn't scrunching his eyebrows at him as he did whenever Wally was stumped by one of the trivia questions or as he did during their fake citizenship test. In a wall in one of the rooms upstairs, there was a bank of computers with a sample civics quiz, the kind that new immigrants needed to take to become Americans. *They have to pass a test that most Americans can't pass.* Clint grabbed a computer, and Mr. Straight-A Zach stood in front of the next one down. The test was hard. Wally and Clint got the one about the first president right off the bat, but questions about the Legislative Branch and how many states had to ratify, blah blah blah, were almost impossible. The multiple-choice format made it only slightly easier. Clint asked his dad for one of the first answers, and Wally winced when "Incorrect" popped up onto the screen. When the computer supplied the right answer, Wally said that that was the one he almost went with. Zach said he was four-for-four, and Wally, standing above and behind his ten-year-old, actually began sneaking peeks at Zach's monitor. He was cheating off an eighth grader. What would he say if his vice principal caught him? Thanks to Zach, Wally and Clint answered the rest of the questions correctly. Clint told him that only three wrong wasn't so bad, and Wally heard a strain of pity.

Then, downstairs, he read the map wrong and accidentally walked them into the cafeteria instead of the gift shop. Before they turned themselves around, Wally saw the picture of the family and instantly came up with his joke. *Because she couldn't get through the metal detector.* That's what he was good with. Fake knowledge. Jokes.

What did it matter if he couldn't follow much of the tour or find his way around a city where he didn't live? Tomorrow they would be flying home, and he might never get up to this part of the country again, so what difference did it make that he still wasn't sure if Broadway ran north-south or east-west? Did anyone fully comprehend New York? It was too big! Did anyone even comprehend Manhattan with all the tall skyscrapers, which he had "come to find out" was not even all of New York. There were five parts of the city. Where they all were, he had no idea. What he thought might be Brooklyn turned out to be Jersey City.

Now, outside, he located Manhattan. How many of the buildings in there were truly famous? How many of the buildings could an *average* New Yorker—not a tour guide, not a taxi driver, just a regular guy—point out and name? Which was the Empire State Building? There were about four that he could see that looked like it. And when did they start putting up these skyscrapers anyway? What did Manhattan look like when the Dutch came? And were they the Dutch, or did he hear wrong? The Danish? No, the Dutch. Well, how did the Dutch take over all of this from the Indians? Were they just really strong guys like the Vikings? Were the Dutch Vikings? Did they storm their way into the harbor and then rape and pillage? He recalled something about a concept of tolerance, so maybe not. There was that purchase of twenty-four dollars, but he thought he heard something about that being a myth. So as best as he could figure it, they bought off some of the Indians, had war with others, and then started dumping landfill into the water to make the city bigger. If you could just keep adding land whenever you wanted to, then the need for Central Park didn't seem so urgent. There were a few bits about Central Park yesterday that still confused Wally, but the one place that really struck him dumb, made him feel like a fool, was the Metropolitan Museum—not the Egyptian section or the rooms with the armor and weaponry, but the modern art that just seemed like someone had gone into a dumpster behind an asylum and framed what they found. He watched other people in front of those paintings and could not see what they did. There was one wall lined with colored rectangles. Clint had moved along that wall, staring at the yellow and then trying out the orange, and he said that his eyes were making new colors as he did that. He hopped from orange to pink to purple to blue. How did he know you were supposed to do that? *Were* you supposed to do that? Was that art? Maybe Clint got that from walking up in the front with the tour guide. Clint knew to look at the nature paintings by rolling up his map and treating it like a telescope. He got that from walking up front.

Wally was now sure that he was missing vital information by having to bring up the rear of the group. On the boat ride back to Manhattan, he was going to send Clint off to play with the Brandons and track the tour guide down for some answers.

12:30 RETURN TO BATTERY PARK

BY THE TIME WE got back to New York, the breezes were no longer blowing, and clouds had swept across the clear sky. It had gotten hot and humid in the last hour. I didn't know if everyone felt this or if it were a symptom of brain fever brought on by Wally's endless interview on the boat. I felt like I'd been defending my graduate thesis in the wrong department. I couldn't tell if he were sincere or messing with me. "Were the Dutch Vikings? Were they really strong guys?" Wally and I were two of the first people off the boat and into the park. I positioned myself on one of the ledges that flanked a small staircase that most of the passengers would take. I asked Wally to stand near the fountain in the distance, and I would send people his way.

"Okay, okay," he said, "but I have to finish about that blotch painting before lunch."

I held the lamppost with my left arm and held up my right whenever I saw someone I recognized. Several of the kids said my pose reminded them of the Statue of Liberty.

Dismal Dina looked up at me and actually smiled. "That would make a great picture. You standing on that thing with your arm up. I have a real photographal eye."

"Do you?" I said with a smile. "I hate your guts," I thought with a scowl.

I saw more of the kids in the flow of tourists, mindlessly following the crowd, drawn to the carts selling t-shirts. I called out their names if I knew them or the name of their school if I didn't. Two of the girls from Georgia were negotiating with a Chinese calligrapher to paint their names; another one was pondering a caricature.

"We don't have time for that," I shouted. "We have to get to lunch."

One of them asked, "Will we have another chance to do this?"

"Absolutely," I lied. The boat was almost empty. How was it that, out of a thousand passengers, three of mine were the last to disembark? The Brandons were the final trio on the gangplank, and they were each holding boxes of miniature Lady Liberties. One of Brandon 2's bags had ripped, and six of the boxes had fallen loose, causing him great consternation. Reunited with the group, several people helped with the stray boxes, opening their shopping bags or backpacks. All of the figurines disappeared among the Georgians, who then teased Brandon, who in turn pouted and said something that got him into trouble with Wally and Nancy, who used her vice-principaliest voice. After he apologized, I got the thumbs-up from Wally and Pete.

I started leading everyone out of the park and was surprised to find Wally lumbering up in the front with me. I needed someone tall in the back, but he had a quick question about modern art, and a case in point rose up in front of us.

"Like that!" he said. "Why in the heck would they put that in a park? What was the artist thinking? What's that supposed to be? It looks like something taken out of a trash heap."

I stopped the group and talked about the sculpture that was bothering Wally, the damaged globe that used to stand in the fountain in the middle of the World Trade Center and was recovered from the rubble of the site and moved to Battery Park six months after September eleventh. The eternal flame was lit on the first anniversary.

"Well, that explains that," Wally said and beat a hasty retreat. After pictures were taken, we resumed the walk out of the park. My cell phone started singing, and a couple of the girls from Georgia asked if I liked that band. I told them no. The ring tone was the result of their screwing with my phone while we waited in line for the last boat. I asked them to reprogram my phone later and answered the call.

It was Carol from the tour company: "Whatcha doin'?"

"Just waiting for the ambulances," I told her. "An eighteen-wheeler just drove over half of our group. Hold on. KEEP PRESSURE ON THE SKULL! DON'T LET HIM BLEED OUT!"

Ignoring my joke, she said, "Listen. Jeff can't do an airport meet today, because he has an audition."

"Good for him."

"Not good for him," she argued. "It's not like he's going to get it. He keeps going on these things just to annoy me."

"I'm sure you're right. This has nothing to do with his dreams or the reason he moved to New York. He prepares monologues and waits in cattle calls…"

"So I have to send Elaine out to the airport, and she might have to stay with them all evening. Can you take the groups to dinner and the theater?" I didn't answer. "Pretty please?"

I told her to wait a second, held the phone down, and used my other hand to point out three things from the northeastern corner of the park, including the Starbucks down State Street which was in the news after 9/11 because the manager charged firemen for water on their way to the burning World Trade Center.

"Firemen get their water from Starbucks?" Clint asked.

"*Bottled* water," I clarified. As my tourists commented on the outrage—several hoped that the manager was fired—I led them across the street toward Bowling Green and then said into the phone, "No, Carol. I don't think so." I couldn't imagine staying with these people past five. I was dead on my feet.

"I don't have anyone else to cover for Patrick," Carol pleaded.

"Did you call Janice, Jim, Maria, Marta, or Hardy?"

"No."

"Or Travis, Mitch, or Elizabeth?"

"Elizabeth is out of town this week."

"Or Walter, Adrienne, Lawrence…"

"Stop that!"

"Mike or Bruce?"

"It would be easier if you just said yes."

"I have plans tonight that I can't cancel."

"You do not."

"Of course, I do. What do you mean I do not?"

"What are they?"

She thought I couldn't improvise my excuse on the spot? How sweet. I rattled off a visit from an aunt and uncle who were taking me to the theater to see *Pal Joey* because Christa Menotto was my aunt's dance student back in Allentown (out of nowhere came Allentown), and we were going for drinks with her after the show.

"Can you get me her autograph?"

"Sure." I could forge one during lunch. "Hold on one sec." I gave a history of the Custom House and the statuary lining the cornice and then explained the significance of the symbols in the four statues that represented the continents down below. They took pictures, and I put the phone to my ear. "If worse comes to worst, I can take the group to

dinner, but that's all, Carol. That gives you the afternoon to find someone who wants the work."

"Deal. You'll get them to dinner."

"No! *If worse comes to worst*, I'll get them to dinner."

"One more favor…"

"One second." I hooked the phone in my pocket and pointed to
Bowling Green, the city's first public park. The Stamp Act repealed,
the King George statue put up, the Declaration of Independence read,
the King George statue torn down, etcetera, etcetera. Fence from 1771,
wrought iron, crowns torn off the tops of the posts. We walked through
the entire park—it takes up less than an acre—and I remembered the
phone. Carol had hung up. We were behind the *Charging Bull* statue,
and the kids slapped each other in the arm and pointed furtively at
the massive bronze orbs beneath the bull's raised tail and at the two
German tourists who were palming those globes and snickering at the
camera as if they were the first two tourists ever to take such a picture.
Lunchtime. I rattled off trivia about the bull, about ticker tape pa-
rades, and about the seventeenth-century streets creeping like streams
through the mountainous twentieth-century skyscrapers. Then I mentioned several spots on Broadway where they could eat. I described our
meeting spot up at Trinity Church, and they looked to their teachers
for their cash allotments just as my phone rang.

"Okay, Janice can do Patrick's job after she finishes *her* tour, so
Elaine will have to get them into the city, but then Elaine can meet
your group at dinner."

"So I have to get them to dinner?"

"Yes. And then you can take off and meet your parents."

"My aunt and uncle." Nice try, Carol.

"Thanks so much!"

I was about to cross the street when Kelly stopped me and asked
if I could take her to lunch away from everyone else. Lunch was when
I usually rested my voice, but Kelly looked so morose in her sunglasses
and baseball cap, and at that point, I still didn't know the story about

Hunter and her phone. The last time she and I were together, we had been shopping for a dress.

"Follow me," I said, and as her fellow travelers posed in front of, behind, and beneath the bronze bull, the two of us slipped away.

12:45 LUNCH IN THE FINANCIAL DISTRICT

DENNIS FOLLOWED HIS DAUGHTER and her friends up Broadway into a large deli. Formerly a bank with a marble staircase, the Variety reminded him of a department store. There were hot and cold buffets, serving stations for salads, deli sandwiches and panini, a Mongolian grill, and sushi, as well as coffee and baked goods. There weren't many tourists in here; most of the clientele were office workers breaking for lunch. There was a purpose in their stride, and he wished for the umpteenth time to be home at his job, having not squandered vacation days for this inane trip to New York whose only thrill was nearly getting into a fistfight with "three Texas frat boy assholes" on the way to Ellis Island. Famished, he opted for the buffet and piled assorted spoonfuls into the plastic container so that his lunch was basically a stew of macaroni and cheese, potato salad, sesame chicken, string beans, mashed potatoes, and penne in vodka sauce. In line for the cash registers, he saw Brittany and her friends walking up a small, almost hidden, staircase to a balcony above the panini and Japanese counters. He paid and followed.

When he reached the top of the staircase, he saw them in the back corner pushing tables together to make room for six: Cody and his suck-up friend, Ryan; the two ditzes, Jenny and Laurie; Dana, the model; and his own dear Brittany, who was sitting with her back to him. It was crowded, so Dennis walked toward the empty two-top table right next to them. He planned to sit down, give a casual "Hi, kids!", and begin lunch. He wouldn't push his table against theirs, he wouldn't try to intrude on their conversation, he wouldn't embarrass Brittany. He just wanted to sit in the vicinity. At the last minute, he reconsidered, turned, and sat with his back toward them at another table catercornered to Brittany. No one saw him sit down. When two people took his intended table, the entire balcony was full except for the seat across from him.

This was better. He would have said something to cause Brittany to blush or cry. This way, if she later noticed him as they left, she would see how inconspicuous her father could be, how he was genuinely trying to give her space and respect her privacy. Also, this way, he could eavesdrop.

Jenny and Laurie were sitting along the rail with a view of the patrons milling about below.

Jenny said, "Oh, guess who just came in, Dana?"

"Who?"

"Your boyfriend."

"The Subway Poker," Laurie said.

Dana whimpered, "Oh, no!"

"Joking!" Jenny said.

Laurie added, "Joking!"

"It's not funny. I'm trying to forget."

Ryan said, "What? How close he got to losing his virginity on your shoulder…"

"I'm trying to eat."

"Hey, you've got to give him props. He's the only one who got some action on this trip."

"Seriously, stop."

Dennis couldn't make sense of any of this.

"Oh my God!" Jenny said, stiffening. "I'm so not kidding. Guess who's here!"

Laurie said, "Tracy." There were sighs of exasperation.

"It's like she has G.P.S."

"She must have put a tracker on one of us."

"On Cody."

Cody asked, "Did she see you?"

"No. We're good."

"She's like a fricking bloodhound," Ryan said. "Sniffing you out."

"Thanks to my mom."

Dennis was still at a loss, but he was more intrigued to hear Cody calling Barbara his mom instead of his stepmom. Cody's real mom was still alive. Dennis thought that if he ever heard Brittany call another man her father, he would be forced to stage a massive intervention.

Dennis was enjoying his mishmash lunch. He had already scarfed down half of it. He kept listening. Their discussion turned to sex and who on the trip they would "bang"—present company excluded—if they had the chance or were forced into it. It was easy for the boys: the teacher from Georgia. No explanation, no argument, no objection. For the girls, the pickings were slimmer.

"Well, if Dana wants a shoulder rub."

"Stop it," Dana said. "I abstain. There's no one on the trip."

"No one?"

Dana paused before saying, "No one not at this table."

Laurie and Jenny said, "Aaaawwww." Dennis almost choked on a string bean. Cody and Dana made a decent high school couple, but she was a year older and way too beautiful to stick with him past the summer. Dana would go on to college and college-aged men; Cody would still be throwing footballs to other high school boys.

Still immersed in their game, Laurie said Jenny would sleep with "the man without teeth" while Jenny retaliated that Laurie would sleep with "Brittany's dad." Dennis hunched over again.

Cody put a stop to that: "Parents are off the table." Laurie and Jenny then chose the student council boys. "Just a one-time thing." "Nothing too involved." Dennis felt the food processing in his stomach as he listened. He wondered how long Brittany had been hanging with them. She was a year behind the rest of them. She was still a virgin.

Then he heard the attention shift to Brittany. It was her turn, and Dennis suddenly wanted to give away his position. He heard her abstain as well. Relief. Good, keep abstaining. Nothing wrong with abstinence. But the shoppers wouldn't let Brittany off that easy. They let Dana get away with it, because Dana was the Queen Bee, but they were going to drag Brittany across the table to get an answer out of her. She knew it too, so after a pause she chose the tour guide. There were some admissions of surprise, quibbling over the rules—did the tour guide count?—and then follow-up questions. Brittany liked his curly hair. She also liked that he was a New Yorker and probably knew his way around the bedroom. Dennis grabbed at his throat. He was going to cough or throw up. Knew his way around the bedroom? This was his baby! He figured her comment could be interpreted in one of two ways—that she preferred someone with experience to match her own or that she needed an instructor to help initiate her. Dennis didn't want to entertain either interpretation! He thought of crawling to the stairs or hurling himself over the balcony.

Then Jenny said, "It doesn't matter. Jack's gay."

"What?"

"Our tour guide is totally gay."

"Really?" asked Brittany.

"Oh my God! Are you kidding me?" The rest of them mulled it over and then agreed. "So he doesn't count."

Laurie added, "And, Brittany, seriously, you need to be careful. My Aunt Kate only dates gay men, and then she's shocked when they come out. After three of them, it's like, get a clue. You don't want to start down that path."

Brittany said, "I was just playing the game."

"They're like the best friends you'll ever want, but you *don't* want to date them."

"Stop yelling at me."

"We're trying to help you," Jenny said.

Laurie added, "And you need it. You don't pick well."

"I do too."

"Randy Brown?" Laurie asked.

Jenny said, "He's on steroids, Brittany. His testicles are the size of peanuts."

"I'm sure she already knows that. They were making out at Gabriel's party…"

This was too much: hearing his daughter picked on; hearing who she would sleep with; hearing of a possible infatuation with a long line of gay men; and hearing about her kissing a boy with shrunken testicles. Dennis looked up at the ceiling and saw two people standing above him with full trays. He gestured to his table and used their bodies to block his getaway.

1:30 TOUR OF WALL STREET

FROM ANOTHER DELI, Pete bought a Cuban panini, won over by the promise of pickles, as well as chips and a Diet Coke. He then walked up Broadway to Trinity Church at Wall Street. Since this was where the groups were meeting, he thought it was where he might as well eat. The air was hot and sticky, and the clouds threatened a deluge; nonetheless, Pete preferred to be outside in a cemetery than inside a deli in the Financial District during the lunch rush. In the courtyard, there were metal tables and chairs arranged around an enormous bronze sculpture of the roots of a sycamore. Another 9/11 memorial. Dedicated a few years earlier. Pete couldn't recall the story behind it and didn't bother reading the explanation posted nearby. He sat down at a table between the twisted bronze roots and the brownstone tomb of James Lawrence, who died during the War of 1812 with the famous last order: "Don't give up the ship."

As Pete pulled his lunch from the white paper bag, he apologized to the memory of Mr. Lawrence, because he had every intention of giving up the ship. This was his last trip to New York with students. He couldn't do this anymore. He would let Lu take over. She was younger, she was energetic, she didn't take their apathy personally. She didn't even *see* their apathy. With her, maybe there would be no apathy.

Would they appreciate the culture, which was the reason he started these trips in the first place? Lu loved theater, she loved music and art. She would find her own way to teach them, and she wouldn't resort to shrieking like a lunatic on the corner of Fiftieth Street.

Pete felt little compunction regarding that tirade, however. His only regret was not having a bigger audience, more students who deserved to hear his harangue. The students back in Seattle, for example. Even David, the Columbia student he had met at the Met. *All you people can be such pains in the ass*, Pete should have told him yesterday in the dungeon cafeteria. He should not have let David ramble on about his life at Columbia when that life wouldn't have happened without Pete's tenacity. Pete should have reminded him: *I had to prod and cajole you into getting the Columbia application.*

Pete was happy he ordered the sandwich with the pickles. Strong, overpowering flavors were the only things he tasted these days, though they weren't enough to divert him from his frustration with college applications, letters of recommendation, and students, who had never been to college, presuming to know more about college than their teacher did. In this regard, Tommy had been the consummate pain in the ass, the high colonic of student aggravation. He gave Pete a week or less to write his rec letter for the University of Virginia. Tommy really wanted to go to UVA and told Pete to "make it good." Pete told him to worry about his own work, not to "half-ass the essay requirements," and to make sure to run them by him, but Tommy didn't. A few days after Tommy sent his application off, he ambled into Pete's room with a copy in his hand and a smug smile on his face. He was absolutely convinced that his essays were superb and told him so. Pete read them, keeping in mind they had already been submitted, and with a smile of his own, no more gratifying than honesty would allow, said something like, "Oh, I think these will work." Because Tommy's letters and official record were so strong, so compelling, Pete was certain he would be admitted, but Pete was pissed off as he had been a few times before at Tommy, for being so goddamned presumptuous and late.

Pete, who had been staring long and deep into the bronze roots of the nearby memorial, suddenly looked around the courtyard and noticed that almost all of the chairs were now occupied by people he recognized. Like a dream, he was suddenly surrounded by familiar faces, and he took a moment to place them all. Lunch was over, groups were being counted. Pete wiped his mouth and beard with a napkin and threw his trash away.

The tour of Wall Street began.

Pete tried to pay attention…

The highest building in your city usually indicates the city's top priority, whether it's religious, political, cultural, financial. Go to Reno or Vegas, it's a casino. In Salt Lake, it's the LDS Church Building. In a college town, it's often a library; in farming towns, it's a silo. In Seattle, it's the Columbia Center, whose tenants include companies like Amazon which is very much Seattle. Trinity Church was once the tallest building in New York, but for almost three decades, the city's tallest structures loomed high above this entire neighborhood. Perfectly named for New York's top priority—the World Trade Center, the center of trade for the world.

…but then the tour turned to Alexander Hamilton's grave, and Tommy once again became the tallest tower in Pete's mental skyline. He remembered Tommy the previous fall, bursting into his classroom, waving a term paper on Hamilton marked with an A+. He had been asked to read his essay in class, and he gave Pete a repeat performance. The thesis (stated a little late for Pete to have given Tommy the plus) was that careers and great leaders were made in times of flux. It was a compelling portrait of a Founding Father who rose the farthest and the fastest and who perhaps more than any of them deserved to have his likeness printed on currency. When Tommy reached the famous duel, he successfully, and memorably, compared the shooting of a former cabinet member (Hamilton) by a sitting vice president (Aaron Burr) to a modern hypothetical of Dick Cheney rowing across the Hudson with Madeline Albright in order to shoot her in the face like the fervid duck hunter he was.

If Tommy had made the trip, he would have posed for a photo in front of the white marble monument with its pyramid and urns, and Pete could now almost see Tommy running along the flagstone path. Visions and memories buzzed through Pete's brain like static, so most of the Wall Street tour was lost. He squinted his eyes and nodded, threw a smile or two, all tricks he had picked up from students who wanted to give the illusion they were paying attention. He heard only snippets as the group peeked inside the church and then headed down Wall to Broad through Federal Hall to Pine up Nassau to Cedar and all the way over to Church. He heard, *The wall was originally built not to keep out the English but to keep out Rhode Island.* He heard, *The only company in the world with more electricity dedicated to its computer system is NASA.* He heard, *There was already a terror attack right here in 1920.* He heard, *That's the wrong Trinity Church in the painting.* He also heard one of the parents from Georgia telling him that some of his high school students were using foul language in front of eighth graders, and could he please stop them. After that, he heard something about a Pine Street building with a Wall Street address, a vault with more gold than all of Fort Knox, and a red statue that was considered the smallest building in New York.

He heard all that, but he saw Tommy. He saw Tommy on his front porch in early May, two weeks before his death. Tommy was trying for a scholarship—he had been accepted at UVA—and this time wanted Pete to help him with his personal statement. It was an incredibly generous scholarship worth twenty-five thousand—and Tommy had a legitimate shot at it. They had gone over his first draft during Pete's planning period, their "unclass," and Pete had made some recommendations. The next night, Tommy phoned and asked if he could come over and have him proof it.

After greeting Pete's wife and daughter, the first thing Tommy said was, "Look, I really worked hard on this, don't cut it up."

Pete replied, "Let me get my scalpel, I'm sorry, pen." And they went to the study. Though Tommy had done a solid job choosing and organizing sections of the essay around a clear objective, Pete pointed out "alternatives, choices" about tone, phrasing, and diction. He made Tommy justify his choices. They were at it for some time. There were glares from Tommy when a perfect sentence was shattered by one of Pete's disapproving clucking sounds, and once Tommy even moaned when he realized he had to replace a paragraph that he couldn't honestly defend. Pete thought he detected a look of concern cross Tommy's face, but he pointed to the page and kept Tommy focused on the work in front of him.

When they returned to the family room, they each had a soda and talked awhile about whatever. Then Tommy looked his teacher square in the eye and said with an expression Pete would describe at the funeral as a mixture of gratitude, admiration, and determination: "Someday I will write as well as you do." Pete took it, for better-or-worse, as a compliment. But more than that, Pete knew whatever it meant to Tommy that he would do it, he would accomplish it. More than anything else, Tommy chose his challenges with a mind to succeed. Pete never knew him to fail or even come up short at anything he was determined to master, and Pete knew him better than most. It frequently occurred to him that every morning, when Tommy left his house and came to school, he had sat in one of Pete's classes—four years, minus three motherfucking weeks.

Pete's chest was empty. The relentless grief of losing this student swelled up in him, almost pitched him off his feet, as the group stopped across the street from a giant hole in the landscape.

2:30 GROUND ZERO

THIS WAS THE PART of the day I most envied my friends in their offices. They didn't have to talk about September eleventh. They might walk by Ground Zero on their way to work, but they didn't have to revisit the tragedy as part of their job description. They weren't asked where the towers stood, where the planes came from, which buildings were damaged, and how many people died. In the spring seasons of '02 and '03, I did not lead my groups to the perimeter. I would talk to them somewhere east of Broadway and use one of the neighborhood maps mounted on the sidewalks to give them their geographical overview—this is how the people reached the Brooklyn Bridge, this is how the boats were used in the evacuation, this is where the school kids were brought, and this is the highway on the east side where all those people walked north. Then I would send them to pay their respects at their own pace, and we would meet three blocks north at St. Paul's. They would take Church Street, and I would walk parallel on Broadway. I frequently had to revert to childhood and stop for milk and cookies at a Mrs. Fields on Fulton.

With each passing year, it became easier to approach the site and the subject. I settled on a crafted speech. I knew which stories I could tell and which would still choke me up. I buried the latter and rattled off the former. I avoided certain topics and built defenses far faster than the actual construction going up at the site. By 2004, an election year when war and terrorism were topics for the campaign, it was obvious that different parts of the country were coping at different rates, had various levels of fear. I never pushed my own agenda. I let people experience what they wanted to when confronted with the gaping hole; however, I could not stomach the racist bullshit I sometimes heard. To keep from subjecting myself to the more offensive reactions, I gave some groups their free time sooner, escaped before they could start up. The Mrs. Fields was torn down around this time, so I had to look elsewhere for cookies.

A couple more years passed. 9/11 became historical. The middle schoolers now arriving in New York had been too young to watch it live. They didn't have the same memories. It didn't have the same impact. And so it was now my responsibility to *remind* them of where they were, to guide them to different memorials, and lend an emotional import to the general overview. But I resented having to do it.

The people in my current group sat themselves on the steps on the western side of One Liberty Plaza. This was where security guards blew whistles whenever a tourist stood on a ledge for a better picture. All day long, they blew whistles. This was also where the tour groups were sniffed out by the parasites who spent their days selling pictures of the burning buildings, of the survivors crying and gasping and choking in the fuel-stenched smoke. They hovered on the periphery and went in for their sales, their albums open to their favorite images of carnage. I chased them off, and they floated ten yards away, waiting for me to finish.

How different was I from these carrion?

We both made money at Ground Zero.

But I didn't want to be here—I didn't want to wake up at five thirty in the morning to brave rush hour with a tour group, endure massive crowds and three boat rides before crawling to lunch and zigzagging through Wall Street only to end, each time, at Ground Zero, where I was expected to grieve anew with every single group—especially (especially!) on Day Three when people were exhausted and cranky and it was hot and humid and threatening to storm. I never wanted to be here. But they sat with faces turned upwards waiting for sense to be made of the empty space in front of them.

Weren't we all?

LASH DAUTENHAHN WAS SEATED at the very top of the stairs. He had purposely avoided Miss Teen Seattle since the incident on the subway. He kept his eyes down, his teeth clenched, his hands in his pockets. He knew that people in the Seattle group were laughing at him, but he didn't know how many of them. He spent the day as invisibly as he could. The fluttering in his stomach made it hard for him to concentrate on anything else. As the day wore on, he grew upset at himself that he was missing so much of a tour that he had looked forward to for so long. This was a vacation, away from school, away from his chores on the farm, and it was ending tomorrow. He only had one day left. He tried to enjoy himself, but whenever his eyes landed on the back of her blonde head, or worse, on her shoulder, the whole city seemed to collapse.

He looked off to his right and saw the guys selling Ground Zero souvenirs. He would have liked a souvenir from Ground Zero. He was the only one in his whole family to make it to the place where the Towers stood, and since he couldn't figure out where any of the buildings stood from where they were sitting, one of those picture books could come in handy. He had saved some of the money from his lunch allotments, so he had a total amount left of thirty-six dollars and sixty cents.

The group was standing and breaking off. Lash hadn't heard what the instructions were. Where were they going and where were they meeting and at what time? He wanted to follow the Brandons, but something was wrong with them. The one Brandon had been in a bad mood ever since his bags ripped and everyone made fun of him, and the other Brandons were not apologizing. The three of them didn't even eat lunch together. That had been a kind of shock for everybody.

So Lash asked Zach if he could walk with him. Zach said sure, but he was walking with Jacob and Sun. Jacob and Sun were the two Seattle boys who hung out by themselves. It was weird, Lash thought, that they would walk with an eighth grader, but Zach read at a college level, so maybe it all worked out. Lash looked at Jacob and Sun as they approached. Did *they* know what happened on the subway between himself and their classmate? Did they talk with the shopping group? He had no choice but to go with them. Everyone else was already gone.

Lash tagged along, eyes down, hands in his pockets. None of them wanted to buy the souvenir books, so he followed them to the memorial for the firemen and then walked along the fence to find a better view of Ground Zero. Lash listened to the three of them talk about engineering, the structure of the towers, why they fell, about a conspiracy theory. He just kept his mouth shut. He took three pictures. They kept walking, and Lash hoped they wouldn't get lost. He hoped he wouldn't be left behind. They crossed the street at the end of Ground Zero and walked through an open gate into another cemetery belonging to another church. They walked past the tombstones into a chapel they called St. Paul's. Inside, it was all white and pink and powder blue. Exhibits were set up around the church, and Lash asked where they were. Zach explained this was the oldest building in continual use in Manhattan and that it didn't close after 9/11.

"This was where the rescue workers came for food, grief counseling, and sleep. Weren't you listening to the tour?"

Lash said, "I couldn't hear everything in the back." Zach started chewing a Starburst, and the four of them looked at scuff marks in a pew made from the boots of sleeping firemen or construction workers. They saw George Washington's booth, some origami. Then they got into line for the bathroom. There were only two toilets. Since Lash didn't have to go, he thought maybe this would be a good time to buy those Ground Zero picture books. He had seen some souvenir tables near the church. Zach said that the whole group would be meeting outside, so Lash returned to the cemetery.

He was almost through the gate when Wally and Clint called him over. They were sitting on a line of benches along a path beneath some trees. Lash looked up and saw the shoppers coming through the gate, and he didn't want to pass right by them—he was trapped—so he hid from them by sitting down with Wally and Clint.

Tracy, the chubby girl from Seattle, walked up to them and said, "Hello, friends!" Lash figured that she didn't know about the subway ride. Tracy sat down right next to Lash on his bench. She said, "My feet hurt so bad, I can't walk another step. This was such a sad stop, don't you think?" Lash nodded, kept his eyes down, his hands in his pockets. "And I think I'm allergic to something in New York. Every time I go back to the hotel, I have a new rash."

The shoppers sat on benches on the other side of Tracy. Lash could hear them talking. He couldn't help but listen in case they were joking about him.

"Oh my God, oh my God," one of them suddenly squealed.

"We were at Century 21," another said.

"And guess who was there."

Lash wondered who they were asking since they all traveled in a pack and all came into the cemetery at the same time.

"Who?"

"Orlando Bloom!"

"Oh my God!" There was more squealing.

Lash heard Tracy quietly say the same thing under her breath.

She looked at her watch.

She looked around.

Lash could tell she was doing an informal count of the people not yet here and of the minutes she had left.

She stood, walked back toward the gate.

Lash turned and saw her exit through the gate and bolt away at a sprint. The shoppers were watching too, and they burst out laughing, giving each other high fives.

SO IT WAS TRACY who was missing during what proved to be the trip's most consequential count. The sky was getting darker. The Georgians were all there, but Pete came up one short.

Grandma Penny screamed, "IS IT BLUE HAIR?!" But then she saw Melanie, who was looking directly at her, so she said, "No, it's all right, she's here." As if someone else had asked for Blue Hair and Penny was calming that person down.

Lash knew who was missing; he told Wally, who told Pete, "She went to Century 21."

We waited and waited, and while we waited, Nancy, the vice principal, sidled up next to me and asked the question posed by someone on every single tour: "Where were *you* on 9/11?"

I looked at my watch and told her that I'd be right back, that I needed to walk toward the store and see if I could find Tracy and hurry her up before the storm let loose. I walked down the path and through the gate, headed south, and crossed the street. I waited there for Tracy's head to appear in the crush of tourists and workers.

Where were you on 9/11? I dreaded the question, partly because I'd have to relive that day, but mostly because I knew what would predictably follow. *Their* story. Where *they* were on September eleventh. After several years, I was just not interested. It was safe to say that I knew where more people were on the morning of September eleventh than 99.6 percent of the human race. Everyone wanted to share with me their 9/11 story, and it was surprising how similar they were. *So-and-so called and said, "Turn on the TV."* Or: *I called home and said, "Turn on the TV."* And: *I couldn't believe it.* And frequently: *We were afraid because forty miles from us is an Air Force base, we were afraid because we have tall office buildings, we were afraid because there's a factory that produces weapons in the next town over, we were afraid because we're near a port city, we were afraid, we were afraid, we were afraid…*

I waited for a few minutes. I saw no sign of Tracy. And then I turned my head. I looked across Fulton Street through the black iron fence surrounding the churchyard, the same fence once covered with posters and letters and quilts from well-wishers around the world, and I saw my group in the cemetery in what appeared to be an all-out fistfight. I turned my whole body, craned my neck, and blinked. It was. It was a melee. Hair was being pulled, arms were being swung, and people were lying on the ground.

My combination group had finally snapped.

PETE NEVER SAW it coming.

He would be the first to admit he was distracted, but he would later blame the close quarters of the meeting place. "The cemetery at St. Paul's" had been their only instruction. There was nothing more specific, so a few people sat down at the first opportunity: on a line of benches that ran along a narrow path near the gate on Church Street. As soon as you passed through the gate, you walked to the right or left and then followed a curve that took you east toward the chapel. These two paths were connected early on by another that ran north-south. There were benches there, shaded by pear trees. Once the first few claimed their spot to rest their feet, the others congregated there as well. After the entire line of benches was filled—and some were even sitting on each other's laps—the rest, the latecomers, stood on the cement in front of the benches.

A Brandon tried to sit down on the grass, but some of the eighth-grade girls expressed their dismay: "Get up! Those are people's graves! Gross!"

Until the fight broke out, the grassy area was treated like boiling, bubbling lava, and the benches and the walk were the only two strips occupied.

As they waited for Tracy, the Seattleites who had seats kept them. The Georgians, however, motivated by a desire to get back to their hotel so they could lie down, shower, stretch, or nap, found themselves standing. Chronically unhappy Dina and Nancy, the overzealous VP, were allied in getting their people up and ready for the final march of the afternoon. They didn't want to lose one second. As soon as the

Seattle group "got their act together," they would be high-tailing it to the subway. The problem was, as soon as they stood up, other tourists, not from their group but from other states or countries, moved in for their seats. They were pushed closer toward the Seattleites, more than half of whom remained seated. Seattle held the general belief that, once Tracy returned, standing up would take no longer than two seconds. Pete realized, though, that their position to the Georgians appeared lazy and disinterested, not to mention unchivalrous—teenagers sitting down while a grandmother stood nearby.

Nancy said to Pete, "This is really inexcusable. We have waited on your group again and again." Pete was taken aback and apologized. He wanted to stand up. Sitting where he was, with Nancy standing above him, made him feel like a student kept after class. "'I'm sorry?'" she repeated. "That won't do. You reprimand the latecomer and apologize to us, and then it happens all over again. There are no consequences, ever, so your students know that they can run wild. If they're late, all they have to do is act contrite. You'll fall for it, and then they can go back to their friends. It is disrespectful on their part and unprofessional on yours."

"I've been bringing students to New York for twenty years."

"If I was in charge of your school, that would probably change."

Pete was flummoxed.

So was Kelly, who was one of the eight or ten who overheard this dressing-down of Pete. Nancy was usually much more passive-aggressive. But everyone was tired, everyone was hot and sticky. Kelly was also aware that Pete had recently lost a student in a car accident and couldn't remember if Nancy knew this or not.

When Kelly put a hand on Nancy's arm, Nancy turned on her, "You're not much better. You're the lead chaperone of our school, and where have you been all day? Why is Wally counting? Why is Ramona giving directions? Why'd you throw your cell phone into the street last night?" Kelly could say nothing. It was as though she had a new boss, an outright hostile one.

She felt hands grip her shoulders from behind. It was Ramona, and Ramona was about to say something in her defense, but as she inhaled, they all heard the Seattle father on the other side of the pack saying, "No, no, no, no, NO!"

AGAINST HIS WILL, Dennis had been eavesdropping again, but this time he had been listening to the three girls from Georgia. He was biting his tongue. He was trying not to say anything he would regret. He was trying not to embarrass his daughter, kisser of a teenaged steroid addict with shrunken testicles. But he couldn't last.

One of the girls asked, "That church is how old now?"

"It's 1766," another answered.

"Wait a second. When was the Revolution?"

"1776."

"And when did Columbus come over?"

"1492."

"Wait a second! What happened between 1492 and 1776?"

Dennis almost butted in, *Oh, nothing much. Only two hundred eighty years of history, the colonization of much of the western hemisphere including the colony now known as the state of Georgia.* What was happening in these schools? What were they teaching? Some of the comments from the high school students were just as asinine. No child left behind! No child is left behind because no child was going forward. Our schools were failing. We were becoming the stupidest people on the planet.

"Missionaries," said one of the girls. "There was a lot of missionary work during that time. They were bringing the gospel to the New World." Dennis cringed. This girl had already held court on how God protected St. Paul's on 9/11, and she had already tracked down the cross found at Ground Zero and taken a photo of the divine sign that God wanted the earth to see: a Christian cross, not an Islamic crescent. "Mainly Catholic priests converting the Indians and the people in Mexico."

Dennis let his tongue go, "No, no, no, no, NO!"

RAMONA WAS ABOUT to tell Nancy to relax, to calm down and go for a walk, when she heard the Seattle man yelling behind her. He was giving history, saying something about mass extermination, smallpox, and imperialism. She tried to figure out who exactly he was talking to, but he was on the far side. She could see only see his head, but he seemed to be looking down. She stepped up onto the grass to see over the people in her way.

Was he yelling at her students?

At thirteen-year-olds?

"Yes, St. Paul's survived 9/11," he said, turning to everyone on the narrow path and benches. "But so did AAAALLLLL of these buildings on this side of the street. Did you notice that? That deli survived, that pizza place survived, that hotel survived. Why? Because the Twin Towers were way the hell over there. And did you know there was actually a church next to one of the towers? Guess what? It's not there anymore! If *that* survived, that would have been a miracle. This wasn't."

Ramona wondered if everyone had forgotten to take their medication. She started making her way on the grass around the others.

"And the cross? The cross found at Ground Zero? The buildings were made of vertical and horizontal beams. Every time they met they formed a cross, so if two towers of one hundred ten stories each fall down, then chances are you're going to find a cross. There are very few buildings in the world structurally made out of crescents."

Ramona interrupted, "The cross was found by a man who transformed an empty space in the wreckage into a chapel. People found solace in the middle of the desolation. It's how the cross was *repurposed*. That's what matters. Didn't you go inside this church here? Didn't you see what it did for all the people?"

"Your students were saying it proved the existence of God…"

"Good for them."

"Sayeth the history teacher."

Ramona later wanted to say that, of course, God exists! He exists in compassion and empathy, in charity, in love, in forgiveness, in all of the acts that the people who worked at St. Paul's performed, but her mind was racing, her thoughts were clogged, and all she could say was, "You're an idiot."

"I'm an idiot?" Dennis asked. "I'm an idiot? The Civil War had nothing to do with slavery?! Are you out of your *fucking* mind?!"

AND THIS WAS WHEN Grandma Penny fell. She wasn't pushed, Wally would later testify. She was not pushed. At least, not by any hand. The word *fucking* might have thrown her. Her foot wobbled off the path and her entire body followed. Everyone was crammed so close together, and no one was sure-footed. Their legs were jelly, their soles sore, and the cement and grass they were standing on were both uneven. This also explained why others fell in the hullaballoo that followed. Grandma Penny fell onto her right side with a cry, her head nearly missing one of the weathered grave markers. She instantly rolled onto her back. Travis, her son, the ironworker, who up until now had been having more fun than possibly anyone on the trip, saw his mother on the ground and saw Dennis above her. Thinking Dennis had pushed his mother, Travis, still wearing his Statue of Liberty foam crown, flew at the father from Seattle. Dennis was bending down to help Penny up when he was hit by Travis's tackle, and he could only wonder what would have happened if Travis had had his arsenal at his disposal. The two men fell to the ground.

BARBARA COULD NOT believe it. She was now even farther away from the trip of seven years ago. She was now in the middle of a brawl. An actual brawl had erupted all around her. From start to finish, it could not have lasted more than fifteen seconds—after their beatings, people soon reclaimed their bearings, realized no one really wanted to hurt anyone else, that much of it was defensive, only some of it retaliatory—but while in the middle of those fifteen seconds all sense of time was lost. When Ramona and Barbara rushed to help Penny and the giant bear known as Wally hurled through space to break apart the two men, the group's mass was displaced. More people fell off the path; others fell into those sitting on the benches. With every push someone else was hit, and someone would come to their defense with a push and end up hitting someone else. An example: Lash stepped backwards where his big shoe landed right on top of a Seattle shopper's flip flop. As his heel crushed her toes, she jammed her hands against his back and yelled, *Get off me, you perv!* When he fell forward off her foot and into the grass, not only did someone else trip over him, but two of the Georgian girls, who saw their classmate rudely shoved, pounced on the shoppers. Cody and Ryan protected their two favorite girls (Dana, the model, and Brittany, daughter of Dennis), leaving the two shoppers to bear the brunt of middle school wrath. Ashley, particularly, the Bible Bee champ, took a chapter out of the Old Testament, where the Amorites slew the Persians and the Babylonians slew the Amorites. In her world, the walls of Jericho were crumbling, and she answered the call of the clarion by picking up a jawbone of an ass and setting to work. She jabbed both of the older girls in the chest before grabbing their hair, pulling them, taking turns kneeing them in the gut. It took both Pete and Nancy to pull her away. Barbara, on her knees, holding Penny's head and shoulders, watched the insanity and joined Brittany in screaming, "Stop it! Stop it!" But the shrieking just added to the chaos, and while people did make movements to stop it, grabbing arms, pushing hands into chests, those were misinterpreted as escalations. It briefly got even crazier: the Brandons were fighting each other!; and the ten-year-old Clint was on the ground in the midst of a stampede as the tourists, who had taken the benches of the Georgians, were running for their lives, shouting for the police.

BY THE TIME I reached them, the Hatfields and the McCoys were all on their feet, spread out on the surrounding graves, squared off between the tombstones. They each had a look of wariness. And weariness. Some panted. They took stock of any injuries while keeping an eye out for cause to run. Would it, could it, flare up again? There were

passersby on the other side of the fence looking in at us. A cop working with traffic on the corner was at the gate conducting an informal
threat analysis.

"Is everyone all right?" was the first thing I asked. Some nodded.
I wanted to say, *Starburst for the person who can tell me, "WHAT THE
HELL?!"* No one looked to be permanently maimed. They all still had
their eyes. There was an abrasion on one side of Dennis' face, and the
shoppers were holding their stomachs. "What happened?" They all
looked at each other.

Finally, Grandma Penny spoke up, "I fell off the sidewalk."

That's all they gave me. Grandma fell off the sidewalk, and that
was somehow a sign to rumble? I saw Tracy approaching on the path
from the church. So did Pete. He stormed toward her. I saw our vice
principal roll her eyes.

"So we're all here now?" I asked. A few nodded. "No one's dead?"

We waited for Pete to finish with Tracy. The sky was now a shade
of green. I asked the drama teacher what the drama was about. She
said she wasn't really sure.

Then she actually said, "It's like the farmer and the cowboy can't
be friends."

"What? WHAT?"

"I'm sorry; we did *Oklahoma* for our spring production."

Useless! Then it broke. The storm, threatening from the sky for
the last few hours, arrived with only ten seconds of preamble—a few
big drops that hit our arms, stained our shirts—before pouring. Some
screamed, some grappled for their umbrellas, and I shouted for them
to follow me. The entrance to the subway was right outside the gate.
The thirty-six of us joined together once again for a mad sprint as our
audience on the other side of the fence disbanded and ran for cover.
The moisture in the air made this subway station smell like a row of
urinals, as if we were entering the subway through the men's room.
People gagged, some were grateful to be out of the rain, while others
almost slipped down the steps.

All I had to do was get them to the hotel. Metrocards were swiped, and we made our way up the platform and into the middle car of a waiting train. It was the terminus for this line, so the car was completely empty. This was Day Three, and the novelty of standing on the subway, balancing without hands as the train rocked, was lost. The tired, sore, and beaten rushed for a seat on the benches that lined both sides. Some sat facing friends, others sat across the aisle from nemeses who, less than ten minutes ago, had them by the hair. I stood. I had to keep on my toes.

The train pulled out of its station. I conferred with Kelly and then with Pete. I pieced together more of the story after consulting with Ramona and Nancy, all the while ignoring Dina who was salivating to share her point of view—this was exactly the kind of disaster that the Dinas of the world relished. Wally was working with me at the far end of the car. He spoke with Grandma Penny and Travis, who was still, *still*, wearing his foam crown. Penny had removed hers and was running her fingernails through her hair, poofing it up. By Spring Street, Wally approached Dennis, and I watched. From what several had told me, Dennis was the pivotal player. Dennis followed Wally to Travis and the two of them shook hands. Travis tried to stand, but the train threw him back into his seat. Penny cringed when he landed on her hip. Fortunately, no fisticuffs followed this fall. The four of them merely chatted.

At West Fourth, an *a cappella* quartet boarded the train. They launched right into their act, a nice distraction. They harmonized to *I Got Sunshine* and were more than pleased to find a car where they were more than welcome. There were a few irritated commuters trying to read, but for the most part, the performers had found benches full of out-of-towners in need of a show, so the quartet stood in the middle of the car and gave it their all. My people cheered, they took pictures, they tipped with bills and fists of coins. The singers gave an encore, extending their run for another station. They exited at Thirty-fourth to ringing acclaim.

Then, for the only time that I can recall, another *a cappella* troupe entered—this time a trio—and they sang the exact same song. People clapped, but the tips had already been paid out. At Forty-second, they bitterly moved on to the next car where the same fate lay in store.

A New Yorker next to me said, "Wow! Sucks to be them."

4:45 RETURN TO HOTEL

WHILE MY THIRTY-FIVE were upstairs changing out of their wet clothes, I sat in the lobby in mine. I tried to think of another Day Three as bad as this one. I wondered if I should have kept the adults downstairs to talk it all out, but after another mad dash through the rain to the hotel, everyone was drenched and dripping with less than an hour to shower before I took them to dinner. It was protocol to notify Carol about the incident, but this was an extremely busy day in an extremely harried week, and I thought that, unless someone had died, she probably preferred to be kept in the dark. Another reason I didn't want to call was because she had wanted me to stay with the group all night, and I had made up an excuse and now couldn't remember where I told her my fictitious aunt and uncle were from—Allentown or Wilkes-Barre? Afraid she might try to trip me up, I texted her instead: *Fistfight @ St. Paul's. Under control now.* Her response was *LOL*, so I let her think whatever she thought. I had made my report; it was not my responsibility to make sure she knew I was serious. What was my responsibility? Maybe I was partly responsible for the clash. Maybe I should have been paying more attention to the friction in the group. Was I expected now to go upstairs and visit with the adults, to make sure everyone was fine? No. No! The lobby was the territory of the tour guide, not the hotel rooms. There had to be boundaries. The tension was diffused. They were all in their separate rooms, part of an itinerary-mandated time-out. Through the lobby window, I watched the rain fade away and waited for my people to come downstairs.

5:45 MEET IN LOBBY FOR DINNER AND THEATER

THE FIRST OFF the elevator, ten minutes early so that she could grab a smoke, was Dina the Destroyer, who looked more chipper than ever, smiling, unshaken, almost euphoric in the aftermath of the chaos. She saw me and took a detour to my sofa. She plopped down beside me.

"It's an interesting city, I'll give you that," she said as if I were a salesman after a forty-eight-hour pitch. "It's a great place to visit, but I would never live here."

Dina wasn't the first to say this, but after all these years I still didn't know how to reply to what was, let's be honest, a veiled insult to where I had decided to reside. I wanted to tell her that no one asked her to live here. I was showing her around for four days and fully expected her on an outbound plane by the end of the trip. "And, by the way," I wanted to say, "I don't even want to *visit* where you're from." But I just smiled, and Dina took my silence as her cue to catalog the merits of where she lived. None of them were original; however, I did get a kick out of hearing her praise the fresh air of the countryside before going outdoors to shove a cigarette in her mouth.

The next off the elevator was Wally. I feared the questions he was about to ask—*Why are the manhole covers round?; Why do they call it the Big Apple?; Where do you store your Christmas ornaments?*—but Wally had no more questions. Instead, he turned out to have most of the answers. He had been busy upstairs, he told me, visiting Travis and Grandma Penny's room to check on her health and to see if there were anything they wanted to say in private. They didn't. They were both enjoying a "pre-dinner wet-the-whistle" and couldn't be happier. He then visited the Brandons who were having their own drama, because "one felt picked on and homesick," so Wally didn't leave until they were laughing at each other and all was forgiven. After that, he stopped by the girls' room where he asked Ashley, the Bible Bee, to step outside in the hallway and explain one-on-one why she attacked the Seattle girls the way she did. She told him that they "called Lash a perv and said nasty things about him," and he told her that she still needed to apologize to them when they met in the lobby. As far as Lash went, Wally said, there was probably a misunderstanding, and he'd keep his eyes open to see if it needed to be addressed.

"Wow," I said. He had done all of this and showered and changed for the theater in under forty-five minutes. I was further impressed when more of our group arrived in the lobby and Wally was able to tell me how everyone felt, what each of them was going through, and not just Georgia but Seattle as well. It was like listening to the director's commentary on a DVD. "Those are the gals that told Tracy Orlando Bloom was at Century 21. That's why she was late." "See Barbara and her stepson? They're arguing cuz she knows that Orlando Bloom was *not* at Century 21 and Cody helped send that poor girl on a wild goose chase." "Just so you know, Tracy still thinks Orlando Bloom *was* at Century 21 and even made a note on her little list. She's also havin' trouble with rashes." "And there's Ashley, who's gonna apologize to Laurie and Jenny, so let me help her out with that." Amazed, I watched him walk over, put his hand on Ashley's shoulder, and take her across to Seattle.

6:15 TOUR GUIDE GOES TO A BAR

THERE WAS NO MORE rain, but the storm that I hoped would clear the air and cool us off was not a forgiving one. It bore a grudge and left a breezeless broth. Dry hair was re-spritzed as soon as we stepped outside. Khakis were clinging to legs by the first crosswalk. Thankfully, Elaine was already at the restaurant, and I was able to hand the group over to her.

I said, "Watch out, they're violent today.

Elaine said, "No! They're angels, they're SWEETHEARTS. Look at their faces!"

On my way out, several of the adults thanked me and said, "Go home, get some rest." I wished I could. Normally, after a day like this, I would have hightailed it to the subway, zipped uptown, showered, and gone to bed. But my day was not yet over. I had made plans earlier that afternoon. At lunch, after Kelly told me what happened with Hunter, I offered to take her out for a drink when we got back to the hotel. When I shared that I had gone through a break-up myself back in February, a break-up I ignored by stuffing the next four months with back-to-back tours, she took my modest offer of one drink and turned it into an entire night on the town.

"It's what we both need," she said. "Ramona will take my group. I'll tell Nancy I have a migraine." It was agreed: Kelly would meet me at a bar a couple blocks from the hotel, and if we both had the energy, I was going to take her to two parties I would otherwise have skipped.

When I passed the window on Fifty-second Street, I saw Kelly sitting at a table in the front. It registered only as I walked through the entrance corridor that she was sitting with someone. The place was full, I assumed, so space had to be shared. Only as I approached the table did I see that the someone was someone I knew. Dennis. Of all people. In the lobby at the hotel, I had been too distracted to notice that Dennis was missing from the count.

Kelly and I hugged, and Dennis and I shook hands, as if we were friends meeting for drinks after a long week at work, as if we hadn't spent the last ten hours together.

Dennis said, "Surprised?"

Kelly explained, "We ran into each other in the hallway. I told him I was sorry that Travis jumped him in the graveyard."

"We started talking and she said you were going out…"

"I invited him along."

"I'm bailing out on *Mamma Mia*," Dennis said. "I didn't mind the musical last night, but I think one show is enough for me." A waiter brought them drinks they had already ordered—a beer in a tall skinny glass and a colorful martini. "And I really don't like ABBA."

The waiter cried, "Blasphemer!"

Dennis, startled, watched him return to the bar.

Kelly sipped at her neon green concoction and said, "Dennis went through a divorce, you just went through a break-up, and I'm going through a break-up right now."

"Well, as long as there's a theme," I said.

"Maybe we can all meet someone tonight," Dennis said, oblivious that the three of us were on different timelines. Less than twenty-four hours ago, Kelly still thought a surprise from Hunter would involve a diamond ring. Dennis took a gulp of his beer and looked around the lounge area, where we were sitting in sleek but comfortable chairs; he looked to the back with the bar and oversized tables surrounded by barstools; and he looked, in between, at a staircase that led upstairs to another lounge and bar area. Then he said, "It's after six. It's Friday. There aren't that many women here."

Kelly said, "This is a gay bar."

"Really?" He looked over the room where men outnumbered women eight to one. "Do we stand out?"

Dennis stood out more than Kelly did. She was wearing a certain black dress purchased at Bloomingdale's. It was intended to premiere in July but was making an earlier debut. The dress, though formal, had a high enough hem to pass for a simple sexy cocktail dress, especially when the wearer had her hair down. Kelly left the second part of the dress, a lacy confection to be worn around the shoulders, back in the hotel room. Dennis, on the other hand, was wearing khaki pants and an olive green polo shirt and, with the exception of the right side of his face, which bore a Neosporin-glazed scrape, a wound sustained in the Battle at St. Paul's, he looked just like any another tourist seeking a local bar, lured in by the décor and assuming it was straight.

Kelly explained that her brother, "who came out as soon as he left home," always took her to gay bars whenever she went through a breakup: "I could let my guard down and dance my butt off."

Dennis admitted, "I'm not really much of a dancer."

Kelly raised her glass, "Well, to whatever we do! A toast to Jack. And one night off from those *people*." Dennis lifted his beer. "I'm sorry, Dennis, not your daughter. We wish your daughter was here with us."

Kelly wished Brittany were here with us? Was that green drink Kelly's first or fourth?

Dennis said, "Brittany will have more fun if I'm not around. Her friends were picking on her before I made a scene down at Ground Zero, and then they *really* turned on her. When we got back to the hotel, I told her for the fiftieth time that she had a key to my room and could move in and take the other bed at any time."

"What did she say?" Kelly asked.

"'Daaa-AAAD!!'" It was a perfect imitation. Kelly and I laughed. The waiter returned and took my order. As soon as he left, Dennis rubbed his hands together and asked, "So what are we doing tonight? Where are we going?"

Kelly said, "Yeah, tell us!'

I understood that I was still the guide or, to be more accurate, the local authority, and they were going to ask me the inevitable: *Take us somewhere off the beaten path; Show us something the tourists don't see; Take us where the real New Yorkers go.*

Well, this real New Yorker had wet shoes and wanted to go home.

"Let's just play it by ear," I told them. "No itinerary tonight."

They seemed happy with that.

7:00 SPLINTER GROUP EATS DINNER

OUR FIRST STOP was a flop. What was once a decorated window belonging to my favorite Mexican restaurant was now empty and framing a sign that promised retail space to lease. When had this place closed? What happened to Maria? Rosa? The guy with the mole? How could the restaurant, one of my preferred purveyors of comfort food, cease to exist? In what city was I standing?

"Well, you're not off to a propitious start," Dennis said.

"*We're* not off to a propitious start," I reminded him. I was off the clock, so unless he wanted to pay me something, we were in this together. I refused to be held accountable for any disappointment.

"That's all right," Kelly said. "We have Mexican in Georgia."

Dennis added, "We should avoid tequila anyway."

We walked down Ninth Avenue with its vast array of relatively cheap international food. Menus were posted in the windows. I encouraged Kelly and Dennis to read a few and choose the place that most intrigued. They wanted me to decide, but after months of making decisions for people—*Let's eat here; Let's go to the bathroom now; Let's take this subway line; Let's cross on this street*—I was sick of choices. It was their dinner.

But they trusted me: "You choose." Kelly wanted to eat something she couldn't find at home. Dennis wasn't up for seafood. I took them down Forty-seventh for Ethiopian. We shared a couple of entrees which arrived on top of the *injera*, the large spongy, tangy flatbread, which we ripped and wrapped around the meat and vegetables.

We talked about the trip so far and, since I was eating with someone from each of the opposing teams, I pieced more and more of their trip together, learned about all of the players, the behind-the-scenes activity, the back stories.

This was where the three of us finally figured out what happened at the Whispering Gallery at Grand Central: Ramona had whispered to the wrong corner, and *that* was how Dennis from Seattle knew what Nancy had said to Ramona in Georgia.

This was where I first learned that Pete had flipped out at his students in Times Square.

And this was where Kelly told us in detail about the texts on her phone and why she thought the texter, a waitress she'd called out for flirting with her boyfriend at McHale's, was "such a spiteful slut."

We asked her what she was going to do when she saw Hunter, and she answered by ordering another round of beer for the table.

8:15 TOUR GUIDE SHOWERS

MY SHOES WERE still wet. I couldn't stand it. Dennis and Kelly had gotten a chance to change out of their wet clothes. Dennis and Kelly had gotten a chance to shower. I told them I needed to go home for a quick costume change. I pointed out a few streets for them to stroll, referred them to a couple shops to while away the time. I wouldn't be long. Kelly didn't trust me. She thought as soon as I got home, I'd be tempted to stay there. Very smart. Probably right. They subwayed with me to the Upper West Side and the apartment I had been subletting since the break-up in February.

After I opened the door and the three of us were inside, I asked if they wanted a tour. This was hilarious twice over—because I was a licensed tour guide and because the apartment was miniscule. Three strategic steps and you'd seen the whole thing. The bathroom and bedroom were separated by the living room and kitchen, which Kelly kept calling "cute." Dennis said it wasn't that much larger than a prison cell. "A spacious cell, a corner cell, but still a cell." He guessed this was why New Yorkers were always eating out. I kicked off my wet shoes in the bedroom. They nosed around my living room while I undressed and wrapped myself in a towel. For the first time that I could remember, I walked half-naked by two of my tourists. Kelly whistled; Dennis looked through the music collection. I showered. I stretched my legs, massaged my neck. Feeling the hot water spray on my lower back was the best moment of the entire day. I wrapped myself again and walked to the bedroom. Kelly whistled; Dennis looked through my books.

8:45 SPLINTER GROUP SUBWAYS TO CHELSEA

ON THE CORNER of the block hosting our first event, I discovered that another of my favorite places had closed. This time a store, a shop for housing supplies. There was a letter posted on the glass door thanking all of the customers and friends for their patronage over the last twenty-two years. How long before the whole city was a series of empty spaces to rent? How much longer, I wondered, could I continue giving tours when all that I knew was disappearing around me? I found myself constantly pointing out things that were no longer there, discussing stories of places and people that no longer existed. A tour, I had to remind myself every day, could not be exclusively a litany of *This was here* and *This used to be there* and *That used to be something else completely*. I needed to touch on what was here now, but I wasn't interested in what so many things were becoming.

Take the north side of Forty-eighth between Broadway and Seventh, for example: It's now another bland glass apartment tower with the M&M store at its base, but did you know that the building it replaced had stood there for over a century? 1600 Broadway was built in 1902 when Times Square was still called Longacre Square and its ground floor served as a showroom for the Studebaker Brothers, who sold luxurious horse-drawn carriages as well as their new automobiles. 1600 Broadway was also the building where three men founded C.B.C. Film Sales Company, which would become Columbia Pictures. It was the site of New York's first Odditorium, the museum and freak show of Robert Ripley, who opened the showcase in 1939 after its debut at the Chicago World's Fair of 1933. Do you care about any of that, or am I really expected to talk about M&M's? Shouldn't I be showing you the things you can't see? As long as there's a sign, I shouldn't need to read it to anyone.

The whole city was changing, had always been changing—it was cliché by now to proclaim that change was the one constant in New York's history—but the latest metamorphosis seemed accelerated. The only thing that was stable was the grid system itself, the street plan that created the real estate lots where we opened and closed our shops and galleries, opened and closed our restaurants and offices, opened and closed our film companies and freak shows.

9:15 SPLINTER GROUP ARRIVES BIRTHDAY PARTY

THE FIRST PARTY was an intimate gathering. There were only ten people in the living room with another four on the fire escape smoking. When we arrived, a woman I didn't know was holding court. She would not be the one to cheer me up. She had been laid off in March, when Bear Stearns was sold off at bargain prices, and she now sat at one end of a leather sofa, forecasting doom, a modern-day Cassandra, neglecting her resume to come here and warn us all that a major financial crisis was going to hit within the year.

A few of the other guests, wrapped up in the election, however, were optimistic. Times were changing. The Democratic primaries had finally come to a close. Hillary Clinton conceded, and Barack Obama became the candidate who would be officially nominated at the convention in Denver. One woman still wore her Hillary button, but two at the party were wild Obama advocates. A buttonless fourth was concerned that the Democrats had made the wrong choice. She kept reminding us of '04 when no one in their right mind would have voted for Bush, but then people did! A majority did!

She then swung to the Kentucky Derby.

In the buildup to that event, Hillary Clinton publicly endorsed the only filly in the race.

The outcome had been outrageous—not only was the winning horse named Big Brown, but the female horse Clinton had endorsed was injured and had to be immediately euthanized on the track.

"You can't make that shit up!" she shouted with bug eyes. "Then Big Brown goes on to win the Preakness, good for him, all right, but now we come to the most important: the Belmont Stakes and the Triple Crown, the general election of horse racing. And what happens? An embarrassing defeat! Big Brown peters out and lopes across the line *dead last*. So the question is obviously will our Big Brown be able…"

Someone with an Obama button said, "Please stop calling him Big Brown."

"All I'm asking is will he be able to win the most important race? Now that it's just Obama and McCain, should we expect another trouncing? Like 2004? I've been nervous ever since the Belmont Stakes, which was the exact same day Hillary officially conceded."

A few seconds passed in the room before Dennis asked the woman he had never met, "Are you genuinely concerned about an election based on the symbolism of three horse races?" Kelly and I wanted to avoid an escalation of hostilities. We both knew what Dennis was capable of. All you had to do was look at the abrasion on the side of his face to know that he thrived on altercations. We hurried to change the subject and wished the birthday boy a happy one.

When the smokers came back in, the conversation broke into smaller groups. Time passed. Somewhere around nine forty, the party reverted to Trivial Pursuit, which I absolutely loved. Bring it on! My guests, however, were unimpressed. How underwhelming it was for them to find New Yorkers spending a Friday night playing board games. Shouldn't we be snorting coke and shooting amateur porn? I already had our plastic playing piece in my hand when I saw the look in their eyes. We apparently had somewhere else to be. I was sad. We left.

9:45 SPLINTER GROUP STROLLS THROUGH MEATPACKING DISTRICT

NEXT STOP: CHELSEA MARKET for the restrooms. Dennis claimed he couldn't use the one back at the party because it was right off the living room and had a thin wooden door.

No soundproofing. No ventilation. Too much Ethiopian food.

"It would have been like going to the bathroom on the middle of the coffee table."

I would not have put that past him.

While we waited for Dennis, I gave Kelly a brief tour of what was once the Nabisco factory where they made Oreos, Animal Crackers, Saltines, Mallomars, and Fig Newtons. I couldn't stop myself. I asked her if she knew how the Oreo got its name.

"No clue." I told her, and she asked, "Is that really true?"

"That's the word on the street."

Dennis returned, and we walked below Fourteenth and over the cobblestone streets into the nineteenth century. I told them about the transformation of the neighborhood: from docks and butchers; through prostitutes and after-parties; to clubs and lounges that sprang up during the *Sex and the City* era. And then I couldn't stop talking about Florent—the legendary diner, the mainstay of the district, the spot that was cool way before the rest of the area became trendy, the restaurant that arguably gave rise to the new Meatpacking District. Florent was closing at the end of the month! They wanted to see it, so we peeked inside. Dennis took a picture on his phone. We wanted to have a final meal there, pay our respects, but we were still full.

I took them to the top of the Gansevoort to see the rooftop pool and for the view of the Hudson and New Jersey. The place was already packed. When a waitress materialized, we ordered more drinks. Looking out over the river, I began to ramble again, giving Dennis and Kelly a history of nightlife in New York—the advent of electricity, the evolution of the red light districts, the birth of the red rope, the guest list, and the innovation of bottle service. I closed with Stanford White, the preeminent architect, the playboy, the gadabout who loved teenaged girls, a *sex offender* in today's parlance. White threw parties where nude showgirls swam in giant glass tanks filled with champagne.

"The Gilded Age," Dennis responded. "That's how they used to do it. Now it's drunk college kids passed out in bathtubs filled with ice and Rolling Rock."

After the dead air that followed so many of his comments, I stupidly replied, "Times have changed."

Kelly said, "Cielo is supposed to be nice."

I told her, "It's too early for Cielo."

Kelly rattled off a number of other lounges and nightclubs.

"How do you know all these?"

"What's your favorite?"

I had never been much of the nightclub type. I loved the history of the nightclubs but rarely wanted to go to one.

"I remember the Palladium; I went there my first year in college."

"Okay, let's do it."

"But it closed in '98. The building was torn down and replaced with an NYU dorm. Before that, though, the Academy of Music stood on Fourteenth where…"

"Jack," Kelly said simply.

Tour vetoed, I said, "It's still too early for nightclubs."

"Then what's next?" Dennis asked.

10:30 SPLINTER GROUP ARRIVES CAST PARTY, LOWER EAST SIDE

NEXT WAS A LOFT party with access to the rooftop and not a board game in sight. Couches and chairs were arranged around a massive coffee table at one end of the apartment. This created four social spaces since the size of the coffee table put real distance between all the furniture. At the other end, was a kitchen and dining room area with a table and several chairs. Temporary walls had been installed to create a bedroom and a walk-in closet directly across from the front door, and we saw that people were already milling about in there. Carrying the beer, purchased at a store on the corner, with Dennis and Kelly behind me, I sought out someone I knew, a connection, to the party, an anchor to justify our presence.

I saw one of the loft's owners, a composer I met in the theater years earlier who had gone on to make a small fortune writing pop songs and incidental music for television. His wife was on the board of the venue hosting a downtown festival playing throughout the weekend.

Each night had different acts, so whoever was on tonight was done performing and ready to celebrate.

"Hey, Jack," Dustin greeted me. "Mandy's on her way. I had to get back and open the doors. I'm sorry to hear about you and Kurt."

"Well, a few months ago," I said. I wondered how he knew, and then remembered that Kurt, focusing more on directing, was working with an actor/singer who was probably part of the festival. I introduced Dustin to Kelly and Dennis, and he told them to have fun. A bottle of wine in hand, he walked toward the other end of the loft, and I whispered a few of the songs he had written. Dennis didn't recognize them, but Kelly did. She smiled. This was exactly the kind of party she envisioned.

Dennis grabbed a soda from the fridge; Kelly poured herself a glass of wine. By this point, I was reminding myself that it was not the weekend for me. I had to be in the lobby of the hotel at eight the next morning. I still had to give a walking tour of Greenwich Village and a bus tour of the Upper West Side before I got a break. I took a glass from a cabinet and filled it with ice from the freezer and then water from the tap. I drank it down and refilled, drank half and refilled.

When I turned from the sink, I was shocked to see Kelly talking to Kurt. My ex. She must have recognized him from pictures at my apartment. I heard her telling him what a terrible mistake he had made, and I saw him trying to figure out who the hell she was. Kurt had just arrived—he was still carrying a surfboard, presumably a prop from the act he had directed. We greeted each other. I asked how the show went.

"Fantastic!" No matter how the show really went, it was always *fantastic* with Kurt. He asked who my friend was.

"Kelly Mitchell. And this is Dennis. They're in town until tomorrow."

Kurt, mysteriously sporting new facial hair, the beginnings of a Van Dyke, asked how I knew them, and from his tone I knew that he knew, and I knew that he judged it odd.

"Did you see the show?" he asked.

Kelly answered, "No, we've been party hopping. We just had drinks at the Gansevoort."

Unimpressed, Kurt stared straight at me and said he needed to put the surfboard down.

I began to plan my exit. I needed to extricate myself from what could prove an uncomfortable evening. I had done my share to entertain Kelly, or to preoccupy her, and now that she was here at her perfect downtown party, my work was done. But could I really just go? Leave Dennis and Kelly alone on the Lower East Side? And it must have been right around this time, as I was wondering whether I could abandon two of my adults, that Elaine Caine up in Midtown lost one of our students.

10:45 K.C. CROWN MIDDLE SCHOOL MEET ESCORT AND RETURN TO HOTEL

ALMOST AS SOON AS the child went missing, Ramona blamed Kelly for leaving her alone to go drinking, as well as for choosing the play that distracted Ramona from safely shepherding their students.

The second play on K. C. Crown's itinerary was an absurd farce full of slamming doors and mistaken identities. The first part of the play was a set-up for the rest, and since that first part wasn't very funny, most of the kids checked out early. They woke up for intermission but were soon comatose again. As the audience laughed louder and doors slammed harder, Ramona found herself getting nervous, agitated by the form itself.

This is what bothered Ramona: Farce asked you to laugh at characters who didn't understand the role they were playing in their own stories. The audience knew what was happening, but the characters had no clue. They were lost in situations that resulted from innocent ignorance. Person A thought he knew who he was, where he was, what he needed to do, and then he walked offstage. As soon as he was gone, other people entered, moved something, took something, dropped something, plotted something, and disappeared. Person A reentered, and the world had changed—Person B despised him, Person C was madly infatuated, Person D tried to kill him, Person E wanted him fired, and Person F placed him under arrest. Ramona could not laugh at this. She felt that farce, far from being outlandish, was the most authentic art form ever created. But it wasn't funny. There was nothing funny about it. It was terrifying, this idea of going about your day, unaware of what people were doing behind your back. It complicated the core of her belief: how do you tell it like it is when you don't know what the *it* is?

These were the thoughts that stayed with her after the curtain fell, when she and Elaine Caine gathered the group and led the way through the mob scene in Times Square. In the front, Elaine wielded a bright pink umbrella. From the back, Wally waved to Ramona at every corner, at each turn and crossing, so she assumed they were together during the several blocks it took to reach the hotel. Inside the lobby, Ramona called back the girls rushing to the elevators. She wanted to do a count just to be sure. Minus Kelly, Ramona counted sixteen, which was the correct number, but she realized as she dismissed the kids for the night, that she had counted Barbara, the mother from Seattle, who had somehow joined up with her group and was standing in the back with Wally and Clint.

"Hang on," Ramona said. "I think we're missing somebody." She counted again and came up one short. Her heart began to race. Her stomach tightened. She told them all to stop moving. She told them all to raise their hands. "Now put your hand down when I point to you." They obeyed. She was still one short.

Barbara from Seattle said, "You're missing the boy I found yesterday."

All heads turned for Lash, the boy who didn't have a cell phone, the boy this city would eat alive. Wally and Elaine hurried back outside to walk down the block. Nancy muttered that she knew something was going to go wrong. She told Ramona to get Kelly down here, migraine or no migraine, but Ramona knew that Kelly was not sleeping off a migraine.

Ramona asked Barbara, "Could Lash have merged with your group somehow?"

"My group's a few blocks away. They went for cheesecake."

Nancy picked up a house phone and asked to be connected to Kelly's room. Ramona thought that even if Kelly were there, if she had come back after dinner, she wouldn't pick up the phone. She was still screening on account of Hunter.

Clint said, "Maybe Lash is already up in the room."

"I was the first inside."

"Maybe Lash had to pee, and he ran past you when you weren't lookin'."

"Okay, Dina and Penny, can you take the kids upstairs and call me if Lash is there?"

Dina said, "If he is, I'll wring his little neck first. Come on, kids!"

"No one's answering in your room," Nancy said. "Could she have taken a sleeping pill?"

Ramona wanted to say that she had no idea what Kelly might or might not have taken, might or might not have done. After two and a half hours, Ramona still felt like she was in the world of that farce—that the hotel lobby had become the new stage scenery and the doors that opened and slammed shut had simply been replaced with elevators and doors that revolved—but now she herself was part of the confused action and no longer part of the all-knowing audience.

Elaine and Wally were back. They circled up with Ramona and Nancy, Travis and Barbara.

"Maybe he found a pay phone and called the number on the Lost Card."

"I'll check with Carol."

"When was the last time anyone saw him?"

"He was sittin' next to me in the theater."

"Did we see him in *front* of the theater?"

"We counted everybody. The number was right on at the theater."

"We were walking too fast."

"I was in the back. I saw everybody."

"There were too many turns."

"It was too crowded."

"These kids are *not* paying attention."

"Where's Kelly?"

"They're just looking up at the buildings…"

"…or in the windows…"

"There was that guy with the python around his neck. The boys tried to stop…"

"Naw, I kept 'em goin'."

"Everyone should have a cell phone."

"He hasn't called Carol."

"It should just be a rule. No cell phone. No trip."

"Maybe someone took him."

"Travis!"

"That's not helpful."

"We have to trace our steps."

"We have to go back."

"He got separated and turned around."

Barbara, who had found him once already, spoke up, "I think he misreads the signs. I don't think he understands that they run parallel to the streets."

Wally said, "Let's go back to Times Square."

Travis said, "And we should split up so we can cover more ground. Wally, you take a lady, and I'll take a lady."

Ramona and Nancy decided to stand in front of the hotel and wait for Lash. Travis and Elaine headed to Times Square via Forty-eighth, and Wally and Barbara took Eighth Avenue.

Ramona's phone rang.

"Hello, Mrs. Harrison, this is Carol. Elaine told me you're in charge because Kelly Mitchell threw her phone into a gutter? Is that right?"

"Yes, and Kelly's not with us tonight."

Nancy said, "I'll call her room again. She *needs* to be in on this."

When Nancy walked away, Ramona said, "She *might* still be with our tour guide."

Carol asked, "With Jack?"

"I know they went for dinner together."

"That's very interesting," Carol said. "Let me make a phone call."

Nancy returned, "Still no answer." She was trembling. "We should've had them holding hands."

"That's ridiculous, Nancy."

"Wally and Clint were holding hands."

"He's a ten-year-old," Ramona reminded her.

"Our kids aren't much older. They're not used to those crowds. Ramona, I've said it before, but it would be nice, especially now, if you agreed with me on *one* thing. That's all I'm asking. Once a year, one thing."

"Well, it won't be telling our middle schoolers to hold hands."

"They should have been right next to an adult on all of our walks."

"They were."

"Someone took him. Someone took him, pulled him into some alley, and did something to him. Did you see those bla…" She stopped herself.

"Oh, say it, Nancy. Just say it."

"Those crazy people dressed up in those outlandish robes and screaming on the microphone? They looked violent to me. They probably grab a kid or two every night."

"And do what? Throw 'em in the back of a van?"

"Was there a van? Did you see a van?" Nancy looked ready to sprint to Times Square at any memory of a van.

"They were in the middle of Times Square. There's no parking in the middle of…"

"But a van could have driven by. It could have stopped at a red light, opened its door…"

"Nancy, the black men in Times Square did not take Lash. You're not helping."

Nancy chewed the side of her thumbnail and told Ramona she was right, adding, "We need more manpower. I'm waking Kelly up." She stormed back into the hotel.

Ramona's phone rang, and she quickly answered it.

Carol said, "I reached Jack. The three of them are somewhere downtown."

"Three of them?" Ramona asked.

"Jack, Kelly Mitchell, and one of the parents from Seattle."

Ramona was floored. There were only two parents from Seattle, and one of them was currently with Wally searching for their lost student. The other was Dennis, the big mouth, the one Kelly swore she never spoke to, even though they seemed chummy on the ferry ride this morning, and now it was eleven o'clock at night, and Kelly was still out with him, "somewhere downtown." She prepared herself for Nancy, who would be back demanding to know where Kelly was. What would Ramona say? Why should she protect Kelly anymore at the risk of her own job? It was becoming clear to Ramona that Kelly could not be trusted. Obviously, Kelly was the one who told Dennis about Ramona's meeting with Nancy—who else could it be?—and she had lied to Ramona's face about it. Had Kelly Mitchell always been this duplicitous, or had she been infected by one of the Bloated Apple's poisonous worms?

Ramona could hear the doors swinging open, the doors slamming shut, and the entire audience laughing at her.

11:00 PARTY, LOWER EAST SIDE

MORE THAN FIFTY BLOCKS away, a boy band sang in my pocket. I had learned that the new ring tone, courtesy of the eighth graders, was sung by the Jonas Brothers. In this loft, which was filling up with more and more downtown theater people, I desperately wanted to silence the Jonas Brothers, so I dove through the front door into the stairwell and flipped open my phone.

Carol, who usually opened with a *Whatcha doing?*, got right to the point: "You're not out with your uncle and aunt. You're with that teacher from Georgia."

"This is New York; things turn on a dime."

"Are you near Times Square?"

"No. Why?"

"Where are you?"

"Way downtown."

"Well, Elaine and several chaperones are in Times Square, where Kelly Mitchell should be, searching for one of her children…"

"Which one?"

"His name is Lash Dautensomething."

I said, "He'll show up. He just got turned around."

"He doesn't have a cell phone," Carol said, "and we can't call his teacher because she threw her phone into a gutter. That wouldn't matter because the teacher is usually with the group she's chaperoning and not drinking with the guide downtown. I thought you were tired…"

"I was ambushed. I had to take them…"

"*Them?* Who else?"

"The father from the Seattle group. He's very provocative. Think of this as a kind of quarantine. I'm keeping him away from everyone else."

"So you're showing *two* people around?"

"We're decompressing after a very tough day. I texted you, remember? They came to blows, Carol. The combo group you gave me came to physical blows at Ground Zero."

"You're with two of our clients, so I hope you're aware…"

"I'm taking care of them."

"Is she standing nearby?"

"Kelly? I don't know where she is. It's a big party."

"I'd like to talk with her when you find her," Carol said. "Have her call me."

When I reentered the loft, I saw Kelly in the middle of half a dozen people several yards away. She was telling a story, acting out something. Dennis was helping her, so I assumed the story was one they both knew, something from the tour most likely. I tried to figure out who they were impersonating, but I stayed near the front door, leaving room for the new arrivals as the party progressively grew more crowded.

A figure in the group around Kelly and Dennis turned away from the storytellers. He was making a cocktail party exit, excusing himself through the lift of his empty glass. *I'll just grab a refill and be right back.* He wouldn't return, though. Kurt had had enough. He was disengaging from the chatter. He saw me watching. But he didn't approach. He didn't want me to finish the story they were telling.

He threw me a look across the floor, over the shoulders of other guests. His lower jaw slid to the right, which distorted the Van Dyke he was trying to grow. He glared at me and almost imperceptibly shook his head. Then he quietly disappeared around a corner. He might as well have thrown wine in my face or pelted me with a cube of cheese. I knew exactly what he was thinking. That look was meant to question everything about this night and the way I was living my life.

It was meant to ask: "Now you're spending your *off-time* with them? You're bringing your out-of-towners to parties where even you have a tenuous connection? You didn't come to the show tonight, you didn't support the festival, you just hit the party with two tourists in tow. You have nothing to do with the creative community working down here. Don't you feel out of place? Tell me: When did this, this, this *tour guide thing*, go from a day job to a lifestyle? You were an actor. You once stopped your bus on Eighth Avenue, told the passengers that you had to pick up their dinner voucher, and then ran upstairs and auditioned! You made your appointment! You had priorities! You would cancel a job if you had a callback, because you were not in this city to give tours of this city. That's not why you came here. But then somewhere along the way you took more jobs, you changed your schedule to accommodate the requests, all the repeat groups who asked for you. For them, you made sure you were available. And with every repeat group, you took a new one as well. You filled up your season. You got choosy with your auditions—some weren't worth the effort—but not at all selective when it came to the tour jobs. In the middle of heat waves, in the middle of blizzards. And despite all the hours you put in, you never clocked out. The more you worked, the more you talked about it when you weren't working. You told so many stories about your day. Each and every day. Long after I stopped listening. Many were funny, some even poignant—the kid in the wheelchair, the old couple with the towel—but, Jack, there's a point of saturation. They're tourists. Tourists. One of the dirtiest words in the English language. Right behind terrorist. Terrorists and tourists, destroyers of cities. Come on, Jack, you were the one trying to make a life in this place, and you've given it away to people who come all the way here to buy bags of candy in Times Square and counterfeit crap in Chinatown. People who eat at Red Lobster and the Olive Garden, people who don't give a fuck about what makes New York original. People who think *Cats* is a theatrical achievement. The people who stand in the middle of the sidewalk blocking anyone with a legitimate reason to walk. Tourists. The people who invade our streets and make fun of foreign accents without a shred of awareness that their accent is almost always the stupider of the two. They come onto our streets, our city, and make nasty comments to gay men and women. Come onto our streets and snicker at the homeless or the street performers. Snicker at those who live here! It's unbelievable. I always thought you would be happy to see them go, but every time one group left, you'd have to give a post mortem. Not just to me, but to our friends, and the novelty wore off even for them. We're busy, we have things we're trying to do, lives we're trying to carve out, and we don't care what the tourists think or say or do or buy. We don't want to see New York through their eyes. We have our own version. And we're not tourists either, Jack. We did not hire your services. We don't care as much as you do about the trivia on every block. A walk with you turned into a history lecture. You stopped listening, you lost the ability to read your audience, and you could barely carry on a conversation because you always thought you had to be the moderator. You turned us into tourists! No matter how fast we walked, you walked one solid pace ahead, always the leader. You held the subway doors open for us. For us! For New Yorkers! You made sure you finished every meal three bites before the rest of the table. You expounded on the state of every neighborhood, told the same stories, polished anecdotes that always got the laugh (the first time around), shared your trivia. Trivial, trivial trivia. At every social engagement, there you were, the life of the party, telling your stories, and weighing in with your opinion on every New York subject. There was always a story from history you could pull out of your pocket, always something bigger, more significant to apply to today. You could have been a lawyer with that memory, that storehouse of precedents, but you chose instead to squander it on tourists. Tourists. The day you threw me a Starburst for correctly identifying the Lever House, well, I knew we were over. It was a joke on your part, I knew that, I know that, but I couldn't live through any more tours. I needed to break new ground. And I am. I wish you could have seen the show. I'm moving into directing full-time. I think I'll be successful. And here I am at a post-show party with some of the most talented artists the city has to offer, and I'm forced to endure another story told by two tourists that you have for inscrutable reasons brought to this loft."

All that.

In one look.

11:00 SEARCH PARTY SCOURS TIMES SQUARE

INSTEAD OF SIPPING champagne at a post-show reception at the Waldorf, or instead of eating cheesecake with Cody and his class-mates in a restaurant near the Winter Garden Theater, Barbara was walking down Eighth Avenue with the giant from Georgia, part of a search party on the lookout for an eighth grader named Lash, and that seemed exactly where she should be.

"I think this is going to be difficult," Barbara said, wondering how to track down a boy you didn't know in a city that wasn't yours.

"I reckon he'll figure out his way back before we find him. All he has to do is ask somebody."

Barbara could see Cody doing that, but Lash was not the same kind of social animal. Lash, painfully shy, couldn't even hold his own against a hot dog vendor or a cashier in a gift shop. She kept picturing him pressed into a corner or a niche, waiting, praying to be found by his teachers. She looked hard into the nooks, crannies, and shadows.

"What's Lash wearing?" Barbara asked.

"Khakis and a white shirt," Wally answered.

"Naturally," Barbara said and then tried to dig deeper into the boy's mind. "Do you think he's a boy who tries to find his way home, or do you think he's a boy who waits for someone to come find him? I think he's a boy who tries to find his way home until he's even more lost. Then he freezes up and waits to be found, but he waits in a place where he won't be found because no one in his group has ever been there."

"Dang! I like how you're usin' your space needle."

She smiled, "Much obliged."

"Let's start back at the theater, and I'll show you the path we took to the hotel. Hopefully, he's still somewhere on it." Wally stopped at a corner. "If I can remember how to get back to the theater. I get turned around up here." Wally looked in both directions as Barbara waited. "I never get lost at home. Well, that way is full of lights and that way is not, so that way has to be Times Square, and our theater was on the other side of that." He led.

Barbara began, "I like how you're using your…" She stopped abruptly.

"Do you see him?" Wally asked. "Oh, I get it. You stopped because you can't think of anything in Georgia."

"I can't," Barbara confessed. "I'm embarrassed. Is there a famous building left over from the Olympics?"

"We've got Stone Mountain."

"I like how you're using your Stone Mountain."

"Naw, that's no good."

"I got it! I like how you're using your Hilton Head!"

"Not bad," Wally raised his eyebrows. "But that's South Carolina."

"Really?" she said. "Now I'm more embarrassed. Savannah, Macon, green jacket…"

"Green jacket?"

"You know, what they wear at the Masters. In Augusta! Um, March to the Sea, *Gone with the Wind*, Scarlet O'Hara, debtors colony, James Oglethorpe. How did I remember James Oglethorpe? I don't know. I can't think of anything…"

"You're forgetting the most obvious," Wally looked down at her. "All you have to say is, 'I like how you're usin' your peach.'"

"Oohhh, that would've been good," Barbara agreed.

"Don't let it get you down."

"What about peanut? 'I like how you're using your peanut.'"

"Well, that one there kind of hints at a small brain, but yeah…we do grow peanuts."

After the two of them reached the theater, they stood for a few minutes in the hope that Lash would step out of a doorway. When he didn't, they began to walk back. They stopped at any corner where the group had turned. Times Square was still full of activity. It was Friday night. He could have been standing in the middle of it all, and they wouldn't have been able to see him. Barbara kept staring up at the signs, trying to imagine how Lash might have misread them, which direction he might have walked. Wally and Barbara looked for places where Lash would have felt safe, places that could have had a pay phone. Wally called Ramona, expecting to be told Lash was at the hotel, but she said she and Nancy were still waiting outside, and Travis and Elaine weren't having any luck either. They asked a few police officers, on foot and on horseback, if they had been asked directions by a lost middle schooler with a very thick accent. None of them had, but one pointed them to a police building at the bottom of Times Square where he might have gone looking for help. Wally and Barbara both doubted it, but they started toward it anyway.

11:15 PARTY, LOWER EAST SIDE

BACK DOWNTOWN, AFTER Kurt diminished my life with a look, I felt a more urgent need to leave the loft. Made to feel I didn't belong, I decided to join the rest of the party on the rooftop, to get some fresh air, to put some distance between myself and my ex. I opened the door and started to climb the old staircase.

I wasn't an actor. I gave that up long ago. There were so many better actors at every audition. Or, more to the point, there were so many more actors whose entire lives were devoted to their *craft*, the practice of it, the business of it. These were people who were more passionate than I was about the struggle, the steps on the ladder. When had I become a full-time tour guide? I didn't know. It was a good job. It let me take time off to travel, and it was a hard job to quit. It was one of the only jobs I knew that ended with hugs, applause, and tips. Kissing, claps, and cash.

And, in another sense, it *was* acting. It was definitely performance, and there was some artistic fulfillment in that. I had been told by corporate executives, who had been on safaris in Kenya and expeditions in Antarctica, that my tour was the single best tour they had ever experienced. To be compared to other tour guides was one thing, but to be compared favorably to animals in their natural habitats? Well, that had to count for something. When I was *on*, there was no better show in town: My show was interactive, both scripted and improvisational, full of jokes, Starbursts, illumination, lectures, and song. I could guarantee you that a tour of the city with me was better than whatever bullshit monologue on a surfboard Kurt had presented to the world that night. And, by *world*, I mean twenty-six people on folding chairs in a basement.

I still stand by it: On the best days, to give a tour of the city is to work in a tradition of storytelling and performance that originated thousands of years ago with Homer and Thespis. But, yes, to be completely truthful, there are other days when working as a tour guide is not so different from working as a dog walker—you pick your clients up at the hotel, take them for a walk, and stop whenever they have to pee.

I pushed open the door onto the roof. The air was not fresh. It was still humid with the recycled breath of millions. The heat had baked into the buildings. It would never be cold again. But I was outside. And I belonged here. There was a sense in the loft that you needed to have been part of the festival, to have at least attended, but there were no such requirements here on the roof above the street lamps and beneath the starless sky. There were a couple dozen people standing around, drinking and smoking. I found a quiet corner.

I looked over the wall down toward the sidewalk and caught myself surprised to find the street below lined with parked cars but otherwise empty. I was on the Lower East Side and half-expected to see a street clogged with hundreds of new arrivals from Ellis Island. Maybe something *was* wrong with me. It was ridiculous that here I was, a century too late, listening for the sounds of the pushcart wheels and the basso profondo of the peddlers. Why did I think I could smell the worn-out coats and the fresh bialys? The more I read about the city, the more I learned, the better I could picture it, and the harder it was for me not to try. I was fascinated by it all, and the fascination only increased the longer I gave tours, the more I walked the sidewalks, the more I imagined the layers and layers that made up New York.

But I was like this wherever I went. Dublin, Rome, Chicago, San Diego. Puerto Rico, London, Virginia Fricking Beach. I annoyed everyone, even the natives, by pointing out things I had learned about their homes. I asked them to tell me everything they knew, to show me, and what they didn't know, I looked up. I read, I explored. I loved to travel. I loved to learn, and I loved to share what I'd learned. How sad not to feel I could tell someone—Kurt Bonner!—what I'd discovered.

Two men and a woman, in their twenties, all with the smell of actor on them, appeared off to my left, taking in the city around them.

Looking east, the woman asked, "What bridge is that?"

I fought the urge to answer. I was off-duty, and to identify bridges for actors would be to prove Kurt right. Let one of her companions answer.

One of them did: "The Manhattan Bridge."

It was the Williamsburg. A building was blocking our view of the Manhattan Bridge.

"The Brooklyn has to be close by."

"It has to be behind those buildings."

So is the Manhattan, I wanted to say. *You're looking at the Williamsburg. It's the Williamsburg Bridge.*

"I thought the Manhattan Bridge was blue?"

That's right, you're on the right track, you've almost got it.

"It looks different at night. With the lights. But that's definitely the Manhattan."

I bit down hard on both my lips and heard a squeak escape through my nose.

11:15 THOMAS LEDCKE HIGH SCHOOL EATS DESSERT

TRACY, WHO HAD TAUGHT me that trick, was one of the sixteen out-of-towners eating cheesecake just north of Times Square. Their teacher was treating everyone to one dessert and one beverage. He said he wanted to discuss some of what they had seen and done. At first, Tracy thought he was going to talk about the kerfuffle down at Ground Zero, but he was more interested in things cultural. He wanted to know who liked *The Light in the Piazza* and who liked *Mamma Mia*.

Everyone nodded noncommittally at both titles, but then he said, "They were good shows to see together because of how different they were." He next asked which show they all *preferred*. Tracy knew what he was going after. Their teacher had chosen one show, and the students had voted on the other. There had been a hot debate that winter about which show to see. They landed on *Mamma Mia* because *Wicked* was sold out on Friday (although they later learned that they could have seen *Wicked* if they had gone on Thursday but they had tickets for their teacher's show on Thursday). Tracy also knew that Pete despised *Mamma Mia*: she had seen him squirm his way through both acts. He asked for a show of hands for *The Light in the Piazza*. Only a few voted. Then again, only a few raised their hands for *Mamma Mia*. The rest said they couldn't choose, because the shows were too different. Tracy agreed. She would have voted for both, and if she were forced to vote at that moment, she would have endorsed the cheesecake as well. It was dense but very creamy, so she didn't chew but rather mashed it up with her tongue, the better to taste every single calorie.

After a brief lecture, which Tracy wanted to listen to, but couldn't, because she was so focused on her cheesecake, Pete began to direct specific questions to each student. He deliberately started on his right, away from his enemies, the shoppers, who were the only ones who had defiantly voted for *Mamma Mia* with the words, "Oh, no contest!" It wasn't too long, however, before they began answering on behalf of the others. They argued that *Mamma Mia* was fun and they were on vacation and they wanted to have fun and didn't want to sit through things that were not fun or were fun only to people who didn't like to have fun and didn't want other people to have fun.

"It's summer break," Laurie said, "we want to turn our brains off."

"Laurie," Pete said, "when have you ever turned yours on?"

Exclamations rang out—*Oo! Burn! No way!*—and Tracy got nervous.

But Pete wasn't done, "'It's summer break, let's turn our brains off.' 'It's the weekend, let's relax.' 'School's out, it's time for TV.' We get you for eight abbreviated periods a day, maybe five days a week, for forty weeks of the entire year, and during those fifty-minute periods, you're asking to use the restroom, you're texting friends, you're sleeping."

"This is crazy! We paid over two thousand dollars for this trip…"

"Your parents paid…"

"…and you get it for free."

"I work for it…"

"For two thousand dollars we should be able to do what we want, and having fun is what we paid for."

Jenny brought the reinforcements, "We have to walk everywhere, listen to all this history about things we've *never* learned…"

"It's been taught!"

"…go to museums…"

"We went to one museum; you knew that when you signed up."

Several said, "I loved the museum."

"And all that's fine, we're part of a group, we know that, but we don't like being yelled at, because we didn't like *Light in the Whatsherface*."

This was when Tracy blurted out, "I LOVE IT ALL!" With the exception of answering the occasional Starburst questions, Tracy had not spoken in front of the group since her Gatsby comment on Day One. But now she couldn't stop herself. She needed to explain what she meant. "I love everything about this trip from start to finish. I loved all the months of waiting and getting more and more excited and raising the money and packing my luggage and making my wish list and meeting everyone at the airport. I loved flying to Chicago and then landing in New York City. I loved the food, the tours, the shows. I can't pick anything out that I love more than anything else. I don't get to travel much, so for me everything is exciting. It's like being in the movies and doing all the things I've read about and watched on T.V. I can't pick one show over the other, because I loved them both. I loved dressing up and walking into the theaters. I loved how one of them was in a glass building with a huge foyer and the other was right in-side the doors off the street. I loved showing my ticket and getting my program and sitting in my seat, which for that night was only mine. I mean so many people have sat in these theaters over the years and seen so many shows, but on this night only I get to see that specific show from that specific seat. Last night I was at Lincoln Center, and tonight I was at the Winter Garden on Broadway, and both tickets are going in my scrapbook. I love the announcements to turn off your cell phones. I loved that last night's was in Italian. That was funny. I love when the lights go down, the music starts playing, and you're in another world in two seconds. I love all of it. I love the stories, the music, the dancing, the clapping. And I love that we're all in it together. We're the only ones seeing that show that night. Then we all come outside and people are walking by who didn't see the show, and there are taxis and horns and people coming from other shows or going to parties or just walking around late at night. There are so many theaters and things to do. And then the *actors* are suddenly outside wearing clothes just like us! And everyone goes on with their night. And I love this cheesecake!"

She heard the whispers, she was aware that her plate was the only one scraped clean. Most were still working on theirs.

"I think New York has the best motto or slogan or whatever you call the thing on the t-shirt, because I do love it and I love it with all my heart and I love it so much I think my heart might pop."

Many were staring at her with different degrees of concern, horror, or embarrassment. She wanted to wrap it up, but now she couldn't remember why she started talking. She was kind of all over the place. What was her point?

"So thank you," she said to Mr. Troiano. "*I've* had a lot of *fun*." Her face felt hot, so Tracy looked down at her plate, but she heard a couple people second her sentiment, a few raised mugs to their teacher, and Ryan told Jenny and Laurie that they had been burned.

Tracy gave up. She hadn't been trying to burn anyone. She wasn't that kind of person.

11:30???12:00??? PARTY, LOWER EAST SIDE

DOWNTOWN, JUST LIKE TRACY, I had been unable to keep
my lips clamped. Of course, I intervened. Of course, I told the three
actors standing near me on the rooftop that the bridge they were looking at was the Williamsburg. Of course, I then provided the dates of all
the East River bridges—who wouldn't want to know?—and explained
what was significant about each of them. All recent transplants, the
three actors were impressed. I told them I gave tours of the city, and
they started talking about their favorite neighborhoods. That, in turn,
required trivia about those neighborhoods, and soon we were off. Others joined, and eventually I was regaling them all with tales of the
tourists themselves.

"For example, Travis. He's an ironworker. He talks about an arsenal he keeps in his house. Travis is someone who almost scared me
when I first met him. What did we have in common? I have never
watched NASCAR, I've never fired a gun. I've never worked with a
blowtorch. I've made my living largely through words, performance.
But I love Travis. I mean, he's eating it up. It's great to see! This man
wore a foam Statue crown for most of the day. You know what I feel
like sometimes? An ambassador. I meet and greet all kinds from across
the country and around the world. I share my passion for this place
and hope I pass it on. And I'm enriched too. From hosting these…
delegations. I mean, I learn about the world outside New York. I knew
about the housing crisis long before it was a main story in the press. I
learned about it from my groups from Nevada and Michigan. And I
can tell you how the electorate is changing in Virginia…"

I kept talking. After years of giving tours, my mouth was able to
go it alone. I was on a roll and couldn't put the brakes on, even after
boredom started registering on the faces of my audience, even after
one couple peeled away to "replenish their drinks," even after I saw
Kurt standing on the other side of the roof watching me ramble, and

even after Dennis stopped by to say he was going back to the hotel. I kept talking and could have talked through the night if it hadn't been for Carol, via the Jonas Brothers, who interrupted me before I could say that I knew more about this country than Kurt and his ilk who put on plays east of the Hudson, who claimed New York should be its own city-state, who dined only with each other, and who did their best to avoid anyone with a different political perspective, with whom even if I didn't always want to engage, I was at least always exposed. I scrambled for my phone to shut the Jonas Brothers up, but in that moment, my entire audience took the opportunity to disperse.

They broke and fled in all directions.

Shocked and mortified, I kept myself from looking over to where Kurt was standing. I ignored the call but still held the phone up to my ear. I could use it for cover. I could pretend that I hadn't noticed my audience's brazen defection. I could use it to make my escape. I should never have been out in the first place. Phone to ear, I made my way across the roof to the staircase. I thought maybe I could still catch up with Dennis, pick up Kelly, and share a cab uptown. I rushed down the dimly-lit stairs, turning and hurrying around each corner until I was one flight above the party.

When I turned that corner, I could see a couple kissing in the middle of the staircase. I froze when I recognized the olive green polo shirt. The wispy beginnings of a bald spot. The bony shoulders rubbed by the manicured fingers of a woman.

In a dress from Bloomingdale's.

I stepped back into the shadows and around the corner.

Blinded by the impossible vision.

I didn't clear my throat or in any way make my presence known.

I didn't want to share a taxi with that.

I waited on the landing above until I heard the two of them moving away, down the stairs, and out of the building. The front door slammed shut and echoed up the stairwell.

I needed to get home. I needed Day Three to become Day Four. My cell phone beeped with a new voicemail message. I dialed it up as I resumed my descent. It was Carol letting me know what had happened to the eighth grader lost up in Midtown.

ON YOUR OWN

IT LOOKED FAMILIAR, Lash thought. But it all looked familiar. It all looked familiar and strange. And just because a street looked familiar didn't mean it was near the hotel. The group had walked all over the city. He recalled that the sidewalk in front of the hotel was busy at night and noticed that these sidewalks were empty. He looked up for a street sign, though he had come to think they were all hung wrong. This one said "5 AV." But the one right under it said "W 48 ST." So which one was it? Which street was he standing on right now? His hotel was somewhere on "48," (or "46"), but it wasn't here. Up a ways was the giant Catholic church from yesterday. This was frustrating. Yesterday he got lost and couldn't find the big cathedral to save his life, and now that he wasn't looking for the cathedral, here he was.

When they had left the theater, Lash stayed smack dab in the middle of K.C. Crown Middle School, and in his mind he went over some of that play, trying to figure out why the woman in the red dress got angry at the doctor when she saw him wearing the handcuffs. He still didn't get it. Unless the woman was the same woman from the first scene who wore the pajamas. If she was the same woman, though, she had to change clothes really fast when the lights went out. Maybe that was why the woman playing that part got it in the first place: because she could change clothes in record time. Maybe that was her talent. Her gift. Maybe that was something you trained for, something you learned in acting school.

When the group had turned at the first corner, Lash was near the back, amazed again by all the lights flashing and moving on the buildings. He made the turn with everyone, though it wasn't easy. There were a lot of people on these streets. It looked like everyone in the world was out in Times Square. Usually, if you're walking in a group of almost twenty, you have control over the path. People get out of the way. But twenty people didn't amount to much in Times Square. He tried to employ the tactic learned on Day One: Don't make eye contact, stare straight ahead, fix your gaze and walk without swerving. Lash also used the bodies in front of him to block and gain yardage.

At the next corner, Lash saw someone selling t-shirts, hats, and buttons for prices as cheap as they had been in Chinatown. The group was waiting for a light to change, and Lash took only two steps over to see the what kind of t-shirts the man had. Lash collected free souvenirs for himself, but his brother would want something bought with money. Lash still had thirty-five dollars left, and if they couldn't stop to shop now, maybe they would come back here tomorrow before they went to the airport. The man next to the table asked a question, but Lash couldn't understand a word of it. The man asked again, and Lash stepped back into his group, but all of a sudden he realized it wasn't his group. It was another group, around his age. He frantically looked around for someone he recognized and then raced across the street. A car honked, but Lash made it to the other side without the car having to stop. He looked up ahead. He saw the McDonald's where he thought they had eaten breakfast that morning. He was pretty sure, but there were McDonald's, Starbucks, and Duane Reades all over the place, and it was easy to confuse them. He kept walking and thought he saw the back of Miss Teen Seattle's head, but he stopped when he remembered that her school went to another theater.

Lash started to jog, but the faster he ran, the more he doubted his group was in front of him. He would have caught up with Grandma Penny by now. So he turned and ran in the other direction, keeping close to the wall where it was easier to slide by people. But then he bumped into a New York teenager stepping out of a store. She swore at him, but Lash was used to that by now.

He made it back to the corner where he lost the group. He stood there for at least fifteen minutes. No one in his group came back for him. They didn't know he was gone, and he couldn't just wait in the middle of Times Square for them to figure it out. By this point in his life, Lash knew that he did such a good job blending into the background that it was possible no one would notice he was gone. The Brandons would eventually figure it out, when Lash didn't show up in their room, but Lash couldn't wait that long. He also felt vulnerable just standing there. He had to keep moving, he had to look like he knew where he was going and what he was doing. If not, someone might try to pickpocket him or sell him drugs.

He was set on finding his way to the hotel. It was near here. He knew that. But the group had walked on a different street every single time. There were too many ways to get to the hotel. He had to pick one of them. He started walking a familiar street but stopped when he didn't recognize it any more. He considered going back to the theater, but now he wasn't positive he knew where that was. There were so many of them. He thought he saw the *Phantom of the Opera* theater, but that was yesterday's show, and if anyone was looking for him, they wouldn't go all the way back to yesterday. It turned out just to be an advertisement for *Phantom of the Opera* anyway. He started walking again in another direction until the street got too quiet and dark. The sidewalks were wide, but there weren't many people at all. He could wait here. He would stand out here. This was better than blending into the crowds of Times Square, but his people might never come this way looking for him.

He told himself that all he had to do was ask someone, but he was too nervous. Too shy. Couldn't stand it. How do people just walk up to strangers and talk? How do some people get on microphones and talk? How do some people get on stages in front of thousands of people and sing and make jokes and remember all their lines? Lash missed his mom. He was panicking. He forgot the name of the hotel and the street numbers. He knew what the sign looked like. He would recognize the front of the building and the lobby through the windows.

This was like the time when he was a little kid, and he couldn't get a lady behind the counter at the swimming pool to give him an ice cream sandwich. He couldn't remember the name of the treat, and the more he panicked, the more he knew, even then, that he would never come up with it. He kept telling her that it was like "graham crackers with vanilla in between." Graham crackers with vanilla. That's where he was right now. He walked down a street with a familiar name, but that name was a number, and all numbers were familiar, so what did that mean? Graham crackers with vanilla.

That's how Lash got to St. Patrick's on Fifth Avenue. There was a police car out front with a policeman sitting inside it. Lash wanted to ask for a ride, but would policemen help boys his age or only grade school kids? He couldn't get the courage up to approach the car anyway. For some reason, he thought he might even get in trouble for being alone. For not being with a chaperone or a "buddy." Late at night. In the city. Did eighth graders in New York walk around alone at night? Was that allowed? Was there some kind of curfew? He decided against asking the policeman for help, but he made a mental note of that police car in case a mugger started chasing him. Lash started walking along the church and remembered instantly from yesterday that that was not the way to go. If he kept walking that way, he would run right into the man at the hot dog cart who tried to steal his money when he bought the Coke.

The Lost Card! Lash could call the phone number and tell that person where he was. He looked up and down the streets but didn't see any phone booths, at least not the kind in the Superman comics. After ten minutes, he found a pay phone on a corner. Too bad he didn't have any coins. But he didn't have to pay anything! It was a 1-800 number. He picked up the receiver and reached for the lanyard around his neck. The lanyard was back at the hotel, in his room, in the pile of wet clothes he took off after the rain at Ground Zero.

Lash almost screamed, but nothing came out. He was seized by sheer terror. Would they leave for the airport without him? No, they had to know by now he was missing. They would call the police. Police would be looking for him. Lash considered sitting on the steps at the cathedral near the police car. They would put out an A.P.B. He could wait for the policeman to recognize him. How long would that take? Could he get through the night? The sidewalks were getting emptier. The place was deserted. Soon it would just be him and the people who prowl around looking for someone like him. He walked back past the church; Times Square would still be busy. Times Square had places open all night. He would sit in that McDonald's or whatever was open and keep an eye out for anyone looking for him.

Lash recognized Rockefeller Center. It wasn't as crowded as it was the day before, but there were people. There were a lot of people drinking down in the hole in the plaza. He felt safety in numbers. No one here was afraid. They were having a good time. They were taking pictures. He started looking for a pleasant face, a face he could muster up the courage to talk to.

"Hey, keed, you lust?" a voice asked behind him. It was one of those bicycle taxi drivers. "I saw you on Seexth. Are you uh-loan?"

The guy had a strange foreign accent, but Lash thought he understood what he was saying. He just didn't know if he should be honest. You weren't supposed to tell a stranger you were on your own. But who could he say he was with? His invisible friend?

"Get een. I take you ver you vant to go."

"For free?"

He laughed, "Fawk no! Dirty bucks."

Dirty bucks? Thirty? Thirty dollars! That was almost all he had left, and the only gift he had bought was a postcard for his grandparents.

"Vere you vant to go?"

"The hotel."

"Vich vun? Dere are too many."

"I can't remember."

"Vat's de address?"

Graham crackers and vanilla. "Forty-eight? Forty-six? Maybe."

"Deescribe vat eet looooooks like."

Lash said it was really nice.

"Nice like de Plaza? Or nice like de Marquis?"

Lash didn't know how to answer that. "It's not the Plaza or the other one. It has windows and uh, one of them round doors that spins in circles."

"Vindows and doors? Dat does not help. Get een, I take you round until ve find eet."

"Really?"

"Dude! Ve'll find eet. Dirty bucks."

Lash took his wallet out of his front pocket and opened it. He handed the guy his ten and his twenty. Then, before the foreigner could pedal off without him, Lash leapt into the seat. He felt more relaxed as soon as he did. The seat wrapped around his shoulders and the smell of sweat coming from the cyclist's armpits made him think of his brother, of chores, of the farm, of home.

At Sixth Avenue, the cyclist pointed to a hotel in the distance, and Lash shook his head. The hotel was definitely not here. His hotel was closer to Times Square. Near all the lights.

Lash said, "The hotel's not far from where you get your group picture took."

"Dat does not help."

"Do you know the guy who takes the pictures on the ladder?"

"I have not met dees man on de ladder." The cyclist looked back at Lash and smiled. He looked forward again and pedaled. Lash trusted this guy. He didn't think he was going to take him anywhere bad, like an abandoned warehouse where he would steal the rest of his money. (Five dollars.) Even if he tried to do something bad, Lash could jump out of this moving contraption at any time. No matter how fast the guy pedaled, Lash could jump out and run. He focused on his surroundings. The streets they were riding on were both familiar and strange.

He could never live in this city, he decided. Lash would never be a New Yorker.

Then there it was! Right there! The windows, the front doors, the sign sticking out above them like the visor on a baseball cap.

And there she was! His history teacher.

Lash screamed, "THIS IS IT! THIS IS IT! HERE I AM!"

Ramona was surprised and confused to see Lash rolling up in a pedicab, but before he could explain, he jumped to her on the curb, threw his arms around her, and broke down into sobs of relief.

DAY FOUR

8:00   Check Out

8:30   Breakfast

9:30   Subway to Greenwich Village

10:00 Greenwich Village Tour

11:30 Subway to Hotel

12:00 Lunch

1:15   Bus tour of the Upper West Side and Morning-side Heights

3:00   Depart for Airport (Harlem Drive-Through)

4:00   Drop K.C. Crown Middle School at LaGuardia Airport

4:15   Drop Thomas Ledcke High School at LaGuardia Airport

DENNIS HEARD THE SHOWER running and was disoriented for the third morning in a row, waking up in a time zone three hours too early. He tried to open his eyes. Too bright. She had drawn the curtains; the sun was streaming into the room. Eyes closed, he rolled over onto his back, dropped a pillow over his face.

He had stopped drinking early in the evening. Sadly, everyone around him kept imbibing and getting stupider. He fell into a discussion with a recent college grad, who laughed at his stories about the religious fundamentalists on his trip. He felt a kinship with her but soon discovered that while she was up for laughing at Christians, Judaism was apparently beyond reproach. He considered her mockery of the Christians, or her complicity in his mockery, distasteful and vile. How was it possible to see the ridiculousness in someone else's religion but ignore the absurdity in your own? So he cornered her and, as quickly as he could, navigated through his fourteen-part proof intended to persuade the listener to renounce any faith-based worldview.

Another woman overheard. She was a Buddhist who didn't worship any deity but started to give the case for faith and the psychological and physiological benefits of prayer or meditation. Dennis nodded as the other one quickly fled. He wasn't interested in any of this one's claptrap—her rehash of something she had heard on NPR while stringing beads and sipping ginger tea—so he zoned out almost immediately. He was also distracted, as he had been all night, by the black evening dress now a few yards beyond the babbling Buddhist.

Kelly Mitchell was utterly charming, very much of the South, and Dennis did find southern women terribly arousing. But she was also someone who could understand why non-southerners looked on the South with disbelief. She was the best kind of southerner: one who had a healthy shame about her home. He loved her drawl, her laugh, her cleavage. He loved her independence. Her teeth. Her long silky black hair. At the party, she flitted from conversation to conversation. Dennis assumed he lost her when she sank into a sofa with a six-foot-six Serb. He was a director, but Dennis didn't catch what he directed. It could have been theater, film, music videos. For that matter, he could have been a director of human resources.

When Dennis got sick of talking to people, he knew it was time to go home. He took the stairs to the roof to thank his guide for a night off the beaten itinerary and headed back downstairs to hail a taxi. Kelly was in the stairway coming up as Dennis was going down. No one was with her. She smiled up at him, the kind of familiar smile you give to a person with whom you came to the party. They had a connection. Others in the loft might have gotten caught in the downpour today, but were any of them involved in a fisticuffs moments before the clouds opened? No. The others in the loft were not acquainted with the thirty-three people from Washington and Georgia who were such a part of Dennis and Kelly's New York. They couldn't envision the exact way Dina spoke out of the side of her mouth or hear the notes that made up the laughter of the student council and their drama teacher. These partygoers hadn't lost a single minute waiting for Blue Hair or had their toes stepped on by a bouncing ten-year-old.

Kelly came up another few steps, and Dennis met her in the middle, where they faced each other and began to kiss. She tasted of red wine with a faint trace of a cigarette. He ran his hands over the back of her dress, which was soft and sleek. She held onto his shoulders for balance. She was wearing heels, and the stairs were small and uneven.

Dennis instantly wished he had stronger shoulders, figuring that her young gardener boyfriend had a v-shaped upper torso. He flexed his arms but couldn't engage his shoulders. The only way he could think of making them expand would be to hold his arms out to the side, but that would knock her off balance.

She whispered, "Hotel."

He almost lost *his* balance. He asked her if she had everything. She held up her purse and took his hand. They tumbled down the staircase and out of the building. There were no taxis on the tiny street, but they remembered the larger one with the two-way traffic and ran hand in hand until they saw yellow cabs coming off the bridge. They both raised arms. Two cabs jerked toward them. They hopped into the first one. He immediately placed his hand over a breast, but Kelly pointed to the driver and took his hand in hers. She leaned into him, rested her head on his bony shoulder. He raised his arm, twisted his body, and held her to him. She placed her other hand on his knee, and he tried to have faith in the physiological benefits of prayer: *Please don't let her fall asleep, please don't let her fall asleep.*

There wasn't any traffic, but the cab ride took forever. They didn't speak: he was afraid he would put his foot in his mouth; he was afraid that even Kelly might say something stupid. If that were possible. No, it wasn't. They decided not to touch as they walked into the hotel. There were thirty-three people (thirty-four, counting Elaine Caine) who might surprise them in the lobby.

As they made their way to the elevator, at around who-knows-when in the morning, Dennis said loudly enough for the security guard and the agent at the front desk to hear, "That was the longest Broadway show I've ever been to." Kelly bent over laughing. In the elevator, they kissed again. When the doors opened, they parted. This was the most dangerous stretch. Their group occupied most of the rooms on this floor. A uniformed woman sat in a chair at the end of the hallway. She was there for them, for their students, hired by the tour company, but Dennis felt guilty, a parent sneaking a teacher from another room, from another state, into his bed. He waved to the guard, who only looked up briefly before going back to her word search. Dennis opened the door, and they stepped inside.

As soon as the door was closed, their mouths found each other again, her arms were back on his shoulders, his hands made their way into her dress. Her cupped her breasts, felt her nipples in the middle of each palm, and moaned into her mouth.

The voice in the darkness was uncertain, "Daddy?"

Simultaneously, Dennis pulled his tongue back and pushed his hands forward. There was some force in his shoulders yet. Between the height of Kelly's heels and the strength of his push, not to mention the alcohol coursing through her, she fell into the door with a thud. He heard her cry out on her way to the floor. He bent down into the darkness. Felt Kelly's shoulder or knee.

Brittany said, "You gave me a key. You told me I could."

"No, I know, that's all right," Dennis stammered. He asked Kelly, "Are you all right?"

Brittany answered, "I'm fine."

"Just wait one second, Brittany. Oh, don't be unconscious. Kelly?"

"Ow."

"Are you hurt?" A lamp turned on behind him. Brittany was in bed, around the corner, out of sight. Kelly was lying on the floor with a hand over her eye and ear. "What happened?"

"What happened?" Kelly repeated. "Are you serious?"

"How did you fall?"

"You pushed me!"

"I mean, I thought you fell backwards, but your eye…"

"I twisted," she said.

"Let me help…" Dennis bent over and took her elbow.

"Is everything all right?" a woman's voice asked through the door. Dennis stood back up, bent his body over Kelly's, and looked through the peephole. The security guard.

"Yes, everything's fine."

"I heard a noise."

"Sshh," was all Dennis could say. He imagined all the doors opening on the hall. This was not good.

Kelly must have been thinking the same and quietly said through the door, "I tripped."

"What was that?"

Dennis felt his anger rise. She was only here to take care of the kids. She wasn't supposed to get into the business of any of the adults.

"Could you open the door please?"

"Oh, damn it," he said. He helped Kelly to her feet and out of the way so that he could open the door a crack. When he did, Kelly pulled the door wide open.

"It's fine, ma'am," she whispered. "I fell. I need to get back to bed now." Kelly took her purse from Dennis, who was somehow holding it, and made her way out of sight and down the hall. He wanted her to get quickly and safely into her room without anyone seeing, so he didn't follow. The security guard looked Dennis up and down. He could tell she was wondering if she needed to write this down in her report. She looked over his shoulder. Dennis turned. Brittany was standing at the foot of her bed in pajama bottoms and one of his t-shirts.

Dennis said, "Good night." He closed the door. "Hey, sweetheart."

"Who was that?"

"That was just the security guard."

"No," Brittany said. "I mean who'd you push?"

Dennis wanted to protect Kelly's privacy, and he couldn't tell his daughter it was a prostitute. He almost told her that it was someone he'd met in a bar, but then, because it sounded more respectful, he said, "It was just an old friend."

"Why'd you push your old friend?"

Dennis had no answer. They stood there facing each other.

"You scared me," he finally said. "I didn't expect to hear…"

"You kept saying I could come here…"

"I know."

"And Laurie and Jenny were mean to me all day." Brittany got back into bed; Dennis stepped farther into the room. "I waited for you, but I was so tired."

"It's fine. I'm tired too. Go to sleep. We'll talk in the morning."

Brittany kept her eyes on him. He went into the bathroom. He wanted to go after Kelly, but he couldn't risk waking anyone up, attracting eyes to peepholes. She was also in her room with that teacher from Georgia who did not like him at all. She would blame him for Kelly's fall. She would be right. He thought of calling her but knew she wasn't picking up the phone and that calling after midnight would give Ramona another reason to hate him. But after throwing Kelly into a door, wouldn't *not* calling be worse than calling too late?

In bed now, beneath his pillow, Dennis mused, *Who knew what other people ever thought? Who could figure them out?*

Brittany was out of the shower. Dennis pushed the pillow away, opened his eyes, shielded them from the sunlight with his hand. She came into the room fully dressed, her long hair still wet.

"We have to take our luggage to Mr. T's room before we go down to the lobby. We have to check out of our rooms before breakfast."

"How much time do we have?"

"Thirty minutes."

"I should shower then," he said, sitting up, stretching his back.

"Daddy?" Dennis looked at his daughter. "We don't need to talk about anything." He nodded. She added, "And you can wear whatever you want today."

Dennis knew what a big step that was, but he couldn't resist standing up and grabbing her by the shoulders. "Even my official Star Trek uniform, replete with boots and phaser?"

Brittany gave a nervous smile. "Did, did you pack those?"

"I'm kidding, I'm kidding," Dennis assured her as he walked to the bathroom. "Nobody ever gets my jokes."

8:00 CHECK OUT

THREE ADVIL, A LITER of water, five hours of sleep, a cold shower, a few slaps to the face, and a cab ride later, I reached the hotel ten minutes before I was scheduled. Today had to be different. Today I had to be at the top of my game. Vigilant. Focused. Attentive. And more cheerful than ever. Bigger smiles. The peppiest of the peppy. Totally in control.

My first obstacle stood smoking outside the front door, a sentry protecting the lobby: "Good morning, Dina."

"Well, hi!" she cheerfully responded and then remembered herself. "Did you hear about last night? We lost one of our boys for more than an hour!"

"I did hear that."

"Y'all New Yorkers walk too damn fast. I said it day one, and I'll say it right now."

"Thank you so much, I appreciate that," I said and slipped into the revolving door.

"I didn't mean that as a comp…"

Inside, the groups were again divided on opposite sides of the lobby, but that was better than being on top of each other in a cemetery. Because it was Day Four, many had relinquished their own clothing and were now wearing the tourist uniform—shirts and hats emblazoned with NYC or I♥NY; sunglasses bought from a stranger's garbage bag; purses snagged from a stall in Chinatown. Elaine was busy collecting keys and reconciling room charges at the front desk. With the broadest of smiles, I infiltrated both groups, asking about their evening, gathering intel, sowing the seeds of diplomacy. Most were exhausted, thankful for the later start. Lash blushed when I asked him about his wanderings and blushed again when I congratulated him on finding his way home. Wally joked that Lash was going to be on a leash until they got back to Georgia. Nancy said he would be holding her hand until the minute she delivered him to his parents. Clint asked for another personalized Starburst question. I realized I had forgotten to resupply. My tour of Greenwich Village would be completely candyless. Keep smiling, keep smiling. The Brandons were playing cards peacefully in the corner. Grandma Penny and Travis were "ready for another great day." The Georgia girls were all half-asleep on one of the sofas, each head resting on the shoulder of the girl to her left. Zach asked if I had seen the play they had gone to and then gave his review—"quite funny with a clever denouement." On the Seattle side, Barbara filled me in on the search for Lash while several of the girls, both student council and shoppers together, quietly sang their favorite lyrics from *Mamma Mia*, and Tracy made sure to tell me that, before their flight home, she still needed a "a bialy, a shmeer, a picture with the Naked Cowboy, and a few more things."

"I'll see what I can do," I told her. The mood in the lobby was pacific; I was encouraged that we could get through the rest of the tour without conflict. Then the elevator door opened, and Dennis, our resident suicide bomber, entered the lobby. He grinned when he saw me and came straight toward me.

"How was *your* evening?" he asked, pretending way too broadly that he hadn't seen me since the previous afternoon.

"Good, good," I said at a lower volume to keep those nearby from listening in and becoming suspicious. "I need to talk to Elaine about luggage." He actually winked at me, and I wasn't sure if that were meant to convey a mutual code of secrecy, which would have been a relief, or an adolescent signal that he had hooked up with Kelly, which I didn't want to know about. On my way over to Elaine, another elevator opened, and Kelly and Ramona stepped out. Even with her sunglasses and the makeup masterfully applied, I was still able to make out the swollen eye and hints of bruising. Ramona was the one who held all the room keys and announced that the group was ready to go. Ramona, it was obvious, was in charge this morning, and Kelly, a disgraced figurehead. As Ramona passed by for Elaine and the front desk, she tossed me a glance that told me she, and she alone, knew I had been the leader of a splinter group and blamed me for whatever had transpired. Kelly and I had only seconds to catch up:

"Dennis?"

"Drunk."

"Eye?"

"Dennis."

"Why?"

"Daughter."

"What?"

"Later."

We broke when another elevator opened. Pete arrived in the lobby. Elaine cried, "That's everyone!" Both groups stood to walk to breakfast, but Pete wasn't done with the checkout yet.

"Where's Melanie?" From a chair next to the front window, our little blue-haired friend raised her hand. "Where are your bags?"

"In my room," she said.

While several groaned, Pete took a deep, deep breath, scratched his beard, and said, "You need to bring your bags to my room. Like everyone else did." All eyes were on Pete, so he announced, "You've also just lost out on the morning tour. Jack, we'll meet you at breakfast. Again." The two of them disappeared into the elevator; the incredulous murmuring began.

—She should've been sent home on the first day.

—It's unbelievable.

—Crazy!

—Oh, you *know* she's on drugs.

8:30 BREAKFAST

HEIDI HUBBARD. HEIDI Hubbard had a new last name. When Heidi Hubbard walked into breakfast on the last morning of her trip to New York, she was shocked to see her boyfriend sitting in a booth

for two. There was a long-stemmed rose on the table and a nervous
smile on his face. His brother and Heidi's sister stood in the back of
the restaurant with a video camera and ear-to-ear grins. Heidi walked
unsteadily toward the rose and could only say, "What are you doing
here?"

"I wanted to meet you for breakfast."

"Oh."

"I missed you."

"But what are you *doing* here?"

"I love you."

Kelly Mitchell. Kelly Mitchell would hold onto her maiden name
a while longer. When Kelly Mitchell walked into the deli on the last
morning of her trip to New York, the smells brought her previous
night up into her throat. The grilling sausage made her eye throb. The
eggs made her head spin. As everyone else headed upstairs to claim
their seats, Kelly walked over to the coffee station, filled a large cup,
told the cashier she was with the group, and walked back outside. She
wandered down toward the corner where she found a row of heavy
concrete planters positioned to protect the skyscraper behind them
from a truck bomb. They were edged with pointy metallic triangles designed to keep pedestrians from loitering. She sat directly on top of the
miniature spikes and readjusted whenever they became too painful.

If she couldn't sit down to breakfast with a future fiancé, then she
didn't want to sit down to breakfast with anyone at all. With whom
could she realistically eat anyway? Ramona, who was being judgmen-
tal, quiet and surly? Nancy, who had already let Kelly know that she
was looking forward to a one-on-one meeting in her office back home?
Dennis Brewer? What had she been thinking? Nothing, she'd been
drinking. And she sobered up as soon as the door punched her in the
eye. Afterward, in her own room, she ripped herself out of her dress.
One of the shoulder straps was already half torn from the way Dennis
savagely groped her breasts. There were smudges and stains from a
cube of lamb that fell from its *injera* at dinner and from red wine that

the Serbian director kept splashing from his glass whenever he made a point. This morning, Kelly and Ramona had double checked all of the Georgia rooms to make sure no one had missed anything while packing, but what Kelly didn't tell Ramona was that, in their own room, in the back corner of the closet, was a crumpled pile of black silk.

A phone in a sewer, a dress in a closet, but it was the image of the charmed Heidi Hubbard, surprised in a diner, that Kelly most wanted to leave behind.

9:30 SUBWAY TO GREENWICH VILLAGE AND 10:00 GREENWICH VILLAGE

ON THE SUBWAY after breakfast, Pete approached and repeated to me that he didn't want Melanie to go on the tour of Greenwich Village. She had lost the privilege. She needed to sit this one out. Because he was the chaperone, he would have to stay with her. On Bleecker Street, I showed him Rocco's, a bakery where they could wait until we came back. As the rest of us soldiered on, Pete quietly pulled Melanie to the side and prepared to cross the street.

Laurie asked, "Where are *they* going?"

Jenny said, "To a bakery."

"What the hell?"

"For punishment!"

"And we have to keep walking?!"

"Yes!"

"Oh my God! She gets to sit down in a bakery, and we have to go on another death march…"

"Well, I do want to see the *Sex and the City* house."

"That's on this tour?"

"Don't you ever listen?"

Pete thought the girls might have had a point this time, but he didn't know how else to punish Melanie. He explained to me in a lengthy email weeks later that he felt it was crucial to show the

Georgians that he took Melanie's tardiness seriously; "otherwise, who knew, a knife fight could have broken out in Washington Square." Pete would not buy her a pastry, however. That was where he would draw the line.

A counter, like the one at Ferrara's in Little Italy, ran on the left most of the way to the back, with tables and chairs lined perpendicularly against the right wall.

As soon as the door closed behind them, Melanie said, "My treat."

"What?"

"I'll buy your coffee."

"No, thanks," Pete said. He was trying to be firm. "You buy yours, I'll buy mine."

"All right. So we're going Dutch?"

"Yes, it's a Dutch Punishment," Pete said. Pete hated the disciplinary side of teaching. He was never good at it. After so many years, he still visualized teaching as mentoring disciples beneath a tree, losing track of time as they debated the birth of American literature. He felt guilty as soon as he snapped at Melanie, but she really ranked up with one of the worst of all the students he had ever brought to New York.

Melanie went to the end of the counter to order her own coffee. Pete looked at the assortment of pastries. He wasn't hungry. He had just had breakfast. But he was on vacation.

"Are you here or to go?" a woman behind the counter barked.

"To stay here."

"Sit down, sit down, someone will come." Pete turned and saw Melanie already seated, having gotten the same directive from someone at the espresso machine. She had her camera on the table and was scrolling through her photos. Pete sat down across from her. The closeness of all the chairs and tables made him think of last night's seating arrangement, the ridiculous conversation he tried to have about theater over cheesecake, and the surprising torrent that came out of one of the students he knew the least.

Pete couldn't just sit there in silence. He felt awkward enough.

He asked Melanie, "How many pictures did you take?"

"Probably about a thousand, but I delete a lot of them. There are only three hundred twelve saved." She looked up from her camera. "Do you want to look at them?"

Pete did. He was curious. What did the students see? What on the trips he was sponsoring intrigued them, stopped them long enough to take a photo? Melanie rotated her camera so that the display faced Pete. He picked it up. The first picture he saw was of the clock at Grand Central. The irony amused him: Melanie taking a picture of a time-piece. He found the advance button and began to click forward. There were railings and light bulbs, tiles from floors and ceilings, counters and finials. They were all from Grand Central, but there was no photo of the exterior façade or of the main room. No photos of other kids. He clicked forward. There were shots of a statue at the Metropolitan. It was familiar, but Pete had to look at a few more close-up shots from different angles to piece it together: the clenched feet of Ugolino, the soft arm of the dead boy, the vertebrae rippling up the strong back. There were also ionic capitals, steps, archways, door knobs, and eleva-tor buttons.

It was almost cubist, this obsession with fragments and the variety of angles. To zip quickly through the pictures was to see the larger image come together. Pete murmured that they were fascinating. It was like looking through an album made up of particles, an atomic tour of New York. There were no pictures of the Statue of Liberty from the boat, no shots of girls posing with their heads against each other in front of the theater. As he clicked forward faster and faster, he almost saw Melanie herself, the photographer, moving around the subject, pressing the zoom, focusing on the detail, and so he clicked even faster. It was a shock when he suddenly did see a person, and an even bigger shock when the person turned out to be Tommy.

He stopped as soon as it registered. It was like a ghost. As if Tommy had made the trip, after all. Where in New York had she taken this picture of Tommy? He looked closer. Tommy was in the tux he wore to the prom. Sans bowtie. Collar open. It was nighttime. Or by the looks of things, very early morning. Pete didn't say anything. He kept clicking through but now felt that he was transgressing. These were intimate pictures. They were at a beach. It had to be Golden Gardens. Close to where Tommy drove into the tree. This was the night or morning Tommy died. Pete's thumb kept pressing the button. The pictures were soon close-ups of Tommy. His eye. His ear. His mouth.

"Tommy was a friend?"

"Yes."

"These are from prom night."

"Yeah."

"He went to the prom with Anissia Griffith. I thought they…" Pete stopped himself. The logistics of the events after prom were fuzzy. He actually never thought there were logistics. They went to the prom, they went to an after-party, he drove into a tree.

"Tommy was my next-door neighbor. He's the reason I came on this trip."

"I had no idea. I don't remember you sitting together at any of the meetings."

"Tommy didn't sit with anyone. He sat with everyone."

Pete agreed. If Tommy had come on the trip, the cliques would not have operated the way they did. Everyone would have behaved differently. Tommy would have changed the dynamic. There was no question Pete would have been a different leader.

A waitress asked what they wanted. They ordered.

"Drunk driving," Melanie said. She shook her head, shrugged her shoulders. "Maybe. But he looked sober when he met up with me, and he died right after."

"Well, you can't tell how inebriated or tired someone is just by looking at him."

"I believe Tommy commit…at least, I think Tommy let the car take him wherever…he felt…destined to go."

"What do you mean by that?"

Pete wasn't the only one who would have been surprised to learn that Melanie and Tommy were together on prom night. His date and their circle of prommers thought he was on his way home to pick up another pair of shoes, though they later questioned why he was so far out of his way. No one would have guessed he was stopping by Golden Gardens to see Melanie.

It had not been a sex-related rendezvous. Tommy and Melanie were next-door neighbors. They had grown up together. Their lawns touched. They spent most of their time together in the summers when the immobility of childhood limited their pool of playmates to the neighboring houses and bordering blocks. The convenience didn't extend to school. They took different classes, rarely shared a teacher, but, during the school year, if Tommy saw Melanie sitting on her front porch, he almost always stopped to chat. And vice versa.

Once upon a time, when they were in the fifth grade, a younger brother of a friend in the neighborhood went missing one evening. A small search party was organized. Tommy thought he had seen Jeremy entering the forested park near their house. Inspired by Harry Potter and Hermione Granger, Tommy and Melanie teamed up together and entered the park as the sun began to set. Tommy was going through a magical phase, a stage when greatness seemed pre-ordained. Of course, he would be the one to find Jeremy. Tommy snapped a leaf from a hanging branch and let the breeze take it. He then walked in the direction of the windblown leaf to find the boy. He would toss that leaf into the air whenever he felt a breeze, even if it meant completely changing course. Melanie laughed, enjoying the adventure, and followed Tommy until they found themselves, well off the path, deep in an unfamiliar, unlit part of the park. Jeremy, by the way, had already been found playing video games at a friend's house, and the search was called off. Stumbling around in the dark, it took Tommy and Melanie twenty minutes to come to a clearing and then to a road they recognized until they found their way home. Once they were safe, Melanie broke into laughter again. Tommy didn't join her. The woods spooked him. He had gotten tearful in the darkness. He asked her to promise not to tell anyone, and she readily agreed. She wasn't gossipy. And it wasn't the first time he cried in front of her—they had grown up together, there had been lots of falls, lots of skinned knees.

But after that night Tommy never again let himself be misled by a leaf.

He never lost sight of the bigger picture, his place in the woods.

And he never changed course.

Their paths parted more divergently in the summer before high school. Tommy spent several weeks away from home with a thirteen-year-old baseball team that looked like it was on its way to the Junior World Series while Melanie's mother and father waged a war that seemed to come out of nowhere. Both were quiet, reserved people who overnight became raging Greeks, screaming and gesturing wildly as they catalogued every slight, affront, and injustice. Another way to understand the sudden transformation would be to see her parents, not as Greeks, but as bureaucrats, accountants entering wrongs in a ledger until the total reached an agreed-upon figure and both decided the other needed to be audited. A dish left in the sink four years earlier earned stiff penalties; forgotten promises were marked under felonious embezzlement. Shortly after the accounting became the shrieking, Melanie was sent to live with her aunt for an entire month as the spreadsheets of her parents' marriage were plastered throughout the house. She came back home just as her father was moving out and school was starting.

Melanie had a difficult time adjusting to high school. The ceilings were higher, the walls were farther apart, but the place was so much more crowded. Tommy meanwhile excelled. He played more sports, he joined clubs, he lit up every corridor he walked down. He slapped shoulders and threw smiles and, instead of waving at friends in the cafeteria, he pointed. He pointed at them like a little CEO or a politician running for office and singling out a donor as someone special. He said good morning to everyone, smiled constantly, laughed all the time. Students loved him, teachers adored him. He was so much happier than she was.

Melanie hoped to be like him one day, but she couldn't help doubt the purity of his happiness. She didn't know Tommy necessarily better than his friends at school knew him, but she knew a different side of him, and she felt there was something inauthentic in his sociability. He was not as rested or at ease at school as he was when he sat on her porch playing hearts on late afternoons in July.

In any event, the more social he became, the more she withdrew. She sometimes felt like she was not the person people thought they saw, that she was in actuality a very tiny person sitting deep within her brain and looking out through the eyes like windows. Her body was a machine, a car she drove to get around, a house where she spent her days. Dying her hair or piercing her lip were just home improvements, alterations that made it a cheerier place to inhabit. She was deep, deep inside looking out.

Melanie thought Tommy was the opposite—spending his life on the outside looking in or, more precisely, on the outside looking at. Looking at himself. Looking at the image he was trying to foist on the world. He looked in mirrors more than most, not to admire what he saw, but to make adjustments to the person he wanted to be. To correct the mask.

He befriended several upperclassmen who would drive him to and from school and to various places on the weekends. Melanie saw him less, even though she spent most of her afternoons on the front porch, avoiding her mother who constantly mumbled. In the spring of their junior year, Melanie saw Tommy in his own car backing out of his family's driveway. The car started to pull away but immediately stopped in front of her house. He lowered the window and shouted, "You have to come to New York with me!"

Once upon another time—they had so much shared history, Pete marveled—a few years before they got lost in the woods, they ran away together for New York but only made it to the I-5. They had seen the movie, *Home Alone 2*, and they thought if that boy could live at the Plaza, so could they. They vastly underestimated the distance to the East Coast. Throughout the years, when seeing a movie set in New York or after reading a book set in New York, they would remind each other of their doomed trip and say, "We'll get there someday." It was almost like a pact, so when Tommy decided he was going on the New York trip senior year, he realized it wouldn't be complete unless Melanie joined him. Her mother was all for it, swore she would make her father foot the bill. "Let's bleed that fucker dry." Melanie was the first to pay her deposit and turn in the initial forms.

In their senior year, Pete held several meetings about the New York trip, and Melanie saw Tommy at these meetings—he even drove her home a couple times—but he was friendly with everyone, so no one noticed what she considered their unique alliance. Again, she might not have known him better, but she knew him longer. She knew a side of him that they didn't—he had cried in the woods when a leaf had betrayed him.

Starting in March, Tommy began spending more time on his front steps. He would sit there in the drizzle wearing his sweatshirt, the hood pulled up. Sometimes she would join him, sometimes he would walk over to her, and sometimes he would just remain alone. His family was having money problems. The housing market was drying up, and his father, a contractor, was watching his business dramatically shrink. Tommy's older sister, who was at school in Oregon, was told she might have to take a year's sabbatical as her parents restructured. Tommy saw this as a potential threat to his own collegiate career. He had been accepted into several prestigious schools, but none near home, none inexpensive. A lot more seemed to be riding on the scholarship applications he was filling out as quickly as he could.

There was even one weekend when his parents floated the proposal that he cancel the New York trip and get the full refund, but for Tommy the trip to New York was as important as prom and graduation. It was a triptych. The family scrimped in other places. None of

Tommy's worries showed through at school—maybe away from his family, he could forget them—but at home or on Melanie's porch, they were all he could talk about. There were no smiles for her, and she wasn't sure to take that as an insult (Had he used up all of his smiles for the important people?) or a compliment (Was he able to let his guard down when he sat with her, his oldest friend?). But as the spring wore on and the sun came out, Tommy's demeanor became bleaker, sadder, and nothing Melanie said could help. She blamed her house, which must have had some grief residue, some drug component, more toxic than meth, that turned people into depressed zombies.

Melanie was never much of a talker to begin with, and since her words did nothing, absolutely nothing, to alleviate Tommy's depression, she just listened and occasionally showed him photographs she had been taking since Christmas. That seemed to distract him. They were shot in various parts of Seattle and throughout their school. She loved to ask him if he could identify where in the city a certain picture was taken. She loved having places outside of the neighborhood that she knew and he didn't. Or she loved having him know that she had a life outside the neighborhood that he wasn't a part of. That's what she realized to her surprise one evening.

In May, their talk turned to prom, the first of the three events that would end their senior year. He didn't know her friends with whom she planned to spend that night—three guys, two girls, three informal pairs, not real couples at all, more of a pack. They were going to hang out afterwards on the beach at Golden Gardens. They planned to build a fire; she invited him to stop by at some point during the night.

Still, she was stunned to see him show up at around two in the morning. Melanie was taking photographs of her friends around the fire when they saw the headlights. They assumed they belonged to the police. They weren't drinking, they didn't have any drugs, but they had piercings, some of their hair was colored, and the girls wore boots with their gowns, so they expected to be harassed. (They had also built a fire and were in the park after hours.) But Melanie recognized Tommy's outline, his posture. She told her friends who he was and waited for him to join them.

But he didn't come over to the fire. She wondered if he wanted to be left alone. He was just standing there in the dark looking at the water, posing, feeling sorry for himself. This was out of his way, though. Why would he have driven here just to look at the water? Where was his date? Where were his friends? She crossed the small beach and hesitated a few yards from where he was standing. He told her he liked her dress. She twirled and then rolled her eyes. They talked a bit about their evenings, and then Tommy made a comment that after he returned his rented tux, he would probably never experience this lifestyle again.

Lifestyle?

Melanie almost laughed. This was a bullshit prom, hands down the stupidest part of senior year. She wanted to tell him not to take it so seriously—only the losers did—but Tommy took everything seriously. He was overwhelmed. His family couldn't afford to send him where he wanted to go. Financial aid was not possible, since the family income had been high the previous tax year. The bank wouldn't let them take out another mortgage. He and his sister would have to sit out a year and see what they could do. He could start somewhere else and transfer, but he didn't want that, he wanted to go to the same place for four years. She had heard all of this before and was irritated that he had sought her out only to have the same conversation they had had again and again and again on her porch.

At one point, she said, "So you're not going to get to go to your dream school?"

"No."

"Which means you'll never get your dream job and have your dream family and live in your dream house."

"Are you making fun of me?" he asked like a hurt child.

"Yes."

"Why?"

"Because it's two in the morning. Because it's prom night and we're all playing dress-up and who cares about all of this? Because there's a fire there and you want to stand over here in the cold."

"I can't help it, I think about it all the time. I have so much to do…"

"So much to do? You don't have anything to do."

No more words.

There were no more words.

This was now totally irrational.

Melanie couldn't think of anything to say to Tommy as she watched him chew the side of his cheek, as she watched his eyes scan the horizon for a way out, for a way to make his perfect life happen. She had been through her turmoil. Her family had their crisis four years ago. She was on the other side of the shocking lesson that the world wasn't fair, that it was heartlessly indifferent to your happiness. She and Tommy were in different places. Their easy talks weren't easy any more.

She remembered her camera hanging around her neck, and she started taking pictures of him. A picture was worth a thousand useless words. She wanted to show him what she saw. She wanted to remind him how young he was, how healthy and handsome. She wanted to show him his real face, the one she loved.

But when she showed him the pictures, his stare was blank and icy.

He hated seeing himself, was too tired to adjust or correct the mask.

Or maybe this was another case of his inability to identify the part of Seattle he was looking at. The part that she knew and he didn't.

The last thing he did, so unusual and memorable because he had never done it before, was to reach up, run his fingers through her hair, and gently press a lock in his grip before letting go. She was taken aback and could only sit there as he walked to his car. She took a picture of herself and looked at the monitor to see if the lock he touched was a different color. Because it felt different. The engine started up, the headlights came on, lighting her alone on the beach. She waved, and the car backed up and drove away.

She slept most of Sunday, watched TV for a few hours, had something to eat, and went back to bed. She went to school on Monday, counting down the days until graduation. She sensed something was wrong as soon as she entered the building. She saw two teachers hugging each other as she passed the front office. Pete was inside talking with their principal. He looked very upset. She thought maybe the trip to New York had been canceled. But there were other scenes throughout the hallways, tiny gestures, inaudible whispers. There were tears. Melanie kept to herself and didn't understand it until homeroom and the morning announcements. The morning announcements were usually delivered by a senior and not the principal himself, and while the principal did not use the word "killed" or "dead," his phrasing was so final, so terminal, that nothing was left uncertain. Grief counselors would be stationed in the cafeteria all day long.

This couldn't be happening. She lived next door. How did she not know there had been an accident? Shouldn't she have had a day's notice? Why was she finding out on Monday morning, like almost everyone else, that Tommy was gone? Melanie did not stop by the grief counselors, not even during lunch when she could see them in their corner trying to comfort classmates who barely knew Tommy. By third period, she had pieced together what had happened through the gossip, some true, some not, and she became more certain that she was the last person who saw Tommy alive. When she went home that day, she avoided her front porch, entered from the backyard. Trapped inside her house, she became furious with Tommy. That weekend, she boycotted the funeral. When her mother insisted that they go together, Melanie lashed out at her with such violence that her mother stumbled backwards. No one had screamed in that house for almost four years. Her mother said she would pass on Melanie's condolences. Melanie said, "Knock yourself out." She regretted her decision the instant her mother drove away, but she couldn't call her back, couldn't call another friend. She went out onto the porch and threw everything off of it. What wasn't bolted down ended up on the front lawn—two chairs, a small table, hanging plants, a croquet set that had been in plain view for so long Melanie had forgotten it was there.

Melanie decided she wouldn't go on the trip to New York. She would back out and get most of the money back. She couldn't go to New York without Tommy. But then, sitting on the floor of the porch, she realized that everything she would ever do would be without Tommy. Everything she would ever do would be done alone. Nobody was completely a part of her life. She knew that.

She finished school.

She graduated.

She packed.

She wasn't sure she would make it through the trip. She struggled with the crowds at the airports, the noise and activity of the city. She couldn't take the idiot girls with whom she was expected to walk or the irrepressible joy of her young, naïve roommate. She listened to her iPod on the bus ride into the city to calm her nerves. Her feelings toward Tommy had gone from anger to guilt, guilt she hadn't been able to persuade him to be happy, guilt that she had finally made it to New York, alone, ten years after they had both set out on foot. She wasn't sure if she could hold it together if she saw a location from a movie or a book that Tommy had seen or read. She didn't know what would happen if she ran into the bridge from *Home Alone 2* or saw the pool where the kids collected coins in *From the Mixed-up Files of Mrs. Basil E. Frankweiler*.

When the group stepped off the bus in Chinatown, Melanie almost had a full-blown panic attack. Very few people were standing still, and if they were, their arms were flailing about. Her classmates were screaming for purses and searching out back rooms and basement stalls or cheap crap that Melanie didn't even want to touch, let alone purchase. She was overwhelmed by the global chaos of the scene until she remembered the camera around her neck, and she began restricting her view to what she could see in the frame. This instantly put her at ease, and she began to wander up Mott Street, away from whomever she was supposed to be "buddied."

She concentrated on capturing stills of an erratic, dynamic, never-ceasing neighborhood and was soon lost in the close-ups of dead geese, exotic vegetables, plastic toys, frogs in barrels, silk scarves, and cheap wallets. She lost sense of time and place and caught herself looking forward to showing Tommy the pictures and asking him to identify the subject's location. This helped her feel much better, relieved her panic, because this way, devoting herself to the details (the trees instead of the forest, the leaves instead of the trees), she wouldn't run into the scenes she would have shared with Tommy. He would have been looking for the big picture, he would not have seen the close-ups, the moments, the life lived at 2 a.m. on prom night. This was how she preferred to take New York—block by block, window by window, corner by corner, brick by brick.

On Day Three, in the cemetery at St. Paul's, Melanie had decided that when she got home, she would visit Tommy's grave and leave the memory card with a small floral bouquet. She reconsidered when she realized that the rain or the sun would destroy that in less time than it took to fill the card or make the gift. She opted instead for another delivery system. She would attach a single picture to an email, and send them all to his account, which she knew no one had bothered to close. She had been writing him emails for three weeks. Full of useless words. Now she would send him pictures from their trip—and it was, after all, very much theirs—so in the midst of all the spam, all the Viagra ads, warnings about a non-existent PayPal account, and pleas from Nigerian widows, there would be three hundred twelve images, all beautiful, of hands, feet, buttons, steps, curves, stones, tiles, and crosses.

11:30 SUBWAY TO HOTEL

"I JUST SAW MY first gay person." This from a Brandon.

"You did not," I told him.

"He ain't gay?" Brandon and the rest of us watched the tall, muscular African American strutting toward the corner of Christopher and Bleecker. He was dressed as a cop, a police officer of an imaginary city, whose regulation uniform consisted of combat boots, shorts hemmed where the leg met the glute, a shirt tied above the midriff, an imposing cap, and a pair of handcuffs dangling from the hip.

"Well, maybe. But he's not the *first* you've seen."

Clint asked, "Where's his gun?"

"He's not an official police officer, Clint. It's a costume."

"I think he got it too small."

Behind me I heard all sorts of comments, ranging from shock to admiration.

Brandon asked, "He's not my first gay person? There were probably some gay people in the plays, huh?"

"At least one or two, but there are gay people all around you."

"Like in *Battlestar Galactica*…you never know who's what."

Our vice principal appeared next to us, behind Brandon, and shook her head at me. She was trying to give me a signal. I realized she wanted me to stop talking about all the gay people in New York. She had asked Kelly about my marital status on Day One and was now afraid I was going to unfurl my rainbow flag and proclaim my Truth. Please. I didn't have the energy. Coming out to a group every three or four days, over and over, would have been like coming out to my grandmother with Alzheimer's. I didn't lie about who I was. I was just me. I let them figure it out on their own. Most did: early on, one of the shoppers told me that she loved gay men because they dressed so well and then, without transition, complimented me on my shoes.

Nancy's eyes were nearly popping out of her head.

"Are you choking?" I asked her. "Raise your hand if you're choking."

"No," Nancy said. "Um, I just wanted to ask you a question about the Village."

"What do you want to know, Nancy?"

She scrambled for a question and then asked, "How much does it cost to live here?"

Late June. Day Four. So, so tired. Same questions. And this was a question that was asked only to change the subject.

I answered, "It ranges."

I had Lu call Pete to let him know we were back on Bleecker Street, so he and Melanie were standing on the sidewalk when we reached the bakery.

Even then, weeks before I received Pete's email and the forwarded photographs, I could tell that something had transpired between the two of them. They shared looks and whispered together for the rest of the day. They saw nothing else on the tour. They were discussing a subject so important that anything unrelated ceased to exist.

—Can we stop for a bathroom?

—I need to go too!

—I was hoping someone would ask that.

"It's hard to find a bathroom in the Village," I said. "Can you all wait until we get back to the hotel?"

—How long?

"Twenty minutes, tops."

—Oh, no way!

—I don't think so.

"All right, you can go inside here, but you'll have to buy a coffee or cookie or something. Only those who have an emergency and truly need to use the bathroom. Otherwise, wait here…" Most of the group filed into the bakery. "There are only two toilets in there," I called after them. "You all have to go to the bathroom? Oh, please! You just smell the cookies…You can't sit down in those seats if you're not buying!"

This was when Kelly pulled me to the side, gave me an envelope with my tip on behalf of the Georgians and then informed me that she wouldn't be going home.

"What do you mean?"

"I'm not going home." Kelly pushed her sunglasses up the ridge of her nose. "Heidi didn't go home on her last day."

"Who's Heidi?" I asked. "Is she the one who got engaged?"

"Yes. She's the one that got engaged."

"So what are you thinking?"

"I don't want to see Hunter's face. Not yet. I want to fly to Atlanta and stay with my brother. When we get back to the hotel, I'll see if I can find a cheap flight. I just want to make sure they don't put my bags on the bus."

"You're not even going to the *airport*?"

"I might have to go to one of the other airports."

"What about your kids?"

"Ramona and Wally'll take care of them."

"Do they know?"

"Not yet."

"Won't you have a problem with your vice principal?"

"I'm done," she shrugged. "I'm resigning. I'll find a new job, start a new life. In Atlanta or another city."

"Wwwwoooowwww."

She added, "This inspired me."

"What did?"

"The Village. Your tour."

"Whoa, whoa, don't drag me into this."

"*You* said it: 'A city is a place to go to be the person you want to be.'"

"Don't listen to anything I say," I told her. "Most of it's raving nonsense."

"All your stories of the people who started a new life and reinvented themselves…"

"I also talked about *The Cosby Show* and gingko trees." I started ticking off other topics on my fingers. "Office design, *'Twas the Night Before Christmas*, pubs and poetry, the *Sex and the City* effect. Thomas Paine and brownstones! I talked about Aaron Burr. Are you going to challenge someone to a duel? No."

"You talked about that Bohemian poet…"

"But mainly I talked about her *house*. Nine-and-a-half-feet wide, that's why we stopped. You can't take any of this too seriously." I looked around for help. I needed to pull someone else into this conversation.

"I'm not that suggestible. I've been thinking of change for a while."

I scoffed, "Since when?"

"There were a lot of cool people at that party last night."

"Oh, since last night?"

"Almost all of them were from somewhere else. I went to college in my home state and then took a job near campus. I want to travel, I want to live somewhere else and now…I just don't want to go home. And I don't need to. It's the summertime."

"Carol's going to blame me for losing a chaperone."

"I'll write her a letter and tell her that it was my decision…"

I put my hand on her arm and said, "It doesn't matter." What was I doing? Arguing? Giving advice? Kelly was a grown woman, and I was her tour guide, not her therapist or career counselor. I had barely remembered her three days ago. Besides, my friendship, our night on the town, had given her a black eye and a mean hangover. It was time for me to reestablish professional boundaries. And as far as Carol was concerned, I couldn't get into any more trouble unless one of the *kids* booked a flight to another city.

12:00 FREE TIME FOR LUNCH AND SHOPPING

AS THE GROUP ENTERED the lobby, people called out the places they wanted to go, and the like-minded formed teams and plotted out their hour. Some wanted to have a sit-down lunch; others wanted to grab a snack to tide them over until the airport. There were all sorts of stores mentioned, most not even remotely near the hotel.

Even though Lash very badly wanted to ride the glass elevators inside the Marriott Marquis Hotel, there was no way he was going back into Times Square. And shopping was not an option. He had given most of his money to the guy who pedaled him home, and the few dollars he did have would probably not even buy a keychain for his brother who had covered his chores. Lash didn't want to leave the lobby where he felt safe, so he was happy when he heard the Brandons whispering that they could pocket the lunch allotment and stay here and play cards. Lash and the Brandons had stocked up at breakfast, wrapping leftovers from other people's trays in napkins and snacking during the tour of the Village. If they could skip lunch and hold out until dinner, they would each make eleven dollars.

Lash watched the Seattleites grab their cash and run out the door. They seemed to have forgotten about yesterday morning's subway incident. Lash had stayed out of their way and didn't hear any more remarks, but he did know that there was one more bus tour and that this time he was sure Dana wouldn't sit anywhere near him. He wondered what he would feel when he got his pictures developed at home and saw all the shots he took of her those first two days. Shame or attraction? Would he tear up her pictures to banish the memory, or would he keep them in a drawer?

After Clint and the adults in his group were given their money, Kelly asked all of her students to gather around her. She held the tens in her left hand, the ones in her right. Lash walked to her side where he could better study the swollen eye behind her sunglasses. Did she really fall into a door, or did she get smacked at St. Paul's?

She started talking. "I just wanted to say how proud I am of your behavior on this trip. All of you. You were punctual, or if you were late, it wasn't your fault. You were polite, you kept your whining to a minimum, you respected your chaperones. You represented your school and your home very well. I'm proud to have been your teacher this year, and

I'm so excited for all that you're going to accomplish in high school and beyond." Lash thought he saw her wipe a tear on the other side of her face, but that didn't make sense. What was so sad about lunch?

She started dispensing the bills, and when she got to Lash, she said, "I'm glad you're safe and sound, Mr. Dautenhahn." He was the only one left. She gave him his ten and his one and gripped him close. "You are a very special guy," she whispered. Lash didn't know what to say, but he made sure he held his hips back.

When she let go, he gave her a nod and said, "Thank you, ma'am." Then he watched as she walked to the elevators, unaware that none of them would ever see her again. When she was gone, he joined the Brandons on the other side of the room. They were sitting on the floor in the corner next to the window, the cards already dealt. Lash picked up his hand.

BRANDON 1: I wonder what's new at home?

BRANDON 2: How do you mean?

BRANDON 1: If it's gonna look different.

BRANDON 3: We only left there on Wednesday.

BRANDON 1: You never know.

BRANDON 3: Yeah, like there's gonna be a brand-new highway paved out in four days.

BRANDON 2: They're supposed to tear down Burger King and the hair cuttin' place.

BRANDON 3: What?

BRANDON 1: Yeah, it's gonna be a Red Robin.

BRANDON 3: A Red Robin's movin' into Sherrod County?

BRANDON 1: You didn't know that?

BRANDON 3: No.

BRANDON 2: Man, don't you ever talk to your mom?

They went on like this, and Lash just listened and either played a card or drew from the deck. It was very calming. He would miss his friends this summer. He didn't see them outside of school that often. He kept busy on the farm. He might run into them at Walmart or at a local pool where his family sometimes spent a Friday afternoon. But he wouldn't be going to plays with them. Or museums. Or on boat rides to look at a giant statue.

After a while, people started coming back from lunch and shopping. Lash looked at the watch on Brandon's wrist—a Rolex bought for twenty dollars in Battery Park—and saw they didn't have too much time to go. Lash played a card and looked up into the lobby. Carts piled with luggage were lined up nearby. He figured it was better than having them lined up outside where anybody walking by could take whatever they liked. He saw his beaten-up suitcase, the only one without wheels. It was leaning into the side of another suitcase at the very top of the cart. Something was weird, though. Something was stuck through the handle. A cardboard tube.

—Where ya goin', Lash?

Lash didn't want to get accused of stealing anything, so he got to his feet and crossed to the cart to investigate. He took hold of the tube and slid it out from the handle. He rolled it around in his hands, looking for a label. Maybe the bellman found it on the floor in the room upstairs, didn't know who it belonged to, and just stuck it here for them to figure it out. He ran his fingernails around the cap until it popped off the end. He peered inside. He still couldn't make out whose it was. There was a piece of paper inside. He wiped his fingers on his shirt before slipping a couple fingers inside and gently pulling the paper out. It unfurled.

It was his.

It had his name on it: DAUTENHAHN, in calligraphy.

He recognized it from Ellis Island—his family's name, its definition, its history.

THE BOY WAS LOST once again. This time, he was lost in what he held in his hands. Barbara was told that Lash was collecting brochures as souvenirs. She had personally seen him collecting handbills from the display case in the lobby. She might not have made the purchase at Ellis Island if Lash had a different last name, but the definition was too rich not to be printed out on cardstock. And she didn't like how the girl behind the counter treated the boy. Lastly, she knew that nothing that she gave Cody or brought back for her twins—one of whom was still refusing to hug his monkey—would be so treasured or appreciated.

Barbara imagined Lash would present it to his whole family as a gift and that they would frame the paper and hang it in the living room right above their most recent Dautenhahn portrait. She watched as Lash gently rolled his name back up and slowly slipped it into the cylinder. He looked bewildered and would probably start narrowing down suspects, but if he approached her, or worse, if he tried to pay her back, she would play innocent and deny everything.

Cody stepped up to her and asked, "What was that about?"

"What was what about?"

"I saw you put that there."

"It's just a little gift."

"Are you kidding?" Cody tried to get her to look into his eyes, but she was still watching Lash. "You know he's the perv, right? He rubbed…"

"He's the dead rooster," she said.

"The dead rooster?"

"It's what his name means. Dautenhahn."

"Oh, that's hilarious," Cody said. "In so many ways. Wait untill I tell the girls…"

"Why would you?"

"It's funny."

"It would be mean."

"Oh my God," Cody sighed. "You're so totally different when you're on vacation. Or when you're in hotel lobbies anyway. Playing Secret Santa with farm boys and pimping me out to chubby girls in white sneakers."

"Ssshh." Barbara put her hand over his mouth, partly to stop him from insulting anyone in earshot and partly because she didn't want to have this conversation. They had been arguing for two days, and that wasn't their dynamic at all. Over the last six years, they had cultivated a very healthy stepson-stepmom relationship. She was a mother to the twins and more like a fun aunt to Cody. She patted Cody's chest and told him to never mind, that she was just tired. She kissed him on the cheek and was surprised again by how tall he was. He would be a senior this fall, the star quarterback. There would be no living with him.

Cody returned to his friends. Barbara crossed the lobby toward a sofa where Grandma Penny and the ironworker were sitting. Barbara felt she owed Penny and Travis, if not an apology, at least some friendly conversation that might pardon her behavior at breakfast that first morning when she ran practically screaming from their table. They had pulled their suitcases from the luggage cart and were packing some of their purchases.

Barbara saw the four "designer" purses in plastic—a Prada and a Gucci on the top. She couldn't stand those purses. She thought it absurd that a person would try to impress the world with a "real" Louis Vuitton bag while wearing cargo shorts from Old Navy. Who were they kidding?

But maybe it wasn't status. Maybe they just liked the style. Let it go, she told herself.

"Consolidating?" she asked. "Those are lovely."

"Thank you," Penny said. "I did get me some nice bags, I'll tell you that. I liked how they did that down there in Chinatown. I liked goin' downstairs to where the chinks had the bags. That's better than'n D.C. where you have to chase the blacks everywhere."

Barbara didn't know what to say.

"You know, down there they carry everything there in those big ol' garbage bags," she explained.

Still didn't know what to say.

"And they roll 'em around and around, and you've got to find where they're at…"

"The stores are more convenient," was all Barbara could come up with.

"The Chinese got a good head for business even if they're communists. Not like the Africans."

Just then—and Barbara never thought this would happen—she was saved by Elaine Caine: "OH! OH! Okay, everyone, the bus is here, THE BUS IS HERE! You take your carry-on bags, we'll bring the carts out with the big bags, but KEEP YOUR EYES ON YOUR LUGGAGE! We don't want anyone stealing another suitcase, do we? Hey, did you ever get that girl new underwear, DID YOU GET THAT GIRL NEW UNDERWEAR?! Where's that girl, THERE YOU ARE, you're a sweetheart, DID YOU EVER GET NEW UNDERWEAR? Someone mentioned…What? Oh, okay, we'll talk about it later."

The crowds on either side of the lobby pushed into the center and began following the luggage-laden carts through the doors one by one, like they were passing through an hourglass. Barbara was impressed by how unintimidated they all seemed to be with the jostling. Shoulder to shoulder, stomach to back, they had all given up their right to personal space.

Barbara, on the other hand, had not. She stayed back and watched them all push onto the sidewalk. She realized she didn't know when or where the next bathroom stop would be, so she took the time to visit the women's room. She hoped Cody would make sure her suitcase got on the bus. She hoped no one would steal it. That's funny, she thought. This was where she was now: no longer pining for the Waldorf, merely hoping no one would steal her luggage from the sidewalk. And she was fine with that.

Barbara was the last to board the bus and immediately noticed two things. The first was that someone on the bus smelled like hot dogs. Or warm bologna. She let that go. And two, the seating on the bus ride to the airport was different from the one into the city. On the first day, people sat in pockets but were spread throughout the coach. Today almost all the Georgians sat in the front, and all the Seattleites sat in the back. Two exceptions: In the empty space in the middle sat Wally and Clint.

Barbara slowly walked toward the back of the bus to join her fellow Washingtonians but stopped before she got there. She hesitated only briefly, and then she turned and slid into the seat across the aisle from Wally and Clint. Wally gave her a smile. Clint leaned forward to look around Wally's stomach and showed Barbara a shot glass from the Hard Rock Café.

"We walked all the way back there for this," Clint said.

Wally said, "You better put that back in the box, so it don't break…"

"I'm just showin' her."

Barbara couldn't resist: "Do you drink a lot, Clint?"

Wally told her, "Five shots before dinner."

"What's your poison, boy?" she mimicked Wally.

"Poison?" Clint asked. "Naw, it ain't for me. It's for Uncle Brett. He'll use it *plenty!*"

Barbara laughed, and she smiled at Wally, who had made her laugh more than anyone else on the trip. She would remember Wally Williams whenever she thought of this trip, just as she remembered Christopher whenever she thought back on her first trip.

She would have to come back some day with her husband just to see what New York looked like with him.

1:15 BUS TOUR OF THE UPPER WEST SIDE AND MORNINGSIDE HEIGHTS

I WAITED OUTSIDE until the driver closed the last luggage bay just to make to make sure no one stole a suitcase. Then I hopped up the steps and asked if everyone were on the bus.

—Miss Kelly ain't here.

—Is she still at lunch?

—I saw her get in a taxi cab.

Ramona, sitting in the front row, gestured for me to explain. I tersely reported that Kelly had another flight to catch and needed to leave early. Even Seattle seemed suspicious. Where had she gone? Why had she left? There was a sense that Georgia had suffered a casualty in the battle between the schools. This wasn't too off the mark when you consider that Dennis was the one who gave her a black eye. Nancy, in an attempt to shore up defenses and to give the illusion that she was in the loop (when, in fact, she was as shocked as anyone), told her Georgians that she would answer all their questions later.

Then Nancy told me, "We can go."

"Is everyone else here?" I asked. She stood to count. So did Ramona. They both separately gave me the go-ahead. All I had to do was get these people to the airport and kill a little time on the way. This was my last day in a twenty-day run of tours, and I had less than three hours to go before I was free. I wanted those three hours to be uneventful, so I turned on my automatic pilot and kept the tour neutral, avoiding anything that might provoke. For the next fifteen minutes, life was all about the Hearst Tower and the world's first one-way traffic circle, about the invention of stop signs, pedestrian crosswalks, and taxi stands, about the pair of Audrey Munsons on the Maine Monument, and about the city's most financially successful apartment building. Life was all about Denzel Washington and Sting, about *Three Men and a Baby* and *Ghostbusters*, about Tavern on the Green, the marathon, and sewing machines. There was such a mellow and somnolent atmosphere on the bus that I myself almost nodded off. Then, for some unexplained reason, somewhere between "Yes, Virginia, there is a Santa Claus" and Richard Hellman's homemade mayonnaise, I decided to add a stop. I told the driver to make a left at America's first cancer hospital (now condos) and a right on Riverside Drive.

Grant's Tomb. I had never had a group who referred to the Civil War as often as this one had, so I thought it would make a nice visit, a reminder that the war was over.

Too bad it wasn't.

After the bus pulled to the curb and I warned them about crossing Riverside, a couple of the Georgians refused to budge from their seats. You can guess who—Nancy and Dina the Disagreeable. They said they were tired. Their feet hurt. Now that they had a bus, they didn't want to leave it. Their butts were planted and didn't need to be repotted until Delta.

Their disinterest in Grant's final resting place could not be more obvious, nor could the antagonism between Ramona and her vice principal. With Kelly's absence, there was a power vacuum, and both were positioning themselves as the new de facto leader of the Georgia faction. All this could be read in their eyes. Ramona, standing, was the second-in-command after Kelly, she was Kelly's roommate, she was a teacher, she knew why Kelly had left, and she had already been leading the group for the last day and a half. Nancy, on the other hand, saw herself as the real authority, the representative from the school's administrative staff, and since one teacher-chaperone had already failed their school by vanishing without a word and since the other teacher-chaperone was withholding information, then she, the vice principal, was going to seize control of this group.

As far as I was concerned, their power struggle was all moot. Because I was in charge. I was the one directing the driver, selecting the stops, keeping us on schedule, reminding everyone to use the bathroom. All they had to do was count their people and make sure we didn't leave anyone.

"Actually, everyone needs to leave the bus," I said, which wasn't true, but I saw this boycott by Nancy and Dina as yet another undermining act of defiance and this one specifically an affront to what they saw as my Yankee identity. "Legally, I can't leave anyone here." I paused. "Because of liability issues if anything happens." I paused. "Ever since 9/11."

Everyone stood up to exit. How could that possibly still work?

THERE WAS NO CROSSWALK where we parked, so everyone had to dash over Riverside in small groups whenever there was a lull in traffic.

Nancy loudly stationed herself on the other side and made it a point to say to Ramona, "I'm going to stay right here and make sure that none of our kids are killed on their way back."

"Good, that's exactly what I was going to ask you to do," Ramona replied. "And I'll be inside educating the children."

After winning that round by two points, Ramona walked with most of the group onto the plaza. She saw that above the portico of North America's largest tomb was the inscription *Let us have peace,* as if Grant and his wife were begging the tour buses to leave them alone. Ramona mumbled the words—written by Grant during the early, tempestuous years of Reconstruction—as she made her way up the twenty-one granite steps, passing between the stone eagles and the fluted Doric columns. She pulled open a door and entered the mausoleum, which smelled of Washington, D.C. and the field trips of her childhood. She looked up at the domed ceiling and then down, through the circle of marble in the middle of the floor, at the caskets for the Grants, positioned with heads pointed north, boots to the south. She was able to make out, down below, the busts of various Union generals surrounding their commander. In the back corners of the tomb were flags from numerous regiments and circular rooms wallpapered with maps of the South marked with famous Civil War battles.

Normally, she would have been inclined to pull a few students together and explain who the generals were, touch on the battles, but she was drawn and tired. This was the kind of stop she appreciated, a teacher of history, a devotee of the nineteenth century, and on Day One she might have asked to stay longer, but on Day Four she just wanted to go home. These stops on the way to the airport—St. John was next—felt fake to her. The trip was over, their bags packed, the bus loaded. After church tomorrow, Ramona planned to go home and sleep all day. Her children, middle schoolers, were away at a camp. Her husband would be working. She would wake up whenever and then unpack. Besides her husband, she wouldn't talk to anyone for the rest of the week. She would pet her dog. She would do that.

She felt someone standing beside her, and she turned her head. It was Dennis, the man who had accosted them at Planet Hollywood, bringing up slavery and the Civil War, ratcheting up the tension between her and her boss, and ultimately estranging her from Kelly.

"Hi, it's Dennis," he said stupidly.

Ramona couldn't stop herself: "There's no reason for me to know your name."

"I was wondering how Kelly was. I thought we'd…"

"Haven't you done enough? I don't know what the two of you were playing at, but…Doesn't matter." She moved away, aiming herself toward the closest exhibit. Whether it detailed Grant's career at West Point or his struggles to finish his memoirs before his throat cancer could kill him, Ramona planned to turn her full focus to the words on that board.

Dennis said, "Hey, did Kelly get a chance to tell you about Grand Central?" Ramona stopped and looked back at him. What on earth was he talking about now? "Your line about slavery?" Ramona stared. "You know, the Civil War didn't have as much to do with slavery…"

"That wasn't my line," she interrupted.

"No, I know. Now I know. It's your crazy vice principal's." He stood there staring at her. "But *you* told me. You're the one who told me. We figured it out at dinner last night—what you were trying to do at Grand Central."

"What are you blabbing about? I never spoke with you."

Dennis explained what was pieced together the night before: namely, that Ramona herself, while trying to share an inside joke with Kelly, whispered into the wrong corner and shared her joke with Dennis, who until last night had no idea why "this crazy woman" was giving him her "whacked-out theory on the Civil War." This meant that Ramona had been blaming Kelly, mistrusting Kelly, for no good reason at all. Kelly had not talked behind her back; Kelly had not stabbed her between the shoulders. Ramona had talked behind her own back. A ceiling downtown had undone her. This devious city, she thought, in its very design, through its architecture, had turned her against herself.

After a long silence, Dennis asked, "Funny, isn't it?"

"Funny as farce," she spat back.

Ramona was still angry, and she still faulted Dennis for a number of legitimate reasons, so she turned on her heel and made for the exit. Tell it like it is. What's the *it*? What's the *is*? This was why she taught history—because it was so much easier to understand the past, to thread the narrative. To tell it like it was. The present was impossible. We could only guess at the present. When you're inside the farce, you have to wait until the end for it to make any sense.

Outside, in the shade of the porch, behind a column, almost lurking there to pounce on Ramona, was Nancy, who had abandoned her post on the curb: "What's going on?"

Ramona almost jumped but quickly regained her composure. "The students are reading about the Civil War."

"You know that's not what I meant. What's going on with Kelly?" Nancy followed Ramona down the stairs. "Did she take a taxi to the airport? Is she meeting us there? Did she book another flight? Where is she going?"

Ramona pulled a destination out of the air: "Brazil."

"This is unacceptable. It's reportable. The Board of Ed…"

"Kelly's quitting," Ramona said, "so that's not an issue."

Nancy stopped following Ramona. She was flabbergasted by this latest thing.

"Because of me? What did I do? I need details, Ramona. What's going on? Her cell phone, the bruise on her face?"

Ramona recognized the need for answers. She understood Nancy's' confusion—the state of chaos, of life inside farce—and decided to complicate things for her by answering with a question, one which she had been wanting to ask since Day Two, since the Metropolitan Museum of Art: "Did you tell Faith Hutsell that she couldn't date Brandon Ellerbe?"

"What?" Nancy stopped walking. "No. Why?"

"Why indeed?"

"No, why would you ask that?" She held her hands against her chest.

"Because Faith told me you called her into your dank little office just like you did me…"

"Well, she completely misunderstood what I was trying to say."

"Nancy, it strikes me that no one ever understands what you're trying to say."

At the bottom of the staircase, between the eagles and beneath the inscription pleading for peace, the two women looked at each other and shook their heads.

At last, Nancy said, "We. You and I. Need our summer vacation."

Ramona threw her arms around her vice principal, gripped her tight, and whispered into her ear, "Oh, Nancy, you see, we *can* agree on something."

NINETY MINUTES, I THOUGHT to myself. Ninety minutes. Little did I know that our final mini-crisis was eight blocks away and would be all mine. The bus circled America's largest mausoleum and headed to America's largest church—the Cathedral of St. John the Divine, a church as long as two football fields with a capacity for eight thousand worshippers and a ceiling so high the Statue of Liberty could fit inside.

This time, as we were pulling up to the curb on Amsterdam, two of the girls in the Seattle portion of the bus announced that they wanted to stay on. They wanted to nap.

Dina said, "Hey, we had to get out back there at the tomb, they better get out here at the church."

One of the girls rationalized, "WE'RE EXERCISING OUR RIGHT TO FREEDOM OF RELIGION."

"NO ONE STAYS ON THE BUS," Dina called back. "WE WENT THROUGH THIS."

"WE'VE SEEN ENOUGH CHURCHES!"

I said, "No matter your views on religion, you can still appreciate a building for its architecture and art…"

"YOU CAN'T MAKE US ENTER A CHURCH. THAT'S ILLEGAL!"

I was losing them. Georgians, Washingtonians, all of them. I smelled a mutiny. I would never make it to LaGuardia.

"Well, you can walk through the garden, go to the Hungarian Pastry Shop, or go to the next corner there and take a picture of the *Seinfeld* restaurant. You just can't stay on the bus." Pete, who had nodded off, woke up and viciously whispered something to the protesters and everyone in the back rose from their seats.

As we were gathering on the steps of the church, Ashley, the Bible Bee, asked me about the denomination of St. John. "Is it Catholic, because I thought you said St. Patrick's was the biggest Catholic church?"

"Exactly right. This one is Episcopalian."

"Oh, then all the atheists can go inside, cuz it's not a real church."

"Yes, it is," I said innocently. "It's very active. It's the flagship cathedral for the Episcopalian…"

"But it's not a real Christian religion."

"Yes, it is," I was growing more impatient, but I still didn't see where she was going. "It's a Protestant denomination that comes from the Anglican Church..."

She declared, "It's not a real church if you have queers for preachers."

On another day, I would have restrained myself as more of the group moseyed over. If I had been prepared, I would have resisted any outburst in front of a full audience. But I was not prepared.

I said, "Shut the fuck up."

The f-word. To a thirteen-year-old.

No excuse.

But here are seven.

I was working on very few hours of sleep.

This was Day Twenty of a twenty-day stretch.

This was Month Four of a four-month season.

Your language becomes saltier the longer you work with middle schoolers.

I didn't get to participate in yesterday's melee and needed an outlet.

I resented the tourists, outsiders censuring the lives of residents.

I resented an eighth grader spitting out the word *queer*. From an eighty-year-old grandmother, bigotry was a quaint reminder of the past and the distance we've come, but from a thirteen-year-old, it showed the distance yet to go.

Everyone was staring. The eyes, all those eyes. I thought I might just have to recuse myself and go home, walk off the job, and let them find their own way to the airport. The driver knew how to get there. Elaine would be there to greet them when they arrived. I would have to write this one off as a loss. Down at Ground Zero, when the first punch was thrown, that's when this tour ended. Or maybe even earlier. In the Whispering Gallery at Grand Central? The first time Melanie was late in Chinatown? When I agreed to work so many back-to-back jobs? When Nancy called Ramona into her office? When Tommy drove into the tree?

One of the Seattle shoppers, the one who liked my shoes, who knew I was gay, heard what the Bible Bee said to me and asked her: "You know Jack's gay, right?" Some people gasped. I had been outed. And outed incomprehensibly.

Her comment only made sense if you heard the whole exchange. If you heard the eighth grader provoke me, you understood that *You know Jack's gay, right?* was in reference to *It's not a real church if you have queers for preachers.* But most only heard my profane response, so they thought *You know Jack's gay, right?* was offered to explain, *Shut the fuck up,* as if it were universally accepted that gay people used inappropriate language.

I had now officially lost the group: *He just cussed at one of our kids AND he's GAY!*

I wanted to get them back. I muttered an apology for the obscenity, started to explain what had been the cause, and then stopped myself. I wasn't hired to stand on the steps of St. John the Divine defending my life to people I didn't know, people who came at me at five hundred miles per hour. I was hired to point out things they might miss if they came here on their own. I jumped into my job. Did they know the bronze doors were cast by the same foundry that cast the Statue of Liberty? Did they notice the Manhattan skyline carved at the base of the third sculpture from the left? There was a watery feeling in my stomach, but I told myself to smile and finish the gig. I was working on behalf of New York. I led them into the cathedral and was relieved to see that they were still following me. Hats were removed, cameras flashed, and the city was able to squeeze out several ooh's and aah's even at the end of Day Four.

St. John the Divine is an impressive environment, just the kind of place you want to take people after you've cursed at them. The dark, solemn immensity upstages all faux pas. It might not make them forget, but it will temporarily distract because all sense of perspective is lost or bewildered inside St. John. And that's what I chose to address at our trip's final stop.

"Yes, this place looks enormous, but it's even bigger than you think it is. Your eyes are deceiving you; your eyes can't grasp how fat the columns are, how high the ceiling is. That tiny circle in the middle of the Rose Window, way up there, where the Christ figure is sitting, looks only two or three feet high, but it's actually almost six feet tall."

There were exclamations of disbelief. Impossible!

"On your first visit to this cathedral, you're overwhelmed by the sheer size and magnitude of the place, but on subsequent visits, you're overwhelmed by the *detail*." I ushered them over to the nearest stall for an example: the Sports Window, high and wide, with thousands of pieces of colored glass. "In the eight large, central circles are depicted biblical sports such as Jacob wrestling with the angel, Esau hunting in the field. The eye easily falls on those. But look at the smaller circles and into the corners where, if your eye refocuses, works a little harder, you can make out contemporary sports like baseball, football…"

—Soccer!

—Boxing!

—Hockey!

—Bobsled!

More ooh's and aah's and camera flashes. More sports called out.

"The Sports Window is one of my favorite niches in the entire city, a city itself overwhelming in both sheer size and detail." People nodded in agreement and continued to admire the window. "Every visit, you just scratch the limestone."

I wanted to give them free time, so I quickly led them to the transept. Here was where the ceiling rose to its full height in a dome where the Statue of Liberty could stand. I talked for a few more minutes about the chapels and about the carvings behind the choir. I told everyone where the restrooms were and asked them to be back on the bus in thirty minutes.

As they dispersed, Zach, the prodigy from Georgia, stood alone looking up into the dark recesses of the dome, trying to locate the curve, the same tilework seen at the Whispering Gallery at Grand Central.

He looked to me and said, "I wonder what the Bard would say about this?"

"About what?" I asked.

He gestured at everything—the dome, the chapels, our people wandering the nave.

"I don't know," I said.

"Don't you wish you had his quill?"

I smiled and told him that yes, I really wish I did.

3:00 DEPART FOR AIRPORT (Harlem Drive-Through)

WALLY SAT IN the middle of the bus and listened to my overview of how Harlem came to be—of the announcement of the subway's arrival, of real estate speculation, of the condemnation of Little Africa for the construction of the original Penn Station, of the relocation of the city's black residents from the Tenderloin to the neighborhood above Central Park. By 1914, tens of thousands of black Americans had moved, for the first time in the nation's history, into the nicest, newest neighborhood in a major city. He listened to stories about the Harlem Renaissance and looked at the brownstones and the grand apartment buildings from the turn of the last century. He saw the wide boulevards and listened to the story of how Ella Fitzgerald made her debut by winning Amateur Night at the Apollo.

This was yet another example of Wally having to reevaluate. What he thought Harlem was was completely different from what he was being told it was. Weren't there gangs and fires? Wide-spread poverty? The itinerary described the ride as a *Harlem Drive-Through* which made him think of a drive-by, a neighborhood so dangerous you wouldn't want to stop and walk around. But the sidewalks were full. People looked normal. He didn't see any gangs.

Beside him, Clint was looking out the window as attentive as he was on Day One. Wally had given up trying to make sense of New York, trying to squeeze it into the world he knew. He had a good hunch that he wouldn't remember most of it anyway. Clint would. No doubt, Clint would be sitting at dinner a year from now and would rattle off information about Wall Street or Ellis Island. He would spot scenes in New York movies and tell his family that he had been there. Wally would probably have to look closer and then just take his word for it.

What bothered Wally now was the separation of the two groups. He didn't like that only he and Barbara made an attempt to sit in the middle of the bus, and he was also acutely aware of the awkwardness palpable since their guide had cursed at Ashley and then been outed by Seattle.

When the microphone was turned off, or surrendered, when the tour seemed to be over, the drive to the airport in progress, Wally rose from his seat and started squeezing his wide hips up the aisle toward the front of the bus. He gave me a pat on the shoulder, took the mic from its clip above the driver's head, and pulled something out of his pocket.

"All right, everybody," he said, wedging himself between the seats in the second row. He fiddled with the switch, and soon his voice filtered through the speakers on the bus. A couple iPod wires were pulled out of ears. All eyes were directed towards this unusual turn of events. "I got the final exam questions. This is a little overview of all we learned this week from our amazing guide and this amazing city." He struggled with his large hands to rip open a rectangular yellow package and then dumped several of the candies into his hand. "So who was the country that took over this place to begin with? Anybody? Anybody?"

—FRANCE!

—ENGLAND!

—THE INDIANS!

—THE DUTCH!

"Exactly," Wally said and threw a Starburst to someone who hadn't answered at all. "The Dutch came over here and started livin' here full-time. Now only eight people were put here the first year. Did you know that? I asked about it. Only eight! So they went through Ellis Island *real* fast. No lines! Now why'd they come over in the first place? Well, the Dutch needed beavers, a lot of beavers. And why?"

—FUR!

—PELTS FOR THE HATS!

"Naw. Because beavers build dams, and the Dutch live underwater. So they trapped a bunch of beavers and brought 'em back to Holland to build dams to save their country. Their first president was actually a beaver. A lot of people don't know that."

Starbursts were thrown indiscriminately throughout the following.

"Now because of all the beavers living over there, it got too crowded in Amsterdam, and more Dutch people had to come over here. They also came here for the theaters and the museums. Even then, they were world famous. The Rockefellers were selling oysters at the time, and the Carnegies were actually Vanderbilts. Steakhouses were very popular, which is one of the reasons the United Nations came here. Anybody know how the English happened to take the city from the Dutch? Anybody? Well, the Dutch legalized marijuana, and before you knew it, everybody here was just stoned out of their minds, so the English just came right in, threw themselves a ticker tape parade, and gave themselves the key to the city. Around this time they built the famous wall. They were actually trying to build a huge house around the whole city, but there was only enough money for one wall. And they also reckoned the roof was gonna be more trouble than it was worth. That's where we get the game handball, by the way, because when those people weren't shootin' at each other in duels, they were playin' handball on that wall. Racquetball came into being in 1876 or 1877, I'll have to look that up tonight. Time passes and the Revolution comes. A giant statue of a bull is put at the bottom of Broadway to scare off the Redcoats, but it don't work, and George Washington has to go to Valley Forge where they actually build a giant horse and wheel it right up to the city. Well, y'all know how that story ended, and New York became part of America. It was actually the capital for about a year, and then they figured the capital should be down in Washington, D.C. because it had the same name as the president. Anyway, Diego Rivera builds Rockefeller Center because he likes ice skating, and the Empire State Building goes up as one of the fastest construction projects in world history. Three hours. It only takes three hours to build the four-hundred-story skyscraper. People are still talkin' about that. The mayor looks around to see if there's anything else that needs to be done. He sees there's a lack of public bathrooms and that's a problem, so they build the subway. Problem solved. And that's the last Starburst I got."

There were cheers. We laughed, and there were smiles throughout the bus, from the front seat to the back, but the face that made Wally the happiest belonged to his ten-year-old, who was kneeling on his seat, looking over the headrest in front of him with a grin of pride.

Wally had told a fib. He had one more Starburst, and he sent it flying to the middle of the bus, where Clint snatched it.

Then Wally thanked us all: me; his fellow travelers; the driver; everyone who made this trip so memorable. He returned up the aisle, having accomplished what no one else on this tour could—he forged a bond of unit cohesion. They clapped. They cheered. This was their vacation; they were going to enjoy it. And all of the craziness? The fights, the arguments, the vanishing teacher, the rashes? They would be turned into stories. To be told at home. And the stories were really the reasons to travel anyway. Not to buy the knock-off purses as much as to tell the tale about how we made the clandestine purchase. The things out of the ordinary, the different and unusual, are what we remember.

"Miss Kelly told us how much she liked us, and then she disappeared in the elevator…"

"We got into a fight at Ground Zero…"

"Our guide was a real, live, breathing homosexual…"

"The ushers who sit you at the theater also give you a book about the play for free…"

"We saw a police horse let out the biggest dump, and then it trotted away and left it…"

"I saw someone snorting coke on a table down at Rock Center…"

"Everywhere you looked was a naked statue…"

"And she walked her daughter, BAM!, right into the wall…"

"There was a guy dressed up as Elmo in Times Square, and he would cuss you out if you didn't pay him when you took his picture…"

"There was a policeman with the skimpiest uniform you ever saw…"

"I tripped down the staircase at the Met, but a gorgeous Italian helped me back up…"

"Manhattan has the nippliest mannequins…"

"Right against my shoulder, just dry humping my shoulder…"

That's the stuff that fills the scrapbook.

4:00 DROP K. C. CROWN MIDDLE SCHOOL AT LAGUARDIA AIRPORT

WHEN THE BUS APPROACHED the airport, Lash spoke, not to the whole bus, definitely not on the microphone, but audibly enough for the first few rows to hear: "I can't believe it's already over." He had looked forward to this trip for two years. For six months, he had counted the days until his first flight, and no matter how many New Yorkers told him to get the fuck out of their way, he wanted to come back. Or go somewhere else. He wondered genuinely when he would. When would he ever be able to fly somewhere again?

The first stop was at Delta for the Georgia group. The two groups gave polite good-byes to each other. They waved. Not unlike shaking hands after tournament play. No love lost. There would be no Christmas cards, no friends added on social media. But Wally and Barbara actually embraced. Barbara also hugged Clint. Wally was the last Georgian off the bus, and he shouted, "Y'all get home safe and stay out of trouble!"

"BYE, WALLY!" came from the back of the bus.

Outside, as the Georgians pulled off their luggage, I posed for some final pictures, shook hands, and hugged. Grandma Penny told me if I ever came down to Georgia, I'd have a place to stay. She would feed me grits.

Travis joked, "We'll give you a tour of our town."

"That'll take all of ten minutes, Dad," Faith said.

"But we got good eatin' down there, Jack. You ever had real southern barbecue?"

"And sweet tea. Y'all got to get some sweet tea up here."

Then I took a breath, wanted to do the decent thing, and wished Ashley good luck on her next Bible Bee. I told her I hoped she'd win, and the crazy little nut job said, "I will."

BRANDON 2: I'm gonna live here one day.

BRANDON 1: You are not, you'd get lost in the subway for years.

BRANDON 3: His whole apartment's gonna be full of little Statue of Liberties.

BRANDON 2: Well, ya'll ain't gonna stay with me, I'll tell you that right here if you keep that up.

BRANDON 1: That's all right, we'll stay at the Plaza Hotel and eat steak, cuz when I'm old, I'm gonna be rich, and I won't be wasting all my money on rent in New York City like your dumb ass...

"Brandon!" Nancy scolded. She thanked me. Ramona thanked me. Then they each, separately, started calling out instructions to their group. Peggy, a representative from the tour company, a milder version of Elaine Caine, came out onto the curb and greeted the group. I turned them over, and they began to roll their bags away.

I hopped back on the bus. I looked through the windows and wondered if Kelly would be somewhere in the Delta terminal, since she was flying to Atlanta. But she could have been anywhere—JFK, Newark, even back in the city, waiting for a later flight. I wouldn't hear from Kelly again. She had taken off into a completely new life. Sometimes I wonder if I'll turn a corner on the Lower East Side and see her walking hand in hand with a Serbian film director, her eye healed, her smile bright, wearing a black dress that's smokin' hot, red carpet hot. Maybe she lives in Atlanta, maybe she moved to Texas. Maybe she sells pharmaceuticals. Wherever she is, I hope she's happy.

I would, however, hear from someone I never expected to. And this is the inspiration, the reason I started telling this whole story to begin with. Months later, after the economy crashed, deep into the following winter, I received a letter from Georgia. I didn't recognize the name. I opened the envelope before I made it inside my apartment. To receive actual mail was such an event. With the letter, came a photograph. Waist-up. Sitting in a recliner. The face was vaguely familiar. It was a woman, but she was completely bald. She was holding a postcard of the Bethesda Angel in Central Park.

The letter read:

> *Dear Jack,*
>
> *I just wanted to write to you to thank you for what you did for me. I was on your trip to New York last June (the K.C. Crown Middle School from Georgia). Right before we came up there I was diagnosed with breast cancer. I almost didn't come but I didn't want to upset my two kids. I had a boy on the trip named Brandon and a girl named Pamela. They still talk about that vacation just so you know. Anyway, when I got back home I had to go through surgery and chemotherapy and radiation, the whole hundred yards. It has been a very difficult many months. I'm sure you can gather that. But I am writing to say how something on your tour helped me through these many months.*

I loved Central Park so much and that angel in the middle of it. How she stood for healing and nature and was taken from a real person who had breast cancer. My children bought me this postcard when they were up there and it was a way of rooting me on. I brought it with me every time I had chemo. It was one of the things that got me through. It's sad the real woman died, but I'm happy to tell you that I beat the cancer. I grabbed it by the neck and stomped it out. So the pictures of me and my kids in New York won't be the last ones of us on vacation together. We're going to Disney World next month. That will be the first vacation since New York. My husband's coming too. We're going to take many pictures of us. I'll be wearing lots of hats until my damn hair comes back. But I'm not going to complain about that! I just wanted you to know. I hope your doing well in your big city.

Thank you with all my heart,
Dina Burns

But that day in June, I didn't know any of that and couldn't be happier to see the bitch go.

4:15 DROP THOMAS LEDCKE HIGH SCHOOL AT LAGUARDIA AIRPORT

ELAINE CAINE WAS CURBSIDE at the Central Terminal to meet the Seattle group. I thought I heard Barbara give a soft whimper. I reminded them not to leave anything behind and said more goodbyes outside. Hugs, handshakes, and high fives.

I saw Barbara smile and heard her say, "Hello, Elaine. How are you?"

"Oh, oh, I'm wonderful, but after I get you all off I'm meeting two more flights at US Air and on Monday I'll be at the airport ALL DAY…" The voice continued, and somewhere in the universe, it continues today.

Pete told me how much he appreciated my work the last four days. He said this was probably his last trip, but he would help Lu organize the next one before officially handing it over. They would make sure to request me for next June. Next June! I almost retched. I refused to think of next year. One at a time. I was almost done with the season, and then I'd have the summer to travel myself and figure out what I was going to do with my life. He handed me an envelope, and I walked inside with them.

Two of the boys said goodbye—the two future computer programmers—and I was struck, not for the first time, by how easy it was to overlook people on the tour. How often had I finished four or five days (four or five days of handing out tickets and Starbursts and Metrocards) and come face to face with people I didn't even recognize. Were they on this trip? Odd, but for every Ramona, Lash, and Tracy, there was a Jacob, Sun, and Pamela.

Seattle was listening to instructions from Elaine. They were ripping off the luggage tags from their flight three days ago and pulling out ID cards. I started to slip away but stopped for a moment when I heard Dennis arguing at the counter. He was trying to check in separately because he didn't want to wait in line. But they were checking in as a group. I almost warned TSA to prepare for Dennis. He had already blackened one woman's eye.

"Oh, and I'm sure it's beyond your skills to just print up my boarding pass," he was telling the agent. "It's not like you do this for a living or anything. God forbid, you just can't pull up my name…" It was the last thing I heard him say.

I took the escalator down, hit the restroom, and then waited for the M60 bus to take me back into the city. I opened the envelope and stuffed the cash into my pocket—a hefty roll with the higher bills on the outside, which made it look to any passerby that I was a drug dealer working my turf at the airport. All the Washingtonians had signed the card, written little notes of thanks and best wishes, and I marveled again at the satisfaction of completing a tour.

Do you know that feeling when you finish a semester or leave a job and walk out into the fresh air? I got that feeling every few days. The gig was over. I had no responsibilities. No school the next morning or paper I had to write. I felt pity for the friends who had to work day in and day out with the people they hated. The people I worked with—the ones I disliked as well as the ones I loved—disappeared within a week.

The Jonas Brothers started singing in my pocket again. Damn them. They reminded me that there was somebody I worked with on a regular basis, somebody I worked for who was unhappy with last night's off-the-itinerary tour of the Meatpacking District and the Lower East Side. I couldn't ignore the call because the tension would have ruined my time off. I flipped open my phone.

"Hi, Carol."

"Whatcha doin'?"

"Just finished up. Both groups are checking in."

"Peggy told me that the lead teacher from Georgia flew to Brazil?"

"No, just Atlanta."

"She abandoned her group?"

"What can I tell you?"

"She was trouble." That was all Carol said on the subject. Then she was on to something else, "Listen, we have a bus scheduled for the Hartselle group on Wednesday. Do you want the pickup to be on Fifth or at the hotel?"

"Um, I don't know. I haven't looked at the itinerary yet."

"Well, call me when you do. It doesn't matter; the pickup *time* won't change..."

I said, "So about last night..."

"Oh, Jack," she groaned. "Aren't the groups at the airport? Aren't they flying home? Next! We have two more weeks to go. Stay focused. Enjoy your two days off. Sleep a lot and get ready to smile on Tuesday."

The M60 pulled up, and I boarded, no longer under the pressure to get thirty-five people on behind me. I no longer had to keep track of any of the sightseers who were now waiting for their flights. I would be home in my apartment by the time they departed. I would be lying on my bed, my feet elevated on pillows, my phone off, my windows open, and my eyes closed. I would be in that delicious end-of-tour slumber, lost in the deep and dark space, so far away, on the other side of dreams, when the flight to Seattle lifted off from the runway at LaGuardia and Tracy Powell, occupying Seat 22A, battled her own impulse to sleep.

She willed her eyes open as the plane ascended into the sky and the metropolis she had lived in for four days started to shrink. She had not been able to check off everything on her list, but she felt now that leaving things to check off for a later trip was a better strategy anyway.

"New York City," she whispered to herself.

She would never be able to watch *Sleepless in Seattle* the same way. First of all, the observatory deck and the elevators in the movie looked *nothing* like the real ones! And how were Tom Hanks and Meg Ryan able to rush to the top of the Empire without being pressured to rent audio guides or pose for pictures with the man dressed up as King Kong? Looking at the city, she tried to pick out as many buildings as she could recognize, but after spending four days at the bottom of the buildings, it was difficult to recognize the tops, especially now that they were so toylike. Central Park she could spot easily, and it made her dizzy to think that there were people like her down there sitting on benches, taking pictures, sunbathing in what was now, to her eyes, just a green rectangle. She thought she could see the cathedral, and it made her even dizzier to think that the little church window, which looked only two or three feet high but was actually six feet tall, was now, when the little window couldn't be seen at all, still, *still*, six feet tall.

There were shards of stained glass down there in the middle of all those boxes, there were rash creams on the shelves at Duane Reade and packages of Starburst candy. Door knobs were turning. There were Broadway tickets, thousands and thousands of them, in pockets and purses so far below her. It was difficult to believe that pictures were being taken, cash receipts printed, lines forming, traffic speeding, and fights breaking out. Impossible to conceive that jokes were being told down there in tiny rooms. Birthdays celebrated. Ambulances rushing to hospitals.

She had to crane her neck now to look behind her. Clouds were wisping by, hiding and revealing the city like a curtain of cotton. She leaned back into her seat and idly watched her window turn blue then white then blue then white. She scratched at the rash on her inner thigh, and her eyelids dipped, rose, dipped, rose.

The last thing she heard before she fell fast asleep was one of the shoppers saying, "Oh my God, this isn't even my size!"

ACKNOWLEDGMENTS

I would like to thank the first readers of this novel, but I can't remember who they all were. The first draft was a decade and two computers ago. I know my brother and mother read it back in the day, as did Nona Lloyd, Tessa Derfner, Colin Winterbottom, and Tom Ledcke. I'm pretty sure Marc Wolf read an early draft along with Peter Flynn and maybe Trish Santini or Laura Clement, and I am almost positive Scott and/or Kelly Proudfit read it. Would Janice Goldberg have read *The Sightseers*? Bruce Racond? Quite possibly. I love all these people anyway, so even if they didn't read an early draft, they should be acknowledged.

More recently, Judy Krause is the reason this book is in your hands. For a diversion, in the depths of the Covid-19 lockdown in New York, I sent Judy a manuscript I hadn't looked at in years. She read it quickly and encouraged me to revisit the novel and share it. From this conversation in early May came the idea to bring out *The Sightseers* as well as three other New York books. After fifty days stuck at the top of Manhattan, aimlessly wandering the hills of Fort Tryon Park in a cloth mask and listening to podcasts to block out the sound of sirens, I suddenly had a multifaceted project to keep me occupied and engaged for the next year. For that, I am eternally grateful.

Thanks to Julie Weinberg who read the revised post-Judy draft. I should point out that Julie was one of my final proofers for *Suspension* and the only person I neglected to mention when that book went to print. Thank you, Julie!

I am indebted to Colin Winterbottom for his notes on the manuscript and the use of his photographs seen throughout this novel as
well as for several others hanging in my apartment. Colin—one of my
favorite photographers of New York and D.C., whose work includes
commissions for the National Cathedral, Green-Wood Cemetery, the
Washington Monument, and most recently Trinity Church—took his
camera around the city for me, playing a part and zooming in on the
details to which a certain character might have been drawn. To see
more of his beautiful work, visit www.ColinWinterbottom.com.

Thanks to the gifted Camille Knop who was there last summer
(and fall, winter, and spring) with support and answers to my many
design questions. Thanks also to Mike Nelson of Type G for his eye
and style. Enormous thanks to Mitch Bach who has been urging me to
undertake a bigger project for a few years now. I greatly appreciate his
unique brand of genius and unrivaled patience as he suffered through
innumerable strategy sessions. And to the talented Mia Heller: your
cover illustration exceeded my expectations.

More broadly speaking, I would like to thank the people I have
met in the New York tour industry, to those who have booked me and
to those I have worked alongside, many of whom I now count among
my dearest friends. I look forward to touring this amazing city with
you again and seeing you "in the streets" or "on the boat."

Finally, I want to express my deepest gratitude to all those who
have taken my tours, who have listened to my stories and shared their
own.

ABOUT THE AUTHOR

Robert Westfield was born outside of Washington, D.C., and grew up in Japan, Hawaii, California, West Virginia, and Maryland. He has lived in New York since 1990 and given tours of the city since 1997. *Suspension*, his debut novel, was published by Harper Perennial and won two Lambda Literary Awards. *The Sightseers* is his second novel.

www.RobertWestfield.com

CPSIA information can be obtained
at www.ICGtesting.com
Printed in the USA
LVHW041231180621
690565LV00005B/217

9 781735 482101